The Other Side of Sanity

DANIEL SHEPLEY

In consultation with Harvey A. Rosenstock, M.D., Emeritus, F.A.C.Psych.

THE OTHER SIDE OF SANITY

ISBN-13: 978-1-7329787-0-6
E-Book ISBN-13: 978-1-7329787-1-3

For my parents…

CONTENTS

ACKNOWLEDGMENTS

Out of legal necessity, this manuscript is a work of fiction; however, my life is very real. This is my story. I lived it in parts.

For telling my story, I globally thank all of the people associated with the writing, reviewing, editing, publishing and viewing of this manuscript. In addition, I want to specifically thank the following seven individuals.

First and second, I thank my father and mother, Paul and Nancy Shepley, for always supporting me, for always being there for me, and for always loving me, no matter how mean and cruel I was to them at times. I could not have asked for better parents.

Third and fourth, I thank my martial arts instructors, Sensei's Dane Sutton and Robert Nyahay, for instilling in me self-control, discipline, and the philosophy, "If I had only started this yesterday."

Fifth, I thank my college girlfriend, Jennifer Hester, for teaching me the valuable life lesson, "There are no second chances."

Sixth, I posthumously thank my best friend, David Ruszczyk, for serving as a role model and for allowing me to live the family life vicariously through his family. I credit David with teaching me the importance of breaking a few bottles.

Finally, I thank my psychiatrist, Dr. Harvey Rosenstock, for intervening and helping me when the whole profession of psychology had written me off to wither away and die. Only through Dr. Rosenstock's care has my once doomed life now taken on new meaning.

And in a small, insignificant way, I also want to thank my enemies because they helped me identify my struggle. In a bizarre, obscure way, they made this possible.

FORWARD BY DR. HARVEY ROSENSTOCK

What could have been the horrendous story of a serial killer and an ultimate suicide was completely reversed and morphed into a productive and contributing member of society whose address is Anywhere, USA.

This fictionalized resurrection of a totally wonderful and productive human being is at once a story of Hope in the face of fear and paranoia; Psychosis in the loss of reality's weakening grasp; and Trust when coping skills were next to nil.

This is the story of what can happen when the strength of a therapeutic alliance between a psychiatrist and a reluctant and desperate patient combine human forces to their mutual growth and faith in the positive expectation of outcome.

The Other Side of Sanity literally shows the path from a suffocating abyss to an enlightened and safe re-entry into normative human experience and social interaction. Impatience, struggle, volatile moments, anger, retaliatory thoughts, recurrent suicidal ideation, and homicidal ideation were seen as obstacles to overcome rather than end-of-the-road signals. In many ways a framework of Positive Psychology served to re-fuel sincere efforts to move forward.

The reader is encouraged to learn from this book – regardless for whom the bell seems to toll – to maintain faith and never surrender to the darkness. Further learn how to people what seems like any empty, totally unpopulated world; learn how to re-engage the social networks that appeared at one time totally rejecting; and learn that non-romantic, mature love is never destroyed any more than a human soul. In the search of everyone's hope for happiness, there are innumerable paths way beyond one's failed path.

In the words of prayer:

"…Yea, though I walk through the valley of the shadow of death, I will fear no evil: for thou art with me; thy rod and thy staff they comfort me…

"Surely goodness and mercy shall follow me all the days of my life: and I will dwell in the house of the LORD for ever." (Psalm 23).

MY WORLD AND MY ANGER

So, my rage. I grew up with humble beginnings. In the northeastern United States where my family lived, there was significant poverty. The town's people who were employed typically worked for one of the local factories making shoes or gloves. My father and my mother both began their careers in this way. My hometown had one grocery store, a Five-and-Dime that sold candy by the penny, and two cobblestone alleys that had not yet been paved. A big day for my brother, sister and me was shucking corn to make corn-on-the-cob.

I look at the calendar. Two years ago this month, I was destroyed and all that I had worked for was ended. Sitting on my cluttered couch, I remove my Taurus 9 mm semi-automatic handgun from its case and load a jacketed hollow point into the chamber. I cock the weapon and put the barrel in my mouth. I close my eyes, my index finger resting gently on the trigger. In a moment of clarity, I realize that I cannot go on this way. I must understand my pain. As I lower the gun from my head, I am somehow changed. Not improved, no less angry, but I have a made a choice.

I still have hopes and aspirations. Growing up, I wanted to become somebody who made a difference, whether it was flying fighter jets for the Air Force or becoming an astronaut or working for the CIA. I knew I needed to have an education, so I studied hard throughout high school, college, and graduate school. Yet, despite the tremendous sacrifices I made to achieve the education that I acquired, the world still wasn't there for me. The degree was not the answer. It looked as if I was not destined to make it after all. If anything, my world looked darker and cloudier. The fire that kept me going is dying.

I am almost extinguished.

Is there anywhere an anger like mine? Why do I not simply curse God and die? In my world, it is always midnight. I no longer hope for sunlight. For a long time, I was crazy, filled with a homicidal rage. Being crazy is like being in an occupied city as evening approaches; curfew comes closer and so does the fear. I am afraid. In darkness, there is only danger: there is no shelter, no escape. I have a dream about a gray city, and I am alone. I am walking backward in the world, no one around but other lost ones: all of us pursued. We all live here; I live here, in this darkening city of pain. One door is open, and that's the one I entered. Paranoia, anxiety, irrational thought: I was psychotic. I had become unreal even to myself. And I have a gun; in fact, I have several guns. I think, I know, I have the right to use them against my enemies and myself.

That evening as I sit in the dark with the loaded 9 mm in my hand, I plan my own death with great precision. I am a careful man, scrupulous about detail. My weapon of choice is the correct one; it will be deadly. With this gun, I am safe; I am comforted. I will defeat my enemies. And then I will kill myself.

I changed into the clothes in which I would die: black bicycle tights, gray martial arts T-shirt from college, white socks and my biking shoes. Such a laughably sporty outfit. I do not know why I thought it was the proper one in which to die. In that moment, I felt completely defeated. I was in a poisonous grip of manipulation and confusion. But this was to be a dry run. I am a methodical man, even in the shadow of suicide. I cocked the loaded weapon and stuck the barrel deep in my mouth, and I tasted the rancid oil taste of the steel. I put my index finger lightly on the trigger. I unload the gun. I need to practice pulling the trigger. Practice, how odd to think I need to practice. I put the gun back in my mouth, as deep as I can into in my throat. I pull the trigger. The hammer strikes the firing pin and the sound travels down the barrel and explodes an inch or so from my ear drums. My ears ring for hours.

But death is not going to be an escape.

I am a witness to my survival, maybe the best one. You see people like me all the time, as you drive down a city street or have breakfast in a coffee shop. We outwardly resemble you, but we, we mad few, organize our lives according to very different principles: cunning, paranoia, and a consuming rage. The city we live in is an occupied one, and you, my friends, are the Occupiers.

It is necessary that I seek help.

As I enter Dr. Janowitz's office, I am at the point of giving up, of surrendering to my madness. If Dr. Janowitz says, "No, I will not help you," I will kill myself right then and there. Is that true? In the rational part of my brain I know that I am not there to threaten Dr. Janowitz and certainly not to kill him. In the other side of my mind, in the deep devil-driven side, I take comfort in the thought that if he is inconsistent in his approach or resistant to helping me, or if he turns me away, I will kill him.

It is evening. Dr. Janowitz's secretaries have left. I am alone with him.

As the first therapy session begins, I reach down and remove the loaded 9mm from my briefcase. I cock the weapon and put the barrel in my mouth – as far back as I can. I spit it out and aim it at my temple, then back again in my throat.

I point the gun at Dr. Janowitz, then back at my head.

I have my finger on the trigger, loosely. I'm pushing it from side-to-side. I don't know what holds me back from pulling it backward and ending it all. I don't know. I keep pushing it from side-to-side and as the metal strikes the side it makes a clicking sound which only increases my agony and sends vibrations down my entire spine. I imagine that I will be experiencing the explosive psychedelic visions of a real Fourth of July firework in my own therapy room at any second.

"No one can help you!" the voice inside my head screams. "No one should help you!"

The sound of the loose trigger mechanism, metal striking metal, again beckons. My destiny will be instantaneous. Someone will have to clean my blood and brains splattered on the rug and walls behind me. Some part of me, some sliver of sanity deeply regrets the thought of a stranger forced to scrape the detritus of my wretched life off the carpet.

Sullenly, I look at the old man sitting across from me, staring at me, wondering.

"It's time to revenge my life!" I shout at him.

"My lawyer be damned!" I yell. "He's not the only one I must kill. There are no second chances, Cindy. You and your superiors knew what you were doing. Your chicken-shit therapy has ruined me. You did not help me; you destroyed me! You will pay the ultimate penalty!"

Dr. Janowitz moves forward in his chair. He looks at me — and the gun — with resignation.

"This is not necessary, Mr. Snyder," the doctor says calmly. "I'm going to help you, but before we can start, you must put away the gun. You don't need the gun here."

"You don't think I could kill you, do you?"

"Oh, I'm quite certain you could. And you might. But, tell me, why exactly are you here? You are terribly depressed, so profoundly, profoundly depressed."

"I need some help. I need someone to help me." I realize that one part of my life is over, and another has begun.

"Exactly," the doctor says. "Help of some sort is what you're seeking. It's clearly what you need. And I'm going to try to help you, but first you must put away the gun."

3

He speaks that final sentence firmly, without fear and with something that resembles kindness. Kindness is foreign to me.

"You've come here for help, James. We're going to start the healing process tonight, right now. This is a safe place. Please put the gun away."

How did I get to this point of self-destruction and homicidal, barely controllable rage?

Now I look at Dr. Janowitz not knowing whether or not he can be trusted. Was it his turn to become one of my enemies? Methodically, the doctor, quietly and calmly, talks me back to reality by explaining the dangerous emotional place I have entered. I listen.

"James," he says, "I have been a psychiatrist for a long time, and I know you are suffering from a serious psychiatric illness. The process of treating a patient — like yourself and like so many others — is difficult. Each case is unique, and there are no guarantees for a cure. First, we have to deal with your terrible, consuming pain. I regard myself as a man of science, but I am also a religious man, an observant Jew, and I believe there are mysteries of the human heart that are inexplicable. We are at a moment of heartbreak. You do not have to do this, my friend. You can survive, we can survive this moment, if you wish it. It's your choice."

My choice.

"My choice is it, Doc?" I resist being carried away in a surge of anger and confusion.

"Your choice, James. This is the moment."

I put away the gun.

IT BEGINS

My Mom and Dad screwed me up. This is my explanation and apology. I thought of myself in the grip of a poison. A product of poverty and the absence of love, maybe depression is in my DNA. When they argued, Mom and Dad, Mom got quiet and Dad yelled. He finally yielded to her, to that silence. I am the first-born male child to a lonely woman and a distant father. They lived in a trailer in the country. Dad was a high school dropout and scraped by with jobs that didn't pay much. I was the oldest boy, and I was expected to carry a torch. Whatever that means. But what torch could I carry for a poor family living in a double wide in the middle of nowhere?

And I had these goddamn big ears. Dumbo, the kids called me. I hated to look into the mirror. It is painful to think about, but I think about it anyway.

As a kid, I made a cave in a storage shed so I could escape my parents and my siblings. I wanted to keep people away. My dream was to get away from all that dreariness: a new country, a new language, a new life.

The truth is I'm not ready for a new life; my history — my resentments, my failures, my pitiful sense of self — follow me like a lost dog.

My deepest fear is the fear of being unloved, of being unlovable. And you can't heal those emotional lacerations until you are damn well ready.

I feel shunted aside. Who will love me, I ask myself, who will know my sorrow?

At 27, after earning an MBA, which I pursued with a single-mindedness that only exaggerated my isolation: no friends, no lover; I was a burned-out case. I was very nearly broke and painted apartments in the complex where I lived just to get by.

I was looking for something or, more properly, someone, and at one point I thought I found her: Natalia.

I've had a lot of bad ideas, but Natalia is among the worst.

She is very sexy, not beautiful, but sexual in a way I had never experienced. I was a not exactly a virgin, but my sexual experience was limited. Hers was not. This is not a diagnosis, but I think she is a sex addict. I know as a certainty she likes to screw.

Natalia is a topless dancer. But, I rationalized to myself, I had become an overeducated housepainter; we all need to earn a living, we all need to make money.

She said to me, the first time we had sex: "Snyder, don't take this too seriously, you're a nice guy and all that but I'm not looking for anything long term."

I didn't say anything. It was a hot night in Houston, and I felt the humidity settle down on me like a fog. We were naked together. She had a beautiful womanly body, a luxuriant body: medium breasts crowned with pink nipples. She smelled of cigarettes and the funky odor of alcohol and sex. The smell of titty bars and desire. My guess is titty bars smell like this all over the globe: Tokyo, Madrid, Fargo. And the girls all carry the same sadness.

"Me neither," I lie.

I try to hold her, but she pushes me away. She is not a girl to be cuddled.

"But I don't think you'll cheat on me," I say.

I'm different. I'm the backwoods boy you were destined to meet: I'll bring you back to the trailer park in the boonies and you can meet Mom and Dad.

She just smiles and pulls the sheet to cover her breasts.

Natalia is neither cruel nor stupid. She is a girl who likes to screw, and just as she promised she moves on to someone else. She stops having sex with me.

I am crazy angry. I try to separate myself from her, but she represents something I cannot understand. She opened a fissure in my brain that took me back to my childhood, something about intimacy and love, I suppose, which I had never received. Those things were something I impose on this sexual interlude: an illusion of love in the doubled-up condoms and the squeak and scent of sex. She is a cold one, Natalia. What I think of as love is simple, dumb longing, the moo cow sadness of a lonely soul. She has a plan, and I'm not smart enough — and I fancy myself as a smart guy, bigshot engineer — to understand that.

Lost again, I plead with people around the apartment complex:

"Have you seen her? Have you seen Natalia?" Have you seen my sex-addict stripper lover who has dumped me for Keith?

The one thing about being a housepainter, you have a lot of time to think. You walk around the inside of a room, sideways, dragging your tray of paint. Walls become white, covering over the stains and dirt of the past. You move your arms up and down in a meter that eventually matches your heartbeat: steady, slow progress. The past can easily fill you up to the brim with the memory of failure. I think about the time I was lost in an amusement park. Now I realize it was not a fancy place, just a sort of mom-and-pop rattle trap backwoods amusement park, cindery and chipped paint on the rides and a sense of being dried up and about to blow away. It is long since closed. I wandered away thinking my parents were right behind me. There never seemed to be a time when I was alone. My mother was always present. She held us all very close, and now suddenly she wasn't there. I remember the utter terror I felt and feel now many years later. My gut is churning with fear. Mommy isn't here. Mommy won't find me ever again. A cop finally found me and carried me back to my parents. My father was grim faced and very angry. I don't want to make Daddy angry. I was terrified and weeping and I buried myself in my mother's coat. She held me very close. I remember, as I do the painter's waltz around the perimeter of the room, being in bed at the end of that day. It was before my brother was born so I was probably still sleeping in the same bed with my sister. I remember burying my face in the pillow and promising myself, that I would never cry like that in front of my parents again. And I never have.

"Have you seen her?" I again ask my boss, a tall, thin, chain-smoking old man named George Carvell. Maybe he just seems old; he has lived a difficult life. I like George and, so far, he seems to like me. But sometimes I get on his nerves, but as long as I am productive, he seems to tolerate me.

"Not today," he responds gruffly in his usual fashion.

"I wonder when she'll be around?"

"You need to let her go!" George snaps sternly. "She's with Keith now." He is rubbing salt in my open wound.

"You're right," I say, the knots turning over and over in my stomach.

"Where should I start?" I ask after looking toward her apartment.

"You'll paint 903 today. And when you finish there, you'll move to 402."

Perfect, I think to myself. From 903 I'll be able to see her apartment.

I quickly gather the painting supplies and, using my master key, enter 903. Once inside, I remove the mini-blinds to have an unobstructed view of the parking lot. I am trapped in the web of desire. I wish to touch her. I wish to slide into her wetness.

"Natalia," I say under my breath as I stare out the window toward her apartment, "Why won't you recognize me?"

My longing is crippling.

I paint slowly, more slowly than usual. Every couple minutes I look out the window to see if Natalia's car has arrived. I need to see her. I am consumed by a hunger for her. I realize that I am also hungry. I only had time for a bowl of cereal for breakfast. I decide to break for lunch, a bologna sandwich on white with a smear of mustard and mayonnaise and a few potato chips. I am a poor boy for the moment and bologna sandwiches are about all I can afford to eat. And beans and watery canned soup. I am almost always hungry these days. Money is short.

At 12:30 PM, just as I am finishing eating, there is a knock on the door. George is stopping by to check on me.

I am reluctant to let him in since the place is such a mess. I only open the door a little, trying to prevent him from seeing in.

"I have to talk to you about a few things, Jim. Let me in, please."

"Okay, but I'm just heading back to 903."

"I just need a minute."

He looks around my apartment in astonishment.

Because I have no money, I have hardly any furniture. The stuff I have is junk people have left in their apartments as they moved out. This is a building with a lot of low income people, poor people, down and outers. And I pick up the junk even they don't want. I have never been this broke, even living with my parents. We had little money, but we had stuff that wasn't held together with duct tape and glue. I smash things in anger, chairs and tables, and then try to put them together again only to smash them again. It was a shambles, as I was a shambles.

"Jesus, James, what have you been doing up here? Poor Jimmy," George says. "You're living like a rat."

"I'll get some new stuff when I have money, George. What did you want?"

He looks at the heaps of my junk in my living room and just shakes his head in bewilderment. He and Grace live like Swiss shopkeepers, neat and organized and a little cluttered. They have a lot of pretty stuff and doilies on the chairs and teacups in the sideboard.

"I checked what you were supposed to do this morning. You haven't made much progress."

"I'm working as fast as I can," I say as I glance out the window yet another time.

"That's bullshit. If you don't let her go, we'll have no choice but to terminate your employment here."

"Are you serious?"

"I'm totally serious," George answers. "In your present state, you're a liability to this apartment complex. You have a master key. What if you lose control and enter her apartment? The owner could be sued for everything he has."

"But I wouldn't do that!"

"Look Jim, you need professional help. I think I can keep management at bay a little while longer. But if you don't get help soon, they will fire you. Think about it. Okay?"

"Okay" is all I can mutter. I can't afford to get fired. The gravity of George's words weighs heavily on my mind.

I return to apartment 903, trying to digest my bologna sandwich. I begin to paint, but the seriousness of the situation is hitting me. I feel a little nauseous with anxiety. I am close to throwing up.

"How will I survive if they fire me?" I ask myself under my breath. "How will I pay the rent and my bills?"

I pace some more. "If I can't pay the rent, they'll evict me, and I'll never see Natalia again. Oh shit!" I say aloud, my stomach turning over on itself at the thought. I decide to call my best friend. I duck back into my apartment, hoping George won't see me. This is important. I have to talk to Scott.

"Hey Scott," I say as he answers.

"Yoooo!" Scott says in response. "How are you doing, Jim?"

"They want to fire me!" I blurt out, the anxiety taking control.

"What?" Scott asks.

"They want to fire me. They say I'm obsessed with Natalia and that I'm a liability to the apartment complex because I have a master key, so they want to get rid of me."

"Whoa," Scott says. "Let's take this one step at a time."

"They want to fire me," I repeat slightly more slowly.

"Got that part of it. Why?" Scott responds.

"Because they say I'm obsessed with Natalia."

"Got that too."

"And that I'm a liability because I have a master key." I have access to everyone's apartments. If George stops trusting me, I'm in a nearly hopeless spot.

"Oh, I see," Scott responds. "Well, you know Jim," Scott pauses, his voice remaining calm and even. "You are obsessed with Natalia. And you do have a master key, so I can understand where the apartment complex is coming from. Did they give you any options?"

"They say I need professional help," I answer.

"That's probably a good idea, Jim," Scott says tentatively. He is cautious. He has seen my outbursts of rage. My anger is unknown to everyone except Scott. I live a walled off life. I am quiet, almost sullen to most people, and they mostly accept that. Scott and a few others, my family mostly, know this other side of me, my rage. I spend enormous amounts of energy struggling to maintain control. How they would fear me if they knew what was inside of me. This is my secret.

"Let me think about it," I respond after an awkward silence. "Please tell Kelly and the kids I said hi."

"Will do, Jim. Take care."

"Bye."

After hanging up, I return to 903 and continue painting, this time a little faster than before. George stops by at 2:15 PM and again at 4:00 PM and is pleased with my progress. I finish at a few minutes before 6:00 PM.

That night I do my habitual push-ups and sit-ups before going to bed; however, I cannot sleep. I toss and I turn, the anxiety weighing heavily upon me. At 4:49 AM the next morning, I decide to get up and read the *Sugar Land Daily* as I watch the sunrise. I stare out the window from my living room, glancing occasionally toward her apartment, my stomach in knots.

At 7:24 AM my phone rings.

"Yoooo!" the voice proclaims.

"Hi Scott," I answer immediately.

"How are you doing today?" Scott inquires, the concern evident in his voice.

"Didn't sleep at all last night," I answer. "But otherwise, the same."

"Oh" is Scott's only response.

After a very long, awkward silence, Scott asks, "Have you thought any more about our conversation yesterday?"

"Yes," I answer.

"And?" Scott asks. His question is almost a demand.

"And I need to keep this job."

"So, what are you going to do?"

"There's an advertisement in the newspaper offering low cost counseling services at Jedermann University, so I'm going to call them."

"And when are you going to make this call?" Scott pushes.

"This morning," I answer, my stomach turning over at the thought of it. "I need to do something," I continue. "This is killing me."

"We're here for you if you need us."

"Thanks."

"What about LT?" Scott adds, abbreviating the words "Long Term," which is our code for my secret ambition to work for the Central Intelligence Agency.

"I mailed the application package on Monday, so unless they come back to me with more questions, all should be well."

"Very cool," Scott says. "Let me know how your call turns out."

Back I go to the window, watching for her to emerge from his apartment. That bitch! Time passes slowly, but my stomach won't stop turning over. I glance at the advertisement I cut out of the newspaper. "Counseling Services Available," it says. "Sliding scale fee."

"Well, screw it" I say aloud. "I've got to do something."

At 8:23 AM, I pick up the telephone nervously and dial the number on the advertisement, then listen to it ring. On the fourth ring, a woman answers. "Psychological Counseling Services," she says.

"Hi, this is Jim Schneider," I announce deliberately mis-stating my last name. "I'm wondering if you can help me. I read your advertisement in the newspaper regarding student supervised counseling services and I'd like to make an appointment to see if I could benefit from counseling."

"One moment please," she says professionally. "I'll transfer you to the Director, Dr. Joseph Monteblanc."

After a pause, I hear a soothing professional voice, like a newsreader on the radio.

"Hello Mr. Schneider. This is Dr. Monteblanc. How can I help you?"

"I read your advertisement for sliding scale counseling services and I think I could benefit from counseling," I answer nervously.

"What seems to be the problem?" Dr. Monteblanc asks with annoying sincerity. His speech has a very subtle lisp.

"Well," I begin, "I met this woman in November 2002, about ten months ago, I think. I don't remember exactly. We became intimate almost immediately; however, she lied to me and cheated on me with my neighbor," I continue, realizing my voice is growing louder, the anger and pain becoming more apparent. "I feel this overwhelming need to see her, to be recognized by her, yet I can't be with her. It's tearing me apart inside."

"Are you sleeping well at night?" Dr. Monteblanc asks after a momentary pause. Maybe he's making notes.

"No, I get maybe three hours sleep a night, if that."

"Are you working? Are you employed?" the doctor asks next.

"No," I answer dejectedly. "I've been unemployed since I graduated from Saint Martha's College a year ago, May, with my MBA."

"How old are you?"

"Twenty-eight."

"Have you been in other relationships in the past?"

"Yes."

"Do you think it could be homosexuality?" the doctor asks next. That question I find creepy, but that's only the first of many creepy questions he will ask.

"No," I answer immediately. "I've thought about that and I don't think that's the case."

"Well, you seem a little defensive," Dr. Monteblanc says with energy in his voice. "Perhaps we need to explore that further."

"Look," I continue, changing the subject, "I've read various books like *The Hard Road Traveled* and *Codependent Be I* and I know that I need to get professional help, but I don't have any money and I don't have insurance. Can you help me?"

"Why don't you come in at 10:30 for a face-to-face? We'll see what we can do."

"Thank you, Dr. Monteblanc," I say as I hang up. "Goodbye."

A few minutes later I walk out of my apartment, go down the stairs, and knock on my downstairs neighbor's door.

"Hi George, hi Grace," I say. Grace is a tiny woman, barely five feet tall with bright blonde hair and long dangling gold earrings that reach almost to her shoulders. Her perfume is very noticeable again today; it is a mist of flowery scent that is almost overpowering. She is a very sweet woman, though, and a tough one, too. George told me that she had once been part of a circus act, acrobats, I think, The Flying Fantuccis or something like that. She was the flyer and her brothers were the catchers. That would be something to experience, Grace Fantucci, airborne. She was a little bottom heavy these days, but as a young woman she must have been svelte, a real knockout. I'm also greeted by their two middle aged dogs, yapping Popeye and Alfalfa.

"Hush," George commands loudly to the dogs to stop their barking.

"Well," I say to Grace, "I made the call. I'm going in to start counseling this morning."

"Oh, we're so glad for you, Jim," Grace says reassuringly.

"I know you both have been telling me that I needed counseling for some time now, so I just wanted to let you know that I heard you and that I'm doing it. George," I say as I turn to face him, "Will you tell the office that I won't be painting this morning?"

"Sure," George says. "We're proud of you, Jim."

"Bye," I say as I turn to leave.

"James," Grace says as I head out the door, "why don't you come over for dinner on Saturday evening and you can tells us what happened. I think this is going to work out well for you."

She is a very sweet lady. Something in her face tells me she has a story or two to tell.

"Thanks, Grace, I'd like that."

I am not totally convinced that counseling will do much good. But there is no alternative now. I have to try to do things differently.

Once back upstairs, I walk into the bathroom, take my shirt off, and turn slowly around to look at the boils all over my back. "Well," I say aloud in a resigned voice to myself, "I've got to do something." I think back to when those boils first appeared. It was right after I found out she was cheating. When was that? Six months ago? March, I think. They are blackish lumps. I go to the doctor to have them drained occasionally. The puss is almost green, with a fleck of blood. Almost green is not good. I never take off my t-shirt. This is what Natalia has done to me. I feel infected with her poison.

"That bitch!" I say under my breath, again becoming angry.

Beautiful women lie, and they are held blameless.

At quarter after ten, I get in my car, a ten-year-old 1993 blue Volkswagen Golf, rusty but a good runner. I wave to George and Grace who are standing at their front window as I back away. In seven minutes, I'm on the Jedermann University campus. In another minute, I'm in the parking lot of the Wasserman Building. I observe that the very front row of parking spaces is reserved for faculty, so I park in the second row back. It is a sunny day with a milky blue sky. It is not hot yet, but it will be soon. I look at myself in the rear-view mirror. I don't look crazy, at least.

I get out of my car, pause, take a deep breath, exhale, and then walk nervously to the two glass entry doors that serve as the main entrance. Once inside, I immediately see "Psychological Counseling Services" written on a glass door just across the hall slightly to the right of the main entry doors. The décor of Counseling Services is trying very hard not to be coldly institutional. There is a large bank of windows that looks out over the lower campus: a rectangle of grass and a few trees. A flag stone path leads off into what I know is the parking lot. The lights are coldly fluorescent, a kind of washed-out green to which I am accustomed having been in classrooms for most of the past decade. There are landscapes on the walls of Texas countryside; a landscape with blue bonnets, a common motif in Texas, an institutional cliché that I, a non-Texan, find increasingly annoying. But they are well executed and seem to be by the same artist. The background music — barely audible, like a whisper — is Neil Diamond's "Hello, Again." I suspect in the next weeks — or however long my counseling lasts — I'll be hearing a lot of Neil Diamond. The boy from Brooklyn's music is filling waiting rooms in every corner of the country.

Instead of going immediately in, however, I walk down the hall pretending to look at the student bulletin boards that are on the wall opposite the Psychological Counseling Services door. I go approximately halfway down the long hallway before gathering the will to return. No quitting now, I say to myself. I wanted to run back to my car and drive away, but I don't. That was a fraught and fateful decision.

As I return, I look through the glass walls of the Psychological Counseling Services waiting room. I observe the utilitarian waiting room couch chairs inside, beige vinyl and chrome legs. They are mostly facing out, and the woman I presume is the secretary is sitting at a desk behind a counter with a three-ring binder on it to her left. She is barely visible at her desk, her head just peaking above the counter. I guess patients sign in and out in the binder. That will be the record for who comes and goes. This public space reminds me of a fishbowl, and I don't like it. After all, I think to myself, I don't really want to be seen here. And I'll be the only one in there once I do go in.

"Hi, Mona Rodriguez," I say as I approach the woman, reading her name off the nameplate on her desk. I try to be casual but I can barely speak. I am truly terrified.

"I'm Jim Schneider. I called this morning and Dr. Monteblanc said to come in at 10:30 AM."

Because I am unsure of the process and the people, I intentionally misidentify myself. More accurately, I don't trust them with my true identity. They're going to have to earn my trust. So, I'm Schneider.

"Oh, yes," Mona responds. "We'll need you to complete these forms first. When you're finished, I'll tell Dr. Monteblanc that you're here."

I take the forms and sit down with my back slightly angled to the entry door and the hallway beyond it. Because it makes me nervous being in the fishbowl, I quickly complete the forms and hand them back to Mona, all the while trying to keep my back toward the hallway as much as I can without looking suspicious. To my surprise and delight, Mona does not ask to see any identification, so I return to my seat as she walks toward the back with the papers. I don't have an ID that says I'm "Schneider." My opening gambit evokes a weak response. I'm going to keep pushing pawns. She returns to her desk about twenty seconds later and about a minute after that a man appears.

"Hi Jim. I'm Dr. Monteblanc," a handsome man, Joseph Monteblanc, says with a soft voice, extending his hand.

"Hi, Dr. Monteblanc," I say confidently, shaking his hand and noticing that his handshake is rather limp. "I'm Jim Schneider." My bravado hides a deeply fearful soul. I hope I'm not all bravado.

Dr. Monteblanc is a slender well-groomed man. He wears his hair long in the back, touching his collar. It is very dark brown with a touch of grey in the temples. He wears reading glasses on a loop and they are off his face, bouncing along his chest as we walk into his office. He is wearing a gray Harris tweed jacket, very professorial except that it is new and not worn at the elbows. He is a man well pleased with himself, and why not? A Ph.D., a good job in a university, and control over his life. I also am sure he is gay. Gay men like me, I've discovered. I don't want to dig too deeply into that though. I think I seem vulnerable to them.

"Please come into my office and we'll see what we can do for you," the Director says, pointing me toward a door marked, "Director, Psychological Counseling Services." His office is located just beyond Mona's desk but off farther to the right.

Once inside, he closes the door. Like an inveterate paranoid I immediately notice that the room is dimly lit by a desk lamp only, that there are no windows in the room, and that the walls are hidden by bookshelves filled with books. There is a pile of books on the floor by his desk. It is as creepy as a wizard's cave. On his desk, the Director has a large metal mug of steaming coffee and files and papers piled neatly arranged, meticulously arranged as if he didn't occupy the space. He sees me looking at his coffee mug and asks, "James would you like something to drink, coffee or water? That's about all we have."

The Director begins by reviewing the forms I completed, then asks additional questions. "When was the last time you spoke to your parents?"

"It's probably been five or six months," I answer.

"Do you have any brothers or sisters?"

"Yes, one of each."

"When was the last time you spoke to them?"

"It's probably been five or six months," I answer.

"Do you have any relatives in this area?"

15

"No," I respond, "I'm here by myself."

"Has anyone in your family ever received counseling?"

"Not to my knowledge." My family would go to jail before they went to counseling.

"You said you met a woman at your apartment complex and became intimate almost immediately. Is that correct?"

"Yes."

"And when did that happen?"

"I met Natalia in mid-November, ten months ago," I answer.

"Do you see her anymore?"

"I see her around the apartment complex, but I don't date her any more since she cheated on me with my neighbor Keith," I respond, the agitation evident in my voice.

"And when did you learn that she cheated?"

"In March."

"And now you say you're obsessed with her?"

"Yes," I answer nervously. "She somehow reminds me of my mother. I need to see her. I need to be recognized by her. But I can't be with her."

"Well you can't have sex with your mother," Dr. Monteblanc quips. "Incest is a taboo in all cultures." I think he means to be funny. I wonder what he would think if I told him I was fucking my mother?

"I understand that, Doctor, what I meant…." I begin.

"Mr. Schneider, sometimes we don't know what we mean, do we?" Dr. Monteblanc says with a smirk. "Sometimes we have to learn to differentiate what we think we mean from what we actually mean. Maybe that's why you are here."

"I suppose so." And by the way, Dr. Monteblanc, I don't appreciate the condescension.

"Do you have a source of income?" Dr. Monteblanc asks next.

"I earn eight dollars an hour painting apartments at the complex where I live, but that barely covers the rent," I respond dejectedly. It's in these moments I realize just how broke I am.

"Okay, that's not much," he continues, "but here's what we can do. It appears to me that you're suffering from a number of issues, primarily relationship issues. I can assign you to a master's level student who has already graduated from the University but who is returning to complete additional training requirements for her state license or I can treat you myself. Either way, your fee will be twelve dollars per session and you'll meet once per week. What would you like to do?"

I think quickly and realize that I cannot share LT with the

Director, who is gay. I don't believe he would understand how much it means to me.

"If you don't mind," I begin, "because my issues are with women—Natalia and my mother—I think it would benefit me more to work with a female therapist to learn to trust women again, all the while under your supervision, of course," I say, hoping not to offend.

"I understand," Dr. Monteblanc responds calmly.

"If you will wait in the reception area," the Director says next, "your therapist will be available shortly. I'll introduce you as soon as she finishes with her current client."

"Thank you, Dr. Monteblanc." I show myself out to the waiting area and sit down.

Despite my growing discomfort with being in the fishbowl, I wait nervously, hoping no one will see me. After about five minutes, two women walk in from the hallway outside.

The first woman to enter has short sandy brown hair, appears to be in her late forties or early fifties, is mildly overweight, stands about five-foot-one, and looks as if she has been crying. Actually, she looks like she's lost her best friend, weepy, unkempt and isolated.

The second woman looks to be in her late twenties, stands maybe five-foot-six, has wavy blonde shoulder blade length hair, is very chicly dressed in designer clothes, carries herself with confidence, and is, drop dead gorgeous. A beautiful woman. Although I try not to stare, she catches me staring anyway, and we both look away. Through my peripheral vision, I watch as the two women shake hands. Then the blonde disappears into the back as the brown-haired woman pays her fee to Mona and departs. I will likely never see her again. Her name is Helen Throckmorton. I saw her name on the sign in sheet. Monteblanc is standing at his office door and says something to the blonde. I'm assuming I'm her next patient. I sit on the vinyl couch waiting. I feel my sweat, despite the air conditioning, trickle down my back, over my boils. I feel like a goldfish in a bowl.

About a minute later, out of the corner of my eye I see the Director exit his office with a file in his hand. He makes some copies at the copying matching and turns toward me in the fishbowl. He waves and mouths something that I don't really understand. Eventually, feeling I have made a huge mistake and planning to bolt, I observe the Director and the stunning blonde walking toward me. They are both smiling, smiles that combine something less than sincerity with a full-blown discomfort. It is clear to me that they have had a disagreement of some sort. She is just short of fuming. Oh, I think to myself, I have really stepped in it this time.

"Jim," Dr. Monteblanc says, signaling me to stand. I rise from my chair, whack-a-mole style. No whacks, but I get a gorgeous toothy smile from the woman. Her old man spent a lot of money on her perfect teeth. "This is Cindy Polanski, your therapist."

"Hello Miss Polanski. I'm Jim Schneider," I say as I extend my hand and shake hers.

"Hi Jim. You can call me Cindy."

"Thank you, Cindy," I respond not knowing what to say next. This is terra incognita to me.

After an awkward silence where the three of us just look at each other, finally Cindy says, "Jim, Dr. Monteblanc has already updated me on you and I've briefly reviewed your intake forms, so if you're ready, we can get started."

"Okay," I respond. "Thank you, Dr. Monteblanc," I say as I take his hand and shake it one more time.

"Why don't you call me Joe?" Dr. Monteblanc says. "We're not very formal around here." Just plain Joe, an ordinary guy.

I smile and nod. No way I'll be calling the creep Joe. The next thing I know he'll be wanting to buy me a White Russian in a downtown cocktail lounge.

With Cindy on my right, we walk side-by-side toward the Psychological Counseling Services' glass exit door. Upon reaching the door, which is hinged on the left, Cindy stops and remains still for a moment, waiting for me to open the door. A little awkwardly I reach past her, pull open the door nearly hitting her with it as it opens, and hold it while she proceeds out into the hallway.

Once in the hallway, we turn left and walk about fifty feet past the student bulletin boards that I had looked at before. As we approach a sign that says, "Educational Development Lab," Cindy slows and signals that we must turn left. At the end of this narrow hallway are two doors, one on the left labeled, "Educational Development Lab," and one on the right that is not labeled. Cindy opens the door on the right and we go inside. The therapy room is much smaller than I imagined it would be. There are two yellow leather chairs that are situated exactly opposite each other, and which are separated by less than two feet. Cindy immediately sits in one of the chairs, and I settle into the other.

As Cindy reviews the intake forms, I sit quietly and look her over. Cindy, who is in her late twenties, is beautiful, to me at least, even more beautiful than Natalia. Cindy's long hair is golden blonde, her green eyes striking. She is pretty as a Texas Prom Queen, all white teeth, blonde hair, and perky boobs. A Prom Queen before the first divorce; before the kids and the long days by the pool, and the just one more martini. I'm being a cynic and an asshole. She's a career woman. Today she is wearing a white, loose fitting, long-sleeve blouse and a black, knee-length, skirt. Her tanned legs are spectacular. I think I'm going to like therapy.

Cindy begins. "For the record, Jim, I'm Cindy Polanski and I'll be your therapist for the next six to nine months, all depending on how long you feel you need therapy. Do you have any questions before we begin?"

I suspect this formal prologue to our actual session means that our conversation is being recorded, either with a hidden video camera or a microphone. Without disclosing that information, I have doubts about its legality. The university will need my permission to record these sessions, I think.

"Yes," I answer. "I'd like to know your credentials—your age, your number of years of experience, and your educational background."

Cindy's response is immediate. "A lady doesn't discuss her age," she states firmly. Who is she, I wonder, Her Highness of Houston?

"Then what about your educational background and number of years of experience?" I ask.

"Oh, a lady doesn't discuss such things," she replies.

"Is that why you stopped at the door and waited for me to open it for you?" I ask next. Cindy responds, "A gentleman opens the door for a lady."

"Well," I state matter-of-factly with a smile, "This gentleman supports women's lib, so you'll need to open your own doors going forward."

This is a little too aggressive, I realize. I'm going to have to settle down into my nice-boy mode.

As I sit there nervously pondering my next question, Cindy begins asking her own questions. "It says on your intake forms that you previously worked for Europe Middle East Africa Airlines as a 'ghost rider.' Did I read that correctly?"

"Yes."

"What exactly is a ghost rider?"

"I was hired by EMEA Airlines to observe and document employee-customer interactions," I answer dryly.

"How did you do that?"

"Well," I pause, "every month I would fly to different cities around the world, usually first class, and I would observe how the employees interacted with the passengers."

"But what did you do?" Cindy interjects.

"The process began when I arrived at the airport," I answer hesitantly. "I would observe whether skycaps were available and courteous. Then I would move to the ticket counter and observe how the agents treated the customers. After that, I'd go through security and next check the gate area and the gate agents. Once on the airplane, I would check to make sure that the first-class flight attendant addressed each customer formally using his or her last name. I would also rate the flight attendants based upon their levels of customer warmth and friendliness."

"Did you do anything else?" Cindy interrupts.

"Yes," I answer. "I would check the lavatories to make sure they were clean. I would evaluate the meal service. And occasionally I would sneak on the airplane without giving up my ticket."

"Wait a minute," Cindy interjects. "You would sneak on the airplane without giving up your ticket? How in the world did you do that?"

"I can't tell you," I reply in a very serious tone. "But I can say that a lot of us were doing it." I used to know a lot of secrets. I've been around the world in a plane.

"But what would you do if you got caught?" she asks excitedly, leaning forward in her chair.

"Well, I never got caught. But I suppose if I had been caught, I simply would have given them my ticket."

"Oh," Cindy says sitting back in her chair. "So, you would always have a ticket to the flight you were on."

"That's correct."

"Can anyone become a ghost rider?"

"I suppose," I answer. "But it takes a lot of time and there are a ton of reports to write."

"But anyone can do it, even me, right?"

"Yes, I suppose even you could do it, assuming you had the time."

"If I wanted to become a ghost rider, how would I do it? Who would I contact?"

"You would contact customer service at the airline, but since 9/11 it has become sort of outdated. With the new levels of security, the airlines don't want to risk anything like having a ghost rider trying to sneak onto a plane. The consequences are much direr. I'm not sure if ghost riders exist anymore. In fact, I know they don't."

"I understand," Cindy replies as she looks down at the intake forms. She seems disappointed.

I have a feeling that Cindy is both hiding behind a façade and that she is very self-centered. I'm not sure I can trust this woman. I need someone to take an interest in me. I need help. I take a chance.

"How did you meet Natalia?" Cindy asks as she looks up from the forms.

20

"I met her in November when she was moving into her apartment. She looked as if she needed help carrying a large box, so I approached her."

"Is she pretty?"

"Yes, she's very beautiful, even more beautiful than you," I answer dishonestly, then continue. "Whereas you have long blonde hair, Natalia has short brown hair. You're taller than she is, and your voice is deeper, but Natalia has larger breasts and a more hour-glass figure."

"James, I think we should skip the comparisons to me, okay?" Touched a nerve, did I, Your Highness?

"Sure, sorry."

"How did you get involved?"

"I saw Natalia later that day at the mail room, and I asked her if she would like to have dinner. She said she had plans that evening, but if I wanted, I could stop by her apartment that afternoon. So, that's what I did."

"And what happened that afternoon?" She probably knows what happened but wants to hear it from me. She doesn't really give a shit, that much I understand.

"I knocked on Natalia's door. She showed me around her apartment. And before I knew it, one thing led to another and we became intimate, which I should've known meant trouble."

"Why do you think that meant trouble?"

"Because I've never known a relationship to last that was based purely upon sex."

This revelation about sex and Natalia seems to have triggered a surge of anger and anxiety. I feel my heart rate increase and my breathing becomes shallow and stressed.

As Cindy once again looks down at the intake forms, I blurt out, "Why did Natalia cheat on me? Why would she do that? I trusted her. I let down my defenses, and she abandoned me."

The pain is bubbling to the surface through gaps and fissures that I don't really understand. "Why won't she recognize me or talk to me?" I ask nearly hyperventilating. "I know I can never accept her back into my life for cheating on me, but still I need to see her. Why can't I get over her?" Calm down, step back, I say to myself.

Cindy recognizes that my questions are about the past and tries to shift to the present. "What do you want from the relationship, Jim? What does Natalia represent to you?"

"She reminds me of my mother," I answer coldly. "But I don't know how. I mean, when Dr. Monteblanc said that you can't have sex with your mother, it was like a flash of lightning went off inside my head."

"Joe Monteblanc said something that made sense to you?" Cindy asks. She raises her eyebrows and smiles as she makes a note on her pad. "You're a lucky guy to have the Director share his wisdom so early in the process."

"He made great sense to me!" I nearly shout. "All this time I've wanted to be with Natalia, but I couldn't be. And then, boom! In five minutes Dr. Monteblanc helps me to understand some of my torment."

"Wow!" Cindy exclaims. "Therapy usually takes longer than five minutes."

"I still need to see Natalia," I say, my stomach turning over on itself at the admission. "But what he said made sense to me."

"I understand from Dr. Monteblanc that you're working at your apartment complex. Is that correct?" Cindy asks changing the subject.

"Yes."

"What do you do there?"

"I mostly do painting. I paint the apartments after people move out. I paint roadside curb in the parking lots Official Traffic Yellow Number Three. And I also pressure wash the aluminum siding."

"So, you're kind of a handy man?"

"Yes, I suppose you could say that. A handyman with an MBA," I add self-deprecatingly.

"Do you have any questions before we end the session?" Cindy asks, signaling that our time is almost over.

"Yes, I have one. Earlier you asked about my ghost rider work experience."

"Yes, I recall," Cindy interjects.

"Well, Conrad Watson, my ghost rider roommate, and his psychiatrist, Dr. Brandon McIvy, who was also a ghost rider, became very good friends after Conrad's therapy ended. If I'm going to bare my soul to you and trust you with my secrets, it's my hope that you and I can similarly become friends after therapy. Do you think that might be possible?"

"We'll see," Cindy says as she gathers her papers and stands up. She opens the therapy room door signaling that we should leave. I guess this is her version of "no."

Together, Cindy and I return to the Psychological Counseling Services room, where I open the glass entry door for her. I'm a gentleman, all right. Or maybe just an asshole. Take your pick. Once inside the fishbowl, I shake Cindy's hand and thank her. She disappears into the back, and I pay Mona the twelve-dollar fee. I then leave the campus.

Once back in my apartment, I call Scott at his work. Scott is my only friend. He has been with me through some rough times. I honestly don't know what I'd do without him. He's been my attachment to a real life. We worked together for a short time after I first moved to Texas. Before he was married we would go out almost evert night to have a beer or something to eat. After he married Kelly and after he had the kids, I became almost one of the family.

"How did it go, Jim?"

"It went all right, I guess."

"And?" Scott pushes.

"And the Director is gay, and my therapist is beautiful."

"One is gay and the other is beautiful," Scott repeats slowly. "Be careful, Jim, you've got to protect LT."

"Roger that," I acknowledge immediately.

"So," Scott pauses, "what are you going to do with your master key?"

"I'm going to give it to George."

"Smart move, buddy."

"I figure George can let me into the apartments I need to paint, at least until Natalia moves out."

"That's excellent thinking, Jim," Scott praises.

"Thanks," I respond. "I'll talk with you later."

"Later," Scott says as we hang up.

I immediately change into my painting clothes, grab the master key, and head downstairs to see George. "Hi George," I say as he opens the door.

"Oh, be quiet!" he shouts to his barking dogs, then comes outside to talk.

"How'd it go?" he asks.

"It was all right," I answer before continuing. "It's going to be a long journey, George. But I've taken the first step."

"We're proud of you, Jim," he says smiling.

"Listen, George, I brought you something," I say as I hand him my master key. "I want you to hold onto this until Natalia moves out."

"Are you sure, Jim?" George asks.

"I need this job, George," I answer very seriously.

"Understand. We'll hold onto this key until Natalia moves out."

"Will you let me into 402 so I can paint it today?"

"Sure will," George answers.

That evening I call Conrad Watson and tell him that I have begun therapy. Because he knows about my dire financial situation, he offers to loan me money to pay for the counseling.

"No, Conrad, I won't take your money. This is bargain basement therapy, twelve dollars a session."

"The offer is an open one, Jim. I know you don't have much money now. You shouldn't let a few dollars and your pride stand in the way of getting healthy. McIvy and I both have real concerns about what's going on with you, about your emotional and mental state."

"I appreciate that, but for the moment I'm okay."

"I'm glad you're getting help, Jim. Keep in touch. I want to know how it's going."

The poisoning, Cindy's poisoning, begins innocuously enough.

POOR JIMMY, HE LIVES LIKE A RAT

I think about my dinner with the Carvels with some concerns. They mean well, but there is much in my life I don't want to talk about, especially with George. He is very old school, pull-yourself-up-by-your bootstraps kind of guy. I know he grew up very poor in rural Virginia, son of a failing farmer. He told me how he learned to fish and hunt at an early age, not for sport, but to survive. He'll point out the local squirrels as we clean the parking lots.

"That's a nice fat one, Jimmy. That one would be good eating."

My dad grew up that way, too. Poor and hungry and ready to stalk anything that offered a little protein. They both—George and my Dad—have a lean and hungry look. At the kitchen table, they can never seem to get enough. George has a pot belly that spills over his belt. Insurance against hard times. He's tough but he's got a heart of gold, as they say. I know he worries about me.

Grace is a mystery. I know she was married at least one other time, and her husband died under mysterious circumstances. George told me they met in San Antonio after he got out of the army. He had been in the army for a long time, ten years, and he was "sort of looking for a wife." He found Grace at a dinner near the Riverwalk. She is much younger than George, it's hard to say how much younger but maybe as much as twenty years. They are devoted to each other in a very charming way. The sense I get is that George went into the army as a hard-drinking hillbilly and came out as an even harder-drinker professional soldier, a Tech Sergeant; a Viet Nam vet with a pocket full of troublesome memories. His one bad habit is that he smokes heavily. His teeth are nicotine-stained yellow, and his clothes smell of smoke.

Grace has settled him down a bit, and seems to have eliminated

25

his drinking. He likes sweet tea and milk. I'm bringing a gallon of milk as my contribution to the meal. I'm happy I can afford it.

I go into the bathroom and start to clean up after a day's painting. I hope there's hot water in the shower. I peel off my painter's pants and shirt. They are splotched with white paint. That's the only color The Dorchester will paint as apartments turn over. This is the worst apartment complex in a relatively good neighborhood, and it collects mostly losers who can't afford more expensive places. Like me. Lots of alcoholics, drifters working on the oil rigs or the refineries. You name it. Not exactly deadbeats, not yet anyway. Everyone seems to be headed somewhere else. The main place our residents want to go to, from my conversations with them, is Las Vegas, the American El Dorado, where credit is available, beer is cold, and even a loser at the tables can be comped at the never-ending buffet. And there's the sex, too, if you're up to it. I'm not going anywhere, broke as I am.

I look at myself in the mirror. I have worked hard in my life and it shows in around my eyes. I have anxious-looking eyes. I was never particularly good looking and I haven't changed that much. I am presentable, at least. My hair is brown, a mousy brown, that lightens in the summer sun, as are my eyes. I burn rather than tan, so I'm careful to put on sunscreen when I'm working outside or riding my bike. Natalia thought I was handsome, or so she said anyway. She was a lot of things, but she wasn't a liar. There was a period, several months, after we had stopped having sex but were still friendly. This was before Keith showed up, of course. We went for walks sometimes and once or twice went to the beach. She slathered sunscreen on my back. I didn't have the boils then. She said I had a nice back, very muscular. I got that from my days when I was training in the dojo. She helped with my "grooming" and took me to her salon to get a haircut. It was a little pricey, but it looked good for about a month.

I have gained weight, probably about twenty pounds from my best condition, my black belt days. I have a little gut and I can grab a couple inches of love handles. I think it's from all the starchy cheap food I eat. White bread and fried Spam sandwiches are not exactly healthy food. I promise myself that I will lose the weight, but I never do. Beers with Scott don't help either. But I would never give up our nights out. The things I dislike the most are my hands and back. My hands are rough and red from painting, mostly because the solvents I use to clean the brushes. Natalia gave me some hand cream, but I used it all. I don't want to go to a drugstore to buy more, even though it helped. My hands look like what I imagine a washerwoman's hands are like. I have a hard time, right now, imagining myself touching a woman, her face and breasts, with these hands. The boils appeared on my back right after Keith appeared and Natalia eliminated me from her life altogether. They range from pea size to one or two the size of a nickel. The open ones seep pus and blood. The ones that are not open are red, almost black and are painful. Sometimes, at night one of these will burst and my sheet will be stained with puss and blood. I don't wash my sheets that often and so there are often several generations of bloody boil junk on them. My general cleanliness is beginning to decline. I no longer shave every day, and I shower when I think of it. George, who is a bit of a mess himself, tells me when I need a shower. My self-esteem is in the toilet, and so is my self-image. I don't really care. I no longer give a shit. Maybe this is the way an eight-dollar house painter should look.

Out of the shower, I carefully towel off my back. I should go to the doctor and have these fucking boils treated but, honestly, I can't afford it. I don't know what I would do if I really got sick. Borrow some money, I guess, but I dread the thought of that. I put on my last clean t-shirt and a pair of jeans, not so clean. I go into the main room, which is the living/dining room and kitchen all in one. This is what The Dorchester calls "luxury living." It is, in fact, squalor in a small space. I've collected "furniture" from all the people who moved out. These are people with very little money, and even they don't want this junk: a kitchen table with a piece of linoleum glued in the spot where the Formica has worn away; two rattan-seated kitchen tables chairs that I have smashed in one of my many rages and repaired, they are mostly duct tape now attached to the chrome frames. I use them for holding newspapers and throwing against the wall. They are a symbol of something, and I refuse to throw them out. I have a badly stained "easy" chair; mostly stain and very little ease, and a black leather sofa George gave me. It has only three functional legs. The third leg has been replaced by Sugarland phone books. Two of them are just the right size. Lamps have all been smashed. I light the apartment with work lights, clip-ons that I paint with. I don't bother to use the silver reflectors. Move on, nothing to reflect here, buddy. No TV, smashed, and when it started to buzz and burn I unplugged it; no radio except for a small transistor that I use when I'm painting. A phone sitting on an unpainted particle board night stand, unpainted and for the moment miraculously undamaged. I have two suits, one black and one grey, badly worn; two pairs of dress shoes, mostly unworn; a dozen pairs of underwear and t-shirts, paint-stained and frayed; bicycle shorts, shirt, and helmet in excellent condition and clean; two pairs of training shoes, one for work and one for bicycling. That concludes the inventory of my life. It is deeply depressing to think about, so I don't think about it. I know Grace will have something for me, shirts or jeans that are hand-me-downs from her son in New Mexico. I've given up refusing them because Grace can be insistent. But I also find it humiliating since I grew up in hand-me-downs. Holy shit, I do live like a rat.

I grab the milk and go downstairs to George's apartment. I knock on the door, and Grace lets me in.

She is very short but attractive in a matronly way. She is not a young woman, but she keeps herself youthful. She goes to the hairdresser every week and gets a perm. Once a month she gets her hair dyed blonde. That's the color men like, she says to me, even if they say they don't.

"Jimmy, I use the same color that Marilyn Monroe used, God rest her soul."

I always say the same thing, always, "You could have been a movie star, Grace." She never seems to get tired of hearing that.

Grace is a good cook. She's Italian, she says, although George told me she was actually Albanian. No matter, the place is aromatic with the tomato sauce, a little garlicky, and there is a platter of meatballs on the stove top.

She takes the milk from me and puts it in the refrigerator.

"Georgie had to leave for a minute, Jim, another problem in 813. It's that crazy Sutherland woman. She's always getting something clogged in her toilet. I think she'd flush that Yorkie of hers down the toilet if she could."

"Do you think I should go help?"

"No, he can handle it. I just don't want her to handle him. I think she's got her eyes on him."

"Mrs. Sutherland? She's only got one leg."

"Jimmy, you don't need any legs to get on your back if you pardon my implication. She wouldn't be the first cripple to try to screw George Carvel."

"I think George would walk away from that nonsense."

"Look, Jimmy, I know what men are like. But George is a good man, and he knows that if he comes in here smelling like sex, I'd slap him one upside the head."

She makes a muscle, and invites me to squeeze it.

"George better be careful," I say.

"I'm strong. I used to be in the circus, you know."

"I know you told me." Many, many times.

"I was a flying Fantucci. Our family was very famous."

"I know."

"I traveled all around the world and met many famous people. I guess you could call me a star. You know, Jimmy, I was very beautiful."

And she was. Truly.

"And then we had that night in Mexico City when those Polish midgets sabotaged our setup, and the boys fell. I could show you the press clippings."

"You did. But most of them were in Spanish, remember."

"Oh yes, those were good days until the last one very sad. But the boys are doing okay back in Albania. You know our real name is Gashi, but the old man thought that no one wants to see Albanian high flyers named Gashi. I guess he was right. Well, something good came out of it. I met my first husband, Carl, Carl Heikilla. He was a Finn and a communist. Very serious fellow, very brave, and very handsome. God, he was a gorgeous man. He was a union organizer and he was trying to organize us circus workers. The owners hated him, but he kept at it. He almost had enough votes to get a union started, if it weren't for the Bulgarian strong man, the drunken bastard. The bosses bought him off with two cases of liquor. I hope he choked on it. Stay away from Bulgarians, Jimmy, they're the worst."

"Far away."

"And then somebody murdered Carl in Oakland. They think it was the mob. He was such a sweet man, sober. Personally, I think he had too much to drink and got into some sort of bar fight. He was a heavy drinker and a nasty drunk. Vodka totally changed his personality, and don't I know it. But that's the past. And then along comes George into my coffee shop in San Antonio, and here I am.

"Now, I have to say something to you Jimmy, and don't say anything until I'm done."

"Okay, Grace."

"You've got to stop mooning over that little slut Natalia. She's not worth it. She would screw the exterminator if she had to get rid of her cockroaches. You need a nice girl. There's that secretary in 414, the Irish girl, Mary Murphy for example. Plenty of them around here. And the other thing Jimmy is you have to stop smashing things. You'll get kicked out if you don't, and George won't be able to do a thing about it. Do you get me?"

"I do. I understand."

"George will be here soon, Jimmy, don't give up going to a therapist. George thinks it's going to help, and so do I. Maybe not as much as he does. But I know a good kid when I meet him, and you're a good kid. You're a nice, clean, sober boy, and you're going to get better. Listen to me, because I have a little gypsy blood in me. I see great things in your future if you can shut the door on the past. Now shut up because I think I hear George in the hallway."

It was George with his plunger and his bucket. He looked tired.

"Okay, gentlemen, come to the table. The pasta will be done in a few minutes and we can eat."

George washes his hands in the kitchen sink and dries them with a paper towel.

"Smells good. I'm lucky to have married such a good cook, Jimmy. I'm just a lucky guy to have a wife like Grace."

I smiled my agreement. He isn't wrong.

SILENCE AND CONTROL

Most things take place in the foreground: the business of a day;
the normal rattle and quake of tasks being performed. Things need to
get done. Even after a disaster — a fire or a war — someone must
reach into the closet or a shed for a broom and a shovel. The broken
pieces need to be picked up and thrown away. Save what you can, as
we build out of the ashes. My life was not that way; my life was
background: the ticking of the clock on the mantle, the sound of a
radio down the hall playing some forgotten tune. Some faces cannot
be seen in the mirror. My face could not be seen in a mirror. The
reason I started therapy was because I felt alone. I felt I knew
nothing, and I was frightened that I would die that way. It was my
expectation — not an idiot's dream — that Cindy would help me. She
did not help me; she was not capable of helping. I forgive myself for
being a fool. The truth is that a pretty woman is always blameless.

The week between my first therapy session and my second passes
in a blur of painted apartments. I want to see Natalia. But whenever I
do see her, my stomach churns with anger and dumb desire. No one's
desire is dumber than mine. I look forward all week to having my
second session with Cindy. I am hopeful that she can help me deal
with my pain.

As I park in the second row back on the Wasserman Building, the
psychological services building's parking lot, I observe Cindy getting
out of her car, a silver Mercedes, which she has parked in the reserved
faculty spaces in the first row. I call to her and she waits for me.
Together we walk into the building. She seems a little uncomfortable
and walks quickly into the building. Doesn't she want to be seen with
me?

Once inside the Psychological Counseling Services fishbowl,

Cindy disappears into the back as I present myself to Mona. Cindy returns about a minute later carrying my file and together we walk to the therapy room. I open all the doors for her, a habit of a lifetime. Something a good boy would do.

We begin. I ask Cindy for her credentials.

She again declines to share them saying, "They're not relevant."

"They're relevant to me," I say.

"I'm qualified to treat you," she says, a little defensively.

"This is my first time in therapy. And you're a graduate student, isn't that correct?"

"Yes."

"And these sessions will be part of your evaluation?"

"Yes."

"If you'd like another therapist...," she begins.

"No, I'm sorry. I'm just a little nervous."

"Don't be nervous."

"What if you flunk?"

"Flunk?"

"What if you screw up my therapy and you fail? And I fail? What happens then? What if nothing helps me, nothing changes?"

She looked at me with defiance. I suspected then that she was as nervous as me. That she was as new to this process as I was; that her rich-girl demeanor was new to her. Maybe she grew up as poor as I did.

"We have to start with a positive attitude, Mr. Schneider. Therapy is not like fixing a flat tire. It's a process, and sometimes it's a long one."

We then engage in a discussion about the differences between beautiful children and ugly children.

"Cindy, you're very beautiful. People must tell you that all the time."

She doesn't respond to that. She doesn't disagree either.

I point out that Cindy dresses conservatively wearing professional business attire and that she wears simple gold hoop earrings. I observe to her that she wears a woman's gold Rolex watch and has short fingernails with clear fingernail polish. She wears expensive shoes — designer shoes — and there is a Louis Vuitton handbag on her desk. She likes nice things, all sorts of shiny objects.

She doesn't acknowledge what I'm saying. She knows what she looks like. She's worked hard at it. No, she is not your typical down-in-the-heels graduate student, eating Ramen noodles and hoping her checks don't bounce. She was something else entirely. She was very finely finished. I was impressed and a little intimidated. I'm the boy with big ears, after all. I'm the poor boy raised in the double wide. At least I knew what I was, that I was real. I may not have liked it, but I understood me. How about Cindy? How real was she?

"Beautiful children are raised differently than ugly children," I state, explaining that when I was young I grew my hair very long to get over what I thought were bizarrely large ears. Sad boy, I also needed braces and medicine for my acne.

"I wasn't very popular," I tell Cindy. "But I bet you were very popular."

She doesn't respond. I press on, right through the silence, the first of many such silences. Eventually, her silences — and the judgments I assumed were behind them — confused me. Then they enraged me. She hid behind those silences. She was stealing my words and not giving anything back.

"Until I grew my hair long," I continue, "I was picked on by other kids because of my ears. I was called 'Dumbo' and 'Mickey.' I was constantly trying to be somebody people liked, but I couldn't quite crack the code."

"I bet that was hard for you," Cindy says, a little coldly. At least she didn't stare at my ears. She was a chilly bitch, that one, an Ice Queen.

"Yes, it was," I say, "it was very hard for me. But it taught me that society rewards beauty and punishes ugliness. It also taught me that beautiful children have an easier path socially than ugly children."

You see, Cindy, that's a little of the old passive aggression: just a knife's nick on your self-esteem. Pretty girls don't struggle. They get it all handed to them.

"How was your childhood?" Cindy asks when I've finished speaking.

"We grew up very poor," I answer. "We didn't have a lot of possessions. I really didn't have anything except the basics until I was old enough to work and pay for whatever I wanted myself. I sometimes wonder if we were as poor as we lived. But it was hard for my parents to buy anything other than essentials. They had grown up in a world without money and assumed it would always be that way. Right now, I have no money. I have substantial debt for my student loans and a minimum wage job. I guess I stay there because of Natalia, thinking she might change her mind and come back to me. My boss, George, says I live like a rat. He's right. It is not exactly squalor I inhabit, but it is damned closed."

I tell Cindy that my mother quit her job as an assistant principal to raise my sister, brother, and me, so I have a tight bond with her. My father, a manual laborer, was unemployed off and on during my early years, so there was a lot of stress. When my father was working, he'd come home and find me and my friends playing in the yard and tell me, "Send those kids home. They're messing up the grass."

"There were power struggles between Mom and Dad," I continue, warming to the topic.

I tried to explain the double game they played with each other and their kids. I told Cindy how each of my parents would respond, "What did your Mother say?" or "What did your Father say?" whenever one of us kids would ask to do something.

If we asked permission, the answer was always, "No."

Everything I know about passive aggression, and I know some, I learned at the feet of mom and dad. It is bred in the bone.

"How did that make you feel?" Cindy asks.

"Not good," I answer. "In many ways, I was socially isolated. I was always the last to be picked for sports teams in gym class. I wasn't very popular."

It is my lament. Maybe she heard it as whining.

Lamentation is a bad habit in my sessions with Cindy.

"How did you cope?"

"I got a job as a waiter in a restaurant and in that way earned my own spending money. I also studied hard to get good grades."

"That's neat," Cindy says, then volunteers that she worked in a grocery store as a cashier to earn her spending money.

"How old were you when you started?" I ask immediately.

Cindy doesn't answer — silence is her lever in our sessions — and instead asks about Natalia.

"Why do I need to see Natalia?" I ask, the pain must have been evident in my voice. "Why do I still want to be around her? I know I cannot accept her back into my life because she cheated on me, but why won't she recognize me?"

As before, Cindy recognizes my passivity and focuses on the active.

"What do you want from the relationship, Jim? Why do you want to see Natalia?"

I should have told what I probably knew to be the truth: I lost something that I thought I possessed. I did not want it back, but I wanted to discard it on my own terms. That was the control Natalia had over me, and is the control that Cindy was beginning to assume.

For every passive question I ask, Cindy turns it into an active question directed toward me, probing. We talk about Natalia for about ten minutes, then Cindy asks about my employment history.

"What jobs have you had?" Cindy asks.

I answer that I moved to Sugar Land, an incorporated city

southwest of Houston, after graduating from Cleveland College to work as an engineer for an oil and gas company. I hated the job so after two years left to pursue an MBA degree at Saint Martha's College in Houston.

"What was your degree in from Cleveland College?"

"I had a double degree in electrical engineering and aeronautical engineering."

"That's impressive," she says.

"Not really. Just hard work. I was a grinder with a great short-term memory."

"All right. Then what did you do?"

"I worked as a ghost rider, as we discussed, for EMEA Airlines while matriculating my MBA degree," I continue. "And after that ended and I graduated without a job, I secured part-time employment as a handy man around my apartment complex. It's not much money," I reflect. "But I'm surviving."

Survived as a ghost rider; barely surviving as a ghost.

"Did you grow up in Ohio?" Cindy asks.

"Yes," I answer. "I grew up in a small town of about twelve thousand people about twenty miles from Cleveland."

"Oh," she says, "I grew up in Los Angeles."

"Really? Which part of LA?" I ask immediately.

She didn't grow up in Malibu or Bellaire, I thought, or she would have told me. More like Santa Monica or out by the airport. Strip malls and cheap residential motels. Parking lots full of rusting convertibles. That's the Los Angeles you don't get to see much. Someplace dreary from which she escaped and now wants to forget.

"Why did you leave LA? Maybe you got married?"

"I like it here better," she says. She glances at her watch again. Time is not my friend, I realize.

"It's funny, James, but you remind me a lot of my dad. He grew up very poor in western Pennsylvania. His father and grandfather were coal miners and he wanted none of that. My dad's name is Bill. He got a degree in chemical engineering and worked for Three M. He invented something — some sort of industrial adhesive — at home on his own time, and he got into a big fight with Three M about who controlled the rights to it."

She is very engaging now, very expressive. It's clear she thinks the world of her old man. I'm flattered that I remind her of Bill Polanski.

"Luckily, my mother's father, Grandpa Berg, is a lawyer and he won the case for my dad. Grandpa Berg said he beat Three M like a rented mule. He was always saying folksy stuff like that. He sold the rights to DuPont and that's when we moved from Minneapolis to Los

Angeles."

"That's a great story, Cindy. I wish I could invent something. It would beat the hell out of the dead-end job I have now."

"You're a bright guy. Something will work out for you, I'm sure. Just like it did for my dad."

A nice moment between us, an interval of warmth. But then she switches back into her ice queen persona. She really won't answer my questions.

"Are you married, Cindy?"

Just a Mona Lisa smile.

"Where do you live in Houston, Cindy?"

She tosses her hair and looks at her watch.

These seem like normal questions, but I am being taught the protocols of therapy. Mind your own business, Jim, is the unspoken subtext. You may remind me of Daddy, but you ain't Daddy. Get your mind right, pal. This is about you — you're the one who needs help and badly — and not about me. Cindy refuses to answer and instead asks another question.

"What activities were you involved with in high school?" Cindy asks next.

I realize that these questions are part of the grad student template. Useful if answered honestly; worthless if the therapist is not paying attention to the tone of voice and body language. This is her classroom, and I am, literally, her subject matter: The Neuroses of James Schneider 101. These are the terms Cindy is comfortable with; the terms that define my therapy. Whether they work or not, she follows the procedures diligently. She thinks she is good at it. Me, not so much.

This is the moment when I answer hesitantly, as befits a troubled soul. "I was in the marching band in the fall. I wrestled over the winter. And I ran track in the spring, but I was awkward and very shy. I was a lonely kid but couldn't admit that to myself, to anyone. That would have been weakness, and my father would not have tolerated that." There was a lot my father wouldn't tolerate. I think about that, too, when I paint. He was an emotional bully, and I was always a little afraid of him. Until I was big enough and strong enough not to be afraid of him. His tolerance expanded in direct response to my lack of fear. Thinking of that makes me sad rather than angry. I love my father, I guess, I wish he were more willing to be loved.

"I was on the yearbook committee," Cindy volunteers, cheerily. Of course, she was.

"Really? What did you do on the committee?" I ask. I think I was sincere.

Instead of answering, Cindy smiles and looks at her watch, signaling that therapy is over. We walk together back into the fishbowl, where Cindy disappears into the back as I pay Mona my twelve-dollar fee. I then leave campus. I guess I got my twelve bucks worth.

At subsequent sessions in October, November and December, we're essentially playing back the same clinical material. I wonder, "Why?"

The answer is Cindy didn't know what else to do. I knew I was a little crazy; she knew I was a little crazy. The problem is neither of us knew how crazy I was and how crazy I was going to be. I guess nobody knows that until they know it. How far would I go? I would go a long way, and I would be driving the bus. That's what I thought, anyway.

Natalia moved out just before Christmas. Brooding, miserable, I painted her former apartment over the Christmas holidays. Gone but not quite forgotten.

The poison infuses me.

COMPETITION AND CONTROL

As January 2004 begins, I finally begin to put Natalia behind me. In her place, I begin focusing my paranoid attention on Cindy. I don't know that much about Cindy, and I still don't know her credentials, but I reason that she helped me to get over Natalia, so I should probably trust her. Yet, trusting Cindy is extremely difficult because she is inconsistent in her moods and in her behaviors from week to week. I feel a discomfort in my chest, a suffocating anxiety. I'm trying to maintain control but I feel the old anger again, like water on the boil.

"I feel like I'm leaving Natalia behind," I say to Cindy in one of our sessions.

"That's good," Cindy says, a little vaguely.

"Why is that good, Cindy?"

"Because you were keeping Natalia's image alive, hanging onto something that wasn't real. I mean, hanging onto Natalia in the long run was bad. But that also means something good can happen."

"And that is?"

"You can focus on me."

As therapy progresses, I observe that Cindy occasionally removes and plays with two interlocking gold bands that she sometimes wears on her left-hand ring finger. I also observe that Cindy has not worn the same outfit twice. Not that I can recall anyway, and I am oddly observant about these things. I am very curious to know how a presumably single part-time graduate student in psychology can afford a Mercedes Benz, a Rolex watch, and a different designer outfit every week.

During therapy, I notice that Cindy doesn't seem to be paying close attention to what I'm saying. Instead, whenever I say something about myself, she volunteers a small snippet of information about herself. When she does this, I immediately ask her a follow-on question; however, she doesn't answer. This frustrates the hell out of me. She's trying to establish some boundaries, which she thinks I've muddled. I've not muddled any boundaries, Cindy. You just don't seem interested in anything I'm saying.

It never occurred to me that the reason she didn't say anything to me was that she didn't have anything to say. Period. I bore her. Fair enough, sometimes I bore myself, sometimes. But then what in the fuck am I doing here?

At the end of January, I finally recognize that Cindy is playing an "attention game" with me. Every time I say something about myself, Cindy volunteers something similar about herself. However, when I ask her for more details, she clams up. I feel that she is competing with me for my attention, and I don't like it, so I confront her.

I begin the next therapy session by telling Cindy that I have something to say to her.

"I believe you are competing with me and trying to best me at every corner of the dialogue, and I want you to stop."

I cite numerous examples, including my extensive martial arts training in Jujitsu and Cindy's brief martial arts training in Tae Kwan Do, my sports activities in high school and Cindy's activities as an aerobics instructor in college, the fact that my mother prepares my favorite banana nut bread every time I go home, and Cindy's mother does the same for her, and the fact that some of my favorite business books Cindy has read.

"I want you to stop competing with me." She twists the gold rings on her finger.

"I'm not competing with you. Why would I want to do that?"

"I don't know."

"I'm just sharing with you some of the things I did. How is that competition?"

"I feel that you're always trying to top me."

"I'm not," she says, as she quickly looks at her watch. Our session, a really short one this time, is almost over.

"I don't want to compete with you, that's all, Cindy. I *really* don't like it." I emphasized really to make my point.

"I'll think about it, James. I'll give what you said some serious thought."

That evening, Scott Todd and his wife Kelly invite me to their home for dinner. Their two children, Rob, age 7, and Amy, age 6, greet me at the door. I pick them up, one in each arm, and give them both a big hug as they ask in unison, "Jimmy Snyder, can we have a lifesavah?" Telling them that they must share, I remove a peppermint roll from my pocket and hand it to Rob. I then give Kelly a big hug and tell her that this is the best part of the evening. She hugs me back, pushing her breasts into my chest. We hold on to each other a little too long. I feel confusion setting in. Something was too intimate about that hug, or was I imagining it?

Scott Todd is the first and almost the only friend I made after I moved to Houston. He is my best friend in life. We worked together briefly at a temp job I had with a computer company. He had worked for NASA, but like many others was laid off when the aerospace program was dismantled. He is a big man, built like a linebacker, with a bristle of red hair and a swarm of freckles. Over time Kelly and the kids have become my vicarious family. He married Kelly just after I met him. Kelly is gorgeous, a Cindy-like blonde with a lovely body. She was an athlete in college, a volley ball player, and was almost as tall as Scott. They seemed to be a perfectly matched couple, and they adored their kids. He is calm, where I am not. He is aware of my emotional difficulties, my tendency towards anger and depression, but he takes it in stride. I'm not sure what he truly thinks of me, although he has never been unavailable to me on the verge of a crackup. A solid man and a good one, too. Grace Fantucci, my downstairs neighbor, thinks he is gorgeous. I'm not sure if I agree with that, but she should know. She's been around the world in trains, planes, and Bentleys with acrobats and aristocrats.

Over dinner, I tell Scott and Kelly that I'm going to get inside Cindy's head. They warn me about doing this, but I tell them that I know what I'm doing. I joke that Kelly and Cindy could be sisters since they look so similar in appearance. I didn't mention that I thought Cindy was slightly prettier. I like women, even the married ones. I just wish they liked me, too.

"Be careful, Jim," Scott said. "Don't make this a drama. She's there to help you."

"What does that mean, 'drama'?"

"It means you can make things difficult for yourself when you don't have to, that's all."

I left that remark stand unanswered. Scott isn't wrong.

I find it odd that, seemingly, Cindy does not audio or video record my therapy sessions for review with her supervisor, Joe Monteblanc. I would find it infuriating; however, if she is recording our sessions and didn't inform me of that fact. Deep in my treacherous heart, at the core of my paranoia, I think she *is* secretly recording every word I say. Protection, ass-covering therapy chatter, for the difficult days to come. And they are coming, count on it. I don't understand a whole lot but I do understand when a big storm is coming. I feel like a canary in a cage.

I wonder what Joe and Cindy say about me.

The poison slowly begins flowing through my veins, seeping into my soul, whatever remains of it.

NO SECOND CHANCES:
INTRODUCTION TO BETRAYAL

Cindy is a study in contradiction. I am having great difficulty trusting her.

"James, I want to talk you about something you said last session, the fact that you thought I was trying to compete with you. Have you thought any more about that?"

"Nothing to think about. It's what you do."

"I think," Cindy says, "you might be correct. I'm going to be more aware of what you said going forward. It's important to me that we establish a level of trust."

"I would like that, too. I'm new to this process and trusting someone has never been easy for me."

"I understand. We can start over with that being our first goal, mutual trust and respect."

"Okay," I answer. "Maybe now you'll tell me more about yourself?"

"What do you want to know?"

"The same things I asked about earlier: your age, your number of years of experience, and your educational background."

"James, my credentials aren't relevant. I'm here to help you, isn't that enough?"

"I need to trust you Cindy. I must trust you if I am to improve, but your contradictions and your pretty professional facade make trusting you very difficult."

In my deeply paranoid state, I warn Cindy, "There are no second chances. Once a therapist violates a client's trust, that's it, her career is over. She is finished."

My words were deadly serious, but crazy. Why do I think her diffidence was betrayal? I am a deeply divided personality, divided against myself. I know that. In this room, talking to this pretty woman, I present a simulacrum of calm. The other James, the James alone and after dark, is a swirling vortex of anger and confusion. I rage at midnight and hold myself awake and aware until I slip into a restless sleep, exhausted. In this moment, I am cold and unrevealing. I repeat, "If you violate my trust, Cindy, your career will be over. You will be finished."

Cindy just looks at me blankly. After about a three second pause, I add, "There are a lot of crazy people out there. You should be careful."

Cindy glares at me, anger in her face. My seed has been planted.

"I'll remember that, James. I'll remember this conversation." You son of a bitch were the words she wanted to say but could not.

I knew she would remember. My words were a mistake, but I couldn't unsay them. I revealed something I did not want to reveal. No time to linger in the shadows of my paranoia. Time to move my knight.

"I have something important to tell you, Cindy. Hardly anyone knows about it."

"Are you sure you want to tell me, James?"

"If you want to know something about my motivation, yes."

I feel I might be making a mistake. I wonder if I can trust her with my secret.

"But you can't tell anyone, under any circumstances, Cindy," I say.

"Our conversations are meant to be private, James, but this a therapeutic environment, you have to remember. Perhaps some secrets, as you call them, can't be kept."

"I need to trust someone, Cindy, can I trust you?"

"Yes, James, I think you can trust me."

Her face shows concern, even panic. What in the world is going on here I know she is asking herself, how did I end up with this goofball in the chair across from me? In this game we were playing, I move another piece on the board, the complicated knight's gambit.

"Okay, I want to work in a position that will require a very high-level security clearance, and I've been working for this since I was twelve years old. I call this ambition 'LT' for Long Term. I want to work for the Central Intelligence Agency. I want to be a case officer, a spy."

"That's admirable, James," she says. "That is a very admirable ambition, your LT. You had some success as a ghost, why not be a spook, too?"

"And my real name is Snyder, not Schneider."

She makes a note of that.

"And one other thing, Cindy, and please remember this well. It is absolutely vital that what I just told you remains a secret. You have to promise me that you will not tell Dr. Monteblanc."

"All right. If that's what you want."

"Say the words, Cindy."

"Why?"

"I want to hear you say the words. With the words, I'll trust you."

"All right, James I promise I'll never reveal what you just told me."

"About LT."

"Yes, about LT."

She made a series of notes on a pad as I was describing LT. She underlined the letters LT twice. Maybe I made a mistake in telling her.

Over time, I think I notice that Cindy's physical appearance is deteriorating — bags under her eyes, disheveled clothing.... Something is wrong with her. I admit to taking a small amount of satisfaction in her dissolution. Maybe the poison has touched her as well. Good, I think, very good.

I wonder if during Cindy's meetings with the Director if he is applying therapy to her. She's always hiding behind a facade. She's hiding from me.

In April, Cindy's deterioration is at its worst. She has very dark circles under her eyes. Her disheveled designer clothes are draped over her frame rather than being worn to make her look attractive. I observe that she communicates her stress level via the tension in her hair, and her hair is very tense — it is tied back in the tightest ponytail imaginable.

"Cindy," I ask, "are you all right?"

"I'm fine. Maybe a little tired because of all the work I must do at the end of the semester. I have my final exams coming up. That's the last of my course work."

At the next therapy session, Cindy is the happiest that I have ever seen her. She announces that she will have a new supervisor next month and describes her decision to leave Joe Monteblanc as "getting that monkey off my back." She seductively puts both feet up on the chair in front of me, and we talk, flirting like college sweethearts. We talk about her father again. She is very admiring of her dad, his strength and kindness and his success in business.

"You know, James," the sweet Cindy says, "you do remind me a lot of him: super intelligent and intense. You both have big dreams. His worked out and I hope yours will too."

In the middle of the session, Cindy suggests that we go outside for a walk to enjoy the beautiful spring weather, so that is what we do. At the end of the session, Cindy hugs me goodbye. I am surprised by this muddling of boundaries. I ask myself, am I seeing something here when nothing actually exists? Am I projecting something onto to the way she treated me? Something arising out of my loneliness and longing? No, she sees something in me that she admires and trusts. She has her own version of longing.

"James, I think we should start meeting twice a week."

"I can't, Cindy," I say. "I have a new job as an inside salesman for an import / export company. It's my first professional job since I got my MBA two years ago."

"That's good news, James. What will you be doing?"

"Have you ever seen video poker games? Usually, they're in bars and casinos. My company imports the monitors from Korea, and my job is to try to sell them to the game manufacturers. I think I might even have to go to Korea for a while to check out the factory. It's not a great job, but it's a lot more money."

"That's wonderful. I love Korean food. There are a lot of great Korean restaurants in Los Angeles."

"I don't know about that. It's a little spicy for me. I liked the kimchi though. Rotten cabbage reminds me of home. The other thing, Cindy, is that I can't do two meetings per week with my new schedule, and, in fact, we need to change our meeting time to Tuesday evenings at 7:00 PM."

"Whatever is best for you," Cindy says. "I just thought we could make more progress."

I thank her for her offer of additional help and say goodbye. Am I making progress? What is her motive for wanting the additional session? Does she think I'm deteriorating? I don't feel like I've made any progress.

That evening, Kelly Todd calls me and says that she won tickets on a radio show to a play at the downtown theatre, but because Scott doesn't enjoy plays and will be out of town on business travel this Thursday, so couldn't go anyway, would I take her. I ask Scott and he says it's okay, so I agree.

On Thursday evening at the play, Kelly and I sit leaning very close to each other. Toward the end of the play, Kelly takes my hand, and we hold hands. On the way home, I stop at her bank's drive-through ATM so she can get money to pay the babysitter. Instead of getting out of the car, Kelly leans very seductively over me to push the buttons. I feel myself becoming aroused. I feel very angry. This teasing isn't fair to me. I want Kelly very much in that moment, and we both know that.

When we arrive at the house, Kelly quickly pays the sitter and then longingly gives me a full-frontal contact hug, pushing her breasts into my chest. Playfully, she brushes her hand against my erection as she pulls away.

"I hope that boner is because of me. Thanks for the nice evening, Jim."

"It was fun, I think" I say. And that boner, I say to myself, is about you.

"You're a great date. We ought to do this again some time. By the way, I really want to have sex with you right now. Am I being bad? I mean, we can't, but I want it. Before I married Scott, I was a sex maniac. I still am, I guess, but it's not so easy with two kids."

No, I think to myself, we ought not to do this again. She is a sexual creature, and she wants to fuck me. I find her very desirable, and I want to fuck her. But she is my best friend's wife! I am deeply confused. And after the confusion will come the anger.

The poison is affecting my brain.

POISONERS AND THEIR POWER

On my second day at my new job, Cindy calls my home telephone and deposits a very friendly, but rambling message on my answering machine to see how I'm doing. I no longer trust her. Because I feel very uncomfortable with Cindy's transparent attention and crocodile friendliness, I schedule a meeting with the Director to discuss my concerns. I am struggling with her motivation for this charade. Have I missed a move?

Monteblanc begins our conversation by observing that I'm not using my real last name. I sidestep this issue and focus on what I believe are the problems with my therapy. I state that I may have bastardized the therapeutic relationship by knowing too much personal information about Cindy.

"Cindy doesn't seem real to me."

"I'm not sure I understand what you're getting at, James."

"My problems with Cindy, that's what I'm getting at."

"She hasn't said anything to me. Are you sure there is a problem? Maybe you're imagining a problem where none exists."

I discuss Cindy's facade of being a lady and my belief that Monteblanc was surreptitiously giving therapy to her during the supervisory sessions.

"Mr. Schneider, it's my job to supervise my students, and I sometimes encourage my students to explore their own feelings about the work they're doing with the people they're counseling. It has nothing to do with you."

I tell the Director that I am uncomfortable with Cindy's seductiveness and that I am not sure if I should continue with her.

"You're uncomfortable with her seductiveness," he says. "My goodness."

47

"Yes."

"I'm also confused and a little pissed by the way she plays with what I take to her wedding band."

"I don't understand, James."

"I don't either. It's obvious to me she removes it, toys with it to make me pay careful attention to the band. I don't know, to make it seem like just another ring."

"I think you're making too much of this. It's probably just a nervous twitch, like swiveling in a swivel chair, for example, which is what you've been doing the past few minutes."

I hadn't realized I was swiveling and I stop abruptly and face him directly. I feel a little stupid to have been subtly, or not so subtly with stiletto silence and precision, embarrassed by him. Something I am unlikely to forget. I do not forget a slight, real or imagined. Subtle or delivered with a longshoreman's brutal force.

"I don't think she does anything without careful consideration. I mean that."

"James, she's an attractive young woman, to be sure, but she seems to me to be very professional. Maybe you're overreacting, being a little paranoid. I think you should give it a little longer since by her account she thinks you have a good working relationship."

"Doesn't it matter what I think?" I say feeling betrayed. "Doesn't it matter that I'm not happy?"

"What would make you happy, James?"

The Director is unhappy with this conversation. He is unhappy with me.

"I'm not sure. Something other than what I've experienced so far."

"Ah," he says, and taps the desk with his pen, "something other than what you've experienced so far." He is stalling for time, trying to think about what to say about Cindy, whom, I feel, he dislikes and distrusts.

"That's right. I'm not happy with her or, frankly, with you." I want to wipe the smirk off his face.

"James, you are with us to find some…some what? Some release from your distress. Is that not correct?"

"Yes. I guess I am."

"James, we are serious people here. We are professionals. Guessing is not really what you're here for. Yes or no, do you want us to help you, whatever 'helping' means in your situation. Yes or no?"

"Yes."

The Director then points out that Dr. Becky Howell is Cindy's new supervisor and any future concerns I have should be addressed directly with her and with Cindy.

"Therapy is a journey, James, not a destination. You must trust the process. And you should be respectful to Dr. Howell and Cindy. After all, we are the professionals here."

I am stunned and infuriated by his arrogance. I want to smash him in his handsome face.

"If that's all Mr. Schneider, I have some work to do," he says, picking up a file on his desk. He smiles at me. "But I'm happy you spoke to me about your concerns. Your wellbeing is of great concern to me."

With that, he opens the file and begins to read. The son of a bitch is showing me the door.

SETTING A TRAP

Prior to the start of my next therapy session, I check in with the receptionist and proceed to the therapy room. I find my clinical file sitting unattended, so I read it as I wait for Cindy to arrive. It seems as if beneath of the veneer of being a young thing, she is actually observant. She has observed my moodiness and tangle of temper. I'm paranoid, she states, and unwilling to surrender much in the way of feelings and anxieties other than anger. She thinks LT is pretty much a delusion. But it is not hopeless, although she is feeling like she is becoming more of a hindrance to me than a help. There is hope for me. Nothing but words and games.

Cindy begins this therapy session by telling me coldly that Dr. Becky Howell is her new supervisor and that any issues I have with the therapeutic process should be discussed with herself and/or with Dr. Howell, not with the Director Monteblanc.

"Okay," I say. "If that's the way it's going to be, that's the way it's going to be. I found Monteblanc to be an empty suit, anyway."

She smiles when I say that and then catches herself. I understand that she really dislikes Good Old Joe.

Cindy then removes a mini tape recorder from her purse, turns it on, and sets it on the table that is on her left.

I politely ask to see the tape recorder, and Cindy reluctantly hands it to me.

I shout into the machine, "Becky, Becky, you fat fucking bitch. If you want to know what's going on in my therapy sessions, you waddle your fat fucking ass in here and join us."

I then turn off the device. Because Cindy quickly grabs for the machine, I hold it above my head as if to smash it to the ground.

"Look what I've got," I say. "I've got the tiny machine that's going to cover your ass. Correct, Cindy? Capture my craziness?"

"Don't do this, James."

"Do what?"

"Act like an asshole and a bully."

Chagrined, I drop my arm and hand it to her.

"If it bothers you that much," Cindy says, "I won't record the session."

"Cindy, remember the trust problem."

"The recording is just meant to help us both. Sometimes things get distorted or misremembered over the course of therapy. I won't use it if it makes you uncomfortable."

"I have a great memory, Cindy. I'll say this one more time. Once a therapist violates a client's trust, once you violate my trust, your career is over. And there are no second chances."

"No second chances, James, that's interesting. Whose rules are those?"

"Mine."

"We'll see, James. There are a lot of rules in play and some of them are mine and some of them are the University's. I am not going to be intimidated by you."

The following sessions grow increasingly combative as Cindy's new supervisor implements rules and boundaries that previously did not exist, rules such as addressing Dr. Howell as "Doctor" instead of by her first name, no foul language, time limits, and taping. When Cindy tells me that we must change therapy rooms to one located inside the Psychological Counseling Services area, I complain vociferously; however, I continue with therapy. I resist and fight every new rule, but ultimately accept each as I am caught in the poison's grip of manipulation and confusion.

Over time, I sense that Cindy is trying to force therapy on me to get me back to the earlier friendliness that we shared. I have changed for the worse. I am very distrusting and growing more paranoid every session. I become convinced that this new room is bugged, has secret recording devises even a camera. When I first enter this new room, I look for a concealed camera. Where would a surveillance pro hide a camera? I ask myself. I couldn't locate one or a mic, but I am positive they are there. I know and fear I am being monitored continuously now. I choose my words with care and try to remain expressionless. I am shutting down emotionally. It is May, I know, springtime in Texas, but I sense this is my emotional autumn. My winter is close behind. Why do they want to record and ruin me?

I wonder what Dr. Howell's family of origin is and why she is acting more like a boxing coach than a supervisor. I wonder what she and Cindy talk about in their supervisory sessions. I must seem a monster to them. I think I am a monster sometimes. Poor Jimmy lives like a rat.

In the waning days of May, I experience moments of great confusion and self-doubt, so I call my "Ghost Rider" psychiatrist friend, Doctor Brandon McIvy, to ask his opinion. Because Doctor McIvy was a former residency director, I believe he will be able to share some insight into what is going on.

"Jim," he says, "it's good to hear from you. How are you doing?"

"I've been better."

"That doesn't sound good. What's the problem?"

"I'm seeing a psychologist. I'm not happy with what's going on."

"What's going on, Jim, is probably just you're having a hard time talking about yourself. It's common enough."

I paused while I tried to think of something that expressed my confusion and anger.

"She isn't honest with me. I don't trust her. I told her something hardly anyone knows about, and now I think she's going to use it against me."

"What was it, Jim. What is this secret?"

"No, I'm not telling anyone again. It's my business." I won't trust him with my secret ambition. He is one of them.

"Jim, if you don't trust the process, you're just wasting time in therapy. You need to trust Cindy and the other people at the clinic. They want to help you, not make your life more difficult. You have to become aware of your problems. You owe that to yourself, and, frankly, you owe it to your therapist as well."

Never, I think, will I lower my defenses.

"I don't know about that. They have another agenda. There is something going on I don't understand. Some sort of plot."

"Jim, give this thing a chance. You owe it to yourself to take a chance and trust those people. It's your duty to heal. I repeat, you owe that to yourself."

I thank him for his time and hang up. Confused and self-doubting, and now instilled with the absolute necessity and duty of healing myself, I vow that I will go into my next therapy session and reveal all to Cindy.

At my last therapy session of May, amid great confusion and self-doubt, I begin the session by humbly talking about LT and what it means to me. I share the real identity of LT with Cindy—my dream to join the CIA.

"I want to talk about LT, Cindy," I say.

"Okay."

"The real identity of the LT is the CIA. I want to work for the Central Intelligence Agency."

"Yes, I know. You want to be a spook, an operative."

"Are you joking? I'm serious about this."

"I was just reminding you that you were a good ghost rider, so you'd probably be a good CIA spook. Relax, Jim. I really want to hear about this."

She seems sincere at least.

Cindy writes something in her notebook. She is smirking, which infuriates me.

"You could at least be sufficiently respectful to wipe that smirk off you face."

Cindy looks up quickly, "What? What are you saying?"

"That arrogant little smirk. I hate it."

"I'm sorry…. No, I'm not going to apologize for a facial expression that you read as a smirk. That's just the face I make when I concentrate. That's just me. I can't do a thing about it."

She is angry. Maybe I'm wrong. Time to begin again.

But I then observe that Cindy is hiding a diamond engagement ring from my view by holding the rock against her pinky finger inside her hand. I'm certain that Cindy has done this before. This outrages me. Why is she doing this? Doesn't she understand a thing I said about betrayal? There are no goddamn second chances. Ever. Because this greatly upsets me, and because our sessions have been extremely combative since Dr. Howell took over, and because Cindy is not exactly warm and friendly anymore, I coldly confront Cindy about what I regard is a deception.

"What are you doing, Cindy?"

"I'm waiting for you to talk about LT."

"Why are you hiding that ring, you stupid, fucking bitch." That took the smirk off her fucking face.

"You are worthless as a therapist because of this, this goddamn deception."

"Jim, this ring has nothing to do with you."

"It tells me you are a liar. And that ruins everything."

"Jim, let's just calm down. I'm not lying to you."

"Your deception means I can never trust you. Why won't you tell me about your credentials?" I could feel the tightness in my chest. I tense my body and move forward in my chair as she falls back in hers. I am frightening her.

"If you had asked, James, I would have told you. If a piece of paper is so important to you, I'll show it to you. Do you think they'd give me a job if I weren't qualified, James? I don't understand why you're being so difficult. If you want a different therapist, why don't you just get one?" Her face is flushed, and she seems ready to leave the room. She looks at her watch.

"I don't have to deal with your misplaced anger, James. Not today and not ever."

I realize that I've made a mistake sharing LT with Cindy. I decide to provide disinformation and so tell Cindy that one-half of all personal information that I shared with her was false. To support that statement, I cite two examples: my first and last names – my last name is false – and my address and Social Security number – the Social Security number is false. I realize that I've made a mistake trusting Cindy about the truth of LT. I also realize that I must end my therapy at the next session.

Cindy is very upset, flushed and on the verge of tears.

"Get out, she says. "Just get out."

Maybe I am a monster, a solitary and vengeful one. Emotionally, I am bereft; emotionally, I am homeless and houseless and haunted by fear.

THE INCIDENT

Beautiful women are blameless.

Tuesday evening, June 15, 2004. I've been in therapy approximately ten months. For unknown reasons, Cindy canceled my appointment for the first week of June. No matter. I know that tonight is the night this nightmare must end.

I arrive at Jedermann University on time as usual and park in the second row back of the parking lot because the first row is apparently still reserved for faculty. Cindy meets me at the receptionist's desk and we proceed without talking to the therapy room located behind the receptionist and off to the right down a very short hallway. As I usually do — I am a man of precise habits — I place my writing pad and my college graduation watch on the table that is to my right. Cindy is restrained and seems a little nervous. As we sit facing each other, she looks weary and not like a Prom Queen. She is frazzled. She has piled her hair on top of her head, and it is held there, tentatively, with a silver barrette. She's not going to the Prom tonight.

Cindy removes the tape recorder from her purse, turns it on as she places it on the table that is to her left, and then begins the session. She tells me that she and Dr. Howell spoke at length about my case and that if I again use profanity or abusive language toward her as I have in the past, she will end my therapy.

"My boss, Dr. Howell, wants you to understand this. Are we clear, James? Any repetition of what happened last time, and I'll terminate your relationship with me and with the University. I don't want there to be any confusion."

"No confusion, on my part," I say with a smile.

I've never been clearer.

Then I ask to see my clinical record, still smiling.

"Why do you want to see it?"

"You said I could see it anytime. I want to see it now."

"I'll repeat, James," with irritation, "why do you want to see the file?"

We go back and forth for several minutes with Cindy raising her voice. It is clear she has been preparing for some sort of confrontation. I remain calm and Cindy finally agrees to let me see the file.

After receiving the file, I briefly glance through it and then set it beside my writing pad on the table that is to my right.

"May I have the file back?"

"No." No, absolutely not, I think. No freaking way. Not just no, but no in thunder, Cindy.

"Are you planning to take that with you? That is the property of the University."

Just to piss her off, I arrogantly answer, "Yes."

"I'm not going to let you do that. That is proprietary information that belongs to the University."

"I have some things to say…"

Cindy cuts me off.

"Give me the file."

I hold it in my right hand and wave it wildly over my head. I'm very happy, especially when I see the look of panic and anger in Cindy's face.

I look at her and say nothing. I open the file and flick through the pages.

"Mr. Crazy Jim Schneider, the spook wannabe," I say. "It's all here. Except, whoops, I'm not Jim Schneider, am I? Had to change the name didn't you. But is that my real name? Maybe I'm Jim Schultz or Jim Schwarz. Take your pick. One name is as good as another, and none of them might be the right one." I was flushed and sweating in my manic mode. "Nobody knows who the fuck I really am? I'm the Ghost Patient."

"I don't give a good goddamn who you are. Either you give me that file back or I'll call campus security. Is that something you'd want on your record? Dragged out of the Psychological Services building in handcuffs?"

"You'd like to see that, wouldn't you, you bitch?"

"You're fucking right about that shit for brains."

Shit for brains. Grandpa Berg must have taught her that one, too.

"I want that file, and I want it right now. And if I don't get it immediately, I am going to call the campus cops. I will destroy you, Jimmy boy, and your adolescent dream about your precious bullshit

LT. I will take you to the gates of hell, push you in, and slam the fucking door. Done and dusted, as the cowboys say."

I just look at her blankly, pretending to be calm.

"Cindy didn't Dr. Fat Ass Howell warn you about using profanity?"

She stands up, red faced and infuriated. Not so pretty now. I felt like I was about to be sick, overcome by nausea. I am overcome by a terror. I am gasping for breath.

I say at last, the words bursting out, close to panic, "Here, take the goddamn papers. Take the papers."

And I tried clumsily to hand them to her. However, Cindy's mind is made up. She opens the door and proceeds out into the hallway telling the receptionist to call the police.

Oh Christ, I think, what the hell have I done? I can't stay here any longer.

I grab my writing pad and the file and follow Cindy out into the narrow hallway. As I attempt to pass her to flee, Cindy steps in front of my path and uses her body to block my departure. Rather than bowl her over the way a charging football player would, I place my right hand on Cindy's right shoulder and firmly move her to the side so that I can squeeze between her and the wall that is now to my back. As I do this, using both her hands, Cindy reaches down and grabs my left forearm with her right hand and the clinical record that is on my writing pad in my left hand with her left hand. To break free of her grip, I feign a karate chop with my right hand. She flinches and let's go. I'm not so proud of that. I run out of the building, get in my car, and flee the campus.

As I'm leaving the campus, the receptionist calls campus security. I imagine that once security has been dispatched, the bitch Cindy calls both the Director and Dr. Howell at home and leaves manipulative messages for each of them telling them that I assaulted her somehow and that was why she called security. This is very bad for me. I was forced into this. She has seduced me into this behavior, that is my internal argument. Tricked me, teased me, trapped me. LT could be finished, and if I didn't have LT what would I have?

A few minutes later, when I arrive home, my shirt is wringing wet with sweat. I strip it off and throw it on the bathroom floor. I use the mirror to check my boils, twisting to catch their reflection. They are black, poisonous looking. Cindy would be proud of her handiwork. I look at my face in the mirror. It is a face, slightly rounder than what I remember and older than it seems possible. I rarely look at myself in the mirror. I know I am not a handsome man, but I don't ever remember looking like this. I have a haunted and hungry look, and my eyes are full of pain. And terror. Poor Jimmy is not just living like a rat, he's becoming a rat, inhabiting the squalor of a wasted life. I do not want this. I want to be strong again.

I look around at my shipwreck of an apartment. It looks like something at the bottom of the sea. All of my furniture, what's left of it, is in a state of decrepitude: tables broken, rattan chairs smashed. The television gives off the acrid smell of melted plastic. Like my life, my furniture sags at the broken places. My attempts at repair are half-hearted. Why bother? I will just smash these things again in a day or two in one of my midnight rages.

I am extremely agitated and upset at what has transpired tonight. I call the Psychological Counseling Services' main number and receive an outgoing message from the Director. I deposit my voice mail message and settle, teetering, into my three-legged sofa. The phone books that are the third leg are missing. I think I remember throwing them at the television in a moment of rage. I try to calm down. I never lose things, and now in a moment of dread, I realize that I left my watch behind in the therapy room. But there are more important things to consider. I have never stolen anything in my life, so I decide that I'm not going to become a thief now. I change shirts, and then return to the University.

As I pull into the Jedermann University parking lot, I see two police cars and several officers shining lights into exiting vehicles, presumably looking for me. I pass them and proceed to park as far away from them as I can.

As I enter the Psychological Counseling Services building, I see the night receptionist talking on the phone and looking at my forgotten and expensive watch. Cindy is standing behind her, triumphant. When the receptionist sees me approaching, she hangs up the phone and motions for me to sit down in the chair in front of her desk. I hand her the file and ask for my watch back. The receptionist, however, hands my watch to Cindy who hands it to me. Cindy then walks over to the glass entry doors of the Psychological Counseling Services' waiting area and looks at the flashing police lights outside.

"I returned the file. You don't need the police anymore, do you?"

Cindy looks at me and says, "Oh, they're not looking for you, they do that every night."

There was no phone call to the cops, is the implication, and there is no search for the miscreant Snyder. The cops are there as part of a nightly procedure, a planned check of campus parking lots. Her demeanor now has changed utterly; she is no longer angry, she seems cheerful. She has me by the balls, and we both know it.

Beautiful women lie, and they are blameless.

Unknown to me, the supervisor on duty is standing close by and has heard my interaction with Cindy; she instructs the receptionist to cancel the police search. The supervisor, Cindy, and I then enter the therapy room to process the night's events. Before we begin talking, Cindy rewinds the audiotape and plays a few seconds of our interaction. I hear my voice on the tape; however, before I can say anything, Cindy appears to rewind it even further before turning it on to record our discussion.

"So exactly what happened tonight, Mr. Schneider?" the supervisor, Ms Sanchez asks.

"His name is Snyder," Cindy says. "Well, tonight anyway."

"We had a disagreement about the course of my therapy."

"He got out of control, Andrea," Cindy says. "He took a file without permission."

Cindy is flushed, her face a bright pink. She seems excited.

"I don't understand," Ms Sanchez says, turning to me. She is Cindy's ally in this one. Ms Sanchez is short and stout; not a happy person, I think. Maybe she would be happier as a teapot. She looks at Cindy, that sleek blonde beauty, as if she were from another planet. In a way, Cindy is from another planet where doors are opened, and problems solved.

"What do you want to do, Cindy?" Sanchez asks. "I mean, what do you want to do about him?"

Sanchez gestures at me, and I smile back at her like an idiot.

"She wants to hang me up by my balls," I spit out.

"No, James, I want…wanted…to help you, but that doesn't seem possible anymore."

"That's what I mean: you wanted to hang me up by my balls, you manipulative bitch."

"Okay, Mr. Snyder, that's enough," the supervisor says, asserting herself in our dialogue.

"Ms Sanchez, I think James and I should terminate our therapy sessions. I'm afraid he might do something violent. He is a very angry man, and I can't seem to resolve his anger. I seem to touch it off."

No, I thought, you fuel my anger.

"Okay," I say. "I agree, it's over. But just note, Ms Sanchez, that I brought back the file. And I never threatened Cindy at any time. That's all in her head."

When I arrive home that evening, as I reflect on what occurred I become greatly agitated and upset. I call Scott and attempt to explain what happened; however, I'm so upset that all he can say is that, if I want to protect LT, I need to document everything.

"You need to protect yourself, Jim."

"I think I screwed up."

"Just write it all down. Think about long term."

So, that is what I do. All night long I sit at my computer typing notes of what transpired. I hope that my phone call to the Director and the night's processing with the supervisor on duty will be enough to contain the situation, but I know that it won't be. I have stepped into the abyss.

At 7:30 AM the next morning, I call the main number for Psychological Counseling Services and deposit a message asking that the Director meet with me that morning. At 8:30 AM, I repeat this action.

At 9:10 AM, I again call the Psychological Counseling Services' main number and this time Mona Rodriguez, the day receptionist, answers and puts me immediately through to the Director, who agrees to see me at 10:00 AM.

At the 10:00 AM meeting, I share my career ambition to work for the CIA — known to Cindy as "LT" for Long Term — with Dr. Monteblanc and I make it very clear to him that I want no more reports made to the police about me, that I want this situation fully investigated, and that I want Cindy punished for what she did. In the spirit of frankness, I share my observation that because Cindy might have erased the tape, it will be her word against mine and — as the client, the outsider — I must lose.

"You want an investigation, about what Cindy did?"

"Yes. Right away. Immediately."

"You know that investigation will include what you did, as well?"

"I guess it will."

"What do you think she did? As I understand it, you refused to return a file that was not your property, and she asked you to give it back to her. And then you took it home. In effect, you stole it. Is that correct?"

"I brought it back."

"Well, that's why we won't need to involve the police."

"I just want it investigated. And I want her punished."

"We'll work that out in time, Mr. Snyder. That is your correct name?"

"Yes."

"First things first, Mr. Snyder. First the investigation, and then we'll see if any punishment is required. In the meanwhile, you understand that your relationship with the clinic has been terminated?"

"Yes."

"Well, then," he says, standing up from his desk and gesturing towards the door, "I'll be in touch."

On Monday afternoon of the next week, I call the Psychological Counseling Services' main number and speak with Mona, who says that she will relay my meeting request to the Director and will call me back at my home number with his answer. I want to get a status on the Director's investigation into the incident. On my answering machine that evening there is a message from Monteblanc inviting me to a second meeting with him at 9:00 AM the following morning. I save this message.

At our meeting on Tuesday morning, June 22nd, nearly one full week after the incident, I ask the Director about the status of his investigation into the incident.

He replies, "I wouldn't really call it an investigation."

From our conversation it becomes immediately apparent that Monteblanc has not spoken with the night receptionist about what she had seen and heard, nor has he spoken with the night supervisor about what transpired when I returned with the file. Even though this greatly upsets me, I remain calm and do not show my emotion. Instead, I talk earnestly about my concerns with Cindy's approach to my therapy.

He nods in what I take to be agreement. Then he says something I find surprising.

Monteblanc says that he has a clinic in downtown Houston and would be willing to treat me there himself.

"This would not be to make up to you for what's happened here," he explains, "but because I think you'd be an interesting case."

"Interesting in what way?"

"From a clinician's point of view, I mean, your issues are compelling."

"I'm not sure I like the idea of being compelling. Cindy didn't seem to feel that way."

"You hit a rocky patch. That happens sometimes. I'd hate to see you give up."

"I'll think about it," I say. I think I seem sincere.

I gather much intelligence at this meeting but depart feeling that the Director is trying to cover up the incident rather than punishing Cindy for what she did, which is what I want.

Over the next two weeks, because I believe that Dr. Monteblanc is not willing to punish Cindy for her conduct, the Director and I exchange a series of escalating answering machine messages which culminate in a follow-up meeting with Dr. Monteblanc and Dr. Howell. A third meeting about the incident.

At my Friday morning meeting — three weeks after the incident

— with the Director and Dr. Howell, I learn that on the morning after the incident, Cindy called Dr. Howell and expressed concerns for her safety, so Dr. Howell gave Cindy permission to again call the police. I also learn that the Director still has not contacted the night supervisor to ask her what she had seen and heard. Instead of answering my questions, both the Director and Dr. Howell attempt to lay the blame for the incident upon me.

"James," Monteblanc says, "The problem from our perspective isn't Cindy's behavior, it's yours. If she doesn't feel safe with you, we must respect that. I know, at least I think I know, that you briefly and unfortunately lost your temper. You meant no harm. Therapy is often an emotionally charged process, so a lot of things get pushed forward: sorrow and anger being the most common. I hope we can get past this without any additional fuss. Sometimes confrontation is a good thing, but not here, not now."

"Director, Cindy played me like a dime-store ukulele. She was very cunning. She is burdened, it seems to me, with a very odd relationship with her father, Bill. She compared me to him a lot. It had this very uncomfortable sexual undertone. I remember her once describing him as a 'gorgeous man, a real hunk.' Doesn't that seem strange to you?"

"Not really. Maybe a little."

"More than a little I think."

"What's your point, James?"

"It's what you professionals call transference, isn't it? Whatever complicated emotions she has related to her father—and I can only guess at them—were placed squarely on my shoulders. Was that what her painfully obvious flirtatiousness was about? And her wanting very badly for me to add another therapy session per week? When I called her out on what I know now was really only faux, make-believe affection, when I saw her hiding her diamond ring behind her pinky finger, that was when she became enraged at me. I didn't fall into her trap, don't you see? She was pissed at being discovered as a cunning lying bitch."

"James, I really think you're making too much of this."

"Really? Because now I realize her intention was to destroy me, calling the cops and destroying any chance I had to have a career in the CIA. She said she would show me my file, but when I asked to see it, she refused. Don't I have a right to see my own file?"

"Of course, but clients rarely ask. It's unusual."

"Finally, after I looked at my file and she demanded that I return it, I refused. That refusal, adamant refusal admittedly, was her opportunity. She knew that. I should have known that but was too confused, I guess, to grasp the moment. It was always about control, Dr. Monteblanc. Her control over me. She intended to get the file back at the moment, without any questions or discussion. Back in that moment or she would call the campus cops. She threatened me with that, unambiguously and with particular venom. I didn't, and she did, the bitch. She called the cops knowing exactly what would be the consequences. She thinks she's won, but I will not accept that. What she did to me, Dr. Monteblanc, makes me very, very angry. I want her investigated, and I want her punished. It's that simple."

"Well, James, let me work on this. It might not be so simple."

I get up to leave and say, "No, sir, it is simple. She is going to be punished."

I depart this meeting knowing that Monteblanc and Dr. Howell will not punish Cindy for her conduct.

But I am willing to take matters into my own hands. There are all kinds of vengeance, all kinds of punishment.

On Monday morning I call Mona and request a copy of my clinical record. The receptionist says that the file is with the Director and that she will call me back if I can have a copy, which she does that afternoon.

But I'm thinking about something else now. Something new.

I need some guns.

PREPARING FOR THE INEVITABLE

On Tuesday afternoon, July 13th, exactly four weeks after the incident, I leave work early in order to pick up a copy of my file. When I arrive at the Psychological Counseling Services Building, I approach Mona and ask her for a copy of my clinical record. She retrieves the file from the Director's office and brings it to me. I immediately notice that the typed last name on the file's label, "Schneider," is crossed out and is replaced with the handwritten name, "Snyder," which is my real last name. Because this greatly upsets me, I ask Mona to also copy the name label when she makes the copy, which she does. Mona puts the copy in a brown envelope and hands it to me. I then depart for home.

After parking at my apartment complex, I walk to the mail room and retrieve my mail, which I notice includes a letter from the Director. Curious, I immediately open the letter and read it.

Dear Mr. Snyder, Thank you for meeting with me on Friday, June 18th, to discuss your concerns about what transpired between you and your therapist, Cindy Polanski, on Tuesday, June 15th. As we discussed in our meeting on Friday, June 18th, I took your concerns very seriously and found them to be unwarranted. These are not issues I take lightly. We take our responsibilities to our clients with the highest level of professionalism. After careful examination of the circumstances, I can find no wrong doing or any actions that could be sanction-able on Ms Polanski's part. I now consider this matter closed.

You will recall that at our meeting on Friday, June 18th, I provided the names of four clinics in the local area that can provide the counseling you sought with us. It is my professional judgment, Mr. Snyder, and my real concern for your wellbeing that you should avail yourself of the services these clinics can provide. Sincerely yours...."

With my defenses up, and with acute attention to details, I notice that in his letter the Director made three references to a June 18th meeting. He further stated that it was that date, June 18th, that I terminated my therapy with Cindy. Lies and more lies, ass-covering untruths. Feeling confused and greatly concerned by this deception, I return to my apartment and examine the clinical record.

The first things I notice in the clinical record are the two typed entries from the Director, one from my meeting with him and Dr. Howell on July 9th and the other from our alleged meeting on the Friday after the incident, June 18th. Both contain false and misleading content about my behavior. In his notes from the June 18th meeting, Monteblanc claims that I admitted to him that I was overly interested in Cindy's personal life, that I had followed Cindy out of the Psychological Counseling Services Building to see what car she was driving, and that I had admitted to him that I assaulted Cindy on the night of the incident. Looking at Cindy's handwritten notes, I see an entry from the Friday after the incident. Cindy wrote, "Please note that one-half of all personal information received is not accurate. Also, the client's real last name is 'Snyder'."

The dates of the meeting are inaccurate and the typewritten notes for the file are mostly lies, larded with a few real facts. He is covering his ass. And it will be my word, a notorious file-stealing madman, against that of the august and much-beloved Joe Monteblanc with his baby smooth skin and his ingratiating sibilant-heavy swishery.

These are lies and now these lies are memorialized in my file. They set a trap, and the trap was sprung. "Snyder/Schneider" is a full-blown nut job: irrational, violent and unrepentant. I was totally fucked. I grabbed the file and threw it into the air, scattering the papers over my living room floor. A blizzard of half-truths and outright lies.

Realizing the gravity of the situation, my heart sinks. I am becoming extremely agitated, angry, and aggressive so much so that the rage consumes me. More than anything, I want to physically attack and harm those people, but I know that if I do, I will retroactively justify everything that they falsely wrote. As I think about my upcoming interviews with the CIA, I become morbidly depressed, so much so that my mind shuts down, and I lie on the floor and black out. I can disappear from the world this way.

When I come to, I sit up off the floor, start becoming agitated again, even more so when I realize that I have no offensive strike capability. I call Scott and try to explain what has occurred, but I'm too upset to speak coherently. To help calm me down, Scott invites me to join him and his family for dinner, but I cannot eat so I tell him that I'll come over after they've finished.

In the next ninety minutes, I pace through my apartment unable to sit still. I look occasionally at the clinical record papers scattered about on the living room floor. I refuse to read them. Ninety minutes drag by, seeming like an eternity. Finally, it's time. I gather all the papers together and leave with the file in my hand.

When I get to Scott and Kelly's house, I am greeted in the usual fashion by their two children, whom I pick up and hug. I then hug Kelly, who says that she's heard that I have a little bit of a situation to deal with, to which we both smile knowing smiles. It is still awkward with her, although she seems oblivious to my discomfort. There is a side to Kelly I don't understand, and I don't think I like. Something playful and devious. I shake Scott's hand, an odd formality for us, and he shows me into the living room. Without a word I hand him the clinical record and the letter, and he begins reading, the letter first, and then the file.

After five or six minutes, Scott looks up and asks, "So, what are you going to do about all this?"

"Be prepared" is all I can answer. "Or better yet, get prepared."

I mention that on the way over I heard about a gun show this weekend at the downtown convention center, and I ask Scott if he wants to go. I tell him that I'm going to buy two weapons, one that can be made to operate quietly and one that will stop a tank. Scott agrees to go with me, and says he'll pick me up on Saturday morning around 9:30 AM. I'm not sure if he realizes why I want the guns. Or maybe he doesn't want to believe that his buddy Jim is thinking about murder. I am doing just that and will proceed, as I always do, like the engineer I was trained to be: scrupulously attending to details, thorough in my research; not cold hearted, but cold in the cruel logic that is pushing me forward to my fate.

The next morning, Wednesday morning, I call the Office of the Dean at Jedermann University and request a meeting to both discuss my situation and file a formal complaint against the Director. The Dean's receptionist schedules this meeting for the following Tuesday, July 20, at 9:00 AM.

On Saturday morning, Scott and I examine all manner of weapons at the gun show.

"You're sure you want to do this? You can't really afford this shit right now."

"Afford or not, I'm going to buy some guns."

We stop by a booth that seems to have everything I need. I looked at the handgun I thought would meet my needs.

"Can I help you guys?" the man behind the table asks. His name tag says he is "Matt." Oddly enough, his last name is Snyder.

He was smiling at us, friendly and attentive. He is in his early forties, his head shaved bald. He has a jagged scar on his head from just above his left eyebrow. He is wearing a much-washed 82nd Airborne T-shirt, frayed a bit at the collar, but clean and neatly pressed. I have the feeling he was studying me. I'm thinking he's a plant from the Federal government looking for potential serial killers. Do I fit the profile? I do, perfectly. A poorly socialized loner pursuing a churning grievance. I must be very cautious with him.

"Yes," I said. "I'm looking to buy some handguns."

"Well," he said with a broad smile, "you've come to the right place. What were you thinking about?"

I look at the table full of semi-automatic hand guns, a smorgasbord of mayhem.

"I think this one looks like the one I want," I say pointing to a Taurus. "I've done some research online, and this weapon is always among the most highly rated."

"It's a good weapon," he says, "but it can be a bit temperamental, especially if you are not experienced. Easy to jam."

He seems to be ex-military, but he doesn't have the calcified hardness of some professional soldiers. He is polite, but cautious. I decide to change the subject.

"Were you in the 82nd?"

"I was but that was a long time ago."

"Why did you get out?"

"The Army made me leave for medical reasons. I wanted to stay but they didn't want me."

He is looking straight at me, his eyes looking into mine. He sees something in me; he seems to know what I was after. Or he feels the poison.

Scott starts to walk away.

I'm not going to let it go. I want to buy my weapons from him.

"Can I ask what your scar is from? Did you get hit in the head or something?"

He touches his scar and laughs, "No, that happened when I was a kid. I fell off my bike. I did a real head plant."

"What did happen? I mean, if you don't mind talking about it."

"I was doing a training jump in North Carolina, and my chute didn't completely deploy. Two hundred feet straight down. I broke both my legs. I was in a medically induced coma for two weeks. After that, I had bad headaches — what a surprise — and I had problems with my vision. The Army more or less forced me out."

"So, you opened a gun shop?"

"No, I'm only helping out a buddy for the weekend. He's a

private seller. His daughter is getting married this weekend, so he asked me to look after his booth. I hooked up with a private security company for a couple of years, and I just got out of that."

"What did you do?"

He stops smiling then, and he picks up the Taurus.

"Lots of stuff," he says, "mostly just looking out car windows at traffic. I was in Africa for a couple of years as a half chauffeur and half bodyguard. Nothing special."

"That sounds interesting. You were what do you call it, a soldier of fortune, a mercenary."

"No fortune," he says, "just a job to pay the mortgage. So, what do you need a weapon for? What do you need *this* weapon for?"

He is not so friendly now, and I can see the hardness in him.

"I live in a marginal neighborhood, lot of break-ins. Lots of gang activity. I really want it for protecting my home. My neighbor woke up one night with a guy in her bedroom. Scared the hell out of her. She screamed, and the guy ran away, but you never know."

"No, you never do. Lots of bad guys out there."

"Have you ever fired one of these things?"

"Not really."

"That means 'no' correct?"

"That means no."

"For home protection, I'm not going to sell you a semi-automatic. Too many things can go wrong, and you really can't afford for anything to go wrong if somebody is breaking into your house, can you?"

"I suppose not."

He turned around and pulled a short-barreled shot gun from the rack of longer-barreled weapons behind him.

"This is what you need. Most of the time you don't even need to fire the thing. Just chambering a shell will scare the shit out of almost anyone."

"What is it?"

"It's a short-barreled Mossberg 590. It's a brilliant weapon. I used this baby in the service and after. Never jams, and it will stop a gorilla. And it's almost impossible to miss from tactical range, and by tactical range I mean someone in your living room while you're standing on the other side of the sofa in your underwear. This is the weapon you need."

I need a gun I can conceal.

"I don't think so. I don't think it would work for me."

He spoke very slowly, looking directly at me, almost though me, "This is the weapon you need, son, and I'm not going to sell you that

Taurus."

"Why?"

He turns and replaces the Mossberg in the rack.

"I can't help you, son."

"I want to buy the Taurus."

There is a lengthy pause as he reorganizes the weapons on the table in front of him.

"Good luck," he says. "It's been nice talking to you."

"You have to sell me this gun. What reason do you have to refuse to sell it to me?"

"I don't need a reason. Good luck to you, but you should move on."

I start to complain. Now I was pissed at being dismissed, but Scott pulls me away. He drags me by the arm down the aisle to another booth.

"That son of a bitch, that bastard...." I begin.

"Take it easy, Jim, the guy jumped out of an airplane and his chute didn't open. That's got to make you a little weird. Besides, you don't want to make a scene at a gun show."

At the second both, a smiling fat man is more than happy to sell me guns. "Ralph P." his name tag said. Ralph shows me everything I want to see.

"I can make you a good deal on any of these guns," he said. "Best deals in the entire show. The one thing that Ralphie Peterson has is first-rate weapons."

We talk about the semi-automatics he has, handing them to me, describing their capacities.

"I like this one," I say, holding the Taurus.

"Well, that's a nice weapon, all right, and not a bad price either. And if you've got cash, it can be even nicer."

Finally, mostly because of its ease of disassembly and cleaning, I buy the Taurus 9 mm semi-automatic handgun. I also buy rubber hand grips, four extra clips that all hold fifteen rounds each, and one box each of Lugar and jacketed hollow point ammunition. I also buy a Browning .22 caliber semi-automatic handgun, which I also buy with extra clips and ammunition. A back-up gun.

On the way back to Scott's place, we stop at a Home Depot store and I buy a four-inch PVC pipe along with the tools and equipment that I'll need to configure the pipe for its ultimate purpose, as a silencer. I buy a cheap hacksaw, duct tape, and a piece of cardboard. I'm going to create a crude silencer, which in theory — as an engineer I knew all about the theory — it should be effective. It just needs to work four times. Scott recognizes what I'm doing, but does not say anything. I sense his concern. It's too late for that; however, I feel I'm on my way.

I am very busy during a hot stretch of Houston weather — weather always seems to be hot in Houston — building my silencer, getting used to the action of both weapons. I am methodical. I am good at this kind of thing. I know how to get from point Alpha to point Zed engineering-wise. It is a steamy time and in this steamy July I obsess about Cindy, sometimes I even dream about her or someone like her. She is always across a room or down a street. Even though I try to communicate with her, in my dreams, I fail. I paint during the day, walls and ceilings, drifting in and out of a vague disassociated state, a fugue state, I think it's called. It is a mild delirium, a dream of cunning and revenge. This painting job is probably the only one I'm capable of at the moment. It requires nothing, only a physical presence capable of steady mindless motion. George is pleased with my work now, but I barely recognize him, lost as I am in my mindless crablike side stepping, this lulling painter's polka around a room. He thinks the therapy has been helpful: I am nearly cured. Grace knows better, of course; we both know I am a man on a high wire, a virtual Fantucci, net-less and terrified of falling. Betrayal has granted me a great freedom. I am free to punish the wicked.

On Tuesday, July 20, exactly five weeks after the incident, I arrive at the Dean's office at 8:55 AM. The receptionist says that Dr. Colwell is waiting for me and so shows me into her office. I introduce myself as I shake Dean Robin Colwell's hand. The Dean motions me to her large conference table where we sit.

"How can I help you, Mr. Snyder," she asks.

Rather than speak, I simply hand her the CIA's interview invitation letter, which she immediately reads. I next present her with the Director's letter in which he makes three references to an alleged meeting with me on the Friday following the incident. I next hand Dean Colwell the Director's file notes from that alleged Friday meeting.

Finished reading, the Dean looks me squarely in the eye and asks, "So, what's wrong, Mr. Snyder?"

I explain that I met with Dr. Monteblanc first on the Wednesday morning immediately following the Tuesday night incident and secondly on the Tuesday morning exactly one week later. I'm angry about Jedermann's stonewalling.

I ask aloud, "But where are those file notes?"

I explain that the only file notes in the clinical record are from an alleged meeting the Friday following the incident. The meeting that didn't happen.

"The fact is, Dean Colwell, the Director's notes about our meeting were full of distortions, half-truths, and outright lies."

"Hold on, James, those are serious accusations."

"I know. What he did was lie about me. He said I called him to talk about the incident with Cindy, Ms Polanski."

"Did you call him and request the meeting?"

"He lied about the dates of the meetings we had. He lied about the supposed admissions I made about my conduct. He is just covering up from his incompetence, his gross negligence and Cindy's conduct towards me, conduct that I regard as psychological malpractice, Dean."

"Are you saying you didn't steal the file, which is the university's property, Mr. Snyder? Are you saying you did not have some sort of physical confrontation with Ms Polanski?"

"No. Some basic facts are true, but they've been distorted."

"I'm going to say something you may not like, James, but it needs to be said. You came to us seeking help for some emotional, psychological issues, did you not?"

"I did. Of course, I did."

"And you, for whatever reason, disguised your true identity and provided other information that was not accurate, not truthful. Isn't that correct?"

"I did, but I had my reasons."

"You see the problem I'm having here. You've been untruthful before, why is this different in relationship to Joe Monteblanc?"

"I am absolutely aware of my position here. I understand that I'm being made out to be the bad guy. But it's wrong. He said I removed the clinical file. I did that but I didn't plan to do it. I made no threat, but in a moment of anger I left unaware I still had the file in my hand, but I returned it later that evening when I realized my mistake. I am not a thief. He flat out lied."

"A different interpretation of events, James. Not a lie."

"Okay, but then he went on to say that I physically tapped Ms Polanski, violently popped her is the suggestion, but I didn't do that. I just pushed her slightly on my way out because she was blocking me from leaving. It is a lie that I did anything more than that. If I had tapped or popped her, she would have been airborne and then would have had me arrested. I am not a weak man, Dean."

"You took the clinical file from her."

"I asked to see it, and she gave it to me. Handed it to me."

"And then you left and took it with you and you pushed her as you left the building. The file that was and is the property of Jedermann University. Isn't all that true?"

71

"I brought it back after I calmed down a bit. Again, I'm not a thief."

"No, but you're acting out aggressively, James. What about the use of an assumed name? Why that deception?"

"That was supposed to be confidential information."

"It is or would have been had not all this happened. James, your situation is not a secret. Your behavior is not exactly undiscussed. You're a bit of a dilemma for us."

"It's because of my ambition to apply to the CIA. I used the name 'Schneider' rather than 'Snyder' because one of my neighbors at the apartment complex where I live is a graduate student in clinical psychology at Jedermann and I didn't want Nina to curiously read my file, should she recognize my real last name. I did not stalk Cindy. I was attempting to establish rapport with her by asking her questions about who she was. I thought it might make the process of talking about my life less one-sided. I had no interest in harming Cindy that night. None."

I ask Dean Colwell how I can possibly be expected to be granted any type of security clearance based upon what Dr. Monteblanc falsely wrote. The Dean looks over the documents one more time.

"Why should the CIA find out about those notes?"

"Because I have to tell them about my counseling."

"I see," she said.

"Once again, Dean, why are the dates wrong?"

She did not respond.

I am getting more and more impatient.

"Mr. Snyder, this is a legal matter. It seems like a complicated one. I'm going to have to talk to the University's lawyers before I respond to you."

"All right. How long will that take?"

"I'll get a response to you by the end of the week."

"I'll look for it, Dean. Please don't disappoint me. I'm tired of being jerked around by Jedermann. There are consequences for these lies."

"Is that a threat, Mr. Snyder?"

"No. It is a simple statement of fact."

"That's good because we don't like threats. Facts can be proven correct or incorrect. Threats get in the way. Very messy, Mr. Snyder, and we want this mess to be cleaned up."

I leave the meeting with Dean Colwell hoping that a satisfactory resolution will come out of it, but also knowing deep in my heart that Jedermann University will attempt to cover-up what Cindy, Dr. Howell, the Director, and now the Dean all know is wrongful conduct.

In a deep depression, I go to work, I go home, go to work, go home, go to work, and go home again, waiting for the Dean's letter to arrive. As promised, I finally get it on Friday. The Dean states that she, "…investigated Mr. Snyder's claims and found them to be unsubstantiated; therefore, this matter is officially closed."

Not for me. Closed is a long way away. I prepare a seven-page response to the Dean's letter in which I outline the University's misconduct and the Director's cover-up. I put Jedermann University on notice of potential legal action.

Rather than mailing my letter to the Dean, I decide that I will present it to her personally. I also decide that I will make her sign for it, thereby documenting her receipt of both the letter and the supporting documents that I attach to it.

I hand deliver my letter to Dean Colwell the last week of July. I also deliver a copy to Mona, the Psychological Counseling Services' day receptionist, so that she can add it to my clinical record.

Things are spinning out of control. Time to get prepared.

I have the guns.

THE SECRET INTERVIEWS

I have had a dream about being a covert CIA operative for as long as I can remember. I'm not sure what it is I find so interesting. Maybe it is the lure of adventure, of being in a foreign place, pretending to be someone other than myself. The CIA is an escape, has always been an escape from the overwhelming ordinariness of my life. The struggle for money and position. I can be invisible and by being invisible I can be whatever I wish to be. I do not have to be Jim Snyder from Buttfuck, Ohio. When I was little, I wrote a very earnest letter, handwritten because I didn't have access to a typewriter, to the CIA. Naively, I addressed it to "Director of the CIA, Covert Operations Division" in block letters. I was probably twelve or thirteen. I remember hiding the letter in my books and slipping it into the mailbox in front of Peters Meat Market on my way home from school. Peters is dead, and his store has been demolished. The lot is overgrown with weeds. Like most of my youth, Peters and his store have turned to dust. A month or so later, I got a letter from the CIA from the Human Resources Department with a glossy four-color brochure included. An assistant director of HR, Maybelle Mary Toussaint, what an exotic and wonderful name, wrote to say that at 13 I was too young to apply, but in a few years, when I was about to get a college degree, I should contact the CIA again. She gave me the address for applicants. She also stressed the fact that ideally I would pursue a degree in science, physics was mentioned, or engineering. She also stressed the importance of learning languages, Finnish, Russian, Farsi, and Chinese were of particular usefulness at the moment. I kept that letter. I have it still, although it is worn in the creases from repeated readings. It was to be a turning point in my life;

but think again Jim. My life took a turn and I ended up in the ditch. I am badly used up with rage, my emotional turmoil, and I have no choice but to follow this to a conclusion. I cannot stop without a deadly sense of betraying my youthful dreams. My expectation is, like Peters Market and much of the rest of my rust belt hometown, little Jimmy Snyder's dream is about to be thrown on the scrap heap, a dream left to rust.

It is Sunday afternoon in the second week of August, almost eight weeks after the incident. Today is the day that I fly to Washington, DC, for my interviews with the Central Intelligence Agency. I've waited a year for these interviews, and, sadly, I'm nowhere close to being prepared for them. My head is filled with Cindy rage, and the fact that I've been repeatedly and maliciously lied to is like a broken tooth in my mouth. I can't help but taste the sharp edge.

My plane lands at Washington's Dulles Airport on time at 7:42 PM. I deplane, collect my bag at baggage claim, and then meet the minivan that takes me to the hotel. Despite being a large minivan, I am the only passenger. The driver focuses on driving and does not talk.

"Nice evening," I say.

He grunts what I take to be an affirmation.

"How far is the hotel?"

"Close."

"Close to downtown?"

"Do you want to go downtown? If that's the case, you're in the wrong van."

He sounded annoyed, and he looked up into the rearview mirror at me.

"No, I'm going to the airport Hilton."

"You're all right, then. But if you want to go downtown, to a bar or something, you're in the wrong van."

He smiles at me.

Another visiting fireman, he must have thought, out of town and chasing pussy on a business trip.

"If you're looking for a relaxing evening, I can probably help you out."

"Just drive," I say. "I'm just looking to get to my hotel." I probably sounded annoyed, but I was just anxious.

I check in at reception, receive my envelope of instructions, which consists mostly of the itinerary for the next few days, and then go to my room where I remain for the rest of the night. Despite the excitement that I should be feeling, I feel only anger and rage and the beginning of the descent into depression. I have a bad headache, and when I turn on the television, the sound is torment. They did this to me. All night long I toss and I turn, unable to sleep. I need someone to talk to, to help me make sense of this churning of anger and emotion. But there is no one, and not for the first time either.

At 7:45 AM Monday morning, the minivan collects twelve of us from the reception area and takes us to CIA headquarters in Langley Virginia. The van is full up with a palpable sense of anxiety and the bitter smell of fear. We are all at some sort of deflection point, some will rise and some of us will fall. We are all on the edge of massive, collective nose bleed. Holy shit, I'm thinking, how did I get into this and how do I get out? Once there, we enter a large conference room where a speaker tells us about the mission, purpose, and history of the CIA. It is a presentation the speaker has made many times, and he drones on in a bureaucratic monotone.

"So," he says at last, buoyed by the fact that he is nearly done with us, "any questions ladies and gentlemen? We're a proud organization with a great tradition and history. Much of that history is, necessarily, hidden. But it's a great honor to serve this country in the CIA, and we take our responsibility in this process with the utmost seriousness. We expect you to do the same."

After this we're divided into three groups of four. With me are three other men - William, Murdoch, and Paul. Paul is freshly ex-military and still has the haircut to prove it. Murdoch is the youngest among us, a recent MBA graduate who speaks fluent Mandarin. William is the oldest, besting me by a year, and is a former police officer from Cincinnati, Ohio.

Following the introductory speech, William, Murdoch, Paul, and I are directed into a room that resembles a college classroom. Once in the room, an instructor explains our schedule for the week. Today and tomorrow, Monday and Tuesday, we'll be taking psychological profile tests in this room. On Wednesday we'll undergo medical evaluations and testing. On Thursday, we'll take polygraph examinations in the morning and begin the interview process in the afternoon. On Friday, we'll conclude the interview process and wrap up with an exit interview with a staff psychologist.

At the first interview on Monday, I find it difficult to answer all of the psychological profile test questions honestly.

I sit across from a paperclip-thin black man, Gerald, my examiner. He wears a thin mustache and gold rimmed glasses. He is decidedly unfriendly, and I don't like him much. He makes no attempt to shake my hand. He has a southern accent, and I ask him if he is from Virginia.

He doesn't answer. He nods and looks at me without expression.

He reminded me of a high-stakes poker player with a winning hand, or thought he had a winning hand. I am finding it hard to concentrate. I would have preferred a woman for the interview. I think I can control my anxiety better if it were a woman across the desk.

Gerald has a pen and some forms in front of him. At the top of the form he writes my name and the date.

"Have you ever wanted to kill someone?" he asks.

"What do you mean?"

"I mean, have you ever felt that you have wanted to kill someone, Mr. Snyder? By the way, these are the easy questions."

I had a feeling this was a trap. Most people have felt angry enough to want to cause someone physical harm, haven't they? Maybe even kill? If I answered no, would that be a lie?

"I've been furious with people," I say, "not enough to want to kill them, though. I guess the answer is no."

"Mr. Snyder, this is neither the time nor the place for guessing. Yes or no?"

"No."

"Have you ever broken anything in anger?"

"I don't remember if I have or not. Maybe as a kid, not lately."

"Is that a yes or no?"

"Yes."

"Have you ever thought about committing suicide?"

"No." A lie, of course.

This is not getting off to an inspiring start.

My headache is almost blinding, and I drink from the glass of water in front of me. Stay calm, I remind myself. I feel helpless and alone.

He goes through the questions with the same affectless expression. He must have done this thousands of times. The room we're in is a dull institutional beige. It is very chilly and chilly in another way, as well. There is no sign anybody actually occupies this room: no photos, no cups of pens on the desk, nothing. It is an interrogation room, and as sterile a place as I have ever been. Maybe the CIA is sending a message. You're not here to learn anything about us, not yet; you're here so we can learn things about you.

Gerald gathers up the forms and straightens them into a neat pile. "Okay, we're done here. Good luck."

"I'm not sure where I'm supposed to go next."

"Don't you have your schedule?"

"I think I may have left it somewhere. Or dropped it."

He looks at me with annoyance.

"Go back to conference room you came from, get a cup of coffee and look distressed. The way you look now is perfect. Typically, we don't let strangers sit around here unoccupied for very long. It's bad for morale. Someone will find you. And try to locate your itinerary, Mr. Snyder. It's sort of, you know, important."

I go to the conference room and am happy to see the other three guys in my group at a table. Murdoch has my schedule in front of him.

After I sit down, Murdoch says, "Here, Snyder. You left this on your seat in the auditorium. Believe me, it's better I found it than the janitor. Wouldn't look good on your resume to lose classified information your first day in the CIA."

It's my itinerary for the three days of the selection process. It's not really classified.

"Stupid on my part."

He smiles at me and says, "I guess we're all a little nervous."

During breaks, I get to know my fellow interviewees. We have lunches together and socialize a bit. I don't share too much about myself because I know that if I do, the anger and rage will pour forth, and that will not be a good thing. Murdoch had been a Princeton undergraduate in Chinese studies. He speaks seven languages, he says, four of them like a native. He was teaching himself Urdu, but it is taking longer than he wished. He is not particularly clean - dirt underneath his finger nails and his shirt is not pressed. He has just gone through a divorce, left the university and is, momentarily, at loose ends. What a surprise, Murdoch, I think you seem to be a happy citizen of the Republic of Loose Ends. Maybe being at loose ends was the best time to go into the CIA. It seems like he could be anywhere in the world and make no sense of it. When he eats, he talks with his mouth full, and tiny pieces of food—spaghetti—appears in the corners of his mouth. I do not like him much.

Paul has just been married and is looking for a long-term career. Another LTer. I like him. He was the calmest of all us, probably because he had been in the Marines and was a cool hand. He had been in a Recon unit, he said, but he couldn't talk about it. But to me, and despite the fact that I really do like him, he is not totally convincing. Maybe I am a little envious of his demeanor, all that officer and gentleman bullshit. He is quite good looking, blond haired and powerfully built. He carried himself like an athlete. His handshake is ferocious, and he seems to enjoy the wince on the face of his partner when he squeezes their hand. Mine is the last of the group's hands he shakes, and I make it a point to return his grip with as much strength as I have, which is considerable. I don't wince, nor does he. But I think he is impressed.

William scares me. He is balding, and he has cut his hair to a bristle around his ears. My guess was that he was actually younger than he looked. He is mostly silent during our meals. No one asks him if he had a wife and kids. He seems to be protecting a complicated and painful secret. Maybe all secrets are complicated and painful. They catch up to you eventually.

"This thing is going too slow," William says, at the end of our second lunch together. "I don't see why we have to be here for five days with all these bullshit questions."

He presses his fingers into the table until they are white.

"Too damn long," he says. William is spooky.

Wednesday arrives in a blur of sleepless nights. During my medical examination, the nurse observes that my blood pressure is 210 over 125. The nurse looks at me with concern, as if I my brain were about to explode.

"Do you have a history of high blood pressure, Mr. Snyder?"

"It's been a little high. Seems to run in the family."

"This is very high, you know. You're in stroke territory. Are you under a doctor's care?"

"I have a doctor," I say, ambiguously. I hope she doesn't press the point.

"Are you under a lot of stress?" she asks.

"I've had a difficult time lately. Some conflict with people who I trusted and who lied to me."

"Here is my problem, Mr. Snyder. You need to relax and get your blood pressure down. You are in a danger zone, and the organization won't let you proceed with the process if it remains this high."

"What will happen?"

"They'll send you to a doctor in an ambulance. After that, I don't know."

"I just have a few problems. There are people who are lying about me. They are trying to destroy me."

She looks at me. This admission is a mistake on my part. She is just there to take my vitals. I felt I had gone too far to stop without looking like a complete fool. She must sense that I am about to have some sort of psychotic break. Christ, maybe I am having just that.

"I tell you what, why don't you just sit here quietly for a few minutes and try to relax. Take some deep breaths, and I'll be back in a few minutes and we'll give it another try."

"That's a good idea."

Her hand is on the doorknob about to leave the room and she glances back at me with a smile, "Deep breaths."

I do not feel well. My head feels like it will explode. But I shut my eyes and breathe deeply. I try to calm myself the way I used to calm myself before a bout when I was a 132-pound wrestler in high school. I imagine myself as pinning my opponent, and the referee holding up my hand in victory. I didn't win very often, and that thought made me smile. I feel better.

The nurse is an older woman, but attractive. She has beautiful gray eyes. After about twenty difficult minutes of deep breathing and trying to have "Happy Thoughts," she walks back into the examination room with a hospital gown under her arm.

"Is that for me?" I ask.

"I hope not. Depends where your pressure is."

She puts on the cuff and pumps it up.

"It's come down to 170 over 125. That's still high, but I guess I'll pass you on."

She rolls the cart with the blood pressure device back against the wall near her desk. When she turns back to me, I realize the need to speak to her directly about my situation, maybe the one that sent my blood pressure skyrocketing.

"It's all in there," I say, handing her a large brown envelope.

"What's this?"

"That's a description of my situation."

"Your situation? I don't understand."

"It's about the people who lied to me and betrayed me."

It is her turn to look a little panic stricken.

"What do you want me to do with it? This is really not my area."

"Can't you give it to someone," I say, sliding into a panic, "higher up? It explains a lot."

"I'll give it to my supervisor. That's all I can do." She desperately wants to get rid of me.

The envelope contains copies of my clinical record from Jedermann University, my twenty-four-page draft letter to Monteblanc that I wrote specifically for the CIA, and my letter to Dean Colwell. The nurse accepts the envelope but does not open it.

I complete the balance of the medical examinations — dental, chest x-rays, review of body scars, etc. — without any further questions from any of the examiners. I have a feeling I'm going to be on someone's radar soon.

On Thursday morning, William, Murdoch, Paul, and I are directed into the polygraph examination waiting room, a room that is protected both by retinal eye scan and armed security guards. On the walls are paintings of ships caught in fierce ocean storms. They are foundering.

I look over the seven paintings carefully before sarcastically commenting to William, "This room is very soothing and very relaxing, just what the doctor ordered before a polygraph examination. I feel like I'm sinking as it is."

He nods and looks around to see if anyone has heard me. But what if someone has? What does it matter at this point? I'm on the gallows waiting for the trap door to drop. I am dead CIA meat.

At 9:40 AM, Paul is called for his polygraph examination. At 10:20 AM, it is my turn. The room is white and institutional; it seems very cold and a shiver goes up my spine as I sit across from the polygraph examiner. The room is dim; I cannot see into the corners. I am connected to the machine by the attending examiner, a woman who identifies herself as Cara. She is dark haired, very pretty, and I am attracted to her. After a quick test of the machine, Cara begins to ask questions, which, as she reminds me, can be answered with a yes or no. Her questions suggest to me that she has read my clinical records.

"Have you ever assaulted anyone?"

"I have not."

"No?"

"No."

"Have you ever been accused of assaulting anyone?"

"Yes, but I didn't do it. It was a false accusation, a lie."

"Have you ever stolen any property?"

Her voice was barely audible, emotionless.

"Can you speak up, please? I can't hear you very well."

I tried not to be irritated.

"Have you ever stolen any property?" she asks again.

"No."

I try to focus my mind to remain calm; nonetheless, I feel the anger welling within me and cannot help but wonder what the effect that is having on the results. She goes through the remainder of the questions in a monotone. I answer most of them, "No."

At the end of my examination, Cara tells me she has found something.

"Mr. Snyder, we have some results that are a problem."

"What kind of problem?"

"Oh, nothing serious. Some of the readings are ambiguous. It happens."

"So?"

"We're going to have to repeat the test tomorrow."

"I thought we would be finished."

"Not quite. We just need a little more time with you."

To find out whether or not I'm a bloody fucking liar, I thought. My gut was gripped with panic; my headache pounded.

Death is my friend. The Devil be blessed. At this moment, I just want to escape this place, over a wall or through a tunnel. I want out.

Following lunch, William, Paul, Murdoch and I individually begin the interview process.

We are mostly silent at lunch. Small talk. I can't speak at all.

"You all right?" Murdoch asks.

"Yeah. I didn't sleep well last night. CIA jitters, I guess."

He nods in sympathy. Loose ends or not, Murdoch notices things. He is very bright and easy to underestimate. Maybe this unkemptness is part of his plan.

I am assigned to a senior staff member who introduces himself as Gary. I sit down in Gary's office, another barren room that is almost completely devoid of personal touches. Again, no photographs of smiling kiddies or beaming bride. There is only a yellow legal pad and a cheap ballpoint pen in front of Gary. This room is chilly, too.

Gary presents a detailed overview of the CIA's Operation Directorate, the clandestine service as it is commonly known. Following this overview, Gary begins the interview process by presenting two scenarios and asks me to role play as if I were the case officer in each situation.

The first scenario Gary presents is a situation where my contact, a janitor, is concerned that he cannot do the job of planting listening devices in the desired conference room. The janitor, it seems, is lacking self-confidence and needs to have his self-esteem built up. I try as best I can to build his self-esteem, but I have great difficulty with this scenario due to my own limited emotional affect.

"I need to know more about him. How can I build his confidence when he is a complete stranger?"

"Mr. Snyder, you will move in a world of strangers, and most of them will be your enemy. That is what we do."

After observing me struggle for ten minutes, Gary signals that time is up, and we must move to the next scenario. He makes a note on his pad. He doesn't seem impressed by what I have said.

In the second scenario, I'm driving a car in a foreign capital with my spy, an important and easily recognized government official as my passenger, when we're involved in a minor accident.

"How should you handle this situation," Gary asks, "as onlookers crowd around your vehicle? What should you do?"

Amazingly, I know just what to do.

"I would jump out of my car and immediately create a scene in order to draw attention to myself so that my passenger could quietly slip away."

I'm excited, and I feel a surge of energy. I jump out of the chair, and soon I'm dancing like a madman in the chilly office, my arms raised over my head, waving them furiously.

"I would shout obscenities at the other driver, Gary, about his mother and his wife and his daughter. Oh, yes, I would fill the air with obscenities, shouting with a madman's joy. I am crazy; I am best so!"

I am hitting a dangerous manic phase now. Gary looks concerned.

"I would insult them in Mandarin and French. I would damn them in every language of the Earth. I would be lonely and crazy. I would damn their filthy souls to hell. I would pray that they die in great pain and alone. I would curse them in words that only God knows."

I take a deep breath and sit down.

"I would be a distraction so that the prime minister of Nowherestan can escape."

"Well done, Mr. Snyder," Gary says with a smile. "Well done, indeed."

He was smiling and leaned close, as if we were colleagues. I think he is relieved I was able to shut down the bubble machine. I feel quite calm.

"Something happened to me like that," he says, "although I was not as crazy as you just demonstrated. It was at the Finnish border back in the Cold War days, and I was trying to get a Soviet scientist— you'd likely know his name—to the West. We made it, too. The problem was we ended up in Paris, and I had a harder time getting him out of Paris than Finland. He liked French women. Can't blame him for that, I guess."

Following this second scenario, Gary asks me several more questions, which I answer as best I can. I'm happy for the moment, and I feel that I have made some progress.

That evening, William, Murdoch, Paul and I have dinner together and compare stories. None of us shares too much. I learn that only William has passed the polygraph today as he was the only one among us to complete the post-exam survey. Murdoch, Paul, and I must re-take the polygraph tomorrow. That makes me feel a little better. I'm not the only liar, it seems. Perhaps there is a tiny, miniscule chance I still could be accepted into the Company. Oh, yeah, and Natalia will come crawling back begging my forgiveness. And my old man will tell me how much he loves me. These are my dazzling delusions.

Friday morning, I check out of the hotel. The mini-van picks up the four of us at the usual time, and we drive to our last day of interviews. I am the first for the polygraph exam, and because I don't do well again—I either fail or am inconclusive—I am not asked to complete the post-exam survey.

For that I blame that bitch Cindy, and I feel I am entering the grip of rage and depression. It is like a knife point in my brain.

Death is my only friend. The Devil be blessed.

Following the polygraph exam, I am introduced to Darrel in Human Resources. He is another CIA cipher, non-person; he's a short white guy with a military haircut, bristly gray hair. He is wearing a pair of khakis, a white polo shirt, and a blue cardigan sweater. He looks like he's on the way to the Men's' Grill at the Club. The only thing he lacks is a four-iron to twirl. He's probably looked this way since he prepped. He seems a Groton type, but my guess is he just couldn't close the deal and get into Harvard. Maybe it is his teeth. He definitely doesn't have Ivy League choppers. They are nicotine stained and crooked. They are the color of wet straw.

"If you're hired, Mr. Snyder," Darrel explains, "your starting salary would be thirty-four thousand dollars per year."

"That doesn't seem like much for a job like this."

He simply smiles at my observation.

"It's not. The way the Agency works," he says, "is that all candidates receive a rejection letter in the mail. Only those candidates who receive a phone call will get a job offer."

"When could I expect a phone call?"

"They're usually made within a month of the interviews, but there is no real time line."

"The problem is the salary," I explain, "I have a lot of student debt, and there is no way I could afford to live in Washington, DC, and work for the Agency this year."

"I know it's tough, but if you do well, you can advance fairly rapidly."

"Tell me, is there such a thing as a deferred enrollment period?"

"Yes, for up to two years, but that would be predicated upon you receiving the job offer phone call. Otherwise, you'd have to re-apply. And it's not any easier on the second go around."

Blah, blah, blah, Mr. Snyder. Now get lost.

Following my discussion with Darrel, I am taken to a staff psychologist for an exit interview. She is an older woman, in her early fifties I would guess, and again very attractive. The CIA has a lot of pretty women on the payroll, it seems. She is quite tall and deeply suntanned. Her grey hair is pulled back into a pony tail. Her name is Judith, and she extends her hand in greeting. Her hands are quite elegant, and she wears a simple gold wedding band on her left hand. She asks me questions about my answers on my psychological profile exam. She is friendly, smiling.

"Now tell me about the situation with Jedermann University" she says. "You seem to have had a hard time of it."

"I feel like they lied to me," I say with some heat. "I feel what they did to me at Jedermann was the emotional and psychological equivalent of rape."

She didn't speak, only paged through the papers on her desk. She seemed almost embarrassed by what I said, my intensity. I desperately need to explain.

"Look, I'll be honest," I say, "I am in no condition to interview now, but I needed to go through with the interview because I worked too hard and for too long not to interview. I've wanted to be in the CIA since I was a little boy."

"You're right. Maybe now wasn't the right time," she says, "maybe a few months later would have been better for you."

"Will I be able to interview again, that is, after I've paid off my student loans?"

"Certainly."

"Should I seek counseling between now and then?" I ask, although I think I know the answer.

"No, were I you, I would stay away from counseling. It complicates matters for us."

"I thought that might be the case. Do you surveil applicants after we go through the selection process?"

"No, of course not."

"I thought you might want to keep track of obvious losers, maybe like me."

"James, we don't think you're a loser. And we don't have the resources to surveil applicants who aren't accepted. I understand it doesn't seem fair, Mr. Snyder, but there are many, many things that are not fair about this process."

She stands up and walks me to the door.

"Thanks for your honesty," I say.

"Honesty is not really the point, Mr. Snyder, but I wish you good luck."

I leave her office with a profound sadness. What else should I feel with the death of a dream?

I wait outside CIA headquarters for approximately fifteen minutes until the hotel courtesy van finally arrives to take me back to the hotel. Because Scott and his family are on vacation in Washington DC, we plan to spend Friday night together.

We had planned this rendezvous in Virginia when I got the letter from the CIA establishing a date for my interviews. It was going to be a festive moment in our lives, Scott and mine. LT becoming, at long last, a reality. That all disappears on the ride back to the hotel. When I check at the reception desk to see if the Todds have arrived, I find they are out sightseeing. I go to the hotel bar and order a beer. I am very upset, slowly sipping my beer and trying to tamp down my anger. The bartender looks at me, "Long day?" he asks. He is the master of faux sympathy.

He must see I'm down. I'm on the verge of tears. But I straighten up on the bar stool and respond, "It's been a bitch. Today was really something, and it's not over."

"A cold beer will help. Can I buy you another one?"

I smile and nod yes. I am disconnecting, willingly now, stony-hearted and alone.

Following a somber dinner, Scott and I go out for drinks while Kelly and the kids stay with her parents. Scott asks me what I'm going to do. I answer that I don't know. That seems to be the answer to most of the questions I am asked lately. I explain to Scott that I can interview again once my loans are paid off. I am very depressed and utterly discouraged.

I felt I was at the end of a bad movie with popcorn stuck in my teeth. I have to get out of here.

Death is my only friend. The Devil be blessed!

SEND IN THE LAWYERS

For the next twenty-two months I am comatose psychologically. I don't know what is happening. To this day, I don't have a clear memory of this part of my life. I got up in the morning and went to bed at night. I functioned with no interest in what is happening around me. I am dead in life. My memory revives in June 2006, two years after the incident. I am done with the painting part of my life, and have left Sugarland in the rearview mirror. Grace and George have moved to Austin to be closer to their daughter. My friend and confidante Grace has been diagnosed with stomach cancer. She has a very short time to live. I said I would go up to Austin to visit them, but we all know I never will. If I were capable of sadness, I would be sad. I should be sad because she is a lovely person and helped me when I needed help. But I am empty of emotions. No, that's not true, my one indulgence emotionally is anger. I don't act out when I am at large in the world. No shopping mall fits for me. At night, when I'm alone, I punish myself with anger and accusations. And then there was the firing range. That was the other reason I left Sugarland for The Woodlands. When I was working as a handyman / painter for George at The Dorchester, I collected newspapers, thousands of them. Not to read but to test my silencer. I made bundles of newspapers, ten inches high unbound. I wanted to test both the .22 short bullet and the .22 long. My judgement was that the shorts would penetrate two or three inches into the pile of newspapers, and I wasn't sure about the longs.

On a Wednesday night, I cranked up the music, Mahler was my choice, the Resurrection Symphony. It was not an accidental choice. In bleak moments I listen to the Finale, the famous "cry of despair." I prefer the alternate interpretation, "death shriek." Somber and fearsome music that got the attention of my roiled spirit. I played the music full volume, and I didn't give a fuck what the neighbors thought. Mahler was my man in the wolf hours after midnight and with my silenced Browning .22, I shoot into the pile. Two rounds of the shorts, one round of the longs. The air conditioner quickly dissipates the smell of the gunpowder, and the music, I thought, would cover the sound of the gun discharging. And I was almost right. I was right about the penetration by the shorts, three inches through the newspaper; the long round went a little farther into the pile. I was wrong about the noise. The long round was very loud, louder than I anticipated. I know I fucked up. The silencer works, that's the important thing, with the shorts anyway. I turn off the music and turn out the lights. Time to pretend I'm tucked up in bed and sound asleep.

In a few minutes there is a frantic hammering at my door. It is George, yelling my name. I crack the door and ask him what he wants.

"What do I want? I thought you had blown your fucking brains out, James. What in the hell are you doing in there?"

"I'm okay. I just dropped something."

"Don't be an asshole, James. I was in the army and I know what a gunshot sounds like."

"I can't talk now, George. Can we do this in the morning?"

"The only thing I have to say to you, Jimmy, is either the gun goes or you go. It's that simple."

In the end, it was smoothed out between us. I promised I wouldn't play Mahler so loud, and I would never again fire the Browning. But the damage had been done, and soon enough I left Sugarland and The Dorchester. I would not give up my weapons; it *was* that simple.

So, here I am sitting in my new apartment on the other side of town, in The Woodlands, unemployed again, as I lost my sales job at the import/export company. It was an absolute dead-end job, trying to sell video screens for gambling machines. Video poker is becoming a big deal worldwide. Casinos and bars are creating a huge demand, and the Koreans dominate the market. I was not a good salesman, although it was a good product. I never met my sales quotas, and that pissed off my bosses. I had a hard time getting along with the Korean owners, who were very aggressive and unhappy with me. They even sent me on a fact-finding trip to Korea, but the only fact I found was that kimchi upsets my stomach. I am glad to be away from Mr. Kim, my old boss, who was a tyrant. I was actually afraid of him.

I am lucky to be employed on a temporary basis with a local computer parts manufacturer. I spend most of my time on the factory floor in quality control. It is a tiresome and tedious job. To escape my pain and to accumulate as much money as I can, I work sixty to seventy hours per week, every week, week after week. It is deadly boring, but it pays the rent. I live as frugally as I can, and my bank account grows weekly. Fried Spam sandwiches on white bread maybe isn't the best diet, but it's cheap. I vacillate between bouts of rage so intense that I want to kill and bouts of depression so severe that I want to die. This is the systole and diastole of my wretchedness. Murder and suicide. It was like being on a swing in a playground, back and forth with no progress. Motion without meaning.

On weekends, Scott and Kelly use me as their babysitter when she wants to go out with her husband because I'm not fit to go out with. Their young children accept me and like me despite my self-hatred for what I've become, so I baby-sit for them. Scott attempts to help me socially by taking me out drinking and playing pool and going to titty bars, but I sense his frustration at my lack of progress. I'm in an endless cycle of anger, depression, anger, depression.

I look at the calendar. Two years ago this month, Cindy and her superiors destroyed all that I had worked for. I remove my Taurus 9 mm semi-automatic handgun from its case and load a jacketed hollow point into the chamber. I choose the hollow point round because it is a bullet favored by police: it expands as it enters the target and does terrible damage to soft tissue. Its other advantage for the police is that it typically won't exit the target, thus avoiding collateral damage to any innocent civilian who happens to be nearby. It's a perfect bullet for close-range mayhem and suicide. I cock the weapon and put the barrel in my mouth. I close my eyes, my index finger resting gently on the trigger. In a moment of clarity, I realize that I cannot go on this way. I must relieve my pain.

I am no longer able to think about working for the CIA. I can't protect a secret ambition that has been destroyed for me by Cindy and Jedermann. The anger takes over. I must destroy Cindy and her superiors for what they did to me. The CIA was in my grasp, I rationalize, and it was Cindy and Monteblanc and the others who stole this from me. My history is corrupted by their lies. I am not going to let them get away with this. I will destroy them, God help me, and kill her.

I call Scott at his work. I tell him that I need a lawyer immediately.

"Why?"

"I'm going to sue Cindy and Jedermann for what they did to me."

"Man, that's going to be difficult. Are you sure you want to do this?"

"I don't care."

"It will be expensive."

"I'll spend every damn dime I have to get satisfaction. I need to start this immediately. I've been checking online and the deadline for filing a suit is only about a week away. Maybe two, max."

He tells me that there's a book at the public library called the Martindale-Hubbell Directory that lists the top lawyers in America. I go there. I find the book. I search under medical malpractice. I find the names of lawyers and law firms in Houston. I photocopy their names and I go home.

I call the number one medical malpractice attorney in town, a man named Nicholas Kadair. I briefly speak with his receptionist who puts me through immediately to him. I explain as best I can. Mr. Kadair invites me to visit for a face-to-face that afternoon. I put on my suit and I go there.

When I arrive, Mr. Kadair greets me with a handshake and ushers me into his beautiful office where we talk. It's obvious that this man is very successful. He looks a lot like a young Nick Nolte, similar build, similar facial structure. A handsome manly fellow. I hand him a small stack of papers to review. He briefly looks over my draft letter to the Director, my letter to the Dean, and my clinical file, and then asks me questions.

"Mr. Snyder," Kadair explains, "there are two extremes of cases that you'll typically find. At one extreme are cases with huge liabilities but small damages and at the other extreme are cases with small liabilities but huge damages. Because of the nature of psychological malpractice and the difficulty with proving damages, your case is likely one with huge liabilities but small damages. The nature and complexity of psychological malpractice makes proving damages very difficult."

"But not impossible?"

"Difficult, but not impossible. However, your case in my opinion is likely one with huge liabilities but small damages. It will be very costly, and even if you win, you won't get much in the way of compensation. Far less than you would think is fair. By the way, in Houston terms, I'm a pretty expensive lawyer. Do you think you can afford me?"

"I have money, and I'll spend it all if I have to. Beg, steal and borrow if I have to. Will you represent me?"

He asks me about Cindy. I give him a brief description, including her Rolex and Mercedes.

"And she's a psychologist or training to be one anyway?" Kadair asks.

"Yes. Very attractive woman. A little crazy, I think."

"That wouldn't be Cindy Polanski, would it?"

"Oh shit, you know her. Of course, you know her."

"It's a small world, even in a town as large as Houston. We had a brief social relationship before she was married. Drinks and dinner, that sort of thing. Nothing intimate. I wouldn't describe her as crazy exactly, but very, very ambitious."

"Small world," I say, not sure if I believe him. "And the bitch is married. Christ, I've stepped into it this time."

"Yes, I think you have. She married money, James. Hey if you can't inherit it, you can at least marry it. It's the American way."

"So, what are you going to do? Will you help me?"

"Sorry, I can't represent you. My advice is to proceed carefully with this case. I think you'll have a hard time with it, and it's going to end up costing you a lot of money."

"I'm willing to spend it."

"One other piece of advice, don't underestimate Cindy, she is very shrewd. And very, very ambitious. She's not going to appreciate being sued."

He offers the names of two up-and-coming attorneys whom he says are very good. I thank him and depart.

When I arrive at home, I call the first attorney, a man named Fred Smith. Mr. Smith says that his plate is full and that he is not interested in representing me.

I call the second attorney, a man named Damian Argantes. I speak briefly with Mr. Argantes and, although he says he's not particularly interested in taking my case, after he learns that my deadline for filing is rapidly approaching, he invites me in for a visit the following afternoon.

As I enter Damian Argantes' downtown office, I cannot help but see the signs: *Argantes for City Council; Elect Argantes - City Councilman At Large.* It is unmistakably obvious Damian Argantes is a man with a plan. And ambitions.

The receptionist announces my arrival. I shake Damian's hand and thank him for seeing me. I'm surprised at how good-looking Damian is. He's a big man with black hair and a very deep tan. It was a perfect tanning bed tan, no gaps or lacunae in the turmeric color of his skin. He dresses well. Today he is wearing a navy-blue suit with a yellow tie. His watch is Swiss, and his shoes are Italian. Put him in a Grand Hotel doorman's fancy uniform—all braids and gold buttons— and he will look like a generalissimo in a banana republic, in exile.

"If you're going to be an at large councilman," I ask, "are you still going to practice law?"

"Of course," he says.

He motions me into his office, which is a little shabby for the man and his ambition.

Somewhat relieved, I get down to business. I show Damian the same documents I showed to Nicholas Kadair, and, like Mr. Kadair, Damian quickly reviews them and then asks me what I want from this lawsuit.

"I want control over those people for what they did to me. I want to destroy them." I feel myself starting to lose control, my anger seething forth, my raw nerves ready to explode in a fit of rage.

"Control? What do you mean by control?"

"I want them to feel the boot of the law on their throats. And then I want that boot to crush them like cockroaches."

Damian sits back in his leather chair and smiles.

"Is that all? Many people who come into my office want revenge, but civil lawsuits are only about money. If you are wronged, you receive money. There is no revenge other than money. Money is the only compensation. A civil lawsuit will not make you whole. It will not bring back the dead or return you to a previous state. A civil lawsuit," Damian reiterates, "is only about money, the dough re mi, my friend."

I quickly calm down and regain control of myself.

"How much money in my situation could I be awarded?"

"Because the overall defendant is the State of Texas with various individuals underneath that umbrella, your lawsuit must be brought under the Texas Tort Claims Act."

"What does that mean?"

"Damages are limited to $250k if you win, but that amount in your case is very unlikely. You'd get a fraction of that."

"What about Cindy. Is she also under the state's umbrella?"

"Probably not. She probably has her own insurance policy."

I tell Damian that I want to file. He tells me to hold on. Because of the probability of losing this lawsuit, Damian advises that no attorney will take it on a contingency fee basis.

"And there's another problem."

"What's that?"

"The State of Texas could assert the principle of sovereign immunity. Simply put, the State can say it and its agents and entities operating under the aegis of the State can be held blameless, not liable in a case of medical malpractice, unless there is a breach of something called the Standard of Care. That 'breach of standard of care' is a shape shifter, and it is being litigated and re-litigated in Texas courts. In short, the folks at Jedermann have to have really screwed the pooch in your treatment. I'm not sure from your file if your case might not be dismissed even before it gets to trial based on sovereign immunity."

"I know they betrayed me, and I know they breached a standard of care."

"Okay, James, here's another fly in our litigious soup. The State can admit liability. Oh, yeah, they can say, we fucked up this poor fellow, and we really feel badly about it. It's a darn shame. We're sorry, but, and this is a big but, the effects of our mistakes were not long term. There were no real damages to this James Snyder. Nothing really bad happened, and those small discomforts he endured were 'acute and transitory.' That's the legal boilerplate you don't want accepted by the Court: acute and transitory. In short, liability but no damages. You get the re mi, buddy, but none of the dough."

I had come too far down this path to go back. I had ridden this donkey into Jerusalem, I was damned sure I wasn't going to turn around and ride it out again.

"That's okay. I understand it's a difficult case, even if I win there may be small damages. I worked about seventy hours a week every week for seven months in a temporary assignment and so I have about forty thousand dollars saved."

That's the "dough" in dough re mi. Damian again sits back in his leather chair and smiles.

"Will you represent me?"

"I'm very busy. But maybe."

"One man against the system could prove to be very good publicity for you in this or any future election campaigns. You know helping the little guy in his hour of need, fighting against the Moloch of the State. You'd be a local hero."

He smiles at the thought of it.

"Local Hero Argantes. That would look good on a poster."

He agrees to think about it. Vanity, I understand is his Achilles heel.

I ask him how I can go about filing the lawsuit on my own. Damian says that going alone can be risky. I respond that I have no choice. He hands me a blank plaintiff's petition, then checks the date that I received my clinical file from Jedermann University.

"You have five business days to file your lawsuit. You should complete the petition and return next week to discuss it with me."

Damian reiterates that he's not interested in representing me but does offer to provide consulting services should I need legal assistance. I thank him and depart.

Exactly five business days later, on the afternoon of Thursday, June 15, 2006, the day that my lawsuit must be filed, I return to Damian's office with my completed plaintiff's petition. Damian reads the first two paragraphs, winces, and says that it will not fly.

"This is no good. It won't work. It's just ranting."

"What should I do? I need to file something."

I felt a twinge of panic.

Damian looks at the clock, realizes that there are only two-and-a-half hours until the court closes, and in a fit of exasperation agrees to help me. Because he's not willing to take the case on contingency, he explains his fee structure: $12K for discovery, $12K for trial, and I pay all expenses. I agree. I couldn't be happier.

Damian prints a contract. We both sign it. I then leave so Damian can work on the petition. He files it that afternoon, ten minutes before the court closes.

That evening I call Scott and share the good news with him. I am ecstatic that I will finally get justice.

I MIGHT BE CRAZY BUT...

I was about to write the phrase, "I might be crazy, but as this lawsuit was initiated, I felt like I was at the edge of a life-altering moment." Some irony there: I was, I now realize, by the measure of any reasonable psychological standard, quite crazy, dangerously so. And it turns out that I was, in fact, at the edge of a life-altering moment, but one I did not — could not — then fully anticipate or understand.

Damian called me the following morning to tell me that he filed the lawsuit on time. He asks that I come in at 3:30 PM to pay the discovery fee and discuss next steps.

That afternoon Damian and I discuss the discovery process.

"James," he says, "before we go to trial both parties exchange information. This is a process known as discovery. It is an important part of the legal process."

"What happens?"

"Discovery begins with requests for the production of documents and other evidence as well as interrogatories, the kind of questions that will be asked. After this exchange, we start depositions."

"What are those?"

"Depositions are a discovery tool. It is testimony, under oath, but not in front of a judge. It can be a bit of a fishing expedition to see just what the other side has in terms of the strength of its case. There is a court reporter, a stenographer, recording the testimony. Usually at the end you have to sign an affidavit attesting to the accuracy of the transcript."

Damian explains that usually the plaintiff goes first; though if the other sides agree, he will take the defendants' depositions before mine. After the discovery period ends, the court schedules a trial date.

95

Damian estimates that the trial in my case will last one week.

"But, James, one thing to remember is that because of the discovery process, the two sides can assess the relative strength of the other's case. Discovery often ends in some sort of settlement and no trial. That would be an ideal outcome for you, I think."

We talk a little bit more about the discovery process and then Damian then asks me for his $12k discovery fee. I pull out my checkbook and write him a check for $12,000.

"Damian, I am not interested in an ideal outcome. I will tell you this directly: I am going to kill each of the individuals named in my lawsuit for violating my trust. This is a warning to you, Damian. It will be the future. I need to beat these people in court. Don't you see, if my case is proven that gives me the right to kill them?"

He took this in very calmly. He looked at the check and put it in his desk drawer.

"James, you're upset and very angry. I see this all the time. This process is not about retribution, it's about justice. You'll calm down and understand that soon. It is a long, boring process."

He doesn't understand! My message was not received.

"I need you to refer me to a psychiatrist for counseling, Damian."

"Not just yet. I know a good psychologist that we'll use as our expert witness."

After pausing to think for a moment, he says, "I don't believe counseling is a good idea right now."

He does not elaborate why.

We discuss the best way to communicate. I explain that because I live so far away from downtown, and because I hope to be gainfully employed soon and will not be able to visit during the day, the best way for us to communicate will be to fax documents to and from my local neighborhood copy shop. Damian agrees and suggests that I start thinking about what questions I want to ask each of the defendants.

That evening, back in my sparsely furnished, arguably barren apartment, I sit down at my computer and begin drafting questions.

THREE THOUSAND DOLLARS' WORTH OF QUESTIONS

Two weeks after filing the lawsuit, Damian receives defendants' requests for production of evidence and interrogatories. So, over the next three weeks, to comply with defendants' discovery requests, I make copies of the answering machine messages that the Director and Dr. Howell left for me. I photocopy the various letters that were exchanged between Jedermann University and me. I visit Jedermann's library where I photocopy the student handbook. And I visit Jedermann's Psychological Counseling Services office and obtain a copy of the Policies and Procedures for Clinical Psychology - the rule book for what constitutes appropriate conduct in a student therapy setting!

Believing that my case is very strong, I fax my answers, after which I call Damian's secretary and schedule a face-to-face meeting with Damian to discuss next steps. The secretary schedules our meeting for the following Tuesday at 4:00 PM.

On Tuesday I arrive at Damian's office promptly at 4:00 PM and his secretary shows me into his office where he is ready for me. After shaking my hand, Damian invites me to sit down. I notice that he has new office furniture, leather chairs and a teak desk. I have a feeling my money was useful to him.

"I like most of your questions, James, and I'm delighted that you have saved as much evidence as you have. I wish all my clients were as careful as you."

"I am organized, Damian. It is necessary to win this case."

My threat against the defendants was not spoken.

"Okay, here's how it will go: after we submit our answers, based upon the evidence that you have saved, I'll submit plaintiff's questions to the defendants."

"Why the delay? I want to get on with this thing."

"You see, James, in civil cases there are no surprises."

"What does that mean?"

"It's simple. Only the evidence presented during discovery can be used at trial. Evidence not presented during discovery cannot be used. So, the order in which questions are asked is really irrelevant."

"Did you read my cover letter?"

"Of course."

"I want a referral to a psychiatrist to begin therapy. It is really important to me."

"I don't think this is the right time, James. It would be detrimental to your case for obvious reasons."

I am about to say that the reasons were not obvious to me, but before I can say anything Damian changes the subject and talks about the billing for expenses. Clearly, Damian doesn't want to discuss therapy.

I pull out my checkbook and put it on Damian's new and expensive desk. My new and expensive desk.

"How much?"

"Three-thousand dollars should be sufficient until the depositions start," he says.

I get up and leave. I wonder what he is going to buy with this three thousands of my dollars.

Dough, re, mi, indeed, Counselor Argantes.

NO SYMPATHY FOR THE DEVILS

It is now August 2006, two months and two years after the incident, and I am working as a temporary employee, a supplier quality engineer, for an electronic parts manufacturer on my side of town. As a condition of my hiring, under the guise of looking for full-time employment, I stated that there would be days when I would need to depart early and/or miss work entirely and, surprisingly, the company accepted my terms. As before, I work sixty to seventy hours per week to escape the pain. I don't mind working to keep my case alive.

Even though the incident occurred more than two years ago, the memories of it are still so fresh in my mind, as if it had occurred only yesterday.

During the last week of August, I meet with Damian to receive copies of the defendants' responses to plaintiff's discovery requests.

"James, I'm going to ask you a very, very important question. What exactly happened between you and Cindy, what kind of physical contact occurred the night of the incident? The truth is critical here, James."

"Cindy blocked my path as I tried to get the hell out of the therapy room. Once I got into the hallway, I moved Cindy to the side, so I could squeeze between her and the hallway wall that was to my back. I did it firmly. As I did this, Cindy grabbed me and tried to physically restrain me, and I sort of faked a karate chop to get her to release her grip."

"Moved her firmly? Faked a karate chop? You don't see a problem with that during a session with a therapist?"

"What this is all about, Damian?"

He hands me the defendants' responses.

"Look at what Cindy swore to under oath."

Cindy claimed throughout her responses that I threw her into a wall in the therapy room and that was why she called the police. I am initially shocked; however, I quickly become angry at these lies.

"She is lying. She is a fucking lying bitch."

Damian smiles at me. He was immune to his client's anger, I suppose.

"I believe you, James, but this is a real problem for us. A major fucking problem. The audio tape from the incident seems to have survived, but it is pretty much unintelligible."

Damian plays it, but all we can hear is white noise with voices hidden in the background. I request that Damian have the tape digitally enhanced to filter out the noise, and he agrees to do this.

"I know you don't seem to want to help me with this, but I want you to refer me to a psychiatrist for therapy."

"Absolutely not. A record of psychiatric treatment with a full-blown diagnosis will be detrimental to your case."

"Why?"

"Jesus Christ, because of what you said. You don't get that? James, you told me that you were going to murder all those people."

I was angry, and I didn't respond to him. He quickly changed the subject.

"Depositions will start in four weeks at Jedermann University."

"Who are you deposing?" I ask, struggling to regain my composure.

"The Director and Dr. Howell have agreed to go first and second, respectively, followed by Dean Colwell, the night supervisor, and then the night receptionist."

"I want that lying bitch Cindy to go before me."

"I'll try."

It is apparent from his body language and facial expressions that he will not. I make note of this. He seems increasingly less sympathetic to my case.

Damian ends this meeting by reviewing the billing.

"James, I want each of the defendant depositions to be videotaped, so I'll need more money. Five thousand."

I'm thinking that this is crazy, and when the meter hits $40,000, I'll be thrown out of the Argantes Car Service. I write him a check for five-thousand dollars. I then depart.

Back in my apartment, I read each of the defendants' responses. I begin with Dr. Monteblanc, then Dr. Howell, then Dean Colwell, and finally Cindy. I am highly agitated and upset at the lies I see in the faculty members' answers. When I read Cindy's responses, I lose control and throw the papers into the living room wall, thereby scattering them about my apartment.

Unable to calm down, I pace back and forth, seething with anger and rage. Finally, I gain enough control over my emotions to telephone Scott for support. I explain to him what had happened.

"Hey, Jim, tough day with Perry Mason I guess."

"Humiliating day with that bastard. I hate him."

I think he finally heard the despair in my voice. Scott understood me.

"Do not do anything crazy."

Scott reminds me that it is my attorney's job to destroy the other sides' credibility, not mine. The truth shall prevail.

"Okay, thanks, I'm feeling a little better."

"Do you want to go out and get a beer? Maybe a friendly face would help."

"No, I'm okay. I'm just going to straighten up this mess and go to bed."

After hanging up with Scott, I regain enough composure to collect and re-assemble the documents in their proper order. I do not look at them further. Instead, I ask myself what if Cindy truly had erased the tape? How would I possibly defend myself?

With these questions weighing heavily on my mind, I become morbidly depressed, so much so that I lay there in the middle of my living room floor and I pass out.

Death is my only friend. The Devil be blessed!

THE PERJURERS' TALES

It's late September. I meet Damian at 8:30 AM in front of Jedermann University's student activities building. We find a small table with two chairs inside and sit down. From my briefcase, I remove lists of questions that I have prepared for each of today's defendants and, because the Director is going first, I hand Damian my questions for him. Damian first looks at me grimacingly, then at the stack of twenty-five pages of triple-spaced questions I just handed him.

"James, do you think this is really necessary?"

"These are the questions that I want you to ask."

Damian reviews the list of questions, then puts the stack down.

"I'll get most of these questions answered during routine questioning. And if I don't get all the questions answered, near the end I'll allow you to select those that you specifically want answered. I'll ask them then. Does that seem okay?"

"I guess so." It seems I don't have much choice.

At 9:00 AM, Damian and I proceed to the conference room where today's depositions will be taken. The conference room is on the Jedermann campus, in the Main Building, and it is used for important meetings, most often invisible ones. Its style is what Cindy called in a casual moment Scandinavian Cowboy Moderne. It is a robust red, red geranium she remembered the color to be, with severe furniture of beech wood and chrome. The chairs around the table are a cherry leather, to match the walls, I suppose. The walls are the Cowboy part: photographs and paintings of lean, mustached cowpokes on horseback heading back to the ranch after a tough day; abandoned farmhouses in an evening rain; and fields of bluebells. Acres of bluebells. Very comforting if you have a big bank account and a cigar in your jacket pocket. A rich man's room. Plenty of rich men sat on the Board at Jedermann and this was where they held their monthly meetings. I didn't have a cigar to my name just then. Inside the room, we find Dr. Monteblanc, looking very bored; Dr. Howell, looking professionally frumpy; Cindy, looking nicely turned out in a navy-blue dress and black shoes. A summer dress with a deep tan. Didn't get that tan in the library, Cindy, I thought. There were others, too: the video recorder, the stenographer, and two attorneys who introduce themselves as Samuel Troutman and Clint Wharton.

As he shakes my hand, Troutman says, "I'm with the Attorney General's office representing Jedermann University and Mr. Wharton is representing Cindy Polanski."

As we sit down, I watch as Damian takes a long look at Cindy and I can only imagine what he is thinking. Cindy wears her hair down. It is shoulder length and flowing. She looks like a model out of a fashion magazine. Christ, she is gorgeous. A sinking feeling comes over me. My big ears against her blonde hair is a lose/lose proposition.

At 9:05 AM, the stenographer swears in the Director for his deposition. He seems nervous and distracted. He drinks water during the questioning and continually clears his throat. He raps his pencil against the expensive Swedish birch table. He can't wait to get out of here. Over the next three hours, Damian grills Dr. Monteblanc. That makes me happy.

"What is your diagnosis of Mr. Snyder's condition, sir?"

"I don't have one. I didn't diagnose him."

"What do you know about Mr. Snyder's therapy sessions with Cindy?"

"Nothing. I have no direct knowledge of their sessions."

"Even though you're in charge of the clinic, you don't know what condition Mr. Snyder was being treated for, and you have no knowledge about whether the therapy was in anyway helpful to Mr. Snyder. Is that correct, sir?"

"Basically."

"Is that a yes or a maybe?"

"Yes. It is correct."

"What is your role with a client like Mr. Snyder and a student therapist like Ms Polanski?"

"My role? I really didn't have one."

"You don't supervise."

"Not really. Not individually."

"You don't instruct?"

"Instructors do that. I'm not an instructor. I'm the Director. I direct."

"Are you good at directing? I bet you are."

At that point, Troutman looks up from his note pad. "Come on, Damian, let's be friendly like, okay?"

"Sorry. Did you offer to see Mr. Snyder in your office off campus as a private patient?"

"I considered it briefly. Very briefly."

"Even though you know virtually nothing about his condition, including a likely diagnosis?"

"Yes, that's not unusual."

"Why?"

"I'm in a helping profession. I suppose I wanted to help."

The Director acknowledges that Jedermann University's training standards were more stringent than Texas state requirements, and that he kept file notes separate from the medical record.

"Did you read the file?"

"I skimmed it. I'm a little confused about the number of and the dates of my file entries."

"Confusion seems to be a mild expression of your state of mind, Director Monteblanc, but perhaps you can be confused and a good director at the same time."

"Did you have a conversation about Mr. Snyder's behavior with Ms Polanski on the evening of June 15, 2004?"

"I honestly don't remember."

"Did you concur with her decision to call the campus police to find Mr. Snyder and recover the file?"

"It's possible, but that was a long time ago."

During his deposition, I observe that Mr. Troutman twice hands the Director tissues to wipe his sweaty palms. Throughout his deposition, the Director appears to be very nervous, and that pleases me.

After a quick break for lunch in Jedermann's cafeteria, we reconvene at 1:30 PM. Damian immediately commences Dr. Howell's deposition. Over the next hour-and-a-half, Damian grills Dr. Howell about her supervision of Cindy.

"Given the situation, the tension between Mr. Snyder and Cindy, why didn't you terminate his therapy?"

"Cindy wanted to continue the therapy sessions, and that is why I did not terminate them. Cindy thought she could help him."

"Everyone seems to want to help Mr. Snyder. And do you think she helped him?"

"I don't know. They were still early in the process."

"Which is the higher priority, Dr. Howell, training the student or treating the client?"

"Training the student therapist is equally as important as the client's mental health and well-being."

I become very concerned with her statement, in fact, it pisses me off. I struggle to keep my composure. The truth comes out in odd ways, in direct blows sometimes or in the matter of factness of someone who doesn't really care.

"What condition do you think Mr. Snyder was being treated for that Dr. Monteblanc didn't seem to know?"

"Depression, I suppose, that's the most common condition we treat, but I can't say with certainty what conditions Cindy was treating."

"Paranoia? Schizophrenia?"

"I don't know. I don't want to speculate here, in front of the patient."

Although Dr. Howell's deposition is beneficial, it is not as useful as the Director's. Dr. Howell refuses to answer certain questions about her age and her level of experience, questions that I specifically want answered. This angers me, but I remain in control of my emotions.

After a fifteen-minute break, the night receptionist, Maryann Esposito, is brought in for her deposition. As expected, she vehemently defends Cindy, Dr. Monteblanc, and Jedermann University.

"Who was the first person out of the therapy room the night of the incident, Mr. Snyder or Cindy?"

"I don't know. I didn't see them come out. I just saw what happened in the hallway."

"What did you see in the hallway?"

"I saw James with a file and Cindy trying to get it from him. They both were quite upset, it seems to me."

"Did you see Mr. Snyder hit or push aside Ms Polanski?"

"Yes. Not hit but he it seemed like he made a threatening gesture towards her. Like a karate chop, but I don't think he actually struck her."

"What happened next Mrs. Esposito?"

"Cindy told me to call the police. She told me that James had stolen some university property, I guess it was the file, and that his real name wasn't Schneider, it was Snyder. And she told me what kind of car he drove. I don't remember the exact make, but it was an older model. I think it was an older Volkswagen of some sort. I think it was a '93."

"Just to clarify things, Cindy asked you to call the campus police, is that correct?"

"Yes."

"And what was Ms Polanski's state of mind like?"

"She was upset, but she wasn't crying or anything. She went back to the therapy room, and I went with her to make sure she was okay. That's when we found Mr. Snyder's watch. Apparently, it was his habit to take it off at the beginning of a session. She said he kept careful track of the time. She thought he was a bit obsessional about timing. She gave me the watch."

"Why?"

"She said it was an expensive watch, and Mr. Snyder would eventually come back looking for it, and she didn't want to deal with him anymore."

"And what did you do with the watch?"

"I went back to my work station, and I put the watch on my desk. Then I called the night supervisor, Andrea Sanchez, and told her we had had a problem. It was all very upsetting to me as well. I get along very well with Cindy. She's been a pleasure to work with. Nothing like this has ever happened at the clinic."

"And did you locate the night supervisor, Andrea Sanchez?"

"Yes. She came almost immediately. She and Cindy had a conversation in the hallway. Cindy sort of showed Andrea what happened, I mean, the way Mr. Snyder ran out of the building with the file. And then I looked up and James came back. He seemed a little strange, sort of angry about what had happened. He sat down in front of me and handed me the file. I gave the watch to Cindy and she gave it back to Jim, and then the three of them went into the therapy room. That's really all I know."

Following the night receptionist's deposition, Andrea Sanchez, the night supervisor is brought in for her deposition.

"You were the night supervisor the evening of June 15, 2004?"

"I was there at the end of the incident."

"Did you hear Ms Polanski ask Mrs. Esposito to cancel the police search because the file had been returned?"

"No, she didn't say that. I told Mrs. Esposito to cancel the police search."

"Why?"

"Because it was no longer necessary. James had returned the file."

"Did you hear Cindy say anything at all to James or Mrs. Esposito?"

"Cindy said something about there not being a police search. I didn't really understand why she said that because there was a police search. Anyway, I think that's what she said."

"If I told you that both Ms Polanski and Dr. Monteblanc in their file notes have said that there was no call to the police, that their presence was part of a regular patrol, what would be your response?"

"I would say it was a very confusing and stressful moment for all of us, but a call *was* made to the police about Mr. Snyder. When he returned the file, another call was made to terminate the search."

"What happened then?"

"The three of us went back into the therapy room. By then, Mr. Snyder was relatively calm. I said to him that because of his behavior as of this moment his therapy was officially terminated. And I asked him to leave the building."

"What did he say?"

"I don't remember. Maybe nothing, but he did leave."

"Anything else?"

"I told Cindy that I was going to write an email to the Director informing him of the evening's events and the fact that I terminated Mr. Snyder's relationship with Jedermann. It was an unusual set of circumstances, and I didn't want to do anything to make things more difficult for Cindy or James than they already were."

"Have you ever ended a patient's relationship with Jedermann before?"

"No, this was a first."

"Did you ever see Mr. Snyder again at Jedermann as a visitor or as a patient?"

"No. I haven't seen him again since that night."

At 4:45 PM, Damian finishes deposing the night supervisor and we take a fifteen- minute break.

Promptly at 5:00 PM, Dean Colwell joins us. For the next hour, Damian grills her about Jedermann University's ethical standards, its policies and procedures, her meeting with me, and her subsequent investigation of my allegations. Dean Colwell's answers are deceiving and very evasive. Dean Colwell dances a fine dance with her answers. I am furious because Damian accepts them without a challenge. My questions go unanswered, just as I anticipated.

At a few minutes before 6:00 PM, Damian finishes deposing Dean Colwell and we're done for the day. On our way out, Damian smartly thanks Mr. Troutman for arranging today's depositions.

"That went well, Sam. Monteblanc is a very impressive guy."

Troutman says, "Fuck you Damian," and flips Damian the bird. Damian just laughs as we head out.

I'm a little panicky thinking that Damian has made another enemy for me. One I don't need at this moment.

"What was that about?"

"Nothing. Just some ancient hurt feelings. Lawyer stuff."

As we are about to exit the building, I stop Damian and hand him a letter I wrote expressly requesting a referral to a psychiatrist. Damian glances at the letter. He seems irritated.

"I'll read it later, but I'll say it again, therapy and whatever diagnosis evolves from therapy will be detrimental to your case. I've told you this before, and nothing has changed. These are very clever people. Very clever lawyers. And they'll move for a dismissal based on a diagnosis of a serious psychosis."

Enraged, I walk to my car, blindly. If there were a little ole lady in front of me I would push her into the gutter. When I arrive home, I throw my list of questions into my living room wall, scattering them about my apartment. Five thousand dollars' worth of questions have become litter on my carpet. This is my fucking life that I cannot rescue, double spaced in a twelve-point font. An old visitor, an old enemy, uncontrolled rage consumes me and is followed by terrifying, crippling depression. I feel utterly alone.

JAMES SNYDER'S TALE:
THE WHOLE TRUTH AND NOTHING BUT

It's early October. I arrive at Damian's downtown office at 7:45 AM for my videotaped deposition. Mr. Troutman and Mr. Wharton are already there, and they are talking with Damian in his office. As I enter, the three of them stop talking and, after I greet each of them, the defense attorneys exit so that Damian and I can talk.

Damian tells me that I should answer honestly and that I should not try to make my case.

"Here is the basic rule of thumb: be truthful; answer yes or no whenever possible; and for Christ's sake don't lose your temper. The defense is there to make their case and that if you volunteer too much information, it will hurt us. If you get wound up and start narrating your life story, it will all come back at you eventually and not in a good way."

I acknowledge Damian's comments, and then Damian and I walk down to the conference room where the others are waiting.

At 8:12 AM, the stenographer swears me in. Mr. Troutman goes first and begins his questioning by asking me about my identity. Mr. Troutman then asks about my family of origin, to which I feel the anger and rage seething within me. I try to contain myself, but the words just flow out of my mouth. To try to silence me, Damian presses his knee against my knee under the glass table; however, I cannot stop. My words flow forth. Damian just lowers his head and listens. This is what he warned me about.

Over the next four hours, Mr. Troutman grills me about my life: early childhood, my earliest memories, my teen years, my parents, my education, my employment history, and my relationship with Natalia.

It occurs to me now that this is a moment I have anticipated a very long time. I have had many rehearsals, many long days and nights when I longed for just this opportunity. Who am I, you ask? Troutman was a slight man with a long, sad face. He seemed sympathetic, even friendly. I noticed his sunburned hands and his lion's head cufflinks. A golfer or a sailor, I assumed. I did not know what to make of his ostentatious jewelry. Maybe a gift from a girlfriend. He didn't wear a wedding band.

I was aware of my lawyer's tension. He bangs his knee against mine: a warning. Careful here, was his silent admonition, here is where you could walk into a trap. Don't be vain, and don't be stupid. Hold your temper and your tongue.

"Mr. Troutman," I begin, "I grew up in a very poor family. My earliest memories are of my father eating cracker soup, which consists of crushed Saltine crackers in a bowl with warm milk poured over them. He dropped out of high school to earn money for his family. My father earned his GED in the Army and was in and out of work during my early years."

Troutman looked at me carefully. I am sure he was surprised at my narration, and he didn't want it to stop.

"My mother stayed home to raise the children. Because the family had no money, I began working as a newspaper carrier at age ten to earn spending money. I did not have a happy childhood, but I persevered. I was involved in sports and band in high school and those activities were a source of satisfaction.

"It was a lonely and contentious childhood. I felt estranged, not really part of my family's life. I was a solitary kid, very shy. One good thing is that because my parents were largely uneducated they stressed the importance of academic achievement, and that influence persisted and sustained me throughout college and even now. They also enforced a certain mental toughness and even physical courage, and I was able to overcome severe injuries to earn my black belt in the martial arts. Oh, and Natalia, Natalia reminded me of my mother and my inexplicable need to be recognized - and I guess even loved - by her. In the end, though, Mr. Troutman, I realized that I was unhappy and confused — ill-socialized, filled with anxieties and anger — which is why I approached Jedermann University to receive the counseling help that I needed. I feel I didn't get that help. In fact, I got just the opposite: more reasons for anxiety and anger which is why we are here today. I did not receive proper therapeutic help."

Mr. Troutman accepts my answers and does not drill into them very deeply. He seems sympathetic, in a way.

At the end of his questioning, Mr. Troutman leans forward,

extends his hand and shakes mine, "Mr. Snyder," he said, "it's an honor to meet you."

He released my hand, and I thought, "Bullshit, buddy." Butter, as a friend of mine used to say, wouldn't melt in his mouth. So, I'm surprised by, but utterly unconvinced of, his sincerity. I felt I just put myself in the crosshairs.

We then break for lunch.

At 1:30 PM we reconvene. This time it is Mr. Wharton who asks the questions, most of which are focused on my relationship with Cindy. Wharton is a disagreeable fellow, slightly unkempt and he has clearly had a beer or two for lunch. I can smell the alcohol on his breath from across the conference table. Wharton is confrontational and does not follow a chronological time line in his questioning.

"Mr. Snyder, after filing the lawsuit why did you send a certified, return receipt requested envelope containing two blank sheets of paper to Ms Polanski's former address?"

"Simple, I requested Cindy's current address during discovery, but she refused to provide it."

"What was the reason you want to know where Cindy lives? How is that relevant to your lawsuit?"

"I was curious to know where a part-time student therapist trainee who drove a high-end Mercedes and who wore a Rolex watch would live."

"You haven't answered my question."

"I was curious, that's all."

"Curious were you. And do you know now?" Mr. Wharton asks.

"Yes," I answer smartly. "It's a $750k house."

"Have seen Cindy's house? Have you sized up the place?"

"I've driven down the street, and it's a beautiful home."

"After you filed the lawsuit, you found out where she lived, and you've driven down her street. Have you been stalking Cindy, Mr. Snyder? Because that is what your actions seem to be. I am concerned about the well-being of my client."

"I have not been stalking Cindy, Mr. Wharton, even though she's made that accusation to the police in the form of a formal complaint. I drove down her street once to look at her house. That was probably in late August or early September of 2004. However, on September 18, 2004, according to a document that is part of the public record, Cindy summoned police to her residence to complain that I was harassing her. That is a lie, Mr. Wharton. The official language of the complaint is that I was "stalking her by means unclassified." That's the chilly language of the police bureaucracy, cop speak. She also alleged that she was afraid of me. But and I can produce a copy of the documents, by the way, something that Ms Polanski was required to do by the terms of discovery and did not do. She said she saw me on September 12 but didn't summon the police until almost a week later. If she were so terrified of Jim Snyder driving down her fancy street why didn't she call the police that day?

"No answer for that? I can give you my theory. This is a little scheme she cooked up to undermine my credibility. 'Here comes Jim Snyder in the stalk-me-mobile, that poor demented son of a bitch.' And I'm poor, cute Cindy, the victim."

I pull out an envelope from my jacket pocket and slide it toward Wharton.

"There you go, Mr. Wharton, these are copies of the documents Cindy was supposed to have provided to me and didn't. What was the reason for that? Because on the face of it, her allegations were spurious. What, did she hide in her closet for a week until the coast was clear and she felt safe enough to call the cops a week later? Or was it going to be obvious that she lied, meaning to embarrass me? Your client lies, Mr. Wharton, and has lied repeatedly. Every damn step of the way."

Mr. Wharton is visibly upset. Damian looks at me, furious.

"Can we have brief break so I can speak to my client?" He nods towards the door. We both go outside into the hallway.

"What in the hell are you doing, James?"

"The job you should have done. I did a little research about Cindy's interaction with the police. It's all in the fucking public record."

"Any more surprises?"

"You'll have to wait and see, Mr. Argantes. If I told you it wouldn't be a surprise, now would it?"

"I'll walk out of here right now, James. Don't push your luck."

"Okay, I have nothing else. That was it."

We go back to the conference room. Wharton is talking to Troutman, and after a serious moment of consultation turns to Damian and me.

"We want to apologize for the oversight in not producing Ms Polanski's complaint about Mr. Snyder. It was an innocent error, I can assure you. No deception was intended. This just sort of fell through the cracks."

Damian shrugs and gestures for Wharton to continue deposing me.

"Okay, Mr. Snyder, we know you did a little research into Ms Polanski's life, including on at least one occasion driving past her house."

"Once. I drove past her house once because I was curious. Curiosity, I believe, is still not a crime."

"What in the world else have you done to learn more about Cindy? Where have your little investigations led you? To her gym? To her hairdresser? I think your conduct, sir, is highly irregular."

Angrily, I answer, "I'm checking every available source for information. Publicly available information. Tell me. Mr. Wharton, is it highly irregular to drive down a public street? Have I done anything wrong? I'll drive where I damn well please to drive, and I won't be browbeaten by a silly old drunk like you, if I choose to drive past Cindy's house."

Wharton stops the deposition. He is seething.

"Damian, I'd like to speak with you in private"

He and Damian and Mr. Troutman leave the conference room and step into the hallway.

When they return, Damian pulls me aside and says in an angry whisper, "James, if you make one more attempt to get information about Cindy, I will quit as your attorney. I know you're angry, but do you also have to be such an asshole?"

Mr. Wharton resumes grilling me about my relationship with Cindy.

"When did you take such a belligerent interest in Ms Polanski?"

"I was never belligerent."

"Why are you so angry at her?"

"Next question."

"Answer that one."

"No."

"Do you mean to say you're not angry at her?"

"Next question."

"I'd like the record to show that Mr. Snyder was nonresponsive to that question."

"All right, Wharton, I'm not angry with her. I'm disappointed in her lack of competence."

"Are you a judge of that?"

"More than you, I think. I was in so-called therapy with her."

Because he repeatedly asks misleading questions, I refuse to answer his questions as asked. Mr. Wharton and I spar angrily, with barely concealed contempt, much to the annoyance of the stenographer who four times interrupts us to say that we must speak one at a time.

At 3:45 PM, we take a fifteen-minute break. After we resume, Mr. Wharton changes his approach and begins grilling me about my relationship with Natalia.

"Did you live close to Natalia at the apartment complex?"

"Yes."

"And you had a sexual relationship with her?"

"How is that relevant? I don't think that's any of your business, sir."

"Objection. Once again the witness is nonresponsive."

And I am not going to respond, you old fool, I think to myself.

"All right, Mr. Snyder, let's talk about something else."

"Okay."

"What kind of work did you do there?"

"I was a painter."

"A house painter. You painted apartments? A well-educated man like you."

"I answered that question already."

"Mr. Snyder, did you have a master key for all the apartments in your complex?"

"Yes."

"Was the apartment manager nervous about your having a master key?"

"You'd have to ask him."

"Did the apartment manager ever take away your master key?"

"No."

"Did you stalk Natalia?"

"No."

"Did you threaten to harm Natalia?"

"No."

"Are you still in love with Natalia?"

"No."

Because Mr. Wharton doesn't ask, I don't volunteer that I turned in my master key prior to starting therapy with Cindy. I don't volunteer how nervous the apartment manager was about me having a master key while I was obsessing over Natalia. I don't volunteer how angry I was at Natalia when I learned that she had been cheating on me with my neighbor, Keith. I don't volunteer how I threatened to kill Keith's dog should I find it running loose around the apartment complex one more time. I'm learning how to play this game.

Mr. Wharton continues grilling me about Natalia until 5:15 PM, at which time we break for dinner.

At 6:30 PM, we resume. Mr. Wharton once again changes his approach and this time grills me about my past relationships. He drills into my personal life like a brain surgeon who is drilling from the inside out.

"How many women have you dated?"

"I don't keep count, Mr. Wharton."

"How many women have you had sex with?"

"I forget."

"An approximate number."

"Okay, more than one but less than five hundred."

"How many women have you stalked?"

"None."

"How many women's houses have you driven past?"

"A question unworthy of you, Mr. Wharton. I'm sure I've driven past tens of thousands of women's houses. I've been driving since I was sixteen."

"All right, how many women's addresses have you tried to locate in order to drive past their house?"

"Just one."

He drills and drills and drills.

At 9:45 PM, the torment ends - Mr. Wharton says he is finished. Saying only goodnight, Damian immediately walks me to the exit door and shows me the way out. Mr. Troutman, Mr. Wharton, and Damian remain behind. Damian refuses to look me in the eye or shake my hand. I'm very worried that I just seriously damaged my case. I am exhausted and very, very depressed.

Before I go to bed, I get a call from Damian. I'm sure he's going to give me hell for my testimony.

"James, I know you like to be kept on top of things. You should be at the courthouse tomorrow, civil part. Wharton and Troutman are going to try to get a restraining order on you, keeping you away from Cindy except during the depositions."

"Can they do that?"

"They're doing it. Ten o'clock. Don't be late."

THE FIRST BETRAYAL

The next morning, at Mr. Wharton's request, Mr. Wharton, Mr. Troutman, and Damian go before the judge to discuss my investigation into Cindy's life. I sit in the back of the otherwise empty courtroom. Mr. Wharton tells the judge that he wants a restraining order issued against me. Mr. Wharton explains to the judge my return receipt letter, and the fact that I drove down Cindy's street directly in front of her house.

"Mr. Snyder, Your Honor, has done everything within his power to discover information about Cindy Polanski, my client. She is very upset by this."

Judge Abraham Morrison is an old man and a reserve judge. He is one of those retired judges who returns to the bench to fill in for vacationing judges. He keeps his hand in and makes poker money. He has a crust of gray beard on his cheeks and reading glasses that perch on his nose like a sparrow on a ledge. He seems to be a very wise and experienced man. He's also an impatient one, it seems.

"So, Mr. Wharton, now you're going to explain to me what laws Mr. Snyder has broken."

"None, Your Honor. Not yet anyway. My client feels threatened by him. Ms Polanski claims he threw her into a wall two years ago."

"Okay, now we're getting somewhere. Where is the police report of Mr. Snyder throwing Ms Polanski into a wall? Or a medical report?"

"We don't have either."

"You don't have them, because I'm assuming none exists. Is that correct, Mr. Wharton?"

"Yes, Your Honor."

"Then what in the world are we doing here, Mr. Wharton? What else do you have to say to the court?"

Wharton stood mute.

"Okay, gentlemen, I was supposed to be on the golf course this morning bright and early, but instead I get called down to a hearing where Mr. Troutman is on another one his fishing expeditions. Nothing doing, Sam. Since you have chosen to waste my time, I will do you a great favor and not waste yours. Request for a restraining order is denied. You know, Counselor Troutman, I didn't like you when you were my student in law school, and I don't like you much now. This hearing is adjourned."

Damian, who had remained silent during this whole interchange pulls Wharton aside and offers Mr. Wharton a protection order in lieu of the restraining order.

"Not good enough," Wharton says. "I think your client is a danger to himself and Cindy."

Once back in his office, Damian calls me and tells me I must meet with him that afternoon at 4:30 PM. Curious, I arrive at Damian's office at 4:20 PM and Damian sees me immediately.

"I'm going to say this one last time, James, if you make another attempt to learn more information about Cindy, I will quit as your attorney. I offered Mr. Wharton a protection order in lieu of the restraining order, but Wharton turned me down."

Shocked, I ask, "Why did you volunteer a protection order?"

"You know damn well, because of what you said. You said you were going to kill Monteblanc, Howell and Cindy."

Angered, I tell Damian I need to get some air, and I leave for home. As I drive, I become more enraged as I think about Damian's comments. Once home, in a fit of rage, I throw and kick anything and everything that is loose in my apartment. In the process, I destroy one of my two cheap breakfast table chairs when I kick the seat out of it. The stuff in my apartment was mostly junk before, but it's all junk now. I throw my thrift store cherry red Bakelite radio at the front door. It's a metal fire door, and the radio shatters into many pieces. I liked that radio. It was from the Forties, I'm sure, almost vintage. What a waste. I'm running out of things to destroy. Three hours later, exhausted, I finally begin to calm down a little. Then the depression consumes me, a severe depression, which is so intense, so black, that I do not move for almost four hours. I lie on the bed and stare at my Bruce Lee poster on the wall. I have traveled with this poster, kitschy black velvet in a black frame of Lee from an early movie. I have brought it with me everywhere I have gone. He is cut and buff, slick with sweat, and ready to strike. I studied karate because of Lee, and stayed on in college an extra year to earn my black belt. Hardly anyone

knows this. I can't talk about it because I badly damaged my right
knee and tore a hamstring, so karate is no longer an option for me.
Just something else I've lost. I have lost the physical conditioning of
my college years, and I feel paunchy and out of shape. My face is
round, and the confidence of my karate days has vanished. Looking at
Lee is an odd comfort, and I feel less lost. This poster is like an old
friend.

I begin to calm down and think about cleaning up the mess I've
created. But I do not move. Tomorrow, I thought, I'll do it
tomorrow.

Death is my only friend. The Devil be blessed!

A BEAUTIFUL WOMAN LIES
AND IS BLAMELESS

On Wednesday, November 8, 2006, the day after the elections, I learn from radio news that Damian Argantes lost his bid for city council. I call him with my condolences and Damian informs me that he will take Cindy's deposition next week.

On Thursday, one week before Thanksgiving, we gather at Mr. Wharton's downtown office for Cindy's videotaped deposition. In the spacious conference room are Cindy, Wharton, Troutman, Damian, the stenographer, the videographer, and me. Just before 10:00 AM, the stenographer swears Cindy in and Damian commences his questioning. The interrogation begins with Damian asking Cindy about her credentials and her educational training.

Cindy's initial answers are straightforward.

"I have a master's degree in Clinical Psychology from Jedermann University," she answers.

"What did you do prior to your time at Jedermann?"

"I got a degree in psychology at Rice University. I wanted to go to the business school, but my grades weren't good enough."

"What did you do after graduating?"

"After Rice, I got a job selling advertising for local radio stations. I did well financially, but I was bored. So, I went to get my master's at Jedermann."

"Did you work while you were attending Jedermann?"

"I worked part-time in three clinics in town before and during the time I was at Jedermann University."

"And how were you supervised at those clinics?"

"In addition to occasionally audio recording the sessions, my supervisors would sit in on them."

"How often would your supervisors sit in?"

"Infrequently."

"Did Dr. Monteblanc ever sit in on any of your therapy sessions with James Snyder?"

"No."

"Did he ever listen to any of your audio recorded therapy sessions with James Snyder?"

"No."

"Why not?"

"Because none of my sessions were recorded while I was being supervised by Joe."

"How did the Director know what was going on in your therapy sessions with James?"

"Joe and I would discuss them during our supervisory meetings."

"What were you treating Mr. Snyder for when he was in therapy with you?"

"He had relationship issues."

"And did you ever diagnose Mr. Snyder?"

Before she can answer, Wharton interrupts, "Cindy isn't qualified to make a diagnosis."

"That might be technically true," Damian interjects, "but she might have had some preliminary ideas about James's condition. She knew him over a relatively long time, after all. I'm not being unreasonable here, Clint."

"All right, go ahead and answer the question," Mr. Wharton instructs Cindy.

"No, I didn't diagnose James," Cindy answers.

"All right. So, without a diagnosis, which you were not qualified to make, what was your treatment plan, which presumably you are qualified to create."

"Relationship issues."

"Without a diagnosis?"

"Yes."

I thought it strange Cindy was treating relationship issues, without even bothering to know my diagnosis. What was she treating? Or was she treating herself?

"Did anyone, qualified or not, ever make a diagnosis of Mr. Snyder?"

Cindy simply answers, "Not to my knowledge."

"Let me turn to another topic then, Ms Polanski, your entries in the clinical file record. When would you write your notes?"

"Immediately following the therapy sessions."

"Would it be ethical, in your opinion, to add file entries at other times, at times when there were no therapy sessions."

Before Cindy can answer, Mr. Wharton interrupts to say, "It would depend, wouldn't it?"

"Yeah," says Cindy, "it would depend."

"What would it depend on?"

"It would vary with every patient. There is no hard and fast rule."

Damian next asks Cindy, "Did you keep any notes related to your therapy sessions with Mr. Snyder other than the file entries in the clinical record?"

Cindy answers, "No."

"Is trust one of Mr. Snyder's relationship issues?"

"Yes, James had a very difficult time trusting me because of what he called my façade."

"That would be reflected in his competition and trust concerns with you. Things he talked about while in therapy with you."

"I'm sorry but I don't recall those specific speeches. I do recall that James felt that I was competing with him on some level. I don't think I was."

"Let me ask you about your supervisory sessions with the Director, Dr. Monteblanc. What would you discuss?"

"We talked about general problems or progress with my clients. Joe and I would spend about ten minutes on each of my six clients."

"Ten minutes. That's all? That doesn't seem like much somehow."

"I was not the only student he supervised. That's all the time he had."

"Why did you change supervisors?"

"My relationship with Joe wasn't a good fit for me, so I requested a change."

"And did you ever describe changing supervisors as, 'getting that monkey off my back'?"

"No, of course not. I would never say anything so unprofessional."

"Did you ever borrow a VCR tape from James titled, *Frightened Silent?*"

Cindy answers, "No."

"Did Mr. Snyder ever share a credit card rewards catalogue with you that had his real name on it? Not Schneider but Snyder?"

Cindy responds, "No. That never happened."

"Did James ever give you his business card with his real name on it?"

"Yes, but I threw the card away shortly after receiving it. It wasn't important."

"Did you ever go for a walk outside with Mr. Snyder?"

"No."

"You're sure of that? Never?"

"Well, I may have conducted a therapy session outside with James. Once or maybe twice, maybe more, but not a walk."

"Once or twice. Or maybe more. Is that a typical practice for you?"

"I occasionally conduct therapy sessions outside when it will be beneficial to the client."

"Did Mr. Snyder give you a framed photograph of a winter scene as a pre-graduation present?"

Cindy answers, "No."

"And have you ever hugged James?"

Cindy answers, "Yes. He asked for a hug after the therapy session outside, so I gave him one."

"Is that something you do frequently? Hug your clients?"

"If a client asks for a hug, I'll give them a hug, but only when they ask."

"Wouldn't hugging be a boundary issue?"

"I don't know. It depends on the client. I felt it was okay with Mr. Snyder."

"How often did you and Dr. Howell review the audiotapes of your sessions with Mr. Snyder."

"We reviewed each one of Mr. Snyder's sessions."

"Each one? Why?"

"Because Jim was a difficult client."

"If James, as you say, was a difficult client, why didn't you terminate your relationship prior to the police incident?"

"I thought that I could still help him. In some sessions, only a little progress was made while in other sessions great progress was made. I felt that by continuing with therapy, I could continue to help him."

"How did you determine his progress?"

"I don't know. It's more of an art than a science, I guess."

"Why did you call the police into your session with James on the night of the incident?"

"I was afraid of him because he had thrown me into a wall in the therapy room that night, and he eventually stole the clinical record."

Damian plays the original, non-digitally enhanced audiotape of that session and asks Cindy to identify for the jury where on the tape the assault occurred. Cindy complies.

"For whom did you make file entry three days after the incident?"

"I made that entry…for the record. I also changed the file name label to 'Snyder' since 'Schneider' was not his correct last name."

"And what grade did you receive for your supervised training at Jedermann University?"

"I was awarded an 'A'."

At 11:54 AM, Damian requests a fifteen-minute break. During this time, I review the twenty-seven pages of triple-spaced questions that I had prepared highlighting those twelve questions that I absolutely want answered.

At 12:07 PM, Damian resumes his questioning. However, rather than asking all twelve highlighted questions, Damian intentionally skips the one that I have marked as most critical: "Cindy, have you made any reports to the police about James Snyder since the incident?" This anger and upsets me; however, I do not lose my composure. Instead, I wait until after Damian finishes deposing Cindy to confront him.

"Why didn't you ask her about the police report? She lied about me to the cops."

"I was concerned about having a police report for stalking in the record."

"But she failed to produce it in discovery. She should be held accountable for that."

"James, I'm not going to chase her down every sewer you manage to discover. You know, I do have other clients. And goddamn it, I don't like surprises, no lawyer does and I don't really know what else you did and didn't tell me about. Just remember what you said. Brother, you scare me some times."

At 12:25 PM, I depart Mr. Wharton's office with mixed emotions — I am both angry at Cindy and Damian, but I also feel a little sorry for her. A twinge. Things don't look good, I think, but I am happy that Damian is afraid of me.

MANIPULATION AND AVARICE
ALA ARGANTES

It's early December 2006, nearly three weeks after Cindy's deposition, when Damian calls me at work informing me that he has retained an expert witness, a psychologist named Dr. Herman Priestley, a man with whom I must meet as soon as possible.

"Why didn't you hire a psychiatrist?"

"Priestly is a solid guy. His objective will be to diagnose you."

"I want a psychiatrist as my expert witness. I also want to be treated by a psychiatrist."

"We've been over this James. It is not a good idea."

Damian ends the call by giving me Dr. Priestley's phone number and telling me to schedule the appointment this week.

Because I'm at work, I know I must control the welling anger that I feel toward Damian. I decide that rather than calling Dr. Priestley immediately, I will wait one hour and then call him, which I do. Dr. Priestley schedules my appointment for Monday at 9:00 AM.

Upon arriving at Dr. Priestley's downtown office, I discover that the doctor shares a receptionist with other doctors in his group, and that he works out of a cubicle. I am horrified at this arrangement and the lack of privacy.

"How do you treat patients in a cubicle environment?"

"I don't treat patients," Dr. Priestley responds. "I read the literature and make my living diagnosing clients for other doctors. I also testify as an expert witness."

Nervous and not liking Dr. Priestley's answer, I look around at his crowded cubicle. In the corner, Dr. Priestley has an old-fashioned coat tree onto which he has hung his tan rain coat. On his desk, Dr.

Priestley has a 1940's style radio, burled walnut by the looks of it. I wonder if it still works. He also has two framed photos of Doberman pinschers, both of which have their ears bandaged. They look docile enough in the photos.

"They're my babies," Dr. Priestley comments when he sees me staring at them. "Beautiful animals, aren't they?"

I look carefully at Dr. Priestley, whose gnome-like appearance is hard to ignore. Priestley seems to be late middle age with the kind of scraggly beard that psychologists seem to favor. Although he wears a wedding band, he has no photos of a gnome-like wife in his office. It's possible that Priestley loves his dogs more than he loves his wife.

"Shall we begin?" Dr. Priestley asks, signaling that it's time to get started. Uncertain and nervous, I agree. He moves his chair away and points to his computer. I slide my chair over and position myself at the keyboard. I feel uncomfortable in his cubicle, hemmed in among other cubicles.

Dr. Priestley begins by having me take the Minnesota Multiphasic Personality Inventory, otherwise known as the MMPI, a two-hour standardized multiple-choice test that assesses personality characteristics. Despite being a skillful test taker, I struggle with many of the questions as I try to comprehend the nuances among each question's four or five possible answers.

After I finish the MMPI, Dr. Priestley dismisses me for lunch. When I return, Dr. Priestley takes me to a small conference room where he administers the Rorschach Inkblot Test, a series of ten ambiguous shapes printed on 18x24 cm cards, in both black and white and color. Dr. Priestley asks me questions about each card.

"What is this?" What might this be?"

Unaware that the ambiguous nature of the cards is meant to provoke free association, I narrow in on specific details of each card. I identify two of the shapes as "people," but I am unable, when asked, to determine their gender. I grow very frustrated.

Just as Dr. Priestley begins asking about the seventh Rorschach Inkblot card, the fire alarm activates, so we exit together down the stairs and out of the building. For me the fire alarm is a happy accident. I needed to get away from the inkblots and breathe. While we are waiting to re-enter, a Hispanic man with two children approaches us and attempts to strike up a conversation. After I politely answer the man's first question, I excuse myself and go wait alone a little further down the sidewalk as Dr. Priestley and the man talk. After the all clear is given and we re-enter Dr. Priestley's conference room, I observe Dr. Priestley furiously writing notes. Is he writing about me or the man who approached us on the street?

Once Dr. Priestley finishes administering the Rorschach Inkblot Test, he dismisses me for the day. Rather than going home, I decide to visit Damian since I am in the downtown area.

At 3:43 PM, I arrive at Damian's office where I patiently sit in his reception area until 4:35 PM, at which time he sees me. His reception area is a small room, with only two chairs, hardly bigger than a closet. It is very dirty and very claustrophobic.

"I met with Priestly this afternoon, Damian, and I'm not comfortable with him."

"He's good, James, give him a chance."

"Good? I don't buy that. I really want a psychiatrist as an expert witness. It is extremely important to me."

"No way, James. Trust me on this. I can get Dr. Priestley to say what I need him to say," Damian tells me.

He changes the subject, "I hate to do this, but we have to talk about money. I've spent the entire pre-trial twelve thousand fee in hours on your case. You have two options: You can say that I have a really great lawyer at a really good price and not pay any more money until the trial or you can pay an additional six thousand discovery fee to cover expenses until the trial."

He is like a hungry snake assuring a frightened mouse that it will be safe. Everything is okay. Trust me. This won't hurt a bit.

"But James," Damian assures me, "whichever option you choose, I will give you the same level of outstanding service that I've given you to date."

I'm not clear about the way he presented his request for more money, so I question him directly, "If you want more money, Damian, why don't you just say so."

"I want you to feel you have great representation."

"Too late for that. You hardly used any of the questions I prepared for you in discovery."

"I know what I'm doing. I have a strategy."

One of the things you're doing, I think to myself, is cleaning out my bank account.

I recognize the lie, and also realizing that I don't have any other option, I choose to pay the additional discovery fee. Damian prints the contract addendum, and we both sign it. I am not the mouse, I remind myself, but the snake. I need to have justice enacted so I can proceed with my revenge.

THE TRAITOR'S TALE

In early January 2007, Damian calls me at work to let me know that he received Dr. Priestley's report and that depositions of the expert witnesses will begin next week. Damian explains that Dr. Priestley's deposition will be held on Tuesday, with Mr. Wharton's expert giving his deposition eight days later and Mr. Troutman's expert giving his nine days later.

"Why the delays?"

"To allow the defense experts time to review Dr. Priestley's testimony."

"Damian, are any of the experts psychiatrists?"

"They're all psychologists. That's pretty standard procedure, James. I've been through this a bunch. A psychiatrist would be the outlier in these kinds of cases."

I am not sure if that is true or not. I do know that I want a psychiatrist, and Damian refuses to provide one.

On Tuesday morning I arrive at Mr. Wharton's downtown office at twenty-five minutes before the scheduled 9:00 AM deposition start time. I find Damian there waiting for me. Damian gives me a copy of Dr. Priestley's two-page report. I quickly scan it looking for a diagnosis. I don't find one.

"Damian, I don't see Priestley's diagnosis. I thought that was the point of my seeing him."

"Dr. Priestley didn't formulate a diagnosis."

"Why?" I nearly shout.

"Look Jim," Damian says with an angry grimace on his face, "there's more to this case than your diagnosis. Trust me on this one."

Trust me is becoming his mantra.

Realizing once again that I don't have a choice, I take a deep breath, calm down a bit, sit down in the conference room, and slowly read Dr. Priestley's report.

At 9:03 AM, the stenographer swears in Dr. Priestley. Mr. Troutman, Mr. Wharton, Damian, the Director, Dr. Becky Howell, the stenographer, the videographer, and I are present. Mr. Troutman goes on record stating that he will allow Mr. Wharton to do most of the questioning.

Mr. Wharton begins his questioning by introducing himself and defining the ground rules for the deposition.

"So, Dr. Priestley, let me ask you about your experience as an expert witness. What sorts of cases have you represented plaintiffs and what sort of cases have you represented defendants?"

"In ten years as an expert witness, I have only been involved in nine legal cases. I have only given two depositions, and I have never testified in a civil trial."

Recognizing the credibility void that Mr. Wharton just revealed, Dr. Priestley quickly continues, "But I have consulted on a large number of situations that never resulted in legal action."

"I see. Have you ever testified against a fellow psychologist?"

"No, I've never testified in a psychological malpractice case."

"So, what do you charge for being an expert, Doctor? How much will you charge in this matter?"

"I charge $275 per hour for legal work, including depositions."

"And how much money has Mr. Snyder already paid you?" Mr. Wharton asks.

Thinking carefully, Dr. Priestley answers, "$3,250. However, Damian paid me, not Mr. Snyder."

"Clint, Is this necessary? We all have to pay the rent," Damian says.

Mr. Wharton asks Dr. Priestley what documents he reviewed in preparation for this deposition. Dr. Priestley looks over the two-inch stack in front of him and lists them beginning with defendants' deposition; the Rorschach scoring guidelines; the MMPI results; and my draft letter of complaint to Cindy's licensing board, a letter that I wrote but have not yet sent.

"Have you reviewed Mr. Snyder's deposition?"

"No."

"Are you familiar with Mr. Snyder's allegations against the defendants?"

"No."

"Are you familiar with the Diagnostic and Statistical Manual of Mental Disorders? I think the current edition is four?"

"Yes, of course, it is a tool for mental health professionals to assist in the diagnosis of patients. I am not expertly familiar with it, however."

"Not expertly familiar with it. But you're here as an expert."

"I'm familiar with it. I don't represent myself as an expert in diagnosis."

"If you're familiar with it, in your words, generally speaking — not as an expert — what kind of personality disorders might Mr. Snyder be experiencing?"

"As I said, I'm not a diagnostician."

"That's right. Just generally speaking, might Mr. Snyder be experiencing a paranoid personality disorder that might have originated in adolescence and therefore be of long-standing duration?"

"It's possible. As I said, I'm not a diagnostician."

Mr. Wharton reviews each of Dr. Priestley's documents in turn by having Dr. Priestley read aloud his handwritten notes and comments. Throughout his answers, Dr. Priestley repeatedly says, "…as I recall," and "…to my knowledge," which I find very frustrating.

"Why did you not formulate a diagnosis?"

"Mr. Snyder is a very complicated and disturbed individual."

"But you did not formulate a diagnosis?"

"No, I was not able to. Mr. Snyder is a very complicated and disturbed individual," Dr. Priestley repeats.

At the end of his questioning, Mr. Wharton pulls a piece of paper from his coat pocket and asks Dr. Priestley a series of seven questions.

"Does Mr. Snyder believe other people are lying to him without any evidence?"

"Yes, I think he does."

"Does Mr. Snyder have doubts about the loyalty and trustworthiness of others?"

Priestley shifts in his seat and reaches for the glass of water in front of him.

"Yes."

"Does he avoid confiding in others due to the belief he will be betrayed?"

"The tests indicate that to be the case."

"Does Mr. Snyder interpret ambiguous or benign remarks as hurtful?"

"I believe he does, yes."

"Does he hold grudges?"

"Yes."

"Does he want to retaliate against people whom he thinks have injured him, despite any evidence to that effect?"

"I would say that's true."

"Is he jealous or suspicious that intimate partners are being unfaithful?"

"Oh, yes. It's a problem for him."

After Dr. Priestley answers affirmatively to each of the seven, Mr. Wharton states that the seven questions were the DSM-IV criteria for diagnosing a patient with paranoid personality disorder.

"Would you agree that Mr. Snyder suffers from paranoid personality disorder?" Mr. Wharton asks.

"Yes," Dr. Priestley responds, "but…."

Mr. Wharton abruptly cuts him off by passing the witness to Mr. Troutman.

Mr. Troutman asks several questions related to my MMPI scores, then passes the witness to Damian.

"Why didn't you review Mr. Snyder's deposition?" Damian asks.

"You didn't ask me to."

"Should you have reviewed it?"

"No, not really. I rely on a different methodology. I trust the science behind the tests. Depositions are not really all that helpful. Many people are unreliable witnesses to their own life. Not purposely, to be sure. But they are animated and misdirected by their delusions or anger or fear. So, no, unless I'm specifically asked, I don't look at depositions."

"Would you say that Mr. Snyder made the right decision in seeking help from Jedermann University's clinic, from Ms Polanski?"

"Most definitely."

"And was he treated appropriately?"

"I have no idea."

"And did his condition improve or worsen?"

"Of course, I know nothing of his condition prior to beginning therapy, but the science indicates he didn't improve."

Damian passes the witness back to Mr. Wharton and Mr. Troutman, who have no further questions so the deposition ends. They have achieved a tactical victory. The record will show that Attorney Argantes' so-called expert witness has concluded that I suffer from paranoid personality disorder. The snake has eaten the mouse, and I am in despair.

Old companions — frustration, anger, and confusion — fill me. I glare at Damian before departing for home. Once home, I fall into the deepest depression yet. I want nothing more than for all this to be over.

I decide not to call Scott. I don't want to bother him with my troubles because he seems to be feeling down about something. He is too prideful a guy, too tough a dude, to admit to doubts or worries.

I'll call him tomorrow, I think, as I settle back into my region of pain.

THE MERCENARY'S TALE

The following Wednesday, I arrive at Damian's office at 12:47 PM, well in advance of the 1:30 PM deposition start time. I tell Damian defiantly that I want a psychiatrist as my expert witness. Damian calmly tells me that he is comfortable with Dr. Priestley and will only employ Dr. Priestley as Plaintiff's expert in this case.

Furious, I demand to know why.

"Because of what you said. Do you remember mentioning murder?"

"Dr. Priestley is fucking incompetent, Damian!"

"That's your opinion. I'm confident that at trial I can get him to say what I need him to say."

On the verge of losing control, I leave Damian's office without saying another word and go outside for a walk around the block. I feel flushed and hot. I'm sure my blood pressure is back in the stroke zone. When I return at 1:28 PM, I find Mr. Wharton, Mr. Troutman, Damian, the stenographer, the videographer, and Mr. Wharton's expert sitting in the conference room. After I sit down, the stenographer swears in Mr. Wharton's expert and Damian commences his questioning.

"Would you please introduce yourself to the court?" Damian asks.

"Yes, I'd be glad to," the expert responds. "I'm Dr. Bernard Walker and I have been retained by Cindy Polanski."

After defining the rules for the deposition, Damian asks about Dr. Walker's educational and employment histories.

"I attended Tourney Hills University for both my undergraduate and my Ph.D. degrees in psychology. I have been employed by Houston's acclaimed Alexander Thomas Hospital as Vice President of Clinical Psychology for the better part of twenty-five years. Recently, I went part-time to concentrate on my private practice."

"Do you know any of the defendants?"

"Yes," Dr. Walker responds. "I know the Director, Dr. Joseph Monteblanc. I supervised his internship many years ago."

"When was the last time you had contact with the Director?" Damian asks next.

"Oh, I don't exactly remember. Probably fifteen years ago," Dr. Walker responds.

"Dr. Walker, are you familiar with the Diagnostic and Statistical Manual of Mental Disorders?"

"Yes. Quite familiar."

"And have you read my client's Jedermann file and Dr. Priestley's report?"

"Yes."

"Do you think my client, Mr. Snyder, meets the criteria for paranoid personality disorder?"

Damian again reads the criteria from the DSM, and Dr. Walker answers affirmatively to all seven of them.

"I think it would be correct to say that your client does suffer from this disorder."

"And do you think he meets the criteria for borderline personality disorder?"

"I'm not sure."

"All right," Damian says, "maybe we can do a short review of the criteria if that's okay with you."

"I'm ready."

"Do you think Mr. Snyder suffers from a fear of abandonment? Is that something he is afraid of?"

"Oh, yes. The situation with Natalia is a good example of that."

"Are his relationships unstable, intense and short-lived, perfect or horrible in his way of thinking?"

"No, I don't think he manifests that kind of behavior. He actually doesn't form many relationships or friendships."

"Does he have an unclear or unstable self-image?"

"I think it may be unclear rather than unstable. He seems to go through periods of intense self-loathing and self-hatred. So, yes, I would say unstable."

"Does he engage in self-destructive behaviors?"

"That's difficult to say. He is a very hard-working individual. I guess you might say he sometimes loses himself in rather mindless work, like working sixty or seventy hours a week to escape his unhappiness. I would give you a tentative yes to that question, I suppose."

"Does he wish to harm himself?"

"I think he has profound thoughts of suicide. It is often on his mind, although I don't think he has ever attempted it. I think he regards it as a legitimate possibility, a way to end the intense pain he feels."

"Does he suffer from intense emotional swings, happy one moment and despondent the next?"

"Oh, yes."

"Do you think he has a chronic feeling of emptiness?"

"Yes, he feels very alone, as if he were in a void."

"Do you think Mr. Snyder struggles with his temper, that he has moments of intense anger?"

"Yes, I think from what I've read in his file and in others' depositions, he can have moments when he is consumed with rage. The incident with the file is an example. Wholly inappropriate behavior. I think he is also angry at himself for the situation he finds himself in. Mr. Snyder is a very, very angry man."

"And, finally, Dr. Walker, do you think James is out of touch with reality?"

"Sadly, yes. Under stress he has moments when he is disassociated from reality."

"So, given your answers to these criteria do you think James Snyder suffers from borderline personality disorder?"

"I think any competent mental health professional would say that is the case, yes, Mr. Snyder meets more than the required minimum number of criteria, and he does also suffer from this disorder."

"And why wasn't that diagnosis made at Jedermann?"

"I don't know."

"And does Mr. Snyder meet the criteria for obsessive-compulsive disorder?"

"That's harder. I'm not sure, sir."

"Is he obsessed by persistent thoughts, urges or impulses that cause him anxiety or distress?"

"Yes, from what I've learned from the files and other depositions, he has a tendency towards obsessions, with Natalia and probably with Cindy as well."

"Does Mr. Snyder attempt to suppress those obsessions or neutralize them with other thoughts or actions?"

"That's not clear to me."

"Does he engage in compulsive behavior like hand washing or pacing in a room or compulsive thoughts like counting numbers or repeating words silently over and over again?"

"Not that I'm aware of, nothing indicates any of those things in the file or testimony. And I'm going to anticipate your next question, Mr. Argantes, and say that again, in my professional opinion, Mr. Snyder does not suffer from obsessive compulsive behavior."

"Thank you, Dr. Walker, allow me to ask one final question, can paranoid personality disorder, borderline personality disorder, or obsessive-compulsive disorder be treated with medicine?"

"No."

"How are these disorders treated?"

"Disorders of affect, like bipolar disorder, panic disorder, and depression can be treated with medicine; however, personality disorders cannot be."

"Do you ever refer your patients to a psychiatrist in order to receive medication?"

"I'm not a proponent of psychotropic medications. I believe they should only be used when the patient is psychotic."

I wonder if a psychiatrist would agree with that.

"Do you think Mr. Snyder suffers from depression?"

"Depression is a complicated diagnosis. It's not just a feeling of sadness. There are three clinically defined types of depression: major depressive episode, dysthymia, and adjustment disorder with depressive features."

"Do you think Mr. Snyder is suffering from, or has suffered from, a major depressive episode?"

"I'm not 100 percent sure, of course, but I would say not. Major depression is all consuming, and I don't think he is in that state. Major depression is actually relatively rare."

"Has he manifested trouble sleeping?"

"No, I don't think so."

"Changes in weight or appetite?"

"He's gained weight but that could be a change in the amount of exercise or diet. He may be eating too much fast food. But I don't think is cause by a major depressive episode."

"Does he exhibit feelings of worthlessness?"

"I don't believe so."

"In your judgement, then, he has not experienced or is experiencing a major depressive episode."

"That's correct."

"What about dysthymia?"

"Dysthymia is like all these depressive states, hard to diagnose. It is a persistent condition, not as intense as major depression, but can last far longer. It's usually characterized by being self-critical and accompanied by low feelings of self-esteem. A person suffering from dysthymia can function in the world. It is very common, especially among well educated people."

"And Mr. Snyder?"

"I suppose he exhibits some of these symptoms, but most of us in this room will exhibit these symptoms at one point or another in our lives. The important element is the persistence of these feelings. My sense is Mr. Snyder does not suffer from this condition."

"And this last disorder you mentioned...."

"Adjustment disorder with depressive features."

"Yes. Do you think Mr. Snyder suffers from this adjustment disorder?"

"I don't think so. Adjustment disorder is really an abnormal, excessive reaction, an overreaction to something stressful like the death of a spouse or a child, loss of a job, a divorce. It can severely impair your life in your job, with your family or in school. It is really very debilitating, and my feeling is that James does not suffer from this disorder. Clinical depression is not an easy thing to diagnose, and these categories in each individual are a bit muddled. In other words, as much as I would like them to be, they are not carved in stone."

"Well, then, what kind of depression does Mr. Snyder suffer from?"

"He may not suffer from any type of depression. It could be that his depressive symptoms, if any, are from one of the personality disorders. Or it could be an adjustment reaction to his condition."

Damian asks Dr. Walker, "What is the treatment plan for paranoid personality disorder?"

"The treatment plan," Dr. Walker begins, "is to make the patient more aware of his condition so that he can adjust his behaviors accordingly."

"Is there a cure?" Damian asks next.

"No, there is no cure," responds Dr. Walker, "only behavioral modification."

"And the same goes for borderline personality disorder, correct?" Damian asks.

"Yes," Dr. Walker responds, "only behavioral modification is possible."

"And the same for obsessive-compulsive disorder, correct?"

"Yes," Dr. Walker answers, "only behavioral modification is possible."

"Dr. Walker," Damian asks, "what do you think Cindy's goal was for Mr. Snyder's therapy?"

"To give Mr. Snyder a heightened sense of awareness of his condition," Dr. Walker answers.

"And do you think she succeeded in that goal?" Damian asks.

"Yes," Dr. Walker responds. "Based upon everything I know about this case, I do."

"Finally, Dr. Walker, in your professional opinion, was Mr. Snyder helped or harmed by his therapy experience at Jedermann University?"

"In my professional opinion, he was greatly helped."

"How?"

"By becoming more aware of his condition," Dr. Walker replies. "He is better equipped today to deal with real world problems and issues than he was when he first presented at Jedermann University."

"Did anyone at Jedermann University violate any rules of conduct during Mr. Snyder's therapy?"

Dr. Walker answers, "No."

"Did anyone at Jedermann University violate any ethics policies or ethics codes in the course of Mr. Snyder's therapy?"

Dr. Walker answers, "Absolutely not."

"Did any aspect of Mr. Snyder's therapy at Jedermann University fall below the standards of care for the State of Texas?"

"Once again, absolutely not."

At 3:43 PM, Damian finishes deposing Dr. Walker and I depart immediately for home. Feeling even more confused than I was last week following Dr. Priestley's deposition, I wonder aloud what my real diagnosis is? Am I really as screwed up as Dr. Walker says? Do I really suffer from borderline personality disorder? Was this really all my fault? Maybe it doesn't matter because a second expert witness, today's good old Bernie Walker, has indicated for the record that I suffer from "paranoid personality disorder" — and more — thanks to my expensive lawyer. I wonder just what in the hell Damian is up to.

Greatly depressed, the only diagnosis I was not given, I lie down on my bed and pass out.

TALE OF THE TAPES

On Thursday morning I arrive at Damian's office at 7:45 AM. Because Damian is busy preparing for the 8:30 AM deposition, I proceed directly to the conference room and wait for others to join, which they soon do. At 8:32 AM the stenographer swears in Jedermann University's expert. In the room are Mr. Troutman, Mr. Wharton, Damian, Dr. Becky Howell, the stenographer, the videographer, and me.

Damian begins by asking the expert to identify himself for the court.

"I'm Dr. Dillard Jackson," the expert says. "I have been retained by Jedermann University and the State of Texas."

"Tell us about yourself, Doctor."

"I attended Broaderdam University in England for my undergraduate degree in psychology and Tourney Hills University in Texas for my Ph.D., also in psychology."

Dr. Jackson continues, "I am Chairman Emeritus of the McKissik School of Psychology at Tourney Hills University, a position I have held for the last twenty-two years."

"Okay, tell us what your responsibilities are at Tourney Hills University."

"I'm responsible for the clinical training of psychology students."

"And these are a mixture of undergraduate and graduate students?"

"All of the students are Ph.D. candidates. There are no master's level candidates in the McKissik School of Psychology at Tourney Hills University. It is strictly a Ph.D. program for psychology."

"And do you supervise student trainees as part of your responsibilities at the university?"

"Yes."

Damian asks, "At what point in the therapy process do you diagnose the patient?"

"Usually at the beginning of therapy," Dr. Jackson responds, "but not always."

"Would you explain that?"

"Yes," Dr. Jackson answers, "a diagnosis is simply a label that we affix to the patient. It's a quick way of triaging the patient."

"But doesn't the diagnosis determine the patient's treatment plan?" Damian asks.

"It's a shorthand way of labeling the patient," Dr. Jackson repeats, "so the diagnosis can determine the treatment plan, but it's not a necessary pre-requisite to determining a treatment plan."

"Does every patient who is treated at the McKissik School of Psychology at Tourney Hills University receive a diagnosis?" Damian asks pointedly.

"Yes, at some time."

"Do you ever require your student trainees to audio or video record their therapy sessions?"

"Occasionally," Dr. Jackson answers.

"And what would that decision depend on?"

"It would depend upon several factors," Dr. Jackson responds, "such as the degree of difficulty the student therapist is having with the patient, the degree or lack of degree of progress being made via the therapy, possibly a complaint from the patient about something the therapist is doing, or sometimes just random sampling so that I know what is going on."

"Do you ever sit in on a student trainee's therapy session?"

"Rarely, but sometimes," Dr. Jackson answers.

"And what would that decision depend on?"

"Well, again," Dr. Jackson responds, "it would depend upon my level of comfort with the student's progress with the patient."

"How do you gauge a student's progress with the patient?"

"Via the progress notes and the supervisory discussions I have with the student," Dr. Jackson answers.

"Are those the only ways?" Damian continues.

"Or by my direct presence."

"How much time do you spend in supervisory discussions of each patient your student trainee is treating?" Damian asks next.

"I spend about twenty minutes on average," Dr. Jackson answers, "sometimes a little more, sometimes a little less. It all depends upon the patient and the situation."

"While at Tourney Hills University, have you ever had occasion to terminate a student therapist-client relationship?"

"Infrequently, but yes," responds Dr. Jackson.

"When would you do that?"

"When the therapist-client relationship isn't working," Dr. Jackson answers.

"Does the McKissik School of Psychology at Tourney Hills University have a mission statement?"

"We do but, frankly, I don't have it memorized, but generally speaking it goes something like this: 'The mission of the McKissik School of Psychology at Tourney Hills University is to help patients by better equipping them to deal with life's everyday challenges in a productive, socially acceptable manner while simultaneously training student therapists to become professional psychologists.'"

"That's interesting, Doctor which do you think is more important, training the student or the patient's mental health and well-being?"

"They're both important," Dr. Jackson answers.

"But which is more important, Doctor?" Damian persists, trying to set a trap.

"The patient's health and well-being are always top priority," Dr. Jackson testifies, glancing in the direction of Dr. Howell who turns away upon hearing his answer.

"Does the Psychological Counseling Services program at Jedermann University have a mission statement?" Damian asks.

"I'm sure they do, but I'm not familiar with it," Dr. Jackson answers.

"Would it would be like Tourney Hills University's mission statement?"

"I believe it would be close," Dr. Jackson testifies. "However, there may be slight differences because Jedermann also trains undergraduate and master's level students whereas at Tourney Hills we train only Ph.D. students."

"Do you think the Psychological Counseling Services program at Jedermann University met its mission statement in its handling of Mr. Snyder's treatment?"

"Yes, I do." Dr. Jackson answers.

"And why do you think that?"

"Because Mr. Snyder was a difficult, demanding patient," Dr. Jackson explains. "I mean, I could go so far as to say that Mr. Snyder was an ass for stealing his clinical file and for assaulting his therapist! That's not how adults deal with problem situations."

"Do therapists ever incite hostility in their patients?" Damian asks.

"They shouldn't," Dr. Jackson responds.

"But can they?" Damian drills.

"Yes, they can. But they shouldn't," Dr. Jackson answers.

"Are you familiar with the phrase 'rupture and repair'?"

"I am. It's not a clinical phrase. It means in a general sense that the therapy is broken through some sort of conflict which allows the therapist to eventually repair the therapeutic relationship and make a breakthrough. It is usually spontaneous and not planned."

"Is that what happened between Mr. Snyder and Ms Polanski?"

"Perhaps. I don't really know."

"Have you had an opportunity to review Ms Polanski's file notes from Mr. Snyder's therapy with her?"

"Yes."

"Did you notice an increase in hostility in Cindy's notes since about the time Dr. Howell began supervising Cindy?" Damian asks.

"There was definitely escalating tension in Cindy's notes," Dr. Jackson responds, "but I'm not sure I would call it hostility."

Removing the digitally enhanced audiotape of the incident from his briefcase, Damian plays a small portion.

"In listening to this tape, would you agree that Cindy was the first to raise her voice?"

"Yes," Dr. Jackson responds, "Cindy did raise her voice first."

"And do you think Cindy raising her voice was therapeutic?"

"It could be therapeutic. It's a hard question to answer."

"And do you think Cindy escalated the tension by demanding the file back rather than listening to what Mr. Snyder had to say?"

"There was a clear escalation of tension," Dr. Jackson testifies, "but I'm not sure who caused it."

Damian plays more of the tape.

"Would you agree that Mr. Snyder tried to defuse the situation by telling Cindy to take the file back?"

"Defuse? I'm not sure."

"Do you mind if I replay the tape?"

"My hearing isn't great. I'm having a hard time understanding it."

"I have a transcript, too," Damian says, handing Jackson a few sheets of paper. "You can follow along."

Damian plays the tape again, and Jackson looks at the papers in front of him.

"You agree that Cindy raised her voice first when she demanded the return of the file. She says, angrily, 'I'd like my file back.'"

"Yes, she raises her voice. She seems angry."

"Then she says, also angrily, 'That's property of Jedermann University. That's not your property.' She seems to be escalating the confrontation, correct?"

"Yes."

"Then she says, 'Have you decided to take that file with you? Is that what you've decided?' Again, she seemed quite angry."

"I would say that's true."

"And then Mr. Snyder says, we are still in the therapy room, by the way, 'Very well, you want the file? Take the goddamn file.' And that statement is followed by a sound that I assume to be the file being tossed on Ms. Polanski's desk. Is that accurate?"

"Yes."

"Does Mr. Snyder seem out of control?"

"He seems upset but not angry."

"And then the concluding piece of conversation, Cindy says, 'I want the file back and I want it right now. And if I don't get it immediately, I am going to call the campus cops.' Then the next part, admittedly, is hard to decipher but she seems to say, 'I will destroy you Jimmy boy…' Or words to that effect. A threat to destroy James Snyder by creating a scene requiring the intervention of campus security. Destroy him by criminalizing his slowness in returning the file. He didn't do her bidding immediately, so she is perfectly willing to damage his reputation and undermine whatever positive things happened in the course of his treatment at Jedermann. Is that your understanding as well?"

"It's hard for me to make that section out. She could be saying that, I suppose."

"Is that appropriate language in therapy, 'I will destroy you?'"

"If she actually said that, it is not at all appropriate. It was a moment of stress and anger for her, I'm sure. We all say things we regret at those times."

"But we aren't all trained therapists, are we? So-called professionals in the business of helping people, not destroying them."

"I have no response to that."

"All right, let me continue. There is the sound of the therapy room door opening and then she continues, 'I'm calling Security right now. Call Security, please.' And then the door slams shut. I'm assuming she is telling Mrs. Esposito, the night receptionist, to call Campus Police. Does that seem accurate?"

"Yes."

"Ms Polanski has testified that Mr. Snyder pushed her violently into the wall in the therapy room. Do you hear anything on this tape that would indicate such an action, violent action, took place?"

"My hearing isn't good, but it doesn't seem so."

I look up at Wharton who has a stricken look on his face. He realizes his client Cindy Polanski has lied during her testimony and has been caught. No lawyer, I assume, wants his client exposed as a perjurer.

"Do you think that Cindy — who initiated the anger in the exchange — was justified in calling the Campus Police because of Mr. Snyder's actions or statements?"

"It would depend upon Cindy's state of mind," Dr. Jackson answers. "If she felt there was a danger to herself or University property, then yes, I believe she was justified in calling the police."

"Did you hear Mr. Snyder make any threats against Cindy on the tape?"

"No."

"Are there any references in any of Cindy's file notes of a threat or threats being made against her by Mr. Snyder?"

"No."

"So, you're saying, in effect, all that is required is for a therapist to believe there is a danger, to call the police?"

"I believe it is," Dr. Jackson responds.

"And Cindy's call to the police the morning after the incident, was that call also justified?"

"It would depend," Dr. Jackson answers. "If Cindy felt that there was a continuing danger, then yes, I believe her second call to the police was justified. Also," continues Dr. Jackson, "Cindy's supervisor approved this call, so I believe it was justified."

"Do you think the therapeutic relationship between Cindy and James was a healthy one?"

"It was clearly unhealthy," Dr. Jackson responds. "Neither Jim nor Cindy could negotiate the process of therapy. They could not agree on where the therapy was going."

"Do you think diagnosing James would have been beneficial to his therapy at Jedermann University?"

"As I said before, Mr. Argantes, a diagnosis is simply a shorthand way of labeling a patient. A diagnosis may have been helpful, but it wasn't necessary for establishing a treatment plan."

"Are you familiar with the DSM-IV criteria for paranoid personality disorder?"

"I am, but I will not diagnose during the deposition."

"Why not?"

"It is my personal preference to spend time with the patient prior to formulating a diagnosis and not off the cuff during a deposition. That would be unprofessional and unfair to Mr. Snyder."

"All right, I respect that, I suppose. How much time do you typically require?"

"Anywhere from one minute to three or more hours. It depends a lot on the symptoms that the patient is presenting."

"A one-minute diagnosis. That must be something to experience."

"Is that a question, Mr. Argantes?"

"No, Doctor, just an observation. What was Jedermann University's diagnosis for Mr. Snyder?"

"As far as I can determine, no diagnosis was made."

Damian estimates the number of hours I spent at Jedermann University and asks if that amount of time would have been sufficient to formulate a diagnosis.

"It should have been," Dr. Jackson concedes.

"If you were treating a patient who suffered from paranoid personality disorder, would escalating the tension and inciting hostility be part of the treatment plan?"

"It would depend upon the patient," Dr. Jackson answers.

"In general, do you try to escalate tension between yourself and your patients?" Damian drills.

"No, I never try to escalate tension or hostility," Dr. Jackson responds.

Damian next asks Dr. Jackson if he believes Plaintiff's symptoms are better or worse today than when I first presented at Jedermann University.

"Mr. Snyder's symptoms are different today," Dr. Jackson testifies.

"That was not my question, Doctor. Are the symptoms better or worse today?"

"Ethically, I can't answer that," Dr. Jackson responds. "Mr. Snyder's problems are ongoing, however."

Damian next asks Dr. Jackson what he thinks is the essence of this case.

"The essence of this case is that Mr. Snyder stole his clinical file from Jedermann University. Mr. Snyder," Dr. Jackson continues, "brought this whole situation upon himself by stealing the file. Had he not stolen the file, I don't think we'd be here today."

"One last question, Doctor, and I thank you for your patience. Do you think, in your professional opinion, that Cindy was properly supervised by the Director and Dr. Howell at Jedermann University?"

Dr. Jackson answers, "Yes, according to every professional standard required by the State of Texas, Cindy was properly supervised."

"Should Jedermann University have held itself to a higher standard than that required by state law?" Damian asks.

"Possibly," Dr. Jackson responds, "but I have no knowledge that a higher standard was required in this situation."

"One last thing. Let me pose a hypothetical question, Doctor. If

Tourney Hills University required in its policies and procedures that the supervisor have direct knowledge of the student trainee's therapy sessions via audio taping, videotaping, or direct presence, would you follow that requirement?"

"First off, I don't deal with hypothetical questions," Dr. Jackson answers, "and there is no such requirement at Tourney Hills University."

"But if there were," Damian interjects.

"If there were such a requirement, then I would follow it. I follow the rules."

At 12:11 PM, Damian passes the witness to Mr. Troutman and Mr. Wharton, who reserve their questions, so the deposition ends.

Feeling good for the first time in all the depositions, I thank Damian and depart immediately for work. Once at work, I call my best friend Scott and invite him and his family to go out to dinner with me to celebrate the apparently good results. Scott readily accepts.

"I'm in the mood for a nice, thick steak," I say.

"That sounds good. The rarer the better. Good and bloody. And the kids can have burgers and French fries."

"Try to convince Kelly to have something other than a salad, Scott. It's a celebration."

"Maybe she'll celebrate with a bread stick. She's going to Mexico with some of her girlfriends next week, and she wants her bikini body back. You know, I guess I do too."

That evening we have a happy time together, the first happy time for me in a long time.

THE SECOND BETRAYAL

It's early February 2007, nearly three weeks after Dr. Jackson's deposition, and despite the initial satisfaction I felt following Dr. Jackson's testimony, I quickly return to my daily pattern of intense anger and rage followed by bouts of severe depression. This is the systole and diastole of my emotional life. I can't escape it, and it is literally destroying me.

On Wednesday morning, February 7th, Damian calls me at work requesting that I visit his office on Thursday afternoon to discuss mediation. Damn him!

"Damian, listen to me, I am not interested in mediation. I don't want it, and I will not support it."

"I need to speak to you, James. It's important."

I reluctantly agree to visit with him.

On Thursday afternoon I arrive at Damian's office at 4:05 PM for our 4:00 PM meeting. Damian is in his office waiting for me. After shaking hands, he tells me to sit down and points to his leather couch. His new leather Snyder-supplied couch. It is as black as Damian's heart. He sits next to me and taps me in a friendly way on the knee.

"How do you think the case is going?"

"Damian, I am not pleased with Dr. Priestley. He's a fucking joke. I want a psychiatrist as my expert witness."

"That isn't possible now that the discovery period is closed. I'm afraid we're stuck with Priestley."

"You mean I'm stuck with him. Did you know he was going to say that I had a paranoid personality disorder?"

"No, Wharton, that bastard, lured him into that trap."

"I'm paying you a lot of money Damian to use an expert witness who doesn't get trapped."

"It happens. How else do you think it's going?" Damian asks, moving away from my complaint.

"I think Dr. Jackson gave the most favorable deposition," I answer. "And I'm really glad the digitally enhanced audiotape of the incident came out so well."

"It worked out well, but there is a long way to go. I know you are opposed to it, but would you consider mediation? It makes a lot of sense from a legal perspective."

"As I told you on the phone, I don't want mediation. I'm not interested in it. I want my day in court. How many times do I have to say that?"

"Going to court will be very risky and potentially very embarrassing for you. You saw what Wharton did to Priestley. Your personal life will be made public, and all your secrets will no longer be secret."

"I guess that's right, but I don't care."

"Your job, any women you want to date, your mom and dad will hear a lot of stuff about you. Nasty stuff. Your life will be scrutinized left, right, and center. Do you really want that?"

"I want my day in court. Juries don't like people who lie. And juries especially don't like people in positions of trust who lie."

"Will you at least think about mediation over the weekend?" Damian asks.

"I'll consider it, but I'm not in favor of any kind of mediation."

"It won't hurt to think about it. The long-term consequences could be devastating."

I look at him and nod. I'm pretty much done talking about it.

"We have to do a little financial business. I need more money to cover the deposition expenses, four thousand dollars."

"This doesn't seem to end, Damian. Don't you ever turn off the meter?"

"I have to make a living."

He looks at me. I don't like him and feel furious to be writing another check. I am working killer hours and, as George Carvel pointed out, living like a rat. I'm running out of money and I feel a little bit of panic creep up my leg into my groin.

I write him a check for four-thousand dollars and leave. He is edging me towards something I don't want. He is a clever guy, but I will kill him if I must. His many betrayals have earned him a death sentence. I will take my time about Damian, though. I wonder if he knows that. I wonder if he is still afraid of me.

"Maybe this one," I say handing him the check, "will get you a down payment on a sailboat."

"Powerboat, Jim, the winds don't always blow in the right direction." He gives me a conspiratorial wink.

"Fuck you, Damian."

"Lighten up, Jim, it's almost over."

You're righter than you know, Counselor. Almost over for both of us.

Once home, I reflect upon Damian's resolve to get this case into mediation, so to counter that, I sit down at my computer and compose a letter expressly prohibiting Damian from requesting mediation on my behalf. I mail the letter return receipt requested the next morning on my way to work.

Five days later, on Wednesday, February 14th, Valentine's Day, I receive the signed return receipt in my mailbox. On this very same day, I learn later from court papers, Damian visits the courthouse and requests mediation in direct violation of my repeated verbal and written prohibitions.

Three weeks later Damian calls me at work advising that the court ordered mediation for my case. Damian asks if I can visit him that afternoon to discuss negotiation strategies since the mediation will be held this Friday, March 9th.

At 4:40 PM that afternoon, I arrive at Damian's office and he sees me immediately.

"Who requested mediation, Damian?"

"The court ordered it," Damian responds.

"Goddamn it, who requested it?"

"The judge ordered it," Damian responds.

"I'll ask you one more time: who requested it? And you're going to tell me this time, you son of a bitch."

Now he's afraid. He looks at me with panic in his face. He sees my rage.

"Cindy's lawyer, Clint Wharton," Damian responds looking me straight in the eye.

"Here's what you're going to do. You're going to go in front of the judge to appeal this order."

"Sorry, the order cannot be appealed."

"Don't lie to me."

"Really, James, it can't be appealed."

I sit there in silence as Damian continues talking, thinking about how I will kill him as he continues his babbling.

Damian reviews the procedures for mediation and then asks if I have any questions.

I ask Damian if he has checked every available information source for data applicable to this case.

"Yes."

"You've checked civil trial histories, criminal trial histories, employment histories, phone calls to the police, and residential address histories?"

"Well, no," Damian responds.

"What the fuck am I paying you for? So, you can furnish your office like a white-shoe lawyer working for an oil company? You need to check those things, and you need to do it right away. I'm losing confidence in you Damian."

"I have a friend, a private investigator who is a former FBI agent, who I can call to do this."

"So, do it!"

"However," Damian cautions, "it will be expensive."

"Of course. You've always got your hand out. How much?"

I remove my checkbook from my briefcase and write a check for eight-hundred dollars, an amount Damian says should be enough. I saw him peek into my briefcase, looking for a gun, I guess.

"Just to be absolutely clear, I will not accept any settlement offers. I want my day in court."

"Think about it and keep an open mind."

I leave in a blind fury.

Once home, my anger surges. To my paranoid way of thinking, it is all very simple. I need a jury to award monetary damages against the defendants in order to justify executing them. If I kill them now, I think, the world will view me as a crazy client striking out against the people who tried to help him. However, if a jury awards damages, their deaths will be justified!

Anger and then a deep depression follow.

I no longer believe much in God, but in this moment, I feel I have been abandoned. I have no facility to pray, but in the grasp of despair I utter the only prayer I have prayed during those long desperate years, "Help me. Please, help me." I guess I am talking to God. I turn off the lights and am enveloped by the darkness. Nothing. An absolute blank. God is otherwise occupied.

CINDY'S ESCAPE

On Friday, March 9th, 2007, I arrive at the downtown mediation center at 9:20 AM. Mr. Wharton, Mr. Troutman, Damian, an insurance adjuster for Cindy's insurance company, and a female mediator are in a large conference room waiting for me. After Damian introduces me, I sit down beside Damian and the mediator begins. Wharton and Troutman seem relaxed. They know they have me by the balls.

The mediator starts by defining the rules for the mediation.

"Good morning, gentleman, my name is Ann Coover and I'm going to be your mediator today. Some of you are familiar faces to me, but we'll all get to know each other over the next few hours. Mr. Snyder, it's nice to meet you."

Ann says she is strictly impartial, and her role is to facilitate communication between the two parties. She can suggest a way to resolve the dispute but cannot impose a resolution. In other words, she says, the agreement must be voluntary.

She is very professional and dressed in a dark blue business suit with a red blouse. I think she is about fifty, a severe fifty, without a trace of makeup or jewelry except a wedding band and a thin gold chain around her neck. I sense she has been through this process many times. Instinctively, I trust her.

"The two sides have chosen to meet separately, so I'll be shuttling back and forth between my office and this room. Damian is this room all right for you and Mr. Snyder?"

"It's fine, Ann. Thanks."

She then asks each attorney to summarize his position. Damian goes first and largely reiterates Dr. Jackson's testimony. Mr. Troutman goes second and states that my therapy at Jedermann University was

150

student training and the supervisors there did nothing wrong. Mr. Troutman adds that I brought this whole situation upon myself by stealing the clinical file.

Mr. Wharton speaks third and asks me, "Mr. Snyder, do you know what malicious prosecution is?"

"Wharton, you know better than that. On the advice of counsel, he's not going to answer that question. Don't say a word, James."

I remain silent.

"Ms Polanski was a student trainee, and Mr. Snyder was paying only twelve dollars a session for his treatment at Jedermann University. You get what you pay for," says Wharton.

He seems on edge

After Mr. Wharton sits down, the mediator explains that each party will go to a separate conference room to negotiate. The mediator states that she will carry messages between and among the three rooms.

At 9:50 AM, Damian and I settle into our conference room. Two minutes later, the mediator knocks and asks what our opening position will be.

"We want one million dollars in damages against each defendant."

She returns six minutes later.

"Both defendants," she said, "Cindy and the State of Texas, offer zero."

Insulted, I stand up to leave.

"There's no way I'm going to get what I deserve in mediation," I say.

"Sit down, James, this is only the start. It's a negotiation," Damian commands.

He is very forceful, and I obey.

"Our offer is two-hundred-fifty thousand dollars from each defendant."

Again, the mediator departs, and returns nine minutes later, "Zero, Damian."

I wonder where she was for the other eight minutes.

"Ann," I say to the mediator, "would you tell Mr. Wharton and Mr. Troutman that juries don't like people who lie, especially people who are in positions of trust."

"No, I won't, Mr. Snyder." She smiles at me. She's an old hand at staying out of the cross hairs.

And just that quickly, I am caught in the negotiation game's vicious tentacles. The mediator departs, and this time is gone for twenty minutes.

When she returns, the mediator states, "Mr. Wharton will offer a maximum settlement of thirty thousand dollars, but the State of Texas still offers zero."

"Damian, it's not enough."

"It's not much, Jim," Damian says, "but if we go to trial you could get zero. Juries don't typically award damages against student trainees."

"It's not enough," I repeat.

"Please consider it," Damian pleads. "These guys have decided to play hardball. We don't have much of a case."

I reluctantly agree to consider it, and then I leave for home.

Once at home in my trashed apartment, I become very depressed. I'm tired of living with the detritus of poor people's lives: the broken chairs, the dog-piss stained couch with a broken leg propped up with a brick. Junk and more junk symbolic of my pitiful self. It should have been obvious to me from day one that Damian was not interested in prosecuting Cindy. Now I have a settlement offer from her attorney.

"Is that good enough to justify killing her?" I say aloud in my paranoid state. "Yes, I think that's enough."

On Saturday morning, I wake up at 7:18 AM and decide that today is the day I go hunting. I load fifteen rounds into the clip of my silenced .22 caliber Browning handgun, and then place the loaded weapon in my college backpack. I don my cycling attire, load my bicycle onto my car rack, and head into town. I am wearing a gray T-shirt and black cycling tights, sufficiently somber and unobtrusive. I don't want to stand out.

I park in Houston's famous Museum District and then cycle casually around River Oaks. Knowing that Cindy lives on Braes Street, I ride past her home looking for signs of activity. Nothing, the shades are drawn.

At around 9:30 AM, I turn right and ride very slowly down the alley behind Cindy's house. I am in a danger zone now. I have moved past a casual ride down Braes Street into stalking by means unclassified. Because Cindy's home is the third house in, I slow down to almost to a stop as I actively seek my target. Out of the corner of my eye, I think I see movement very near the back fence on my right. I approach the wooden fence slowly. The spaces between the pickets are very small, and I have a hard time seeing through them.

"Cindy," I say in a whisper, "where are you?"

I ride to the gate and try to open it, but it's locked.

"Cindy," I say softly, "there are no second chances. Once a therapist violates a client's trust, that's it. Her career is over. She is finished!"

I continue looking for signs of movement in the back yard. I see nothing, so I casually proceed down the alley and then turn right twice to head back up Braes Street.

Once back on Braes Street, I see a grey Mercedes C class quickly backing out of a garage and speeding away from me. Cindy's Mercedes, I assume. I speed up to try to catch it, but it is too fast. When I reach Cindy's house, I see that the front gate is now open, and a shovel and loose dirt are in the back of the yard where I thought I had seen movement.

Cindy has escaped, for now.

My target escaped me, and I return to my car, disappointed but undeterred. Murder is still in my heart. I head home. My destiny is before me. Once home, I think about Wharton's settlement offer and Damian's insistence that I accept it. I suffer, we all agree, from paranoid personality disorder. And out of disorder will come order.

Death is my only friend. The Devil be blessed!

THE THIRD BETRAYAL

On Monday afternoon, March 12th, I arrive at Damian's office at 4:00 PM for our scheduled 4:15 PM meeting. Damian sees me waiting in his lobby and motions me to join him in his office.

"Have you thought any more about the settlement offer?" Damian asks as I sit down.

"It's not enough," I answer.

"Well, how much is enough, Jim?"

He is clearly angry at me.

"How much is a nightmare worth?" I answer. "How much is a year of your life worth? Now multiply that by sixteen. How much is that?" I ask in defiant response.

He recognizes my reference to the CIA, of course.

"If you will be truly honest with yourself, Jim, you'll acknowledge that the CIA probably wouldn't have hired you anyway. They don't hire people with personality disorders. It's that simple."

The fact that he is right doesn't improve my state of mind, and I become silent. He's a smart fellow is Damian, smart enough to have seen from the start how weak a case I had. He was the organ grinder and I was the monkey, that's how well he played me. He saw my anger as a vulnerability to exploit, just like the others. But I won't be disposed of quite so quickly. They'll all discover that eventually.

He is in lawyer mode now, and he does most of the talking.

"Civil lawsuits are only about money, Jim, and a victory in a civil lawsuit won't bring back the dead. It won't right the wrong. It will only give you money to compensate you for your pain and suffering."

"But those people knew what they were doing!" I insist.

"Maybe they did, maybe they didn't," Damian counters. "Either way, it's still only about money."

"Why isn't the State of Texas offering a settlement?"

"Troutman wanted to offer a settlement; however, his boss in the Attorney General's office wouldn't let him."

"What evidence do we have against Cindy?" I ask.

"She was a student in training, Jim," Damian answers wearily. "No jury is going to award damages against a student in training. We've been through this."

"Did your FBI friend investigate all of the defendants as I asked you to?"

"Yes, there's nothing out there."

I look at the lying bastard in disbelief.

"Nothing? Really?"

"Nothing," Damian repeats.

"But Cindy committed perjury!" I shout. The anger, confusion, and depression all weighing in on me, surging.

"That's your opinion, Jim," Damian responds. "A judge and jury may not see it that way. Good luck trying to prove it. Everybody lies, James, that's the dirty little secret about practicing law. Everybody lies. Only the dumb ones get caught, and these people are not dumb."

Feeling overwhelmingly defeated, I ask Damian, "What are the terms of Wharton's settlement offer?"

"They're standard terms," Damian answers, "and by accepting the settlement, you acknowledge that Cindy denies any wrongdoing."

"Oh, there's one more thing," Damian says, as he removes the settlement document from a folder on his desk. "As a condition of the settlement, you are prohibited from filing any type of claim against Cindy with the State Licensing Board."

"No fucking way!" I shout. "That's a deal breaker!"

"Look, Jim," Damian responds angrily, "you heard the experts. The State Licensing Board isn't going to punish Cindy. The most they'll give her is a slap on the wrist."

"Well," I respond, "that's a slap I want to give her."

"Jim," Damian says, softening his tone, "try to think it through. You file a complaint with the Licensing Board. Cindy hires an attorney, you hire an attorney. They'll bring out Walker again who will testify that neither Cindy or Jedermann did anything wrong. That when you stole the file you fucked the whole thing up. And do you know what, he's probably right. And all we have is Priestley who is already on the record as saying you suffer from paranoid personality disorder, as in, you're looney tunes. In the end, the whole process costs you a lot of money and you get no satisfaction out of it when the Board decides that Cindy deserves nothing more than a letter that says, 'You screwed up, honey, do better next time.' Is that really what you want?"

Believing that there is some element of truth in Damian's argument, I reluctantly acquiesce and sign the settlement agreement, thereby releasing Cindy from all claims and causes of action that I could possibly have against her in this matter. In perpetuity. Forever.

When I arrive at home, I am already morbidly depressed. I go to my dresser, remove the Taurus 9 mm from its case, load a round into the chamber, cock the weapon and put it to my head. I sit down on the edge of my bed and close my eyes.

Why not do this? Why not just get it over with? I've held this gun to my head many times with my finger on the trigger. One infinitesimal gesture, just a tiny amount of pressure on the steel of the trigger and it's over. Game's up.

Death is my only friend. I put the gun down and remain alive. Why? I'll be damned if I know. Or maybe I'll just be damned.

JAMES SNYDER VERSUS
THE STATE OF TEXAS

In the months that follow, I find myself repeating a pattern of waking up, going to work, coming home, becoming homicidally angry, suicidally depressed, going to sleep and doing it all over again. I have almost no contact with Damian and even less contact with the outside world. Time is a blur until Damian calls me in late September.

On Tuesday, September 25th, Damian phones me at work informing me that the court set a mid-October trial date for my case. The complaint against Cindy has been closed, but the complaint against the State of Texas and Jedermann University and the eventual trial is still going forward. Damian requests that I visit him on Thursday to prepare.

On Thursday afternoon, I am able to leave work early and I arrive at Damian's office at 3:50 PM for our 4:00 PM appointment. Because Damian is with another client, I wait impatiently in the reception area. At 4:10 PM, Damian invites me into his office and we talk.

"How have you been, Jim? I have to say you don't look well."

"Not good," I answer, explaining my cycle of work, anger, depression.

"It's almost over," Damian says reassuringly.

"I'm going to ask you one more time for a referral to a psychiatrist."

"Priestley is our expert, and he'll do just fine."

I ask Damian if he is ready for trial.

"Almost," he responds. "We need to subpoena Cindy, and I need to call Dr. Priestley."

"Anything else?" I ask.

"Well, I need you to review your deposition and prepare yourself for trial. Will you do that for me? You need to be clear about what you testified to and the deposition. If you begin to freelance, they'll catch you, and your credibility will be blown."

"My credibility is fine."

"Other than the fact you suffer from a Paranoid Personality Disorder?"

"That doesn't mean I'm not intelligent with a great memory. And I'm not a liar."

"Okay, but stick to your story, no embellishment. The less you say on the stand, the better off you will be. Any confusion or contradictions, and Troutman with chop you up."

"Yes, but all the details are still fresh in my mind." I know my review will be very quick.

"When will you subpoena Cindy?" I ask.

"I'll process the paperwork today and the server will deliver the subpoena tomorrow," Damian promises.

"Will you call me tomorrow and let me know that she's been served?"

"Sure, Jim, no problem."

At 4:28 PM, I thank Damian and depart for home. That night I try to sleep but cannot. In my mind I repeatedly re-live The Incident, the moment when I grabbed the file and left Cindy standing in the hallway at the clinic at Jedermann as I ran into the parking lot. The anger and rage consume me before the depression finally takes over around 4:00 AM. And old exhausting pattern.

On Friday at work I wait anxiously for Damian's call. At 3:20 PM, I decide I've waited long enough and so I call Damian.

"There's a slight problem with serving Cindy," Damian responds. "The server went to her work, but Cindy refused to meet with him, so she hasn't been served yet."

"Can you serve her at home?"

"The server will try that this weekend."

Agitated and upset, I leave work early. Once home, I am deadly angry. I consider going hunting again but know that would not help my case. So, I remain in my apartment. I am extremely angry until the depression takes over and I sleep.

At around 9:30 AM Saturday morning, the server approaches Cindy's house and knocks on her door. Cindy's husband, some mook named Steve Balboni, answers and, even though the server can see Cindy at the top of the stairs in the house, Steve says that Cindy isn't home. The server says he'll come back that afternoon.

At around 2:25 PM, the server returns to Cindy's house, knocks on the door, and again Cindy's husband answers. This time, however, Steve hands the server a temporary restraining order and tells him to get off their property or he will call the police. The server departs.

At 3:32 PM, Damian calls me at home, "They've taken out a restraining order against our subpoena server. He couldn't serve her."

"What does that mean?"

"It means we need to get a different person to serve Cindy on Monday."

On Monday morning, October 1st, the original server and a new server are waiting at Cindy's work. When Cindy arrives, the second server approaches Cindy and serves the subpoena while the first server acts as a witness. Cindy was visibly upset, according to Damian.

Midmorning, Damian calls, "She's been served. I'm not sure what they thought they were gaining with that restraining order."

"And what about Dr. Priestley? Is he ready?"

Damian hesitates and clears his throat.

"We have another little problem. Priestley resigned as our expert witness."

"He's done what? How can he do that?"

"He faxed a letter of resignation stating that he changed his practice and is no longer interested in representing you. Very strange."

"How can we go to trial without an expert?" I ask.

Damian answers, "We'll use Dr. Priestley's videotaped deposition and that should be sufficient."

"No, I need a referral to a psychiatrist," almost spitting this out at Damian.

"There isn't time. The trial is scheduled for next Monday."

"Can the trial date be pushed out?" I ask.

"Perhaps," Damian responds, "but usually the court is so backlogged that the trial date will be reset without any intervention from us."

"When will we know?" I ask. I feel kicked in the gut by anxiety.

"By Wednesday," Damian answers.

For the rest of the day, I am agitated and aloof. It takes all my roiling mental capacity to not become angry at work. By the time I arrive at home at the end of the day, I am already in a rage. I throw anything and everything that I can inside my apartment. All the junk I have, anything light enough to pick and toss, ends up smashed. I even toss the TV against the wall, and it sizzles and pops on the floor. It sounds like my brain in meltdown mode. More stuff to end up in the dumpster which is very likely my destination as well. Then the depression takes over, moving in like a fog bank, and I am filled with a grinding and haunting sense of the inevitability of failure.

IRRECONCILABLE DIFFERENCES

On Wednesday afternoon, Damian calls me at work informing me that the trial date has been reset to April. Greatly relieved, I thank Damian and hang up.

On my drive home that evening, I hear an advertisement on the radio for a private investigator. I listen to the ad and make a mental note of the investigator's name. When I arrive at home, I think about Damian's reluctance to prosecute my claims against Cindy. I grow angrier and angrier the more I think about the lack of data in my case. I decide that I will call the private investigator in the morning to see if he can help me.

At 9:17 AM Thursday morning, October 4, I call Gonzalez and Associates Private Investigators, and Luis Gonzalez answers. I explain what I'm looking for and I ask Luis if he can help me. Luis invites me to visit with him that afternoon, so that is what I do.

When I get to his office, Luis greets me with a firm handshake. He looks like an ex-cop, or what I imagine an ex-cop to look like: he is heavy set with a thick mustache that covers most of his mouth. He is friendly, though, and seems anxious to help. His office is more cubby hole than an office. It has two black file cabinets and a gunmetal gray desk probably from a second-hand business furniture store. The only things on the wall are a Dallas Cowboy calendar and a photograph of Gonzalez in a cop's uniform. He was a very young cop in the photo and about thirty pounds lighter.

"So, Mr. Snyder, how can I help you?"

"I need some assistance in a civil action, medical malpractice. I lack data in my case and I'd like you to look at civil trial histories, criminal histories, residential histories, phone calls to the police, and any other data that you can find that will help me against Cindy

Polanski, Joseph Monteblanc, and Becky Howell. Cindy was a graduate student at Jedermann University and Monteblanc and Howell are administrators there."

Luis thinks for a moment. I suspect he has chased down some medical malpractice rabbit holes in the past.

"I can do that Mr. Snyder," he says at last, "but it will take some time to research all this information and it could be expensive."

"How expensive?" I ask.

"The bill could approach two thousand dollars."

"Do I write the check now or later?"

Luis smiles, "I just need a down payment. Two hundred fifty dollars will be fine."

I hand him a check.

"Will you write down their names and addresses if you have them and their titles at Jedermann. Come back next Wednesday at 3:30 PM for the results. This should be relatively simple." I shake his hand and say goodbye.

On the following Wednesday, October 10th, I return to Luis' office at the appointed time. He is on the phone as I walk in. He looks up at me and points an index finger upwards indicating he will be done soon.

"Right," he says, "of course, I'll check it out tonight. I'll try to get a photograph."

He put down the phone and laughs to himself.

"One of my clients thinks his wife is cheating on him. Man, has she been cheating on him. He's not happy now, but he's going to be very unhappy when he reads what's going on. Crazy woman he's married to. She's the queen of cheap motels. Like a drive through at McDonald's: easy in and easy out."

Luis seems to enjoy his work.

"What have you found?" I ask.

"Quite a bit, actually. For example, I found a police report that Cindy filed against you alleging that you were stalking her."

"Yeah, I found that myself."

"It looks like the cops didn't do anything. I also found something you might be interested in. Cindy worked part-time as a therapist in a practice near Montrose, for your buddy Joe Monteblanc, who has a very large private practice that caters mostly to students. She worked there for almost a year and there was a dispute about money. After a certain number of cases she claims she was supposed to get a raise and a bonus. Monteblanc, who has a reputation as a bit of a deadbeat, refused to pay. He's got a reputation for a lot of other things, too. He seems to like to date young Hispanic guys. Anyway, she sued him, and during the course of the lawsuit, she revealed the names of one-hundred-three of her clients."

"How could she do that? She's breaching client confidentiality."

"I don't know. I just find the information, I don't figure it out."

"In my case, Cindy is claiming she was naïve with patients due to being an inexperienced student in training and here she is breaching confidentiality of one-hundred-three of her clients? This is extraordinary. And Monteblanc is part of it, too. That old fraud. I'm going to fucking crucify them both."

I examine the police report again and ask, "What does this mean? Is this bad? No cops ever talked to me."

"No, lots of unhappy ex-wives and girlfriends make a police report. Cops don't pay them much heed. But I talked to one of Cindy's co-workers at the Monteblanc clinic. Apparently, she is furious with you. It looks like Cindy was planning to countersue you. Something called 'malicious prosecution'? That's what she will allege anyway. The police report was meant to strengthen her case. It's a bit of a con, and that's why the cops didn't take it very seriously. Why wait a week to file a complaint? But she's going to say that you were out to get her one way or another."

"Malicious prosecution," I respond. "I've heard that term before. Her fucking fat-faced lawyer brought it up. May I have copies?"

"Of course. That's what you paid me to find. They're yours."

He hands me the file and an invoice, and I happily write him a check.

"Thank you, Luis, this is money well spent. You did a great job."

When I arrive at home I attempt to carefully read the police report and the names of Cindy's clients; however, the more I read, the angrier I become.

"Why didn't Damian find these?" I question aloud.

My anger grows and grows as the night wears on.

At around 2:30 AM, I call Damian's office. "God fucking damn you, Damian!" I shout. "I found the evidence that you didn't even look for. You incompetent fucking whore!" I scream. "I never would have accepted a settlement offer had you discovered this evidence. God fucking damn you, Damian! You're an incompetent fucking whore!" I repeat.

After hanging up, I try to calm down but cannot. I am consumed with rage. I call Damian's office two more times and deposit similarly vitriolic messages. I am a maestro of vitriol, a dervish of obscenities. Mom would not be happy with her Jimmy.

At 8:28 AM Thursday morning, Damian calls me at work.

"Mr. Snyder, I just want to inform you that as of today, I am no longer your attorney due to irreconcilable differences."

I don't respond, but I am not surprised.

"My law partner, Suzanne Withers, heard your messages and is very upset over them. How would you like to come into work and find messages like those on your machine?"

I don't answer. Damian says that he will send me the forms needed to file a motion for continuance so that I can continue my lawsuit without him, and he hangs up.

"Oh, shit," I say under my breath as I hang up my phone. "Now what do I do?"

MY MISSION IS MURDER

On Tuesday, October 16, Damian's letter arrives. I open it immediately. In addition to Damian's instructions to the court that he is withdrawing as my attorney, the letter contains a motion for continuance that Damian states I must complete and submit before 5:00 PM Wednesday, November 7th, if I want to keep my case alive.

Feeling betrayed, I place the letter on my kitchen table and do not read it again until Monday evening, November 5th. That evening, I come to the realization that if I do not file the motion for continuance, my case will end. Believing in my paranoid state that I still need a jury verdict against the defendants in order to justify killing them, I sit down at my computer and begin preparing the motion.

The next evening, I finish the motion, review and edit it slightly, and print it for submittal on Wednesday.

On Wednesday afternoon, November 7th, I drive to the courthouse, find the court coordinator's office, and at 3:23 PM file the motion for continuance. The court coordinator explains that if a judge grants the motion, I will be *pro se*, that is, I will be acting for myself, against the State of Texas and will have only three months to find a new attorney before proceedings resume in my case. I acknowledge my understanding, thank the coordinator, and depart for the Houston Public Library.

Once at the library, I go straight to the Martindale-Hubbell Directory of the Best Lawyers in America. I photocopy seventeen pages of medical malpractice and tort litigation attorneys. I then go home.

The next morning, I call in sick to work. From my apartment I begin calling medical malpractice attorneys, starting first with Nicholas Kadair, the attorney who referred me to Damian. Mr. Kadair's number is out of service, and there is no forwarding number. I begin calling the "A's" on the list.

I speak to three lawyers at three different firms, but none of them will take my case. I continue calling, and my calls result in the same answer: sorry, not interested. I struggle to find motivation to continue. Then the old pattern returns: anger and rage followed by a severe, crippling depression.

The next morning and every day thereafter I call at least seven attorneys. And every day I get rejected at least seven times. I grow increasingly despondent as the weeks and months pass.

As I begin calling the "T's" on the list, I decide to write a letter to Damian to see if he will take my case back. Scott helps me to draft it. In the letter, which outlines my mental degradation over the course of the litigation, I explain the rage and anger I felt toward Damian over the evidence my private investigator found, and which Damian did not. I also note that at Damian's direction, I did not receive any counseling despite repeated requests for a referral to a psychiatrist.

On Monday morning, January 7, 2008, I mail my letter return receipt requested.

On Thursday morning, January 10, I call the law firm of Tran & Associates, LLP, and leave a voice mail message. On this same afternoon, Damian calls me at work inviting me to visit with him and his law partner, Suzanne Withers, the following afternoon.

"Why do you need to involve your partner?"

He responds, "Because of what you said."

The next afternoon I leave work early to prepare for my meeting with Damian. I go home and draft a suicide note to my parents apologizing for ending my life that day. I place the note on my kitchen table. I then remove my Taurus 9 mm handgun from its case, load fifteen jacketed hollow point rounds into each of five clips and place the loaded weapon and the clips in my briefcase.

At 3:53 PM, I arrive at Damian's office for our 4:00 PM meeting. Damian immediately shows me into Suzanne's office where Suzanne begins the meeting by discussing the attorney-client relationship. Suzanne looks over my letter to Damian and then addresses each of the allegations it contains.

"Why didn't you receive any counseling, James?" Suzanne asks.

"I repeatedly requested a referral to a psychiatrist; however, Damian refused to get me one saying that therapy would be detrimental to my case."

"That's not true!" Damian says loudly.

I look at Damian, who is sitting on the edge of his seat, as if he were ready to pounce. He is flushed and sweaty.

Suzanne is looking at me with pity and contempt. I look down at my briefcase, knowing the firepower it contains. The death that it could bring in a few seconds. I look again at Damian. In a moment of clarity, I realize that Damian, despite his overarching ambition, will never amount to much in life, and I feel nothing but contempt for him. He will always be a chiseler, ambulance-chasing loser in an expensive suit and a suntan. He'll make a handsome corpse in an open casket. Unless he takes a bullet to his brains. I look at Suzanne and again at Damian.

Instead of reaching in my briefcase and killing each of them as I had planned, I say softly, "Perhaps I misunderstood your instructions."

"You're damn right you did!" Damian responds angrily.

I have wasted my money and my life listening to this moron. Who is to blame for that but me? This makes me unspeakably sad. The truth is hard to take, and the truth is I was cheated by a cheap hustler on the make. Accepting this fact, I am filled with sorrow. I am absolutely exhausted and humiliated. I'm profoundly tired of my rage. I screwed the pooch, as my old man used to say. Another fuck up. I am not going to waste my bullets on these two. I have more important targets to attend.

Suzanne continues asking about the allegations in my letter; however, for me the rest of the discussion is a blur of white noise as I have zoned out, consumed by depression. I just don't care anymore. Their voices are like a conversation in another room in a cheap motel. Whispers through the plasterboard, old lies, new confessions, tired excuses. Hey, you cheated me out if my money, fair and square, what the hell else do you want? More money and to rub my face into a pile of legal shit.

I drive home that evening in a fog. At home, I look at the suicide note on the table, remove the 9 mm from my briefcase, cock the weapon and put it to my head. In a daze, I sit on the living room floor still holding the weapon to my head until dawn, a pointless exercise.

Death is my only friend, but I am a failure as a suicide. The poisoners have won. I feel utterly defeated.

THE DISSOLUTION OF DAMIAN

On Monday morning, January14, I go to work where I discover that Thomas Tran of Tran and Associates, LLP, returned my call late Friday afternoon. Because Thomas expressed interest in taking my case, I call him back immediately. Mr. Tran invites me to visit with him that afternoon. I readily accept.

At 3:45 PM, I arrive at the downtown law offices of Tran and Associates, LLP. The receptionist informs Mr. Tran that I am there, and he comes out immediately and greets me. Mr. Tran invites me into his office where we talk.

I show Mr. Tran the documents I brought with me, which include the new evidence, the settlement agreement, the original court petition that Damian filed on my behalf, and numerous depositions. As I hand each document to Mr. Tran, I tell him the history behind each.

"I'll look at these later, Mr. Snyder. First perhaps we should talk about the case."

"Okay. That's good."

"Have you received any therapy since filing your lawsuit?"

"No," I reply. "I repeatedly requested a referral to a psychiatrist, but Damian felt that therapy would be detrimental to my case."

"Why would Damian feel that way?" Mr. Tran asks next.

"Because I initially told Damian that I was going to physically harm each of the individually named defendants. He repeatedly referred to it, somewhat indirectly."

"How?"

"I asked him for a referral and he would refuse to give me one. When I asked why, he would say, 'Because of what you said.'"

"I don't know, but it seems to me that what you said would be even more reason to get you into therapy," Mr. Tran comments.

167

"Not for Damian."

"Do you still plan to harm the defendants?"

"No," I answer, untruthfully, I think.

"How much money have you spent so far?" Mr. Tran asks.

"Forty-four thousand dollars," I respond.

"You're serious. Forty-four thousand dollars. And you haven't had any therapy?" he asks.

"No not a minute."

"Damian's got some balls. I'll give him that."

"Not if I have my way."

"Let's leave that for now. Damian is clearly ethically challenged. What do you want from this lawsuit?"

"Some level of control over those people's lives!" I answer loudly, the anger welling within me.

Tran gives me a concerned look.

"You know that's not possible, Mr. Snyder."

"Yes, I know," I respond more calmly. "Damian used to say that civil lawsuits are only about money and not revenge."

Mr. Tran and I continue talking for another ten minutes. He then outlines his payment structure should he choose to take my case. As with Damian, I will be responsible for all expenses. In addition, I will pay him five-thousand dollars for his time, and he will receive thirty-five percent of all proceeds from the litigation.

Mr. Tran's receptionist calls informing him that his next appointment has arrived. Mr. Tran agrees to review my documents and says he will call me in one week to let me know whether he will take my case. I graciously thank him and then depart.

On my drive home, I feel hope for the first time in two-and-a-half months.

In the following days my thoughts fluctuate from hopeful ideation to extreme anger and rage to suicidal depression. Even though I go to work, I cannot concentrate. At times I am a live wire, ready to snap at the slightest provocation. At other times, I am somber and restrained.

On Friday morning, January 18, Damian calls me at work informing me that he will take my case back, subject to involving his partner in the litigation. He invites me to visit him that afternoon to discuss his new trial fee. Realizing that Damian countered every allegation I made against him with his partner, Suzanne, as his witness, I decide to secretly record our meeting in the hope of undoing some of that damage. I need a record that Damian cannot dance way from. I want to catch him in his lies and have him disbarred.

In the parking lot outside Damian's office, I turn on my mini-cassette tape recorder, which is the size of a pack box of cigarettes.

Before getting out of my car, I place it in the inside pocket of my suit jacket, and then walk into Damian's office. Damian sees me arrive and immediately ushers me into his office. I ask if Suzanne will be joining us, but Damian answers that she took the afternoon off. He doesn't need her anymore. She has accomplished what he wanted her to do.

Damian begins our meeting by defining ground rules for our interaction going forward. "No more angry answering machine messages. Agreed?" Damian asks.

"Agreed."

"No more accusatory letters. Agreed?"

"Agreed."

"We're going to do this my way. Agreed?"

"Agreed." We both can hear the resignation in my voice.

"And my partner is going to be involved. Agreed?"

"Why does Suzanne need to be involved?"

"Because of what you said," Damian answers.

"What about our expert witness?" I ask, interrupting Damian.

"We'll use Dr. Priestley's videotaped testimony," Damian answers.

"I want a psychiatrist as my expert witness."

"We'll use Dr. Priestley's videotaped deposition," Damian counters, raising his voice. "My way, remember?"

"I want counseling," I demand louder.

"Look Jim," Damian says, the anger growing in his voice, "you and I have been over this. Counseling is not a good idea for you at this time."

"Why?" I demand.

"Because of what you said."

Because of what I said! How I hate that fucking sentence. I should have shot the bastard, the lying weasel when I had the chance.

"Do you want me to take your case back, Jim?" Damian asks pointedly. "Because I don't have to. The judge granted my motion to withdraw. I'm a free man."

"The judge made a mistake, Damian."

"The trial fee for your case is fifty-thousand dollars," Damian states.

"Fifty-thousand dollars? I've already paid you forty-four thousand."

"Fifty-thousand dollars," Damian responds, explaining that this amount is needed to pay both him and Suzanne.

"But you were all ready for trial already," I counter. "What value is Suzanne adding?"

"Fifty-thousand dollars, James, take it or leave it."

"Fifty-thousand dollars!" I exclaim. "It's too much. I don't have

169

that kind of money anymore."

"Go ahead, make an offer," Damian says with a laugh.

I get up out of my chair and head toward the exit.

As I show myself out, I say to Damian, "I'll consider your offer and get back to you next week." Or maybe I'll blow your brains out.

At home, I turn the volume up on my cheap stereo to mask the noise and the destruction I am creating. I throw anything and everything. Nothing is sacred. I would throw myself against the wall if I could. Instead, I bang a cheap pot against the stove and chip the finish and dent the pot. I sit on my bed, pot in hand, looking for a target. I throw it against the bedroom doorjamb and it spins to a lopsided stop on the floor next to me.

Because of what I said, magic words that seem to slow me down. I need to be quiet now and just move forward. I don't need any more planning, I need action.

Death to the Devil Damian! He's not going to put that on a campaign poster.

THE WHITE KNIGHT

On Monday, January 21, Thomas Tran calls me at work informing me that he will take my case. He asks if I can visit him that afternoon to sign the contract and get the paperwork out of the way.

I answer, "Yes, and thank you for your help."

I arrive at Mr. Tran's office for my 4:30 PM appointment at exactly 4:30 PM. I announce myself to his receptionist, and she summons him from his office. After shaking hands, Mr. Tran invites me into his office. I see several documents on his desk.

"Are those for me?" I ask.

"Yes," he answers, getting right down to business.

Mr. Tran hands me his one-page contract. I read it quickly, sign it, and then hand it back. He next hands me an attorney transfer form. He explains that this form is needed both by the court in order for him to take over my case and by Damian in order for Damian to release all of the court filings. I read it over quickly, sign it, and hand it back. Mr. Tran next asks for his five-thousand-dollar trial fee. I write him a check, hand it to him, and receive back a pre-printed receipt.

Mr. Tran says he'll contact Damian in the morning and make arrangements to pick up my case files.

"Then," he continues, "I'll find a competent psychiatrist and get you diagnosed. Any questions?"

"You don't have to pick up the documents, Mr. Tran. I'll pick them up myself. I don't trust Damian at all."

"Okay, but if Argantes is there, just treat him with courtesy. I know you don't like him. Believe me, a lot of people don't like him."

"We have a lot of work to do, you and I, but I think it will be fine."

After I have departed, Mr. Tran faxes the signed attorney transfer form to Damian along with a cover letter requesting the case files. Damian calls Mr. Tran back about twenty minutes later advising that he will be tied up in court until Wednesday afternoon and will need that much time in order to organize the files.

On Thursday morning, I retrieve the files from Damian's office and I take them home and place them on my kitchen table. It is a formidable pile of legal papers and deposition testimony. I have kept a copy of most of these papers for my own record. I have a talent for organization and detail. I was trained as an engineer, and I prefer organization to chaos, although the current state of my ruined apartment would indicate otherwise.

"All right," I say aloud, "let's see what we have here." I flip over the pages one by one.

"I can't believe what this asshole has done," I say aloud to myself. I'm astonished and angry. A cursory examination of the two piles of documents, mine and Damian's, indicate that instead of organizing the case files, as he told Mr. Tran he would, Damian went through the files and purged all communications from me to him.

My review process is interrupted by the phone ringing.

"Yooo," Scott says in his typical greeting. "What are you up to Jim?"

"I just picked up my files from Damian's office. I'm looking through them carefully. Damian has removed every fax, every letter, every note that I ever gave him. He's purged the files."

"Why?"

"Because he's a lying bastard, and I've caught him in some lies. He didn't think I would be so careful at my end. Tran, my new attorney, would have no reason to question what Damian gave him, and I shouldn't be aware of what he did, but I am."

"That must be illegal or something."

"Damian is a clever character, he has covered his ass in some way that I'm not aware of. He probably shredded the documents thinking no one would be the wiser."

"What are you going to do?"

"I'm going to talk to Tran and give him everything I have."

"Well, just be cool, Jim. I think Tran will do the right thing. I'll talk to you later this afternoon."

"Okay."

Damian instructed, I assume, his administrative assistant to prepare the now-sanitized files to give to Thomas Tran. I think he assumed that I would never see the files and wouldn't notice what he had done. I'm a careful man, well-organized. I carry grudges. I doubt the loyalty and trustworthiness of others. I am suspicious. I'm suffering from paranoid personality disorder, but in a world of bottom feeders like Damian, who can say I'm truly crazy?

Early Friday morning, I drive to Tran's office and drop off the files. He is busy with another client, so I drive to work rather than trying to speak to him. I will call him when I get to my office.

I call Tran's office and he answers on his private line.

"Hi, James, I got the paperwork. I'm going to spend most of the day reading it."

"Damian committed a felony, at least I think it's a felony."

"I'm not surprised," Tran says with a laugh, "what did he do this time?"

"He destroyed all my personal communications with him. He even destroyed his invoices to me. He has erased my input from the record. But I have copies of all the stuff he destroyed. I'll make copies and give them to you when we meet again."

"What an asshole. It's probably not technically illegal, but it is an ethical breach, no doubt about it. By the way, I thought of a psychiatrist who might be helpful."

"Great. Let me know what happens."

Mr. Tran calls a psychiatrist named Dr. Solomon Janowitz, and, after describing my case to him, asks Dr. Janowitz if he will be my expert. Dr. Janowitz agrees to review the documents in my case.

That afternoon, a courier service delivers the requested depositions to Dr. Janowitz's office. Dr. Janowitz's secretary, Leti, receives the documents and calls Tran's secretary saying that the doctor will review them over the weekend and will call Tom on Monday.

That evening, Mr. Tran calls me at home informing me of these facts and that he is almost certain that he has retained a psychiatrist as our expert witness. Tran suggests that I will likely have to meet with Dr. Janowitz early next week. I thank him profusely, then hang up.

I immediately call Scott and share the good news. I am more than happy. I am ecstatic for the first time in more than two years. Scott encourages me and is very glad that I finally received some good news. We talk for about fifteen minutes, then hang up.

As the night wears on, my mood changes from happiness and joy to anger and rage at Damian's betrayal. Then, like every rage episode, this one is followed by an intense depression. I have some faith in Tran, though. He found a psychiatrist.

IF MADNESS IS A MOUNTAIN,
I NEED A GUIDE

On Monday morning, January 28, Dr. Janowitz phones Mr. Tran and advises that he is very interested in working with me. Dr. Janowitz requests that I visit with him as soon as possible.

Tran calls to give me Dr. Janowitz's phone number and says that I should coordinate the meeting through Leti, Dr. Janowitz's secretary, and that I should make the earliest possible appointment. I call immediately and discover Leti has scheduled my first meeting with Dr. Janowitz for the next evening. For the rest of the day at the office, I am distant in my thoughts. Two of my co-workers independently ask me if I feel all right. I answer simply that I have a bad headache.

On Tuesday evening, January 29, I arrive at Dr. Janowitz's office at 5:15 PM, just as the staff of the Janowitz Clinic is departing for the evening. I introduce myself to Leti. She is a middle-aged black woman and exudes a sense of control and efficiency that is comforting. She is not maternal, not at all, but seems utterly in control. I think she must have a flak jacket or a life ring under her desk. Prepared for any eventuality, she is ready and poised for action.

I look above her head and see an enlarged photo of a dachshund on the wall behind her.

"Is that your dog?"

She smiles, and smiling she seems quite beautiful. She rests her head on her chin, "That is not my dog. My dog would eat that dog for supper."

"That's Dr. Janowitz's dog?"

"It's more like his wife's dog. She does love that creature."

"Does he have a name?"

"She has a name. Lucy. She's a friendly little thing, although just between you and me and Dr. Janowitz, she's getting a little old."

"I guess we all are."

She hands me a stack of forms to complete, which I do in short order. And then I wait. One of my obsessions is being on time, so waiting is something I do often.

At 5:35 PM, Leti has cleaned off her desk and is beginning to put her coat on. The intercom buzzes, and I hear a voice that says, "Send Mr. Snyder in."

"Okay," Leti says, "Dr. Janowitz is ready for you now. Second door on your left."

I knock tentatively on the metal door. Janowitz is partially hidden behind a computer monitor. His desk is empty except for a manila file in the corner. He motions for me to take a seat and we begin to talk. The first of what will turn out to be many conversations.

"I've read most of the depositions in your case, James, as well as a lot of the case filings. My role now is to diagnose you. I will provide expert witness support for your causes of action against Jedermann University and the State of Texas."

"So, James, how are you feeling?"

I explain my wild emotional swings, from homicidal rage to suicidal depression. To emphasize my point, I remove my Taurus 9 mm handgun from my briefcase, chamber a round, and hold the loaded, cocked weapon to my head. With my index finger gently rocking the hairpin trigger from side to side making an audible clicking sound, I say, "I just don't care anymore, Dr. Janowitz."

After a brief pause, as I look squarely into Dr. Janowitz's eyes, I ask, "Will you help me?"

What can he say? I am the madman with a gun in his hand. I am resigned to killing myself, right then, right there. I am indifferent at that moment to my death and to his.

Janowitz shows no fear, and that surprises me. He is a shortish man, about 5'4", tending towards stoutness, with a belly hanging above his belt. There is nothing heroic about him physically. His demeanor is one of great self-awareness and kindness, although I distrust nothing so much as kindness which I read as patronization. I feel displaced momentarily from my anger with him. I am leaving a comfort zone of anger.

Dr. Janowitz responds calmly, "You are telling me that you are very depressed and that taking your own life is not beyond you. We have some real work that we have to do."

"I guess we do."

"But I don't do my best work with someone waving a loaded gun around. And I presume it's loaded?"

"Yes, it is loaded."

"Well, then, probably for us to continue it's best for it to go back in the satchel," Dr. Janowitz says.

"Okay. But it's not a satchel, it's a briefcase."

He shakes his head and smiles. "Very well, James, put it back in your briefcase."

Madness is a mountain, and I begin the dangerous descent from the icy place I had achieved. It's not the mountain we conquer, it's ourselves. That's something I remember from my early, secret boyhood studies. I think Edmund Hillary said it, I think. I am no mountaineer and Janowitz is not a Sherpa, but we have little choice in the matter. We descend. If I'm going to kill Janowitz, it won't be today.

I am not quite sure what has just happened. I unload the weapon and put it back in my briefcase. If truth comes in torrents, it may also come in a whisper, in a calm conversation with a reasonable man at the end of the day.

And with that, we begin the real healing in my life.

THE JANOWITZ REPORT

On Friday morning, February 1st, Thomas Tran calls me at work requesting that I visit him that afternoon.

"What's the meeting about?"

"I'll discuss it with you in person."

At mid-afternoon, I arrive at Mr. Tran's office. His receptionist notifies him that I am there, and he comes out immediately and greets me. After shaking hands, we proceed to his office.

Mr. Tran begins the meeting by stating that he received Dr. Janowitz's report with my diagnosis; however, the real purpose of the meeting is to discuss Jedermann University's request for summary judgment.

"Your lawsuit was filed under the Texas Tort Claims Act," Mr. Tran says, "which only permits lawsuits against the State of Texas under certain conditions. Jedermann University is challenging the basis of your lawsuit under this Act."

"Can you defeat the motion?"

"I don't think so, not this time," Mr. Tran answers.

"I don't understand."

"The courts have recently tightened their stance on the Tort Claims Act. When you first filed your lawsuit, the courts had a broader view as to the types of cases that could be brought under the Act. The State is asserting sovereign immunity. It looks like they'll win."

"Is there nothing we can do?" This seems like the end of the road. I am frustrated.

"Nothing legally. Maybe sue Argantes for malpractice but that is a waste of time and money. He should have known all this by the way."

"He told me about it. He did warn me that this was a possibility,

177

but the issue was being litigated in the court cases. He said it wasn't settled law yet."

"It is now. It's been resolved. Did he say anything about 'breach of a standard of care'?"

"Yes. He said it was something that I didn't want to hear."

"I've examined your Jedermann file, and I don't find anything that would disqualify the assertion of sovereign immunity."

"So, it's over?"

"I'm afraid so, James. Look, I know it doesn't mean much but I'm really sorry. The legal profession did you no favors. In fact, we did you a good deal of damage."

"You didn't. You've been a great help."

"I think the best thing you can do at this point is devote yourself to therapy with Dr. Janowitz. I certainly wouldn't spend any more money on this lawsuit," Mr. Tran responds.

"You said you received Dr. Janowitz's report with my diagnosis?"

"This copy is for you," Mr. Tran says as he hands me a two-page document that has Dr. Janowitz's letterhead at the top of the first page.

I quickly scan the report: Depression, Paranoia, Suicidal Ideation, all secondary to Post-Traumatic Stress Disorder.

"What does this mean?"

"When is your next appointment with Dr. Janowitz?"

"On Tuesday."

"You should discuss it with him, James."

"Would we have won the lawsuit with this report?"

"It's hard to say. The report is advantageous to our case; however, the final decision would be up to the jury. Janowitz points out the inconsistency in Monteblanc's testimony and the obviously doctored file notes. But the bar in tort cases is a high one, and I'm not sure Jedermann or Monteblanc or Cindy actually breached a standard of appropriate care. Then there are the damages. They would have been minimal even if you had won, I'm afraid. But it would have been up to the jury to decide, both the verdict and the damages. And juries are funny things."

"It was never about the money. It was about something else."

"What was that, James?"

"I don't know. In the end, honor. The truth, I guess."

"Not much of that around these days, James. I'm sorry."

"Is there anything else for me to do?"

"No."

It was not just about honor, it was also about murder. Vengeance. I thank him and go home.

Once home, I try to read Dr. Janowitz's report; but I cannot concentrate. The words will not register in my brain. Depressed, I remove the Taurus from its case and chamber a round. But rather than putting the weapon to my head, I simply hold it in my hand and look at it. It has begun to feel strange in my hand.

What is my fate? In the morass of my precise paranoid logic, I feel defeated. No guilty verdict means no righteous murders. The poisoners will live on to poison others. This does not seem right, but it is the impenetrable calculus of my hopelessness.

LIFE IN THE PRESENT TENSE

I am ruined, that is the sentence going through my head. I had tried to climb out of the dark place into which I had fallen, and I had failed. I have been pushed and prodded to confront my demons and only found more demons. I have spent most of my available cash pursuing a profound grievance against people whose purpose was to "help" me and found them to be wretched manipulators and poisoners; my lawyer is a liar, a narcissist, and a fraud. I am disconnected from everything except the past and a handgun and a pocket full of lethal ammunition. I am left with a handful of dust, nothing more.

But then something happened, something always happens and lately it has almost always been bad for me. Scott called.

"Hey, Jim,"

"Hi, Scott, what's up?"

"How did it go with Tran?"

"State of Texas won, the judge dismissed the suit. I have officially achieved the end of the road. Janowitz's report would have been helpful. He did point out what a total fuckup Joe Monteblanc is, but it doesn't matter."

"Can you appeal?"

"I don't think so, and I don't have the money right now anyway."

"I'm sorry, Jim, I really am. But I have some good news."

"What's that?"

"Kelly took the kids out of town to visit her mother for the weekend. Actually, they're going to meet in Las Vegas. You know her old man likes to play cards. He always loses but it doesn't matter to him. Frankly, he's an idiot, but it's not my dough."

"So, you want to go to another titty bar? We could have done that whether or not Kelly was in town or out of town."

"I know. But I'm also aware of the fact that you would like to go places that are a little higher toned, so you could meet some classy women and get away from strip bar skanks, I think you call them."

"Not tonight, Scott, I'm a little down about the legal news."

"No, I'm not going to let you brood in your so-called apartment. Kelly reminded me she got a gift certificate for the restaurant at the Houstonian, a fancy old hotel, as a Christmas gift from her boss Corey, that wanker. You know the way she eats, which is hardly at all. And so she suggested that I take you out for a proper drink and a meal tonight while she is spending our hard-earned money on the slots. She said, 'Jimmy is probably just going to scramble some eggs for supper again. He deserves a nice meal and a nice glass of wine.' I made a reservation for 7:30. I'll pick you up in a half hour. Wear a collared shirt and a jacket. I don't think you need a tie."

"But…"

"No buts. Meet me in your parking lot. We are going to a nice place and you are going to meet a classy woman. End of story."

I realize I don't know anything about this hotel even though I've driven past it many times. I think part of the property includes the old G. H. W. Bush house. I assume its clientele are "the newly wed and the nearly dead"; old Houston money, or as old as money gets in Houston. I can picture Damian at the bar drinking a "dirty martini" and plotting his next political campaign.

Scott seems enthusiastic as we walk into the lobby, "We're going to get a drink at the Great Room Lobby Bar, buddy."

The lobby is surprisingly empty at 7:00 PM, although I guess most people have checked in or checked out. It is dominated by large stone fireplace with a rustic, roughhewn mantel piece. A gas fire is burning brightly, and large men in cowboy hats are sitting in the leather club chairs, waiting for their wives to meet them for dinner. This is not a world I know. I'm a poor boy who has had a very bad day, and a drink in a fancy hotel bar is not going to do much to lift me out of my depression. I don't know what in the hell I'm doing here, although I appreciate Scott's effort to cheer me up. This is not going to do it. We take a place at the bar, which is Carrara marble. It is a long bar with a graceful inward curve at the opposite end. The bar is almost empty, and we take seats at the end toward the entry. The bar stools are dark wood, mahogany probably, with plush red seats.

The bartender is a young guy, probably thirty, with a well-trimmed goatee. His hair is combed back and loaded with hair gel. He is slightly overweight but seems energetic, and as tense as an uncoiled spring.

"Gentlemen," he says, putting down coasters, "what can I get for you tonight?"

"Yeah, hi, may I ask, what's your name?"

"Paul," he says putting his hand forward to shake Scott's hand. "Paul Leventhal."

"Paul, I'm Scott and this is my friend James."

"James, pleasure to meet you," he says shaking my hand in turn.

"Here is our situation, Paul. My wife was given a gift certificate for this place for Christmas. She can't use it, but James and I want to tonight. Is there a problem with that?"

"None at all. Are you having dinner or just drinks?"

"Both, I think, but we'll probably just eat at the bar, if that's okay."

"Absolutely. Just give me the gift certificate when you want to settle up."

"Perfect."

"What would you like to drink?"

"I'm going to have a Dewar's rocks," Scott says.

"I'll just have a house Chardonnay. Is it any good?"

"For a house wine, I'd say its drinkable. Not great, but it's one of our biggest sellers at the bar."

Paul returns in a moment with the drinks, "Would you like to see menus now?"

"I think we'll wait a bit. We're going to sample the ambiance, aren't we, Jim?"

"Sure," I respond.

"It's quiet tonight, but things should get busy later. Let me know when you're ready to order," Paul says, returning to the back of the bar.

Scott looked past me down the bar and turned to look at the room behind us.

"I don't see many women here tonight. We need some classy women here tonight. Got to get you away from those lap-dancing bad girls."

"They're all right."

"All right for me, but then I have someone to go home to. You need some feminine companionship to take your mind off Cindy and Jedermann."

"And Damian," Scott adds.

"Him, too. That fucking liar."

Neither Scott nor I are serious drinkers. A few beers while playing pool or watching girls dance naked is our usual quota. We nurse our drinks and, as Paul predicted, the bar gradually fills up. Finally, there is only one seat remaining, and I notice Paul puts a coaster, a glass of water, and an empty wine glass on the bar in front of that seat.

I look at him and he says, "I'm saving that seat for a Friday night regular."

It is getting louder as more people filter in from the lobby and the pool area. It doesn't really matter as I have very little to say. For once silence suits me as well as a conversation.

"I'm going to find the bathroom," I say to Scott. "We should think about ordering some food."

He nods in agreement.

When I get back the empty seat is occupied by an older woman, probably in her seventies. As I sit down, Scott smiles and raises his eyebrows. No, this is not the high-toned woman I've been promised. She is nicely attired, I can't help but notice, in a light gray sleeveless dress. Her arms are tanned and toned, without the old lady's arm wattle. She stays fit swimming or playing tennis. She has a matching jacket on the back of her chair. Her hair is quite short, and she wears it brushed back away from her high forehead. The only jewelry she wears is a silver bangle on her left arm, and small silver hoop earrings. Lately, I haven't seen too many women I would call elegant, but she is elegant.

"The usual, Mrs. Bowman?"

"Yes, please. And how are you tonight, Paul?"

"I'm fine. I haven't seen your friend yet."

"Oh, Louise is running late again. She's on the way. As they say, she'll be late to her own funeral if she has one."

"How is your husband?"

"If it's Friday, Paul, he's playing poker with the boys. I'm sure he's gambling away the money I was saving for a face lift."

"Maybe he'll win tonight."

"Paul, I love my husband very much. We've been together for fifty years, but he was a bad poker player fifty years ago and age has not altered that one bit. His luck was in finding me, and my luck was getting him out the door every morning to go to his office."

She looks at me and says, "Good evening."

Before I could respond, Scott leans forward and says, "Ma'am, I don't want to be too forward, and pardon me for overhearing your conversation with Paul, but you're one of the only women in this room who doesn't need a face lift."

"Well, thank you, young man. You're a wonderful liar, but it's a nice compliment. And my face is one of the many things this old lady needs lifted."

"I'm Scott, by the way, and this is my friend James."

"I'm pleased to meet you both. My name is Vera. Are you staying in the hotel?"

"No," I say, "we live in Houston. We're just here to get away from the honky tonks we usually go to. Trying to move uptown a bit."

"I must say you don't look like guys who go to honky tonks, and I've been in some. You live in Houston, but I don't think you are native to Houston. Am I right? You're probably engineers with NASA."

"Scott was before he got laid off, and I work for Texas Computers as a temporary employee. I'm a kind of an engineer, second grade. Originally, I'm from Ohio and Scott is from California."

"My husband and I are both Midwesterners. He's from Illinois and I'm from Wisconsin. We met because we were both in college in Chicago, but that was a long time ago. He was a banker, and we lived all over the world. We ended up in Houston, and now we're trying to figure out where we want to live in our dotage."

Scott says, "You seem to have a slight accent."

"You have a good ear. I was born in Berlin, Germany in 1934. I moved to America in 1946. My mother was what used to be called a war bride. Not many people catch my accent. I have worked very hard to eliminate it. I want to sound like an American from Wisconsin, U.S.A."

"Your father died in the war?"

"Yes, he was an officer in the German army, the Wehrmacht. He died or was captured in Stalingrad. I only remember him a little. I never saw him after 1939. He was a highly decorated officer. My mother was very proud of him."

"I'm sorry."

"Oh, that was long ago."

"My mother met an American officer in 1945 while she was working in a hotel in the American zone in Berlin. She liked men in uniform, I guess. He was very handsome, so skinny and tall. Next to us malnourished Berliners, the Americans were like gods."

"They fell in love."

"Something like love, at least for my mother. My American father adored my mother, however. But his commanding officer would not give him permission to marry my mother, and we thought that was the end of it. We Berliners were held in low esteem, I'm afraid, because of the Nazis. Goodbye, Captain Jack Duffy. But no, he left the army and came back to Berlin and married my mother and took us away to New York City. And then the train to Chicago and a stay in the Drake Hotel and then the train to Bayfield, Wisconsin. That is way up north. My American father's family — Jack's family and eventually my family, too — owned a hardware store there. What an adventure that was. I remember the day Jack took my hand and we walked up the gangplank of the SS Northern Star, an old tub of a boat, when we sailed away from Hamburg. Such a great day. Such a kind and generous man."

"Was it bad in Berlin during the war?"

"Not so bad, James, but horrible. That's what Berliners used to say. They were a tough lot with the bombing and destruction and no food. And Hitler kept saying we would win, all we needed to do was to believe. And then there were the Russians, of course. My mother was alone, with me to care for and to feed. There was little food, scraps really. I don't know how she managed to keep us alive. And then the Russians came. They were beasts. Worse than beasts. Drunken animals. But we managed somehow."

"You seem to have lived an amazing life."

"A lucky one. But I'm just a talkative old woman. What are you gentlemen celebrating, if I may ask?"

"Not a celebration. More like a wake," I say. "I had a complicated lawsuit, a medical malpractice suit, that was dismissed recently. I spent a lot of time and money and it all came to nothing."

"I'm sorry to hear that. But you seem healthy."

"Not in my head I'm not. Don't worry," I say as she looks a little alarmed, "I'm okay. I just had a few problems."

"There are always those."

"Mine don't seem to want to go away."

"James, let me tell you one more story, and then I'll be quiet. My life in America has been a happy one. There are always problems. We had two children, a boy and a girl. The boy was killed by a hit and run driver in Paris. He was only five. His nanny, a silly woman, let him out of her sight. But it was my fault, of course, I was his mother. She was not. My mother worked as a maid in the American sector in Berlin, but we lived in what would become the Russian sector. This was before the Wall, you see. She had an old friend named Michael Kruger who lived close to us. He had been her teacher in high school, a literature teacher. He had been in the Great War and badly burned. The right side of his face was terribly scarred. But he was a wonderful, sweet man. I would stay with him after school, and when she was finished with work she would take the tram back to our neighborhood and pick me up at Michael's apartment. Miraculously, his building was intact despite the bombing. The first weeks and months with the Russians were horrible for women in Berlin. If you were a female, regardless of your age, the likelihood was that you would be raped, many times. Women stayed off the streets as much as they could, but it didn't help. My mother was never touched, thank God.

"Finally, it got a little better. But then many Russians began to desert, usually in twos and threes. They lived in abandon buildings and stole and scavenged. If the Russians caught them, in uniform or out, they were executed, often in the street and left to rot. The dogs ate them.

"Michael gave my mother a bayonet, finely honed. He said to her, 'Maria, if one of the Ivans comes after you or Vera, slit their throats. Don't be afraid to use it because they will rape and kill you and Vera'.

"My mother was a remarkably homely woman. Horse face, bad teeth, and very tall.

"My mother told Michael, 'I'm too ugly for the Ivans. They'll want something pretty.'

"Michael said, 'They'll want you and Vera. Kill them if you can or yourself and Vera if you can't'.

"You see, James, what you've gotten yourself into. A long, sad story."

"I'm listening."

"One night she had to work overtime and missed her tram. She had to walk to Michael's apartment. It was late when she got there, and he begged her to stay overnight. But my mother was more stubborn than ugly, and she refused. We were almost home when the two of them crawled out of a basement, their lair, you might say. Russian deserters, wild men.

"My mother whispered to me to run back to Michael's, get away now. I ran but I hid behind a pile of bricks across the street. They dragged her into their basement, and then it was silent. No one was on the street, no one to help. No screams, nothing. I assumed she was being raped and then she would be killed. But after a few minutes I saw her crawl out of the basement and walk in the direction of our apartment building. Her dress was torn, and she was bloody, but she seemed okay. She was holding the bayonet. I ran to her and held onto her legs. I was sobbing, as you can imagine.

"'Stop crying', she said, 'stop. Those drunken fools. They couldn't find their vodka; they wanted one more jolt of courage before they murdered me, I guess. They had dropped their pants and turned their backs to me. I did what Michael told me to do. They didn't rape me, and this is their blood. Vera, you must never, ever tell anyone about what happened tonight. Eventually, they will find those pigs, and cops will come around asking question. You must never tell anyone about this. Ever.'

"She wiped the handle clean and threw the bayonet into an unexcavated ruin.

"After my son died, I went to Berlin to see Michael Kruger. He was an old man, of course, but an amazing survivor. I brought him a bottle of schnapps. He loves schnapps as do most Berliners. He had moved to the American Zone and was living on his pension, getting by, nothing more. He never married. I assume he was a homosexual which was a capital offense under the Nazis.

"I told him about my son, and we had a good cry. The pain was overwhelming for me. There was nothing he could say.

"'By the way, Michael,' I said to him, 'do you remember those two Russians they found in the basement of a building down the street where we lived? My mother killed them.'"

"'Yes, of course, I knew that, and she did a proper job of slitting their throats, too. Everyone knew, Vera. She killed more of them, too. She was an angel of vengeance. That was so long ago. I am an old man. I have seen things too dreadful to remember. History has overwhelmed me in many ways, yet I survive. The past is too painful to dwell upon, and I have

186

no future. Soon I will disappear, un-mourned. So, Vera, I choose to live in my moment. I will smoke my pipe and drink a glass of your excellent schnapps. And that is enough. I choose to live this way. No past, no future. I was a teacher, and a good one, too. A grammarian. As a grammarian, I choose to live in the present tense. Only that.'

"He's dead now, of course. I mourn him after my fashion.

"So, now I have to meet my friend Louise, so we can gossip about our sons-in-laws and brag about our grandchildren. She is annoyed that I haven't joined her at the table behind us. It was nice to meet you boys, and I hope I haven't bored you with an old woman's chatter."

We wished her goodnight.

After she left, Scott turned to me. "That was a surprise," he says. "Do you believe it?"

"Not a word of it. None of it."

But we were no longer hungry, and we settled our bar tab. We drove back to my apartment complex without speaking with the windows down. It was a warm night in Houston, and I could feel the humidity building. Scott turned on the radio. Rain tomorrow, says the announcer.

At home, I lay in the dark in my own ruins trying to sleep. I want to believe that old woman's story about the valor of her mother and her rescue by Jack Duffy. I want to believe her about Michael Kruger. But I don't. I do want to live in the present tense. Maybe that would make me happy. But I don't like happy endings. As far as I can tell, I'm not meant to have one.

THE HEALING BEGINS

On Tuesday, February 5th, I begin my second meeting with Dr. Janowitz by asking him to tell me why my coping skills enabled me to function and fit into society before I met Cindy and her superiors. When I first enter, I sit in a chair facing him across his desk. His desk is empty except for a pile of papers turned face down. He is very careful about privacy and protecting his work product. I notice close to his right hand is a Bible, well used with yellow Post-It notes sticking out like budding leaves.

"How are you today?"

"I'm confused, Dr. Janowitz, mostly. Why did I seem to be doing better before I ever met those people?"

"When you started the process at Jedermann, you probably had unrealistic expectations of what was going to happen. When they failed, James, or you felt they failed, something was destroyed for you. We're going to try to be realistic about what can happen in this room. You'll start a regimen of medication that should help. We are just starting this process, but I would say your considerable intellectual capabilities and your coping skills will help you succeed."

He stood up and went to a circular table behind his desk. There were two chairs at the table, and a manila file; my file, I assume.

"James, why don't you join me over here? I don't like talking with a desk and a computer monitor between us."

He has been at this a long time I sense, and he seems to be a kind fellow. This may be a professional demeanor, developed over many years. Maybe he's sincere. He is unthreatening certainly. Short and round-faced, his office walls are filled with pictures of nature and natural scenes. But they seem generic, nothing much personal about them, as if they were from a decorator's catalogue. We sit in leather office chairs at the table, which is a light oak and a little dusty. I can see it is my name written on the file, the correct one this time. I have trouble making eye contact. I feel exposed. He is careful with me. He's on bomb disposal duty, in a dusty ruin, trying to figure out which wire to cut, the red the blue or the black. He knows that I am a threat. I have left all my weapons at home, and I feel like the sole POW of a lost cause. The cause is me, and I am the dusty ruins.

"The sooner you treat a serious psychiatric illness, the more likely it is that you will have a better, enduring result. The sooner you attack a disease, the better your long-term prognosis. Does that make sense?"

He is very direct. He is the first person — psychiatrist, psychologist, lawyer, friend, or enemy — to tell me that I have a serious psychiatric illness. That's the truth it seems, and everything else is bullshit.

"I think so."

"The first serious episode of psychosis or depression should be treated to remission with a great deal of attention and force. When you attack a first-time presentation or one of the first-time presentations of a major illness, you get a better chance for full recovery. In principle, it's quite simple."

"This is what is simple for me, Dr. Janowitz. I want those people punished for what they did to me."

"I realize that, James."

In a moment of psychotic clarity, I say, "Your job is to get me well enough to withstand a police interrogation. Nothing more. Nothing less."

In my mind, as soon as I get well enough to think clearly and plan the attacks, I am going to kill Cindy and Damian and as many of the others as I can for violating my trust. Verdict or no verdict, I could not let the poisoners survive.

Janowitz leans forward, listening intently. He makes no notes. My nerves, my soul, are on fire.

"I must avenge the wrongs that those people have done to me," I scream wildly.

Dr. Janowitz sits back; superficially, he is very calm.

"Well, what were those wrongs?"

"That stupid fucking bitch knew what she was doing! And I know what I'm doing!"

"Those are serious things, James."

"Because Cinderella Psychobitch became emotionally involved with me, and because her superiors protected her rather than punishing her for what she did, I have no choice but to kill them all!"

189

He says nothing, makes no notes. His silence is discomforting to me. He uses silence as effectively as conversation.

Frustrated, I tell Dr. Janowitz that he's only in this profession for the money. My tone is one of contempt. I am certain in my paranoia and rage that it is only money that motivates him.

"I'm not actually, but let's save that discussion for another day, James."

"I didn't mean that you're only in it for the money because you're Jewish. I hate those country club prejudices."

"I wouldn't know since I don't belong to a country club. I am Jewish, and my religion is very important to me. As we get to know each other better, you'll discover that. I don't think you'll mind. Judaism contains great wisdom and comfort to tormented souls. In the dark nights I have endured, it has sustained me."

The doctor acknowledges my anger and attempts to talk me back into reality, but my nerves and brain are so wired for rage, it is difficult for me to calm down. To help get my anger under control, Dr. Janowitz starts me on normal doses of Prozac and an anti-paranoia medicine.

"I'm going to start you on a relatively low dosage of Prozac, and we'll monitor how you're doing. Eventually, you'll probably need a higher dose due to the severity of your symptomatology. You should contact me immediately if you notice any adverse changes once you start taking the medicines."

He also prescribes Risperdal, an antipsychotic.

"It's important that you read about the possible side effects for these medications, James. Weight gain, change of eating habits, like being hungry or thirsty all the time, that kind of thing. Let me know about any side effects. They're powerful drugs, but they are very helpful."

Prior to ending the session, Dr. Janowitz goes to his samples cabinet and retrieves some Prozac samples, which he sets in front of me.

"I don't want those. I don't want your pity. I pay my own way. I will not accept this charity."

"I'm not going to force you, James, but this is sort of standard practice with me. Not pity, not charity. But if you prefer, I'll write a prescription. But you should take these samples of the Prozac. We need to get the process started right away."

I pay the doctor his fee in cash and I depart leaving the samples behind.

Once home, I try to calm down, but cannot. What had been semi-contained rage is now fully exposed. The low starter dose of Prozac doesn't seem to help. The anger consumes me until well into the night. Then the depression takes over and I sleep.

I repeat this pattern nightly. It is only by hiding in my office with my door nearly all the way closed that I can avoid confrontation in the workplace and thereby remain employed.

A TIME TO SOW

On Tuesday, February 19, I begin my third meeting with Dr. Janowitz by exploding with rage toward Cindy, her superiors, and Damian. Even though Dr. Janowitz speaks to me in calm, even tones, I cannot calm down. My nerves are perpetually exploding. The rage blinds me.

Dr. Janowitz attempts to assuage my intense anger by planting a seed in my mind, but I won't have it.

"James, I think under all this torment there is a really nice man waiting to be discovered."

"You're full of it. If anyone is crazy, it's you."

My anger and self-hatred for what I've become pour out. I am out of control. The drugs are not touching the deep wells of my rage.

Dr. Janowitz moves the conversation to get me away from Cindy and those monsters.

"What about your job? You're a full-time employee now, no longer a temporary, correct?"

"Yes."

"And you're no longer on the factory floor, correct?"

"Yes, but my job is boring. All I do is follow a cookie-cutter recipe."

I describe how I remain in my office the whole day with my door practically shut.

"I want to quit. I can find a job anywhere."

Alarmed, Dr. Janowitz raises his voice to match my volume level.

"It's important that you remain employed. The economy is bad now and you need the experience. Is the Prozac helping?" he asks.

"No. It's worthless."

Dr. Janowitz increases the dosage and again offers samples;

however, I vociferously refuse his kind gesture. Throughout this and every therapy session, I closely watch Dr. Janowitz for signs of inconsistency. Dr. Janowitz says I'm hyper-vigilant. All I know is that if I ever see even the slightest inconsistency in behavior like what I saw with Cindy, I'll quit immediately.

The next months pass in a blur. I continue my pattern of flying off the handle, shouting obscenities, the rage and anger pouring out of me. Dr. Janowitz remains steady in his attempt to nurture the seed he has planted; however, I still won't hear of it. Because of my intense self-hatred for what I've become, I grow a full beard and I don't bother to groom it. Underneath the beard are pimples that I pick at. I feel hideous. But the uglier I look, the more comfortable I feel. I can't stand the sight of myself in a mirror. My beard is my disguise and distortion. I gain weight and none of my clothes fit anymore. The medication has affected my appetite, and I can't seem to get enough to eat. I look like a caricature of myself. I was never thin, but I was fit, a second-degree black belt in karate. No Bruce Lee, oiled up and ready to roll, but strong and flexible. My depression and rage are undiminished. I seem to be making no progress.

"I want to quit my job. My boss, Christian is making my life a nightmare. He's building a case against me. Lies and distortions about how I'm performing."

Despite my strong desire to quit my job, I follow Dr. Janowitz's advice and remain employed.

"James, it's really important that you don't quit your job. It's your connection to reality and a real lifeline. Isn't your annual performance review coming up? Maybe you can clear the air. We will monitor this very carefully. You always have recourse to HR if this guy is really that bad. That's part of what they do."

"You don't believe me when I talk about what a prick he is?"

"Of course, I do. But you are scrupulous about details and you need to keep a precise record of what transpires. Here is where your great skill with details will come in handy. If you complain to HR it has to go beyond a simple angry or anxious complaint. You need facts."

"Do you think I should shave off my beard for the review?"

He smiles at me and laughs, "James, I tried growing a beard many years ago, and I was a dismal failure. If you want to keep the beard, keep it. If you want to shave it, shave it."

"Do I look like an Old Testament prophet?"

"No."

"Do I look like a hillbilly from the Deep Woods?"

"No. You look like a nice fellow who has something to hide."

"I wonder what that is?"

"I think, as I've told you earlier, it is an intelligent, kind and useful human being you're hiding. He's been through a lot, too much. James, it's okay to come out from the shadows."

I'm not ready for the sunlight, not just yet.

CHRISTIAN PLACES THE NOOSE
AROUND MY NECK

My fiscal third quarter performance review is scheduled for Friday, June 20, I learn from my director, Patricia Wallace. We are all very worried about the next shoe dropping after our struggling company was acquired by a much larger and more successful one. This is the food chain in the tech business, the computer business, the strong consume the weak. We all assume that after the two workforces are combined and redundancies are eliminated, a lot of us will be out of a job. I'm taking Janowitz's advice seriously, and I'm going to do everything I can to keep mine. One problem is my direct supervisor, Christian Battaglia, who despises me. I completely reciprocate the emotion, but he has all the leverage and I have none.

He is a tiny man, about the size of a jockey, with a chubby Italian wife and four chubby children. He seems to be a devoted husband and father. He is active in the Catholic Church, and one of the pictures on his desk is him accepting an award from the archbishop of the Houston Diocese, some cardinal or other. I don't keep track. He likes to listen to Frank Sinatra in his car driving home. I know that because he gave me a ride to the garage where my car was being serviced at the end of the day. He had Sinatra cassette playing on the car's sound system. He drove a very family friendly SUV.

"Do you like Sinatra, Jim? This is *My Way*."

"Your way to where?" I was going to play with this moron for a bit.

"No, the song. It's his signature song."

"Oh, yeah. What's not to like?"

"You know what they used to say about him when he was a kid? That he was 119 pounds and nineteen pounds was between his legs. I think it's an Italian thing."

At around 1:45 PM on Thursday, June 12, Christian's manager, my director, Patricia Wallace, stops by my office and tells me that she received my request for a one-on-one meeting and that her secretary will be scheduling our meeting for some time tomorrow. She is wolf-like in her appearance, thin with a rapacious eye. Her dark hair is always pulled back and fixed with a platoon of barrettes. She is quite fit and at lunchtime goes to her gym around the corner. She comes back looking thoroughly exercised, with her face flushed and a dew of perspiration on her skin. She wears no makeup and seems to survive on celery sticks and black coffee. A fully-fledged careerist.

"I'm having a really hectic week with the merger, so if you could be flexible it would really help."

"Of course," I say. Patricia is a straight shooter, and she had helped me in the past.

On Friday morning, I arrive at Patricia's office at the anointed 10:00 AM start time.

"Come on in, Jim," Patricia says warmly. "What can I do for you today? I hope it's nothing serious. A lot of crazy things are going on around here."

"I'm concerned about my relationship with Christian. He seems to have it in for me. I know he keeps a file on every memo or email that I write that he has been cc'd on. I have no idea what is going on."

"I can't really talk about this without telling Christian about this conversation, Jim. He is your boss, after all."

"I'm not trying to make trouble."

"Jim, a lot of things will change around here very soon. None of us may be around after the dust settles, including me. My advice is to have the performance review, get his comments, and then we can talk about it. It may be a moot point anyway."

Before this meeting, I had very high hopes that something good would come out of it; however, deep in my gut I feel doubt.

"After all," I tell myself under my breath, "Patricia has protected Christian thus far. Why would she change now?" The answer is she wouldn't.

I decide to call Dr. Janowitz to discuss my reaction to the meeting. Leti answers my call, puts me on hold for several minutes, and then Dr. Janowitz comes on line.

"How did your meeting go?" the doctor asks curiously.

"I want to believe that it went well; however, I'm not sure anything will change."

"Why is that?"

"Well," I say with a pause, "Thus far Patricia has been so focused on getting herself promoted that she's largely ignored the people management issues under her. For example, she's allowed her managers to make all the hiring decisions with very little oversight. She just doesn't seem to care."

"Oh, that's not good," Dr. Janowitz says.

"Yeah, I know," I add.

"What did Patricia say would happen next?"

"She said she would discuss my concerns directly with Christian this afternoon. Until then, I guess I wait."

"Well," Dr. Janowitz says as he searches for a positive spin, "At least now you've gone on record with your concerns. Let's wait and see what happens next."

"I'm going to get completely screwed by this guy. He's going to do it his way. Him and his twenty pounds of penis."

"I'm not sure what in the world that means."

"It's a private company joke. Okay, thank you Dr. Janowitz," I say as we hang up.

I spend the rest of the day Friday and all night mentally reviewing my meeting with Patricia, grasping for hope that she will effect change but knowing that the odds are against it.

At work the next week, Christian is particularly negative toward me. He barely acknowledges me on the way to the break room. "Big storm coming," I think to myself. Better find a life raft.

At my third quarter performance review, Christian again tells me that I need to find a new job. This is not an encouraging way to begin my review.

"James, your future is not with this company. It's pretty obvious that a lot of people are not going to make the cut after the merger. Time to go, I think."

This time rather than taking this abuse, I respond, "Really? I'll tell you one thing Christian, you need to stop sabotaging my internal job search by telling fellow managers what a terrible employee I am. That is unfair, incorrect, and unethical."

"All I'm doing is reciting facts," Christian says, half smirking. Rather than losing my cool, I decide to not say anything further.

As he always does, Christian takes out a manila folder that has my name on, sets it on his desk, opens it, and begins by first reviewing his Post-It notes and then, when he's finished with those notes, he reviews the e-mail messages on which he was copied regarding my accounts. He questions me about each issue. If the issue is closed to his satisfaction, Christian throws the note or e-mail away; however, if it is not closed to his satisfaction, the note or e-mail remains in the folder to be reviewed at a subsequent date. Very few things are finished to his satisfaction. He has distorted and lied about my work product. I am astonished at the thoroughness of the hatchet job he performed. Based on the blizzard of untruths reported as truth, I'd fire myself at once.

When there are no more notes or e-mails to discuss, Christian looks at me and asks, "So, do you have anything for me?"

Furious, I answer, "No," and that ends my mid-year performance review with Christian.

Once back in my office, my heart sinks as I realize that nothing is going to change despite anything that Patricia may say to him. Prudently, in a mood as dark as the night sky, I spend the rest of the work day re-writing my resume.

At my next therapy session on Tuesday, June 24, I tell Dr. Janowitz that it's pretty clear I'm going to be terminated.

"Whatever Patricia may have said to Christian doesn't appear to have had an impact. We're all on a sinking ship, and it's every man for himself or woman for herself. Glug, glug."

"Are you sure?" Dr. Janowitz asks.

"As best I can tell," I answer. "Should I go complain to Human Resources?"

"At this point, if you do, the company will definitely get rid of you," the doctor responds. "Once you're viewed as a complainer, no matter how legitimate your complaints, no other manager will want you working for him because of the fear that you may complain to HR about him. Going to Human Resources is a last resort."

"Understood," I acknowledge. "So, what should I do?"

"You should continue documenting Christian's behavior every day. Send yourself a confidential email, that way it will be time-stamped. And if you can tape record his statements, so much the better as those recordings will be irrefutable evidence."

"Okay," I say. "I'll do that. I have my mini-cassette tape recorder."

"Be careful and don't violate any company policy."

"Our fiscal year ends on September 30th, so in mid-October Christian will be giving us our final 2008 performance reviews."

"How do you think you'll do?"

"I'll be really lucky if I receive an 'S' for satisfactory," I answer in a resigned voice. "I know I won't receive an 'E' for exemplary. And the only other choice will be an 'I' for incomplete, incompetent, inferior, improvement needed, and so forth."

"What happens if Christian rates you an 'I'?"

"Anyone rated an 'I' automatically goes on probation for six months. If at the end of those six months the manager still feels that you're an 'I', you get fired."

"Oh, that's not good," the doctor says, stating the obvious.

"The third quarter is over now, so it'll be what it'll be," I say softly.

"You have to stick to the plan for the next few months. You simply have to do everything with your typical attention to detail. You know what this guy is like, so you need to anticipate what he'll not expect in the next few months. You have some time, at least."

For the rest of June, July, and August I follow my plan scrupulously. I'm aware of how deeply Christian dislikes me and how much he wants to see me fired. Accepting the fact that he is a sleazy little shit, a member of his personal Rat Pack sans the Pack, I set out to erect defenses against his ill will and lies. I keep a daily record of our interactions on my computer, writing memos to myself, memorializing his demands and attitude. I am pleasant to him, although he makes my skin crawl. I feel utterly hypocritical, but I'm not going to be his victim. As one familiar with anger, I anticipate his. I'm attentive and agreeable: mystify, mislead and confuse. That is my indirect approach to defeating Christian. I'm unsure whether or not it will work, probably not, but the old frontal assault didn't work either. Mystify, mislead and confuse. And defeat.

I'VE GOT HIM UNDER MY SKIN

On Wednesday, October 22, I receive my final fiscal year 2008 performance review. I know it cannot be good. In this regard, Christian does not disappoint. I receive an 'I' (improvement needed) rating. Christian is only too happy to inform me that I'll be on probation for the next six months, at any time during which he can terminate me if my performance does not improve.

"James," Christian says with an evil grin, "I'll just remind you that I'm the boss, and that it's my way or the highway in this organization."

Because I anticipated this result, I remain silent. He's doing it his way, all right.

When he has finished, Christian hands me a hard copy and asks if I have any questions. "No, I think your points are clear," I respond, after which the meeting ends.

Once in my office, I carefully read my review. Noticing that virtually all of my major accomplishments are missing, I print out the three-page accomplishments document that I sent to Christian as my inputs to my review. I then compare the two side by side. Within seconds it becomes undeniably obvious that Christian is deliberately trying to fire me. Whereas I received a $350 monetary award from my vice president for traveling to Asia upon very short notice in August to resolve a supply crisis, Christian barely made mention of this. Instead, Christian listed my primary accomplishment for the year as having updated all non-disclosure agreements with my suppliers. Whereas I solely negotiated a four percent cost reduction on one of my highest volume products, a cost reduction for which I received a congratulatory e-mail from my director, Patricia Wallace, Christian listed my second accomplishment as having uploaded all of my contracts into the online repository tool. Wherever I had a major accomplishment, Christian either downplayed it or trivialized it in favor of insignificance.

Enraged by the lies and distortions in front of me, I remain in my office for the rest of the day with my door closed. In order to funnel my growing hostility in a positive direction, I begin composing a rebuttal letter to Christian's review. I make this rebuttal letter my priority and work on it every day for the rest of the week and into the following week. Rereading it, I think it is complete, accurate, and filled with contempt for Christian and his management style. He is a one-man Rat Pack.

On Tuesday, November 4th, I discuss Christian's review and my rebuttal letter with Dr. Janowitz. I am highly emotional during this therapy session and Dr. Janowitz spends as much time calming me down as he does discussing the documents.

"When is the deadline for submitting your comments?" the doctor asks referring to the section of the performance review where the employee can upload comments.

"Friday, November 21st."

"Well, then, we have some time," Dr. Janowitz says confidently, noting that he and I will have one more regularly scheduled therapy session prior to then. Dr. Janowitz and I discuss the rebuttal letter for the next twenty or so minutes. I feel better after this discussion.

At my next therapy session, I arrive with the letter in my jacket pocket.

"Have you finished your rebuttal letter?" Dr. Janowitz asks as we sit down. He is anxious to deal with my work situation, too, it seems.

"Yes," I respond. "I took your advice and enhanced the letter like you said I should. Here it is," I say as I hand over the document.

The doctor takes his time and carefully reads paragraph by paragraph. Every now and again he stops and makes a comment, but otherwise he stays focused until he has read the entire letter.

"I think if you choose to, you could make a very strong case with Human Resources against Christian," Dr. Janowitz says confidently.

"But I thought you said going to HR was a last resort?"

"It is a last resort, one that we shouldn't have to exercise. Based upon this letter, I'm confident that Christian's manager will recognize the seriousness of your allegations and take action to avoid having her department embroiled in a HR inquiry."

"Are you're sure?"

"If Patricia is seriously seeking a promotion to VP, she won't want this on her record."

"So, you're sure?" I ask again.

"Yes, I'm sure," the doctor answers. "But you can't do anything stupid or you will get yourself fired."

"Understood," I acknowledge.

"What happens after you submit your letter?" Dr. Janowitz asks, probably already knowing the answer.

"Nothing," I respond. "The letter goes in my file and it doesn't change anything. For all I know, it may never even get read."

"Then what happens?" the doctor asks again.

"Once the appeal process closes on November 21st, Christian will provide me with a corrective action plan, each element of which I will need to satisfy else Christian will have liberty to fire me."

"When do we meet next?" the doctor asks.

"In two weeks, on December 2nd," I advise.

"Will you have the corrective action plan by then?"

"I suspect I will."

"Very well, let's see what that entails then."

I have a moment of blind, psychotic anger at Christian and Cindy. Obscenities flow from me with volcanic intensity. I am wild with rage. Janowitz, who I thought was inured to my anger, seems seriously alarmed. He knows anger from rage, and I am at the upper level. He says nothing and waits for the storm to abate.

"Those motherfuckers are killing me, piece by piece. I can't take it anymore. I want to die. I want to kill them and I want to die."

At last, exhausted by my outburst, I look at him and say, "I'm sorry, Dr. Janowitz."

"Yes, it is troubling dealing with these people. You are still in great pain, James."

"I don't want to be in pain. I want it to end."

"We have more work to do."

My firing, should it happen, will probably come as a relief. Relief is what I'm after. I feel, momentarily, in the aftermath of my outburst that I have to be willing, as willing as I have never been before, to contemplate the impenetrable sadness of a human heart, my own.

HOW DO YOU SAY "TRUST" IN HEBREW?

On Tuesday, January 13, 2009, I arrive early for my therapy appointment. Possibly because I had a really bad night last night, I am feeling particularly distrustful this evening. I've been having a really difficult time at work. My boss, Christian, is perpetually giving me a hard time. He's been trying hard to get me fired, but I'm doing everything I need to do according to the corrective action plan, so he cannot fire me, at least not yet. Apparently, as a result of my letter he had a meeting with HR which did not go well for him. He is like a junkyard dog, growling at me from the other side of the fence. One of us has to go.

Dr. Janowitz begins the therapy session, "How are you doing today, James?"

"How am I doing," I say leaning forward in my chair, "how can I be doing anything other than awful when I have to deal with fucking liars and assassins? These bastards are butchers and thieves."

"There will be a day of reckoning. I'm confident you'll find some sort of justice."

I ignore his attempt to talk me back into the moment.

"That stupid fucking bitch, Cindy, knew what she was doing!" I shout. "And the Director protected her, and my lawyer wouldn't prosecute her. And that son of a bitch Christian with his smarmy Sinatra songs is trying to bankrupt me!"

At the top of my voice, I yell at the doctor that I have no choice but to kill them all for violating my trust, "I will kill them all!"

Dr. Janowitz sits back in his chair, looks me over carefully, and calmly begins talking me down from my nearly hysterical rage. After about twenty minutes of dialogue, I have calmed down enough to allow the depression to begin to take over. It creeps in like a cat.

"Why is it that Cinderella Psychobitch can pursue her dream of working in psychology even though she and Monteblanc destroyed any chance I would've had to pursue my dream of working for the CIA?"

I demand an answer that I can accept.

"I don't know, James, maybe it wasn't their intention to do that."

"If they couldn't help me, they should've turned me away. Instead they chose to hurt me. It's not right!" I am sounding like a petulant child, but the answer was important, even critical, to me.

"When I started therapy with Cindy, my depression and paranoia were relatively mild. I had some level of self-confidence and self-esteem. Perhaps they were low, but I had them. But then the therapy progressed from the initial stages where I actually needed help to the friendly, the faux friendly stages with Cindy. She also did this weird transference thing. She told me many times how much I reminded her of her father in California. He was a chemical engineer, very precise, very organized, and brilliant. I think his name was Bill. I don't know what his business was, but he invented a super glue and was very successful. Does that happen often, Doctor?"

"It's called countertransference, and it's rare that a therapist would engage that way with a patient. It most often happens the other way around with the patient transferring feelings for a spouse or parent onto the therapist. But it happens. Cindy seems to have been a curious kind of therapist."

"I felt she was trying to seduce me. Make me her boyfriend, and I found that very confusing."

"I'm sure you did."

"That was really the beginning of the manipulation. When Monteblanc stopped supervising her and was replaced by Becky Howell, I felt like new rules were being imposed and boundaries established that had not existed."

"Like what?"

"I just had to act in a certain way. Becky was like a boxing referee. I also felt that Cindy was trying to manipulate me back to our earlier, friendlier state. But by then my paranoia and distrust of all them had bloomed, like flowers in a hothouse. Yet I couldn't quit therapy until the incident. I was caught up in the manipulation and I was severely confused."

"Maybe you misinterpreted some of that."

"That's what Monteblanc said, too. But I was there to get help for my issues and I got none. I was only made less healthy and more vulnerable. I felt Cindy had her own agenda, and the transference of her father onto me was part of it. She tried to shape me into what she wanted me to be — a potential boyfriend."

"I thought she was engaged."

"I don't know what her status was. But I saw proof of her wanting to seduce me into loving her when I saw her hiding her 'engagement' ring in her hand, shielding the diamond from my view with her pinky finger."

"And as a result, you lost your coping mechanisms, most typically projection and introjection. The first basically is projecting your perceived faults onto someone else, and introjection is the opposite, projecting someone else's faults onto yourself. Both are powerful and common defensive mechanisms. It seems they had been displaced for you."

"Transference, countertransference, projection, introjection — they are all synonyms for misery as far as I am concerned. I'm not sure if I understand you completely, but where once I was able to cope with my life — imperfectly, I know, but I still functioned — after Cindy's intervention, I was a lost soul. By the time I filed the lawsuit...."

"And just before Tran sent you to me," Janowitz adds.

"Yes. At that point of filing the lawsuit, my depression and paranoia were at an extreme. I had no self-confidence left nor any self-esteem. I was easily manipulated and suffering from psychosis. I was ready to die."

"What I realize now is that at a certain point Cindy realized that I had figured out her little game with me. All that phony friendliness, that faux flirtatiousness was just a ploy. She is an intelligent woman and a beautiful woman, too. Women like that can lie and be believed. And be held blameless. On the night of the incident, I asked to see my file. I have a right to see it. I know that. But that was the irritant she knew would provoke me. I'm sure she could sense my anger, even though I tried to tamp it down. I was in a weakened state. What should have been a helpful, supportive process turned out to be just the opposite. That was her finding a way to diminish and control me. I made a huge mistake: I told her about LT and how much it meant to me. All that bullshit about how much she admired me because I reminded her of her old man was another shiny object like her Rolex watch and her diamond ring to distract me. It was another strand in the web she was weaving. I get that now. As I held the file, she demanded, with a lot of profanity, that I return it to her immediately. And if I did not, at that moment, she would call the cops and destroy me. That I was going to be taken out of the building in handcuffs. That this moment would appear in my file and damn me. Ruin me. And it did."

Janowitz studies my face. It is very quiet in his office. I can hear the phone ringing at the receptionist's desk down the hall. I take comfort in the silence.

"Her face was contorted into a mask of hatred and rage. When I rushed out of the building, I knew she had won. I was confused and frightened, I suppose. But I am not going to let her beat me. Every dog will have its day, and I know in every fiber of my being, I will have mine. What's the line from that old poem, 'my head is bloody but unbowed?'"

"'Under the bludgeonings of chance….' That's from *Invictus*, a poem that every British schoolboy once committed to memory. Not an inapposite poem for you tonight, James."

"I'll look it up. I sure as shit have been bludgeoned." The quiet settles down on us again.

"And here we are," he says at last. "And how are you sleeping, James?"

"I had a 9-mm night last night," I respond, explaining that I held my loaded, cocked handgun to my head because I was feeling down.

"Oh, that's not good," Dr. Janowitz says, as he begins asking more questions to understand why I felt suicidal again.

I don't have any real answers for him. It is just what I feel. A weariness with life and a willingness to end it.

He talks about righteousness. *Tsedakah*, he said, is the word in Hebrew. He has never been overtly religious in our sessions. I am no longer religious at all, but I like the notion of righteousness. Tonight, because of my distress, he reads me something from Psalm 91 about finding the protection of the "Almighty."

"*You will not fear the terror of the night, nor the arrow that flies by day, nor the pestilence that stalks in the darkness, nor the plague that destroys at midday. A thousand may fall at your side, ten thousand at your right hand, but it will not come near you. You will only observe with your eyes and see the punishment of the wicked.*"

"I want to see the punishment of the wicked, that's a fact."

"But it's not up to you to punish the wicked. You have to trust in something other than your anger and your handgun. You will be vindicated."

"I hope so."

"How was your Christmas, James?" I think Dr. Janowitz is trying to walk me away from my anger.

"It was okay. My parents wanted me to come back to Ohio and spend it with the family, but I stayed here. I spent Christmas Eve and Day with Scott and Kelly and the kids. Kelly made a turkey with all the trimmings, and I got to help the kids put together their toys."

"Were you able to speak to your parents, at least?"

"Yes, we had a short phone call on Christmas Day. It's the best one we've had in a long time, since I moved to Houston, for sure. How was Paris?"

"Paris during the holidays is glorious. It really is the City of Lights then, very festive. The food is unbelievably wonderful. I practically had to drag my wife to the airport. The only bad part was that it rained almost every day, and I really felt the damp in my bones."

"I'd like to go there again someday, when things settle down for me."

"You should. Are you taking your medicine, by the way?"

"Yes."

I'm, suddenly, feeling very tired. I want the session to be finished.

"Why did you feel down last night?"

"I don't know. I get angry sometimes and then the depression takes over and I feel really down. Last night, I just felt down. I get that way sometimes."

"How often do you get that way, Jim?"

"Probably once a month."

"Well, we obviously still have more work to do," Dr. Janowitz says, as he writes notes in his folder.

"Can I see my file?" I ask.

Dr. Janowitz pauses, thinks for several seconds, "Why do you want to see it?"

"I want to see what you're writing."

Dr. Janowitz answers that he's taking dynamic notes of what we're discussing.

"What are dynamic notes?"

"Notes in the moment. I try to catch the ebbs and flows of what is going on in your mind and what is coming out of your mouth. And mine, too, frankly. It's kind of a map, a tool to help me keep track of a patient's progress or lack of progress."

"Can I see my file, please?" I ask, slightly more forcefully.

Dr. Janowitz again pauses for several seconds as he gauges my intention and thinks about what to do next, then with a truly pained expression on his face, hands me his notes. I look carefully at them; however, I cannot read them. They are as mysterious to me as Sumerian.

"What are these?"

I'm staring at shorthand notations with Hebrew characters mixed with some English letters.

"I can't read these," I say aloud, as I flip through the pages.

"To protect the confidentiality of what we discuss," Dr. Janowitz says calmly, "I use my own system of abbreviations, symbols, and characters. No one but I can understand what's there. Sometimes, frankly, even I can't understand them."

"It's a mystery to me," is all I can say as I hand the file back to him.

With relief on his face, Dr. Janowitz attempts to introduce the concept of group psychotherapy, but I won't hear of it. Dr. Janowitz says that I could benefit immensely by working through some of my issues in a therapy group.

"I don't want to be around a bunch of crazy people!"

"James, I'll tell you again, I think you're a really good guy underneath all these issues."

But this just makes me visibly angry, so he backs down immediately.

Dr. Janowitz ends this session by asking if I need any medicines. When I answer affirmatively, Dr. Janowitz once again offers samples; however, I again adamantly refuse his kind gesture and insist that he write prescriptions. I am a difficult person.

I pay Dr. Janowitz his fee in cash to blind the outside world to my transactions and depart for home.

CHAOS THEORY WORKS

On Wednesday morning at work I cannot concentrate. My brain refuses to block the fire within that I feel toward Cindy, her superiors, and Damian. Rather than risk exploding at my co-workers, I stay in my office with my door nearly all the way shut the whole day and try to remain calm.

Thursday is no different.

On Friday morning, Ruth Wilson, a woman from HR, who has always tried to be friendly and concerned about me, stops by and asks if everything is okay. I feel she is a genuinely nice person.

"Yes, Ruthie," I respond. "Everything is okay. I'm just feeling a bit stressed this week."

"Well, you really need to get out of your office and interact with the team," Ruth advises. "People want to see your smiling face. It would be good for you, too."

It occurs to me that this visit is not an accident. People have been noticing my attitude and my closed door, I suppose. But I don't think Christian sent her.

"You're right. I'll do that, although I don't think I've been smiling much lately. That reminds me, where's my old pal Christian? He usually crawls out from beneath his rock and gives me a hard time about now. I haven't seen him yet today."

"You haven't heard? No, of course, you wouldn't with your door closed. There is a general email going out later. Christian has left the building. He was fired last night."

"Fired! You're kidding. Why in the world was he fired?"

"He was caught with a girl from the Copy Office doing the nasty on a Xerox machine. Do you know Tracy?"

"I don't think I know a Tracy. But people come and go in that

209

office all the time. It's hard to keep track of them."

"He kept track of her."

"That son of a gun. Got caught with his pants around his ankles. Who says that God doesn't have a sense of humor."

"I know our new VP, Patricia, doesn't have one. She's the one who caught him."

"Thanks for the info. I'm happy to get some good news."

Ruth and I leave my office, and I see Mary Lou, my Procurement Specialist and Business Lead, coming down the hall toward me.

"Good morning, Mary Lou," I say. She is remarkably thin. Her skin is like porcelain, and you can see the blue veins around her temples. She is strikingly beautiful but seems to be unaware of it. I have had a secret crush on her for as long as she has been my lead. But she is married and is preoccupied by caring for an autistic son. She seems to be preoccupied today.

"Good morning, Little Jimmy."

"Hey, Mary Lou. Ruthie just told me about Christian."

"Yeah, isn't that something? But he was riding for a fall, that arrogant little shit. Sometimes, things work out."

"Have you seen Big Jim this morning?" Mary Lou asks, referring to our Director, James Aird. There's another Jim in our office, a large man, and to distinguish us Mary Lou has designated us as Jimmy Big and Jimmy Little. Jimmy Aird, as far as I can tell, is a good guy and knows his stuff. He is not a head case like Christian.

"No, not yet. Is he looking for me?"

"Yes," Mary Lou answers as she passes me. "He wants to know when your electronics module supplier will be qualified."

"They're qualified. Just found out this morning. I'll go see him now."

Before approaching Big Jim, I quickly step back into my office and grab my supplier qualification binder notebook, then walk down the hall and around the corner to his office. "Knock, knock," I say, as I approach Director James Aird's open door, my apprehension camouflaged by my calm outward appearance.

"Come on in, Jim. What can I do for you?"

"Mary Lou said you wanted an update on my supplier qualification progress for the electronics module, so here I am."

After I review and explain my progress, Big Jim asks if I'd be interested in becoming a Procurement Specialist like Mary Lou.

"Yes, I'd like that a lot." I respond. It would be a promotion and out of the manufacturing area I have been in, and more into the business side.

"Well," James says, "I have an opening coming up and I think you'd be a good fit. We'll put you through the interview process starting around the middle of next week."

"Thanks." I'm surprised by this offer, and pleased, too. But the possibility of promotion and success makes me anxious, too. I am caught in the sweaty grip of a panic attack.

When I return to my office, I file the binder notebook, then stare at the e-mail messages on my computer screen. Almost instantaneously, the agitation in my stomach intensifies, the nuclear reaction starting all over again. I cannot escape it. I rush to the men's room and kneel in front of the toilet. I want to be sick, but I just dry heave. I wash my hands and face before I leave. In the mirror, I look awful, ashen-faced and angry at the same time. I can't stand the way I look. The knot in my stomach tightens. Rather than risk confrontation, I remain in my office the rest of the day. However, to accommodate Ruth, I leave my door all the way open and say hello to my co-workers as they pass by. With Christian gone, I'm no longer on thin ice. Christian, tiny little Christian, would have loved to have fired me. I could not have afforded that. But now he's home in his underwear watching *The Price Is Right*, not me.

But over the weekend my anger toward my old enemies, Cindy, Monteblanc, and Damian intensifies. I recognize that I cannot go through job interviews and expect success with this level of uncontrolled rage roiling within me, so on Monday morning I call Leti and request an unscheduled appointment with Dr. Janowitz. Leti tells me to come in at 6:00 PM.

I arrive early for my appointment and pace in the waiting room. At about 6:20 PM, Dr. Janowitz finishes with his last scheduled patient and is ready to see me.

"How are you doing tonight?" he asks as we walk down the hall toward his office.

"Christian got fired."

"Well, amazing. That's good, right?"

"That's one problem down and many more to go. He was caught having sex on a copy machine."

Janowitz just shook his head, "That makes sense somehow."

"Yeah. That's amore in the office. The moon hits you right in the eye."

Once in Dr. Janowitz's office, I explode. "Why is it that Cindy can continue working in her chosen profession of psychology, but she can destroy me and my dreams? Why is it that Monteblanc can get away with falsification and murder, all in the name of covering up his own incompetence?"

Sitting on the edge of my chair, I yell that I have no choice. "I need to kill those people for violating my trust! That's the only way I can become whole again!"

"Becoming whole again is something new, James. It's all good but certainly there are better ways to become whole. You must change your life, James. The great energy of your anger has to be channeled in a new way."

Dr. Janowitz listens intently as the rage flows out of me, then as before calmly begins talking me back down into reality. After about twenty-five minutes of dialogue, I have almost calmed down enough talk rationally; however, the fire still circulates within me.

"Are you getting any exercise, James?"

"No."

"What about going back to karate?"

"I'm afraid I'll tear a hamstring again, plus my knee isn't great."

"You have a bicycle. What about joining a touring club?"

"I'm not a good enough rider. I'm terribly out of shape. I could ride by myself, I guess until I lost some weight and got my wind back."

"Think about it. How are things at work?"

"I feel like I hit the Daily Double. Christian was terminated because he porked one of the girls in the Copy Office. Couldn't keep his big Italian sausage in his pants. He was walked out of the building by security with his personal belongings in a cardboard box."

"Well, well. Another Christian fed to the proverbial lions. But you said Daily Double, what was the second thing?"

I tell him about the opportunity with Big Jim.

"Wonderful. How do you feel about becoming a Business Lead, Jim?"

"It's a desk job!" I say loudly. "It offers nowhere near the excitement and risk of being a covert operative for the CIA. It offers nowhere near the thrill of recruiting and running spies in hostile territory. I mean, how exciting is it to say that I received a two percent cost reduction on my products. Big fucking deal!"

"James, this is a good thing," says Dr. Janowitz. "You won't be following a cookie-cutter recipe any more, will you?"

"No."

"And you won't be a supplier quality engineer any more, will you?"

"No."

"And you'll have more opportunities for advancement, won't you?"

"Yes."

"So, I don't see this as a bad thing. It will be an opportunity for you for professional development."

"It's not the same," I respond dejectedly.

Dr. Janowitz talks about the positive aspects of my opportunity for another fifteen minutes. He reinforces the fact that I need this job, that I need to advance and overcome, and that I need to remain calm. To help me stay focused, Dr. Janowitz suggests that I try breathing exercises and meditation.

"One, two, three. Deep breaths, James. Maybe you should try yoga."

"I'm not a Downward-Facing Dog kind of guy, I don't think."

"It's done wonders for some of my patients. Something to think about." He then ends the therapy session.

Once again, I pay Dr. Janowitz his fee in cash, cash is king and untraceable, and depart for home feeling better for having had the session, but still frustrated and angry.

LETTING GO

The next seven months pass quickly. At work I immerse myself in training and learning the skills needed to become an effective procurement specialist. Because work is very, very busy, it is as much an escape from my private hell as it is a job. After work I go home and torment myself about what might have been. On weekends I go out with Scott on Friday nights and then babysit for Kelly and Scott on Saturday nights. When I visit Dr. Janowitz, I always explode emotionally. I can't help but wonder why he continues working with me. I certainly wouldn't work with me. My soul wonders, "What does he see that I don't see?"

It's Tuesday, August 18, 2009, and I arrive at Dr. Janowitz's office early for my 5:30 PM appointment. Leti informs me that the doctor is running late again, so I take a seat in the waiting room.

At around quarter past six, Dr. Janowitz shows his last patient out and simultaneously signals for me to enter his office. The doctor is particularly cheerful this evening, and that annoys me as I'm feeling somewhat down.

"How are we doing tonight?" Dr. Janowitz asks, breaking the uneasy silence between us.

"Do you really care, Doctor Janowitz?"

"Yes, in fact, I really do."

As has happened in every prior therapy session, my emotions take over and I hemorrhage about Cindy, her superiors, and Damian. Dr. Janowitz listens for a while, then talks me back down into reality; however, today Dr. Janowitz's talk is different. He wants me to pause in my rant and think about the progress I've made. I don't feel like I'm healing, however.

"But I don't seem to be getting better."

"Better, as you term it, is not a final destination. Your symptoms are less intense, less lacerating. Don't you think you're a different person than the man that plunked his satchel down on my desk and pulled out a loaded gun and asked me why you should not kill us both?"

"It was a briefcase, not a satchel, but I suppose I am. I don't want to be crazy."

"You're here. You haven't run away, and I would say that is better."

He makes some notes furiously in that odd, unreadable, untranslatable Janowitzian script. He looks up from his notes and smiles. He takes off his glasses and rubs his eyes, looking tired. He seems younger when he smiles. I realize I have no idea how old he is. Older than I think he is.

"James, do you know why therapy has been successful for you?"

"No, I really have no idea."

"It's simple. Therapy has been successful for you thus far because you have been in control."

"I'm not in control of anything."

"Of course, you are. Do you remember at the beginning when you said that if you were paying for an hour of therapy, you wanted an hour even if we talked about the weather?"

"Yes."

"Well, you received your hour because you were in control. Control, or more specifically, your need to control, is one of your major issues."

Dr. Janowitz pauses before continuing. "And that's something that we definitely need to work on."

"I see. Maybe." But a light goes off inside my head. "But I've always believed that when I relinquish control, I will lose."

"That's probably true in some situations, Jim. However, in your case, you try to control every element of your life. And that's just not manageable. Things happen that are beyond our influence or our control. That's life! It happens to all of us. But when it happens to you, it can be very traumatic. What exactly is it that you believe you will lose?"

"I will lose....myself. I will stop being James Snyder."

"You'll stop being a version of James Snyder. The James Snyder with a gun in his briefcase and murder in his heart. But isn't that why you're here? Isn't that why you sought treatment so desperately? Letting go of that profoundly conflicted and unhappy version of yourself is not a bad thing. It's a necessary thing, James."

I lean back in my chair as if struck by a cosmic meteor. The awareness and the vision that Dr. Janowitz just shared are undeniably clear. We sit uncomfortably for a few moments. I cannot think of a response. I feel exposed.

"Jim, entering group therapy might be a good way to learn to become less controlling."

"I don't want to be around a bunch of crazy people," I say loudly, hoping that my anger will mask the fact that Dr. Janowitz has penetrated the carapace that I had spent so many years constructing, that cocoon of anger and mistrust.

"Crazy people," I say without irony, "make me nervous."

Dr. Janowitz laughs, "Well, welcome to my world, Jim. I sometimes feel exactly the same way."

Dr. Janowitz tells me again that he thinks there is a really good guy waiting to be discovered underneath all this hostility. That suggestion, as in the past, just makes me angrier, so he abandons the thought immediately.

As he always does at the end of every therapy session, Dr. Janowitz asks if I need any medicines.

"Yes."

"Do you want some samples?"

This is the conversation we always have at the end of a session.

This time, rather than aggressively refusing his kind gesture, I calmly say, "Maybe some other time."

After Dr. Janowitz writes prescriptions, I pay him his fee in cash and depart.

A TEST OF TRUST

"How did he talk me into this?" I ask myself under my breath, my fear and anxiety getting the best of me.

I'm sitting on a chair in an oval of small couches and chairs in Dr. Janowitz's group therapy room. I chose a chair directly opposite the entry. It is a burgundy fabric, a little worn, the kind of furniture you see in waiting rooms in doctor's offices everywhere. Tran had chairs almost identical but his were navy blue. Hard-wearing and not uncomfortable. The couches are upholstered in a striped fabric, deep green and blue. There is some art on the walls, again generic decorator's idea of how this kind of room should feel, welcoming but still a little institutional. There is a print of a map of the world prior to Columbus's voyages and a painting of hands in various poses of supplication. It's a journey we're embarking on, I suppose is the point, and don't forget you might need to pray because the world is a dangerous one. It's 5:43 PM on Thursday, February 18, 2010, and the session is scheduled to start at 6:00 PM. Tonight will be my first group experience and I'm not looking forward to it. Only six months ago Dr. Janowitz's seed germinated in my mind. And now, here I am.

The conference room is empty except for me. Soon, a woman enters. She is rather tall, somewhat heavyset, and wearing purple hospital scrubs. She sits in the corner opposite me. We exchange glances and nod to one another, but neither says anything. Then a man and two women enter. They sit far apart from each other. Like the first woman, we exchange glances but don't say anything. Soon, another man and woman enter. These two appear to know each other. They talk jovially like long lost friends while the rest of us sit silently, alone with our thoughts.

At a few minutes past six, Dr. Janowitz enters with three other women and one man, stragglers in this Long March towards Attitude Adjustment. He seems very cheerful and as always wears his suit jacket and tie, navy blue and yellow respectively. He looks prosperous and proper. The rest of us have come from work and we are dressed in what Houston considers business casual, no jeans and, except for the woman wearing scrubs, the women wear skirts or slacks. The new comers are welcomed to take a seat. Dr. Janowitz rolls his chair into place at the long edge of the oval, the far turn on a racetrack, just across from me. I cannot help but notice, among the dowdy ladies of the group, one dark haired beauty.

"Welcome everyone," Dr. Janowitz says. "I'm so happy to see you all here tonight. I just have a feeling this is going to be a good group. I think we're going to have some fun together."

The room we are in is pleasant enough, pastel yellow wall with a white chair rail. The ceilings are off white acoustic tiles and the lighting is panels of fluorescent tubes that provide a light with a greenish cast. No one looks good in this light, at least I don't, although looking good is the last thing I'm thinking about tonight.

This is this group's first meeting, and Dr. Janowitz begins by describing the purpose of group and what we can hope to accomplish by being there. The purpose, he says, is to have an open and honest exchange of ideas. No topics are off limits, but he wants us to be thoughtful and respectful to one another. This is not meant to be work, but it does have a purpose, a long-term therapeutic goal.

"So, why don't we get to know each other? Tell us just a little bit about yourselves, your career, why you're in group, and a comment or two about your personal lives. We only have an hour," he says with a laugh, "so I would encourage the Reader's Digest version and not the War and Peace version of your story."

That drew an uncomfortable laugh. The large man to my left seems to enjoy it the most.

"Hey Doc, don't you know I'm a budding Tolstoy?"

"I hope you are, Rick, but maybe not tonight."

"Okay, who would like to begin?" the doctor asks.

When none of us volunteers, Dr. Janowitz selects the woman in hospital scrubs and asks her to go first.

"I know this is a little awkward at first," Dr. Janowitz says, "but you have my word that after a while I'll have a hard time to shut you up. You are all my patients. I selected this group because I think you will like each other and be compatible and empathetic. Melissa, why don't you start."

"Hi everybody, my name is Melissa Stevenson and I'm an orthopedic surgeon. I'm in therapy to change my life. I'm here tonight because Dr. Janowitz asked me to be a part of this group. I don't really expect too much from this type of therapy. Let's see," she pauses, "a comment about my personal life. I'm married but it's not a good marriage, and I'm not happy. It is straining my value system and making me very confused. And that's all I think I'll say." She looks tired to me, but I like her.

"Thank you, Melissa. We'll work on those problems you've shared. Marriages are complicated, aren't they? Even happy ones."

"Who would like to go next?"

When again none of us raises a hand, Dr. Janowitz says, "Jerry, how about you go next?"

"Okay," the man says. "Hi everybody. I'm Jerry Whitmire, and I'm an attorney and a recovering alcoholic. I've been sober for more than twenty years."

"Let's give Jerry a big hand everybody!" Dr. Janowitz exclaims, signaling that we should clap. Jerry seems a bit worn down by life. It's hard enough being an alcoholic, and I imagine it's harder yet, knowing what I know about the law, being an alcoholic and a lawyer. He is wearing black slacks and a blue dress shirt without a tie. The shirt has a stain near the pocket, tomato sauce that has been unsuccessfully blotted with a napkin.

I feel like an idiot but join in the desultory applause. I give Jerry a tiny hand.

"What brings you here tonight?" the doctor asks.

"I have a very bad temper and I'm here to learn how to better get along with people when I'm tired and irritated. I find myself alienating people because of it. My practice is not going well, and I realize I need to find a better way to deal with people."

"I think the group can certainly help you with that." Dr. Janowitz says. "Your anger may have something to do about why you were addicted to alcohol. It's all part of a piece. Sometimes you need to dig a little deeper."

Dr. Janowitz next turns to one of the women. "Margo, how about you tell us a little bit about yourself? You don't need to say much, just share a little."

"Hi everyone," the woman says shyly. "I'm Margo Portenski and I'm a writer and a single mom of a pre-teen daughter. I'm here tonight searching for ways to reduce the tension in my life."

"What kinds of tension?" Dr. Janowitz asks.

"I have writing deadlines, school deadlines for my daughter, the pressures of being a single mom, and the pressures of living everyday life." Margo does look a little haggard. She is dressed nicely, though, with a tan business suit and a blue blouse. Black flats. She wears no

219

makeup. Maybe she's given up on that part of her life.

"Thank you. That's a good start."

"Rick, why don't you go next?"

"Okay," says a surprisingly cheerful older man. "I'm Rick Liebowitz and I'm really happy to be here tonight. It's nice to see you again, Cassandra," Rick says to the woman he was talking to before the session started.

"Oh, it's really nice to see you again too, Rick," Cassandra says smiling back.

"I need my family," Rick starts to say before being interrupted by the doctor.

"Without going into too much detail," Dr. Janowitz instructs, "Tell us a little about what you do and your personal life."

"I'm a retired dentist," Rick says looking around the room at each of us. "I'm working contract for other doctors when they want a little time off. My personal life? I don't have a personal life! My wife won't leave the house. The house is always a mess, so we can't have people over. My daughter won't talk to me or my wife. And I have a grandson whom I've never seen." He is dressed like the golf pro at a down in the heels country club: tan chinos, a white polo shirt with the collar turned up, a red cardigan, and spectator shoes. Why spectator shoes? I suspect he will be the one to try to dominate the conversation, which is fine with me. I'm going to try to fade into the wall paper, except there is none.

"Is it fair to say that the group means a lot to you?" Dr. Janowitz asks.

"The group is my family!"

"By the way, Dr. Janowitz, I have an idea that might be a fun, bonding exercise. When I had a full time dental practice, everyone in the office put a dollar into a pool and we would buy a lottery ticket. We never hit the jackpot, but we won enough to make it interesting. Since we meet every other week, I think we should put in two dollars each. I'll buy the tickets and I'll divvy up our winnings. What do you think?"

"Rick, I think that's a splendid idea. Any objections, group?"

None were offered so we tried to ante up the two bucks. It was a little complicated because hardly anyone had one-dollar bills.

"Okay," Rick says, "I'll cover the first two weeks. Just bring some ones in when we meet again."

"Very good, Rick, this will be fun. And you never know, we may hit it big," says Dr. Janowitz.

I'm having deep misgivings about being here and looking around for a back door to escape. Just don't call on me, I think. Please just leave me alone. I look down at my lap, my arms folded across my chest.

"Okay, that's a lot you're dealing with," states the doctor. "I think we'll stop here with Rick for today. Thank you, Rick."

"Cassandra," Dr. Janowitz says turning to face her, "tell us a little about yourself."

"Hi everyone. I'm Cassandra Blackhart, and I'm an executive secretary. I'm still working, but Dr. Janowitz is trying to get me to retire. He's been trying for a while now. I really should retire, I guess, I just don't know."

"Why would Dr. Janowitz want you to retire?" asks Jerry.

"I have health problems. I can't sit still for long periods of time. My arms, shoulders, back and body hurt — I mean really hurt! — by the end of the day."

"Can you tell us a little about your personal life?" Dr. Janowitz suggests, changing Cassandra's focus.

"I'm married and have two children, a daughter, Melanie, who's married, and a son, Henry, who's engaged. I guess I should say that I've — we've — known Dr. Janowitz for a long time. I think he saved Melanie's life from an eating disorder when she was a child."

"No, no, we all saved her, Cassandra. She saved herself, in the end. But that was another time. What would you like to accomplish in this group?"

"I'd like to, no, I need to learn how to be more assertive."

"Well, the group can certainly help you with that. One of the techniques is role playing, when you can rehearse being direct and assertive. It can be a bit difficult at first, but it works." She has a long history with Janowitz. Her sadness is like a song poorly remembered, lingering but barely remembered.

He turns to the woman on my right.

"Nita, let's come to you," Dr. Janowitz says as he turns to face her.

"I'm Nita Hammerly," says the woman. "And I'm a petroleum and natural gas engineer. I've been feeling depressed lately, ever since I lost my engineering job. The good news, I guess, is that I'm now working at Office Supply. Maybe that's the bad news, too. But I don't know how long this job will last. I can't seem to keep a job for more than six months."

"Can you share something about your personal life?" asks Dr. Janowitz.

"I'm single and would someday like to re-marry."

"Okay, that's sounds like an achievable goal," says the doctor before turning to me.

"Jim, why don't you tell the group a little about yourself?"

I sit more rigidly now so as to not invite any interaction at all and look directly at Dr. Janowitz. His face is the only one I remotely trust. I feel the eyes of all these strangers, crazy strangers, on me.

"I'm Jim Snyder. I'm not sure why I'm here. I guess I'm here because Dr. Janowitz asked me to come. I don't think any good will come out of my being here. And Dr. Janowitz promised me I wouldn't have to say too much."

After I stop talking, there is a long silence before Rick comments, "Well, I'm glad you're here."

I remain stiff and do not acknowledge his statement. I can't think of anything to say. I don't recall what happened for the next forty minutes. Lots of conversation. A little laughter and some tears, but I am comatose, unfeeling.

"And finally," Dr. Janowitz says, "Leigh, what's your story?" A wee beauty is this Leigh.

It makes me uncomfortable to be in the presence of a woman of such beauty. I think all of us felt that way, especially the other women in the room. If they had any insecurities about their appearance or demeanor, this Leigh person, would make them feel like frumpy hausfraus. It's not fair, of course, but she is stunning. Dark-haired and blue eyed, an extraordinary combination. There was something else, too, she seemed utterly lost. I'm good at picking out a fellow citizen of an emotional Desolation Row, a citizen of the Occupied City, and she was one of us. The others in the group seemed like well-educated garden-variety neurotics, but Leigh seemed pushed to the edge of something. I had a radar for people like we two at the edge of a very black hole.

"Hi, everyone. My name is Leigh Hoffman, and I recently moved here from Chicago. I teach mathematics at a local community college, which is something I'm really enjoying. I like Houston, but it's so different from Chicago that I'm having a little trouble adjusting. It's so humid here! I joined the group at Dr. Janowitz's suggestion because I have just gone through a very difficult divorce. It's hard for me to be alone because I do miss my husband and everything we had together."

"You'll do fine, Leigh," Melissa says. "It takes time to work things out. I wish I had the energy to leave my husband."

"He left me, Melissa. I think that might be part of the problem."

"I'm sorry, dear. We'll be here for you."

"Okay," Dr. Janowitz says, "that was a good start. I think we'll stop here for tonight. It really does get easier as we get to know one another. We'll do this again in two weeks."

One by one we silently file out of the group room and, except for Melissa, each of us pays Dr. Janowitz his fee. I am the last to pay, which I do in cash. I will go home where I'll slip into my familiar depression. On the way to the parking lot, my brain involuntarily reminds me that I am not comfortable; a little bit angry; don't want to be in the group. Group therapy will be a test of trust. It doesn't feel good; and I can't see anything positive about it. Babbling, lachrymose crazy people. That's not James Snyder. I have a feeling deep in my stony heart that what happens in group therapy can't be good. Maybe for them, the weak ones, not for me. I will be in fucking control. Always. I am not like them. But I am like them in one way: I, too, am well educated and white. Dr. Janowitz says he put this group together for my benefit, and we all are similar: we are all Caucasians; we all have college degrees, some have advanced degrees; all of us are well spoken. We all seem to be functioning heterosexuals. No outliers among us. I seem to be the only one who has advanced beyond neurosis into psychosis. I wonder if any of the group is as full of psychotropic medication as I am. And we all sounded a lot alike in group: serious minded and full of good will. I'm serious minded, I suppose, but don't possess a gram of goodwill. My guess is none of the guys in the group has hung out in Barbutto's Bikini Bonanza. I have plenty of good will in the Triple B.

As I am walking toward the exit, I notice that Leigh Hoffman is standing by the door. She seems to be waiting for someone. It shouldn't have been me, but it was.

"Hi, James," she says.

"Hi, Leigh, what's up?" Clever conversation, Jim, keep it up.

"I think we have a friend in common. I teach with Thomas Tran's wife Dotty, and I had dinner with them when I first got to town. I don't know if this is a breach of legal ethics or not, but he told me about Dr. Janowitz and that's why I started therapy with him. He mentioned that he's referred a couple other of his clients to Janowitz. He said that Janowitz was as good a psychiatrist as he's ever dealt with — a brilliant, insightful, kind man. He said he also referred a guy named Harry and one named James. I put two and two together, and I thought you might be the James. No sign of Harry, though. I hope we can be supportive of each other. I don't know about this group therapy stuff."

"I feel the same way. I feel lost in there."

"Maybe we can have a drink some night after group. I don't know a soul in this city other than the Trans."

"We should do that. Get to know one another."

"Okay, goodnight."

"Goodnight."

I started the evening full of trepidation and anger. The evening ended with my being smiled at by a dark-haired beauty. Life is a mystery.

WORKING AND WORRY

Very early on Friday morning my best friend Scott calls me at home asking how I am doing. When all I can muster is a low grunt, Scott replies, "Oh, boy. You don't sound good."

Scott then invites me to his home for the weekend. "I've got some small tasks around the house that I'll need your help with. I'll tell you about them when you get here."

Friday at work passes quickly. After work I rush home, pack my clothes, and drive over to Scott and Kelly's house.

"Jimmy Snyder, can we have a lifesavah?" Rob and Amy Todd ask in unison as I pick them up and greet them, one in each arm.

"Yes, you can," I say putting them down and handing Rob my car keys. "But only one. You don't want to ruin your appetites for dinner."

"Where's Casey?"

"He's in the garage. He pooped on the floor again. I know he's an old dog, but we are going to have to figure out something to do with him"

Casey is the German Shepherd Scott found as a stray. Just a puppy and we both raised and trained him. I feel he's as much my dog as theirs.

"If I didn't live alone and work such crazy hours, I'd take him. But he would be worse off with me than here."

"I know, Jim, I guess I'll just have to keep a closer eye on him."

Scott and I watch as the two children unlock and open the passenger door of my car, then open the glove compartment and remove a roll of peppermint lifesavers, which they quickly devour.

Kelly joins us from the kitchen just as the children are returning my keys.

"This is the best part of babysitting," I say as Kelly and I hug.

"How's your new job?" I ask after we separate.

"It's going great. I love it."

"And you're doing marketing for oil and gas, correct?"

"That's right, Jim. And I love it!"

"Love is a pretty strong word, Kelly. Why do you love your job? It's just work, right?"

"The people I work with are wonderful. I've been with babies and toddlers for years, I love them, Jim, but I need to interact with adults about something other than diapers and daycare. It gets a little lonely. And work provides that interaction. Come on now," Kelly says, anxious to change the subject, "dinner is almost ready."

After dinner, while Scott and I clear the table and load the dishwasher, Kelly announces that she is going to check her e-mail. Scott looks puzzled.

"You just checked your e-mail, Kelly."

"I'm expecting something from my mother," she says, smiling, "a recipe. I'll just be a minute."

"I don't know, Jim," Scott says after Kelly has left, "I don't know what kind of recipe she's expecting. Kelly's mom can barely boil water."

"Scott, she's back at work, and she seems happier than I've seen her for a long time. Happy wife, happy life, right?"

"I guess so. Maybe I'm a little jealous of her job. She thinks about it all the time."

He seems distracted.

"Something else bothering you?"

"She's password protected her email. She's never done that before. We were always able to read each other's emails."

"Maybe her company makes her do it. Some sort of proprietary information might be restricted to Kelly only. Not even her husband should see it."

"Maybe. I don't know."

"Why don't you ask her?"

"Because I don't want to seem paranoid. She's really glad to be back at work, and I don't want to spoil it for her."

The three of us then huddle and decide that Scott and I are going out again — it is Friday night, after all — while Kelly watches the kids.

On the way to shoot pool, Scott shares his vision for the tasks he mentioned this morning. He wants to turn the unused attic space into a playroom for kids, their own special clubhouse. It's a big job, and daunting for me. Scott is much more experienced in construction and has a workshop full of tools.

"That attic is a bare space. There are no walls, there isn't a floor."

"I know. It's a blank slate. It'll be great!" he says excitedly.

"You'll be working with someone who knows nothing about plumbing, electrical, HVAC. I can tape wallboard and paint, but really I'm just barely okay if truth be told."

"Yeah," replies Scott, "That's what'll make it fun."

"Fun? I don't know, Scott. What kind of plumber are you?"

"I guess we'll find out, won't we? Come on, Jim, it will work out."

"You're a masochist," I utter, before adding, "When do we start?"

"How does next weekend sound?"

"Sounds good to me," I answer. "Let's do it."

It did sound good to me, but I was there to be a laborer. Scott was going to have to supply the expertise. I decided not to worry about it; I had enough on my mind as it was.

Scott and I drink lots of beer and shoot pool for about two hours all the while talking about the project. At Scott's insistence, we then visit a gentlemen's club, just as we have done every Friday night for as long as I can remember. Scott calls them Gentlemen's clubs; I call them titty bars because there are a lot more tits than gentlemen in them. I tell Scott that I'd rather go to a fern bar where we can meet women who are not strippers of the hard-eyes variety. Scott likes them a little nasty. But because he always drives, we always end up at a gentlemen's club, a titty bar of which Houston has more than a few. There are four or five in the rotation but Barbutto's Bikini Bonanza, Western-themed with girls in leather G-strings and cowboy hats, is our go to place. I guess that's a Western theme. Mostly it's a smoky old joint with a bad air conditioning system and lots of white guys with tattoos. The girls are pretty, though, and Scott knows most of them by their name, or what they say is their name.

The parking lot is full when we get there, and we are met at the door by the bouncer/owner, Larry Barbutto. He had a brief success as a musician in Nashville, a session guitar player before he discovered heroin, which lead him to jail, his wife Noreen, and the Bikini Bonanza. Noreen's father owned the building, a hardware store as I recall, but she loved Larry, and that was it for the hardware store. Initially, Noreen wanted all the girls to be in bikinis, but that was not a good business model. Now it should be called Barbutto's Boob Bonanza because there were plenty in evidence, not any of them the saggy variety either. Larry liked them pert, pretty, and willing to work hard. Scott liked them that way, too. Larry got rid of the bikinis a long time ago.

"Gentlemen," Larry says, as we walked up to the countertop with his cash register, "you fellows are going to get your twenty dollars' worth tonight. Lots of *carne fresca* in there. Just off the bus from Denver and ready to dance their darlin' little hearts out for you."

He stamped the back of our hands and gave us each a token for a free beer.

"I'm glad to have regulars back. Have a beer on the house, boys."

"I'm going to have to record this in my diary tonight," Scott says. "Big Larry Barbutto bought Scott and Jim a drink. That never happened before."

"There's always a first time. And a last time, boys, and you got both tonight. Enjoy."

We call this joint in the private language of Scott and Jim the Triple B. Whenever Scott mentions the Triple B, he always adds, "And I don't mean the cup size." And laughs at his own joke, although neither of us finds it particularly funny anymore. Barbutto's is many things, but luxurious is not one of them. But we're both a little short of money tonight, so this is the bargain basement alternative. Cheap, cold beer and big, bare boobs. Friday night in Houston. Scott has got his lap dance antennae up, but he doesn't see the kind of dancer he likes: he likes them skinny, blonde, with real boobs, no silicone.

"I hate phony tits, Jimmy. Don't see why women use that silicon shit. Why, it's a dangerous industrial product not conducive to good health, long term. That's what I tell Kelly, anyway."

"I don't think she needs any enhancement."

"You've noticed that, too? If the subject comes up at the dinner table, I'm going to expect you to back me up."

"Do you think it will really ever come up, Scott?"

"Probably not. But I've got something that will come up but it looks like it won't be here, tonight. Looks like the good-looking ones went back to Austin."

"Let's get a beer. I see Laurie is one of the bartenders tonight."

Barbutto's is a worn-out place, but I like it. It's cheap. It needs a facelift. The finish on the floor has been scrapped off by cowboy boots and dented by high heels, and the walls which might have been white and bright at one time are a smoky tan. It's got a great bar, though. Barbutto got it out of a downtown hotel that was being torn down for the cost of dismantling it and driving it a few miles north. I've heard a lot of stories about it, but the most frequent one was it was hand built just before the First World War by German carpenters imported just for the job. Despite the wear and tear and the damage from demolition and reinstallation, the workmanship is extraordinary. The bar top is Brazilian black granite, new in the last few years. It's not in bad shape. Laurie, one of Barbutto's daughters, looks after it.

She's managed to put a shirt on tonight although she often works without one.

"Hey, Laurie, what's the matter, the girls a little shy tonight?"

It is one of Scott's habits to call boobs, "the girls."

"If isn't my old buddies, Scott and Jim. New regulation in Houston for tonight, bartenders have to cover up their tits. I think it will be repealed tomorrow night though. Where have you guys been? Dangling at The Dingle again?"

The Dingle was a gay club around the corner.

"You know, Laurie," I answer, "we'd only go to that place if you got fired from here, and your daddy isn't going to do that."

We throw down the tokens on the bar top.

"The old man is squandering my inheritance, I see. Can't make any money giving the inventory away. Those will get you two cold domestics. Budweiser, boys?"

"What does this place look like when the lights are turned up?" Scott asks.

"You don't want to know. The place is crawling with cockroaches."

We can look at the mirror behind the bar and see the girls dancing on the stage. One is on the pole and the other is working the tables in the front. A skinny black girl is inviting an old man to drop a dollar bill into her G-string that he's holding in his mouth. He doesn't seem interested. It's a slow night for everybody.

"Where is all the talent tonight, Laurie?"

"I don't know. Maybe they went to the movies."

She moves to the end of the bar, and, I notice unbuttons her shirt. She has small breasts with dark brown nipples. She is the kind of girl I prefer. She doesn't chew gum and she doesn't want to know what I do.

I've noticed that Scott doesn't like to tempt fate by flirting with the prettiest strippers. Since he's married, he probably shouldn't be flirting with any women. But he is a good-looking guy, very charismatic and funny. His laughter and energy are infectious. Women like him; they always have. He'd pay for a dance, get all excited, and go home to his wife, but he doesn't like the sweet little buttercups from Duluth or Dubuque. Or college girls picking up rent money. He likes professionals, sharp tongued and sharp eyed who were playing a losing hand. No subtlety about the way they wiggle their butts into his lap. It is great for him, but it doesn't do much for me. I like the buttercups who look a little scared. He declines all offers from the girls, no lap dances tonight.

"Let's get out of here, Jimmy. I'm tired and I want to get home before it gets too late."

On the drive home, he is silent. We arrive at a few minutes past midnight. I immediately hit the couch as Scott heads upstairs to bed. The dog settles on the floor next to me. I can hear Scott and Kelly arguing a little, but then I hear the percussive sound of their love making. Just another Friday night at the Todd house. The walls and ceilings are pretty thin, and they are both large people. Kelly is a screamer, and she starts screaming early. It was a couple of her orgasms before I got sleepy. Casey is on the floor next to me. I think he smelled the sex smells of Barbutto's on both Scott and me. He is uneasy, and so am I. The difference is that he's been neutered, and I haven't been. Old Casey can dream of old dogs, my dreams are of bouncing boobs.

What did Kelly think about Scott's Friday night lap dances? She likes the Friday night sex, that is a certainty. This was my family, and I was worried about them, maybe for the first time. I didn't want to lose what I had. Something felt wrong.

At sunrise on Saturday morning, I'm awoken by the feeling of two small children climbing on top of me.

"Jimmy Snyder," asks Amy, "can we watch TV?"

"Sure, but first you have to walk Casey, okay?" I say, as I roll over and attempt to go back to sleep.

"We're not allowed to walk him," Amy says.

That explains Casey's pooping, I think.

I pull on my pants and shoes and grab the leash. Casey was anxious to shit, and we were back quickly. He is a nice dog, great with the kids. I join Rob and Amy for some Saturday morning cartoons. Eventually, Kelly and Scott come downstairs. Kelly immediately begins preparing breakfast as Scott and I review his drawings.

"Scott, this is going to be a massive undertaking," I tell him as we enter the living room on our way to the breakfast table.

"I know. But it'll be worth it."

"Have you ever done anything this big?"

"Not really."

"You seem pretty calm about all this. I'd be worried about starting and not being able to finish."

"Jim, let me worry. You have a strong back. I'll be the brains and you supply the muscle. How does that sound?"

At Scott's insistence, the kids join us for a family breakfast of scrambled eggs, bacon, toast, and juice.

"That was delicious, Kelly," I say, complementing the cook.

"Thanks," Kelly responds. "What are you two guys going to do today?"

"We're going transform an empty space into Aladdin's cave. For my babies. And in order to do that we need some stuff. Wallboard for the walls and ceiling, plywood underlayment for the floors to start. We're going to take some measurements and make a run to Home Depot to order the stuff. Agreed, Jim?"

"Agreed!" I answer.

After breakfast, Scott and I clear the table as Kelly checks her e-mail. We then head out to Home Depot. Scott has ordered a lot of stuff over the years he has been in his house, so he goes to the contractor's station.

"Hey, Scott, how have you been? What are you guys up to?" Larry, the sale's associate, asks.

"We're going to renovate the attic in my house as a playroom for the kids."

"Just the two of you?"

"Just me and my buddy, Jim, here. He is going to be the Robin to my Batman."

"How long do you plan for it to take?"

"Not sure. But it will take longer than I think it will take."

"And cost more money," Larry says. "That's what all you do-it-your-selfers are always complaining about. So, what do you need?"

"I need some electrical cable, some electrical boxes, outlets and switches. We're going to have to pull some wire before we can put up the wallboard."

"You can get that over in the electric aisle. I think Bobby J is over there today."

"Okay, I know him. I also will need some underlayment for the floor and some wallboard for the ceilings and walls. It will have to be delivered by Friday, though. Maybe you can give me a hand figuring out what I need. I have a drawing."

Scott pulls out an elevation of the renovated attic he had done on the computer. He was a dap hand with CAD software.

"Scott, can you leave this with me?"

"Sure."

"I've got a manager's meeting in a few minutes. It will last most of the morning, and after that I can take off the square footages and figure out what you need."

"That would be great, Larry, thanks."

"You still have a house account and live at the same place?"

"Yes, to both."

"Good. I'll have this stuff to you by Friday. I'll give you a call before I send the truck out. Can we put it someplace for you?"

"In the garage. Give me a call so I can leave one of the garage doors open. You're the best, Larry, thanks."

Driving home, the tools clatter in the back of Scott's truck.

Just as Scott planned, we spend the rest of the day organizing the attic. There was a lot of junk left over from the renovation of the kitchen. It was very hot, and we both sweated through our shirts quickly. We work well together. Without a word, Scott was in control, and I followed his direction effortlessly. We alternated trips down the stairs with black garbage bags filled with insulation and flooring from the kitchen and bathroom. We learned not to fill the bags too full. The stairs were the kind of pull down access stairs to the attic common in most Texas homes. Eventually, Scott said, we were going to build a new staircase. There was no air conditioning in the attic and soon we peeled off our sweat-soaked t-shirts.

Scott and I took a break after a couple of hours. We each drank one cold beer quickly. It's amazing how good it tasted. I put the cold bottle to my forehead. We each got another one out of the cooler.

"How are you doing, Jim?"

"I'm a little hot, but I'm doing fine otherwise."

"No, I mean about the other stuff. The therapy with Janowitz."

"I don't know. I've started group therapy, and I feel like the biggest loser in the bunch."

"You're not a loser, at all. You're trying to get your life going in the right direction."

"I feel very awkward sometimes, but I'm getting used to being there."

"That's good. And meanwhile," he said with a laugh, "we've got the GW."

"The GW?"

"The grunt work, Jimmy. Let's get cleaned up," he said. "Kelly said dinner would be ready about now. I'm trying hard to keep her happy. Happy wife, happy life. Right, Jim?"

"She's happy, Scott, why wouldn't she be?"

He didn't respond right away, but just nodded and smiled.

"Yeah, she's happy," he said, finally, "why shouldn't she be?"

For dinner, Kelly prepares steaks, baked potatoes, corn, and homemade rolls. It was a heavy meal after all that work, but I was hungry.

After dinner, Scott cleaned up as Kelly again checks her e-mail. Shortly thereafter, the two of them depart for their night out while I babysit the kids. The adults return from their movie at around midnight only to find Rob, Amy, and me asleep on the couch. After putting the kids to bed, we talk for a little before calling it a night.

We talk about the job, the scope of the job and how Scott is going to pay for it. Kelly looks worried.

"I'm glad I'm working. I didn't realize it was going to cost so much," she says. "We have to think about the kids' college."

"We'll get it all back when we sell. And your parents can help us with the college tuition. They're loaded. Beaucoup bucks."

Scott winked at me when he said that.

Money was always a problem within Kelly's family.

Kelly kept calm. She yawned, a lengthy, very theatrical yawn.

"I'm tired, and I'm going to bed," Kelly said. "Thanks, Jim, for putting up with this guy."

On Sunday morning, the kids again wake me wanting to watch TV. This time, however, I am able to fall back asleep. It's only when Scott and Kelly come downstairs that I really wake up. We all eat cereal for breakfast. Because Scott and I are exhausted, we choose not to do any more work until the afternoon, so we spend the morning reading the Sunday paper and idly talking.

Sunday afternoon finds Scott and me doing some light demolition.

"Jim, I just have to warn you that until we get the underlayment done, you have to make sure you step on the floor joists. Beneath that layer of insulation is just a layer of the wallboard on the ceiling. I wouldn't want you to fall through and crash into my bedroom feet first."

"I'll try to pay attention to where I step, Scott. I actually didn't think of that."

After another nice dinner — fried chicken and mashed potatoes, Kelly's specialty — I depart for home. I was not completely sure what was happening with Kelly and Scott. I was a little worried. More than a little. As always, I drive home and try to put Scott and Kelly out of my mind.

CURATIVE FACTORS

My second group experience begins with less anxiety than the first. Seven of the eight of us arrive early and sit quietly in the waiting room. The group therapy room is locked tonight, so we are all squeezed into this small anteroom. Leigh is the last to come in, and she waves to me.

Dr. Janowitz emerges from his office at a few minutes before 6:00 and invites us in. We enter the group room and take the same seats we sat in the first night, as if they had been assigned. As I did before, I sit in the chair across from Janowitz and the exit. This is my safe spot.

"Let's begin, shall we. First, a little news about the group. Margo won't be joining us any longer," Dr. Janowitz says. "She's a very sensitive person and she felt that dealing with the group dynamic and all of the issues involved would be too much pressure for her."

Turning to Leigh, Dr. Janowitz says, "Leigh, why don't we start with you tonight?"

"Good evening, again" she begins, quietly. "Last time I forgot to mention that this is my first experience in group, in fact, my individual sessions with Dr. Janowitz are my first experience with any kind of therapy so, I'm a little nervous."

She looked at Dr. Janowitz, with a strained expression.

"What should I talk about?"

"Anything you want, Leigh. As much or as little."

"Okay, well, I'm recently divorced, quite a difficult and painful divorce. I've had some health problems lately. Physical problems that have I think created a few emotional tics, as well. That's why I'm here. I don't think I'm up to talking about it just yet. Not tonight. I just had a very difficult day with my lawyer."

234

"That's fine, Leigh, I think I can speak for the group, and say you should feel free to share as much as you feel comfortable sharing."

"Glad you're here with us, Leigh," Rick says. The group beams at her, including me. I am certain I have a goofy smile on my face.

"Let's see, who has some good news to share tonight?" the doctor asks as he looks around the room at each of us.

As before, I sit very rigidly, my body language unmistakably withdrawn and un-inviting. No one seems to have any good news.

"Cassandra, why don't we come to you?"

"Hi everybody," Cassandra says.

"Tell us some good news," Dr. Janowitz directs.

"Some good news. Well, I guess some good news would be that my son's wedding date is fast approaching."

"That is good news!" the doctor interrupts. "When is the big date?"

"Henry will be getting married in three weeks, on Saturday, March 27th."

"Let's give a big hand for Cassandra everybody," Dr. Janowitz directs, signaling that we should clap.

"I guess," Cassandra pauses, "I probably shouldn't say this, but this is really bothering me. Ted and I, we don't think that this marriage will last."

"Why don't we save that for next time?" Dr. Janowitz suggests.

"Oh, okay," Cassandra responds.

"Jerry, why don't we come to you next?"

"Hi again, everyone," Jerry says.

"Do you have any good news to share with the group?" Dr. Janowitz asks.

"No, I'm afraid I'm out of good news today."

Jerry seems downcast and weary.

"Tell us what's going on," the doctor encourages.

"I can't seem to get a date. What I mean is, I think I'm a really nice guy, but I just can't get a date for Friday night. I'm putting myself out there. Where are all the available women?"

"Can anyone help Jerry?" Dr. Janowitz asks the group.

Rick volunteers. "Where are you going to meet women, Jerry?"

"Church is one place. I'm active in Sunday school. And I'm even taking country western dance lessons during the week."

"And there are no available women there?" Rick asks incredulously.

"None that want to date me!"

Dr. Janowitz speaks. "Country western dancing is an excellent way to meet people. It's neutral. You're there to learn how to dance.

If you happen to mingle at the Coke machine seven or eight times, pretty soon it's not mingling any more. I think it's only a matter of time, Jerry."

"I don't think you're trying hard enough, Jerry," Rick says. "You're too passive."

"I try hard."

"Knowing you, you give up at the smallest hint of rejection. You have to be less insecure and go for it."

"I don't know what that means, Rick," Jerry says sharply. "You've been married forever. You don't know what it's like out there."

Jerry's temper is getting the best of him. He does have a short fuse, and Rick likes to prod him. Rick has an edge that is being revealed. Rick and Jerry are not going to have a happy ending.

"Okay," Dr. Janowitz says, "let's move on, Jerry and Rick. Jerry, it's good that you're trying to get dates. You're trying, and something will work for you eventually."

He looks at the group. I keep my head down and my arms folded across my chest.

"Melissa let's come to you."

"Hi everybody. I guess tonight I'd like to talk about my practice." Her scrubs tonight are a powder blue. I think I like the purple ones better. Melissa stares at the ceiling, which she does, absentmindedly, when she talks. She rarely makes eye contact with anyone in the group.

"I'm trying to focus on building my practice, and it's hard, especially because I'm doing it all by myself."

"What is it that you do again?" asks Rick. Rick is the chatty one, the I-want-to-be-heard guy. He knows what she does, of course. He just wants not to be neglected.

"I'm an orthopedic surgeon. Dr. Janowitz has been helping me to focus on building my practice, but marital issues keep getting in the way. I'm probably going to get a divorce. It's just so hard!"

"How are you doing otherwise?" Dr. Janowitz asks.

"Other than struggling to build a practice and dealing with marital strife, I'm doing great!" Melissa answers dryly. "Just really, really great."

"Do you have a specialty, Melissa?" asks Leigh.

"Knees. I'm the knees person. I'm beginning to hate knees. I see them in my sleep. You're going to have trouble with your knees, Leigh, later in life. Stand up."

Leigh stands up and lifts her skirt to expose her knees. Her skirt is blue with cornflowers, very springy although it isn't spring.

"Bad alignment. Sorry, I can't help myself."

"Maybe we'll have a consult someday, Melissa," Leigh says.

I think Leigh has great knees. She's got great everything.

"It's difficult, I know, Melissa, with your work and your husband. But it looks like we're developing an agenda," Dr. Janowitz says.

Dr. Janowitz turns next to Nita who is just to his left.

"Nita, how are you doing this evening?" Dr. Janowitz asks.

"I'm doing okay. I like my job working at Office Supply, supervising the duplication center."

"Excellent."

"I really like that it's low stress, although my boss is a real pain."

"Could you explain that?" Dr. Janowitz asks.

"My boss jumped all over me yesterday because I had the audacity to bring a cup of coffee into the duplication area. She said that I was very unprofessional for doing that because coffee could have spilled on something important. She also has been snapping at me for not being fast enough at my work. As I said, I don't think she likes me. My boss is a real pain."

"And how are you doing financially?" the doctor asks.

"Not well," Nita answers. "I make slightly more than minimum wage."

"Hang in there, and maybe something will turn up and you can get back to being an engineer," Dr. Janowitz responds, before turning to face Rick.

"Rick, let's come to you."

"Hi again, group mates," Rick says cheerfully. He adjusts the collar of his polo shirt.

Jerry coughs, theatrically, and shifts in his chair. Rick looks at him, smiling.

"Tell us some good news," the doctor encourages.

"I'm afraid I don't have any good news tonight either."

"Oh, what's going on?"

"I'm not working as much relief work as I'd like. The house is always a mess, so we can't have anyone over. My wife won't leave the house, so we can't go any place."

"Tell the group a little about your house."

"There's floor to ceiling junk. I mean boxes and newspapers literally piled high! We have pathways from one room to another. It's that full!"

"Are you a hoarder?" Jerry asks. "That sounds like hoarding to me."

"No, but my wife is."

"So, is it fair to say that you're lonely?" the doctor asks.

"Yes, I'm very lonely. I need my group."

237

"Maybe you're not trying hard enough to get your wife to throw out her junk," Jerry says.

"It's a sickness, Jerry, and I'm trying to talk to her."

"Maybe you should call the Health Department."

"Screw you, Jerry. You shouldn't take this stuff so personally. Do you think you're the only guy in Houston who can't get laid?"

"That's good. Let's try to stay on point here, gentlemen. We're here to help each other and not create more conflict."

"Sorry, Jerry," Rick says, reaching around Melissa to shake his hand.

"No problem," Jerry says. "We're just getting used to this process, I guess."

Dr. Janowitz says, "That's right, this is new to most of you. There will be some tension and maybe even some conflict, but we'll deal with it. We won't ignore it."

"Thank you, Rick," Dr. Janowitz says as he turns to face me.

"Jim, can you give Rick some support?"

"Hi, I'm not sure that I can be of much help to Rick," I say as I sit even more rigidly and stare straight at Dr. Janowitz. "I live in a very sparsely furnished place, so I don't know anything about clutter."

"That's fine," the doctor says back to me. "How are you doing this evening?"

"I'm not sure why I'm here," I respond tersely. "I don't think any good will come out of this."

Seizing my cue, Dr. Janowitz talks about the long-term benefits of being in group therapy. It is a speech, I sense, he has given many times to many groups. I've heard part of it about individual therapy as well. When he has finally finished, he says to the group, "We seem to exhaust the time frame for group too soon."

Turning to me, Dr. Janowitz asks, "Jim, would you consider biblio-therapy? I'd like to recommend Yalom's *Principles and Practices of Group Psychotherapy*, especially those curative factors, for you to read and bring back to the group."

"Maybe" is my one-word non-committal response.

"It would be useful for you, and it would be useful for the group to hear about it."

"I'm not sure. I'm not good at book reports."

"Think about it. And, Leigh, we'll talk to you more next time. I'm sure we all want to know more about you."

The doctor says, "I think we'll stop here for today. We'll meet again in two weeks."

We file out and I follow Leigh toward the exit. Oh, boy, I thought, it would be easy to fall in love with her. I wonder if that's a proper protocol for group therapy?

"Are you going to read that book," Leigh asks, as we exit the building. "It might be interesting James. It's something I'd like to know about."

"Leigh, Dr. Janowitz has talked to me about the Yalom book in individual therapy. He lent me a copy. It's a textbook written for professionals in the field. It's six hundred and fifty pages long. The reviews in scholarly journals says it is a masterpiece, but I'm not going to read it and give a report. No way. I don't have the time or the energy."

"There's a reason Janowitz wants you to do it, you know. He wants you to integrate with the group."

"I know, but it will take me a year to read it. The problem is if I start it, I will have to read it all, even the footnotes. I'm a little obsessive that way."

"I guess you know best."

"How are you, by the way? Are you okay?"

"My life sucks, James. Maybe when the divorce is final, I'll feel better. Hey, do you want to get a drink next time after group? There must be a place around here."

There were probably a hundred places in the blocks surrounding us. My mission was to find just the right one. That and maybe skim the Yalom book, concentrating on the curative factors, whatever they are.

THE REVELATION

The months of March, April, May, June, and July 2010 fly by. During this time in group, Melissa announces that she is seeking a divorce; Jerry struggles with his temper and with securing dates; Leigh talks about her husband leaving her and her breast cancer scare, she is alone for the first time in her life and it makes her uncomfortable; Cassandra's son gets married despite his parents' concerns and Cassandra decides to retire; Rick struggles to find relief work and leans heavily on the group as his only social outlet; Nita quits her job at Office Supply and is still unemployed; and I say as little as is possible but do slowly begin to share more with the group as time goes on. It is obvious to everyone in the group that something is going on between Jerry and Nita. They still sit in their traditional seats, but they come in together and at the end of the session they leave together. It seems okay, but Jerry, I think, would be a difficult person to be with in a relationship. He seems altogether too volatile and too needy. Of all the group, I like Jerry the least and Nita, frankly, the most. She is very sweet and very lonely. I was wrong, it turns out.

"Leigh," Dr. Janowitz says, "how are you tonight?"

"I'm a bit down. I met with my lawyer today. I'm trying to get my divorce over and done. The problem is my husband won't speak with me. He won't answer my phone calls or messages. It is as if I no longer exist."

"And why is that?"

We all turned toward her. Tonight, she wore her hair in a French braid. She was very tan and wore a white blouse that made her tan look even deeper, and a pair of jeans. What a lovely woman she was at that moment. She paused before she spoke, wondering, I suppose, if she should go on.

"Why is that, why is that, why is that?" she repeated, like a mantra. "Because I broke his heart, I suppose. Because I had an affair and broke his heart."

"An affair," Rick says, "what's the big deal? I've had many affairs."

"I didn't, Rick, it was a big deal to me. My husband is a good, funny, and kind man. His name is Jacob, Jake. We met each other in graduate school. He was in law school, and I was getting my Ph.D. in mathematics. He wanted to be a musician. He is a talented cellist, but a pretty average one. And he knew it. His mother, by the way, is a famous teacher of piano at Oberlin College. She is a bitch on wheels and looks like she was run over by a milk truck. Jake lacked the confidence to pursue a career in music, so he studied law. I was a very good student of mathematics, very serious and very shy. We fell in love. I'm ashamed to say now he fell in love with me more than I him. I have always been pursued by men because of my looks. It was not my intention to be pretty. My mother was a beautiful, alcoholic slut and my father was an empty-headed and handsome trust fund dissolute. He jumped into a river and drowned. I think it was the Delaware River. My mother is still alive, apparently, but I have no idea where. I found myself alone in the world, truly alone, and then along came Jake."

"Are you okay, Leigh?" Dr. Janowitz asks.

She waved her hand to suggest she was going on.

"Jake saved me from my wretched family, although I never told him that. There were many things I never told him. I was not comfortable with the intensity of his love and desire then, although I miss it now. I was a fool. I would do anything to be naked in bed with him again, almost anything. We lived in Chicago, and Jake got a job with an insurance company there and I got a job teaching at a local community college. Jake, by the way, is very handsome. He has a wonderfully kind face, and people thought we were a perfect couple. We were, I realize now.

"But then I met this man, the dean of arts and letters, Jay. Well, I won't tell you his last name because it doesn't matter, does it? He was spectacular. A rock climber, a black diamond downhill skier. He jumped out of airplanes, and he was brilliant. He was a gorgeous man. He read everything and knew everyone. He pursued me; he seduced me. The first time I fucked him was on his desk late at night after a basketball game. I told Jake I had an evening out with the girls.

"His wife, Rochelle, also worked at the college. She was chairman of the philosophy department. She was a Wittgenstein scholar, and a famous one at that. We were friends. We had lunch together.

Somehow it all seemed normal, but it wasn't, of course. And every time I fucked Jay, I realized, I must have smelled like sex, and Jake must have known something was going on. But he never said anything. I think he knew what was happening, but he was embarrassed for me. He knew Jay, he knew Rochelle; we were all friends.

"This went on for several years. Many times, I promised myself, I would get out of it. But Jay was a powerful man, and he kept me close by. He said he hated his wife and needed to get away. He was desperate to get away. But, of course, nothing happened until, finally, something happened. Rochelle caught us in an embrace in his office. How convenient, now, I realize, to be caught that way. It was horribly humiliating, and I scurried away.

"Jay called me the next morning and said we needed to meet to deal with this, our 'affair.' It was necessary to clear the air. We met in a parking lot near Lake Michigan. It was bitterly cold. They were both dressed in black. It was their ending an affair outfit, I think.

"Rochelle was there. She wasn't furious, just distant. It was not enough just to send me away; it was also necessary to humiliate me. Jay was part of that. I had become a clingy, needy and unnecessary part of his life.

"'Leigh,' she said, 'you are not the first woman in your position with Jay, do you know that? Don't answer that. Do you know what fellows like my husband, Jay, call women like you? They call you their 'fuck girls.' Lovely phrase, isn't it? You are their piece on the side. I told Jay last night that he could leave me for you — please leave me for you because you are so exquisite — but he won't. He never does.'

"I looked at Jay then and his hands were behind his back and he was staring at the blacktop. He never once looked up. He never said a word. I realized I had been his fuck girl, nothing more, and I was angry and ashamed.

"'So,' Rochelle said, 'here is my advice: leave the college and never have any contact with my husband again, ever. Dear, sweet Leigh, he is a piece of shit, but temporarily at least he's my piece of shit, not yours.'

"'I don't want Jake to know,' I said.

"'You are a silly woman, Leigh. Jake knows; everyone, for fuck's sakes, knows. What do you think my asshole husband talks about in barrooms and the sauna in the college health club? He talks about you and your perfect tits.' We got into our cars and drove away. And that was it, over and done. I cannot undo what I've done, but I am broken hearted.

"Jake is still in Chicago, but he is lost to me. Lost forever, I guess, although I love him. I'm trying not to dwell on the past, but it is in me almost all the time."

"Oh, Leigh," Melissa says. "I'm so sorry."

"That's very sad, Leigh. Those people, how horrible," Rick adds.

"No, I'm the horrible one. I betrayed my husband, and I can't forgive myself."

After a long pause, Solomon Janowitz finally speaks.

"Thank you, Leigh," Dr. Janowitz says quietly. "I think we should call it a night."

Leigh rushes out and doesn't look back. I felt sorry for her. I guess we'll wait to have that drink another night. I could wait, because I felt a little intimidated by her. I'll have to think of something to say. Or not. I'm learning from Janowitz that silence can be as important as words.

I feel less an outsider and begin to trust the group a little. My anger has lessened, I think, and my paranoia has subsided. I'm less fearful. I begin to realize how fearful I have been in my life. Gradually, I begin to look forward to our sessions. Not enjoying them exactly; I am still the stiffest and most resistant one in the group. But I'm not fighting it. If there is a tide in these groups, a push and pull of empathy, I'm not swimming against it anymore. I talk to Leigh a little after session as we leave the group room. She is friendly, sad but distant. What can be said? I guess I'm becoming less self-involved and more empathetic because I sense in her a deep hurt. Often after group, sometimes with the others but mostly alone, we end up in Rolf's, a German restaurant around the corner from Janowitz's office. She has a glass of wine and I have a beer and we talk about the group or her job at Lone Star College, a job that she is seriously overqualified for. No romance is possible with her, I realize early on. I'm going to be her beer-after-group buddy. Someone to gossip with about Jerry and Nita. That's okay with me. Her fragility is tangible, and I don't possess the skills to deal with that. She is a rare creature: a kind woman willing to be my friend. That I love her is my truth, but it will be something I will never disclose. Not to Janowitz, not to the group. Not to her. I feel awkward with her, with my little pot belly and scraggly beard. I decide to do something about both. I have to get back to my bike riding. I used to enjoy that feeling of rolling through the Texas landscape. Two-tired Snyder, that was me.

During this time, I spend every weekend at Scott and Kelly's house working on the project. Scott and I finished the demolition. He pulled the electrical cable and installed the boxes. He's good at that stuff, and I'm not. Often, I mostly handed him tools and tried not to get in the way. We put down the plywood underlayment for the floor. This was not complicated, using more muscle than brains, and I'm good at it. In a few weeks after our initial efforts, this raw space began to look like a room. In May we started sheet rocking the room. We do what we can by ourselves but for some of the mechanical systems — plumbing for a bathroom and the HVAC — we need licensed professionals. The city won't sign off on the job without those credentials. It takes time to coordinate all those details. Even so, the two of us working alone, for the most part, make great progress in only five months. Scott occasionally has to work weekends and that slows us up. Sometimes I work alone taping and mudding the sheetrock. I discover, because I am a meticulous worker, that I am good at it. It has a rhythm and logic of its own. When I don't feel like working by myself, I use Scott and Kelly's house as a jumping off point for my bike rides. Even with the delays, I figure that by the end of August, the kid's playroom will be done.

Because I'm spending every weekend at Scott and Kelly's house, I get to live the family life, vicariously. I've developed a plan for the weekends. I ride my bike to their house on Friday evening, and ride it back home on Sunday afternoon. From The Woodlands where I live to Spring where they live is about an hour's ride. Almost always, I take a longer ride on my way home on Sunday. I have lost weight, and I've shaved my beard. I look younger, fitter. I'm beginning to like the way I look now.

"Jim," Kelly said to me before dinner one weekend when Scott was playing with the kids, "you look great. So thin and handsome."

"I wish I were."

"No really. This is the best you've looked in a long time. Do you have a love interest?"

"Not really. I was just tired of being out of shape."

The kids, Rob and Amy, have adopted me as family, as have Scott and Kelly. During these hard-working weekends, it makes me wonder if I couldn't be a real part of the family. During our time together, it makes me wonder if I couldn't step in and fill those shoes and carry the family flag forward if anything were to happen to Scott. It makes me wonder if I couldn't someday have a family life like Scott and Kelly have. It makes me wonder if I should try to start a family or if I should find a single woman who already has a family and adopt it as my own. It makes me wonder about all the fabulous joys that can come from parenthood. It makes me wonder.

On Friday nights during these months, Scott and I work until about 8:30 PM. We then clean up and head out, either to just drink beer or sometimes to shoot pool, but always to a gentlemen's club at the end of the evening. Despite my ambivalence toward titty bars, I really enjoy socializing with Scott. Were it not for him and his project, I would probably be sitting at home alone every weekend. Scott is my social life.

On Saturday nights, Scott and I work until dinner. Then he and Kelly go out on their date while I tend to the kids. I really enjoy Rob and Amy's company. They're great kids and generally well behaved. And while they'll soon be old enough to not need a sitter, they're still young enough to not be too rebellious, so they listen well, which makes sitting for them a joy.

It's an odd life being a kind of honorary uncle and semi brother and brother-in-law, but a good life. It is as close to happy as I have ever been.

THE SORROW OF JAMES SNYDER

On Wednesday, August 11th, 2010, a date that I will remember forever, Kelly calls me at work at 10:12 AM and asks if I can come over to their house right away.

"What's going on?" I ask.

"Scott's dead!" Kelly answers, as she begins to cry.

"What are you saying?"

"I'm saying that Scott died this morning at work. I don't have any more details, but I really need you here."

After hanging up with Kelly, I immediately go see my new manager, Mike Brow, and explain what little I know.

"Absolutely, you have to get over there. Don't worry about it."

"Thanks."

"Just keep me in the loop about what's going on."

"I will."

My hands are trembling as I start the car. I'm short of breath.

When I walk in the door of Scott and Kelly's house, Kelly greets me with a hug. I can see that she's been crying.

"How are you holding up?" I ask.

"I don't know. I'm numb," Kelly responds.

"How are the children?"

"Amy's taking it really hard," Kelly answers, explaining that last night Scott sent her to her room for misbehaving and she said she wished he would just disappear from her life.

"Every child does that at some point in their family life," I say, trying to comfort Kelly.

"Where are the kids?"

"They're upstairs in the playroom."

"Let's go see them."

Upon seeing me, Rob and Amy run to me and I give them both a big hug. It's obvious that they've been crying, so Kelly and I comfort them as best we can.

Throughout the day, various friends of the Todds stop by the house to share their grief and sadness with Kelly and the kids. Some of their friends I know, but most of them I don't, so I look after the kids as Kelly interacts with her guests. I am in shock, stunned by the suddenness of it. There are plenty of tears in the house, but I shed none of them.

For dinner that evening we order pizza. After dinner, as Kelly checks her e-mails, I sit with the children and we talk about what it means to lose your father. I try to be as supportive as I can, but because I am unable to fully express my own emotions, I'm not sure how effective I am being. No, I'm sure they look at me like I'm a zombie because I'm so disconnected from my own grief.

That night I sleep on the couch in my work clothes. Actually, I stare at the ceiling and think about Vera Bowman. I wonder if she would talk to me if I sought her out in the Houstonian Hotel? I would like to speak with that old woman again about her life. And her mother, Maria, was it?

Because we all wake up early the next morning, I help Kelly prepare breakfast for the children, after which, the kids go outside and play, and Kelly and I sit and talk.

"Because Scott died so suddenly at work, the coroner has to perform an autopsy. I'm going to have him cremated."

"That's probably for the best."

"Will you go with me to make the arrangements?"

"Of course," I answer.

After a quick trip home to shower, I change clothes, and pack for the rest of the week, not sure about how long I'll have to stay with Kelly and the kids. I return to their house where I try to be the steadying force they need. I don't how I'm going to keep it together.

On Friday afternoon, Kelly receives a call from the coroner's office. The coroner finished the autopsy. Scott's cause of death was a previously undiagnosed brain aneurysm that ruptured. His death was almost instantaneous. Dead before he hit the ground.

Kelly explains to me, "Scott stroked out."

"Jesus, I'm so sorry," I say as I give her a comforting hug. She doesn't feel in my arms that she wants to be comforted.

For the next two hours we talk about Scott's recent headaches. They didn't seem serious at the time.

"He would take a lot of aspirin for them, but it never seemed to help. I should have made him go to the doctor."

247

"You couldn't know. It's not your fault."

"Maybe if I had been more vigilant, James, this wouldn't have happened."

"I think it would have happened one way or the other."

"I shouldn't have been so busy at work. I should have been a better wife."

"You were a great wife. You had a great marriage."

She had an odd, perplexed expression and she looks away.

"I was a great wife. Do you really think that, Jim?"

"Of course. You had the best marriage I've ever been around. You guys adored one another."

That evening, I tend to the kids as Kelly checks and responds to her e-mails. Because no one seems interested, I walk the old dog Casey. Even he seems to sense something is wrong. She spends a long time in her office space, and when I look at her I can see she's been crying.

"I'm going to bed, Jim. It's going to be a tough day tomorrow. We have to go to the funeral home and make the arrangement for Scott."

"Goodnight. We'll get through it."

On Saturday morning, as a neighbor watches the children, Kelly and I visit the funeral home to plan Scott's cremation. After greeting us, the funeral director quickly excuses himself only to return shortly with a cup half filled with water and several tissues, all for Kelly in case she needs them.

"I'm all right," she says.

I'm surprised at her coldness. Maybe this is the way she deals with grief.

"They're there if you need them. It's a hard time."

To my surprise, Kelly is very businesslike in her dealings with the funeral director. She doesn't shed a tear, nor does she need the water. In less than twenty minutes, the arrangements are made. Scott is to be cremated on Sunday, and his ashes placed in an urn that Kelly picked out from a photograph. It's the least expensive one.

For the rest of the day Saturday and all day Sunday, I remain with Kelly, Rob, and Amy. On Sunday evening before I go home, Kelly and I talk about how difficult it will be for her to go through Scott's clothing.

"I'll need to donate all of his suits, his favorite jeans, his beloved cowboy boots," Kelly says as she begins to cry.

"You don't need to do anything right away," I tell her. "You have plenty of time to do that when you're up to it."

Kelly nods her understanding. When the time is right, I give her another comforting hug, I hug the children, and leave. The world is upside down. I am filled with anxiety, and feel the tug of my old companions, anger and depression. I have trouble sleeping and lay awake thinking about what will happen to Kelly and the kids. And what will happen to me.

On Monday at work I cannot concentrate, so I decide to leave early for the Todd's house. When I arrive there, I am greeted again with warm hugs from Kelly and the kids. Casey is back in the garage in his kennel. I then learn from Kelly that she finished going through Scott's clothing earlier in the day and the donation van picked them up that afternoon. The only thing she kept of his was his cowboy boots.

"Really? That's pretty sudden isn't it?"

"No use in waiting, James. What's the point? It won't get any easier."

"It must've been hard for you to do this so soon after his passing," I say, trying to comfort myself than more Kelly. She seems different, not the old Kelly. I'm not sure if I like this version.

"I cried all morning," she responds, "but it had to be done, so I did it."

She is very composed. I guess this is because she is in shock, but she seems almost indifferent.

"Some friends of ours would like to hold a memorial for Scott on Wednesday evening at 7:00 PM at the Community Center."

"That's a wonderful idea."

"Will you be the emcee, or whatever they call it?" she asks.

Without hesitation, I answer, "Of course, I'll be honored to do it."

It is something that I do not want to do. I feel uncomfortable speaking in front of people. All my anxieties operate at full strength. But it is something I can't run away from. I'll do it for Scott.

We have a sad dinner, Chinese food, with very little conversation.

"Jim, I'm going to be okay, I think, but I'd like to be alone to collect my thoughts."

"I understand."

I'm a little hurt by her asking me to leave. I am grieving, too. I feel the old tug of anger but resist it for Scott's sake. I will miss him, I realize, every day for the rest of my life.

On the drive home, I consider what I will say on Wednesday evening. Fortunately, I have an appointment with Dr. Janowitz tomorrow after work, so I decide to ask him for help.

On Tuesday evening, Dr. Janowitz and I discuss Scott's passing.

"How do you feel?"

"Confused. I think I should have noticed something."

"Like what?"

"His headaches. Sometimes he would have to lay down when we were working because of them. He thought it was the heat or the stress. After a few beers, he would be confused. Not drunk, but just a little spacy. Clearly, there was something wrong, and it wasn't heat or stress. Maybe if I had insisted that he see a doctor."

"That's magical thinking, James. It's very unlikely that there would have been any outcome other than this one."

"I'm just terribly sad."

"I know. Scott was your beloved friend. But now you have a larger responsibility."

"What's that?"

"You need to spend as much time with the children as you can," he instructs. "This is a vital time in their young lives. You need to show continuity and that life continues."

On Wednesday evening, a group of about forty-five people assemble for Scott's memorial. I am nervous, but I feel the need to rise to the moment.

I begin the memorial by sharing stories about how Scott and I bonded at work and after work to become best friends, about how Scott and Kelly accepted me as part of their family. Because of my own limited emotional affect, I have great difficulty conveying emotion, but I try my best.

"I've been trying to think of a way," I say, "to talk about Scott that would be meaningful to me and to you his friends and family. He was an extraordinary man, and I'm sure we all have a story about something Scott said or did — an act of generosity or a word of support or kindness — that we will remember about him.

"My memories of Scott will involve the project we started this year, the Renovation we called it. We all know how much Scott loved his children, Amy and Rob. He decided that they needed a playroom, a kid's space that would be theirs alone. A hideout, a clubhouse. He decided that he and I would do the work — and there was a lot of it — by ourselves. We were not builders, at least not in the traditional sense, and we were certainly not carpenters, electricians, or plumbers. But Scott was undeterred — he was fearless about trying new things. He was convinced we could learn enough of all those trades, with a little help from true professionals, to do the job. He was right, as he most often was, and we almost finished it together. He died before the final details were completed. To finish those final details is my sacred obligation to Scott.

"We worked at a pace that reflected our ages. We were not old men, of course, but we were not young men either. Office workers, now in early middle age, and all this work was a stretch for us.

However, it is my belief that God protects home handymen and fools, and for those five months of the Renovation, we were both. We worked steadily, with many breaks for consultation. During the consultations, we drank a few beers, as I recall.

"And then, except for some sanding and painting, the job was done. The skeptics — some of them are in this room — who shook their heads at our hubris are proven wrong. It ain't hubris if you can do it. We were pleased with ourselves.

"On the last day we worked together, and on one of the last days Scott was alive, as we were putting away the tools for the day, Scott said to me, 'Jimmy, can you believe we did all this?'

"'You did it, Scott, I was just a grunt on this job.'

"He laughed in that typical Scott way, holding nothing back, full of energy and affection.

"It was a splendid evening, with a thick yellow dusky light. He was a good-looking guy, as you know, and very powerful, and not just in the sense of physical strength.

"'We did it, buddy. I'll tell you a little secret. I wanted to give up months ago. I knew you wouldn't let me,' Scott confided.

"The truth is, I probably wouldn't have let him quit, as I found the time spent working with him in the heat and the rain, early in the morning and late into the night, with our bone-headed amateur mistakes — I'm not going to tell you about the time I stepped off a floor joist and through the sheetrock in their bedroom — and our awesome successes was a very happy time for me. I had a good friend, and I was part of his family. So, Kelly and Rob and Amy, this is the Scott Todd I loved, will always love and honor, and will remember."

After I finish speaking, I invite others to come forward and share their stories. To my surprise, about ten people do just this, relating how Scott positively influenced their lives. I find it quite moving to hear about his good humor and generosity. He was well loved and respected.

After the memorial ends, Kelly gives me a big hug and introduces me to several of her co-workers. We all talk for a little while, then round up the kids and head back to Kelly's house.

At around 10:00 PM, Kelly puts the kids to bed. She seems very weary and sad. We both are.

"I'll be back this weekend to finish taping and mudding the unfinished drywall in the attic to get it ready for painting."

"Are you sure you don't want to take some time off."

"I'll take time off when it's done."

"Okay, Jim, I guess I'll see you Friday. And thank you."

"For what?"

251

"For today. It was special."

She seemed oddly disconnected from me. We then hug goodbye,
a very chaste nonsexual hug, and I drive home. I am exhausted and
confused. Something is happening, and it is making me deeply
unhappy. Not angry, not yet. I don't like surprises, and at this
moment I don't like Kelly. I feel something that is new territory for
me. The things I had felt for the past years, anger, depression,
paranoia are present but muted. They will never go away. But these
enemies of mine, the affectless burden of someone suffering from
mental illness, me, were shunted to the background. I feel something
at last, something that feels like the truth: a deep sadness at the death
of my best friend. The sorrow of James Snyder.

THE ENGAGEMENT

On Thursday evening, August 19th, I remain at work a little later than I should and so arrive late for group. Upon entering the group room, I take a seat and listen as Nita talks about how frustrating it is to be job hunting. When she has finished, Dr. Janowitz turns to me and says, "Jim, let's come to you next."

"Hi," I say to Dr. Janowitz in my usual fashion.

"Hi," Dr. Janowitz says back to me. "I understand you have some sad news to share with the group tonight."

"Yes, I think I do," I say softly after a pause, "my best friend Scott died last Wednesday."

The group members all express their sympathies and condolences.

Rick leans forward and taps me on the knee, "Sorry, buddy."

I explain how Scott died. "It was a total surprise. It seems totally unreal."

Dr. Janowitz asks, "How are you dealing with the loss?"

"Well, to be honest," I answer, "I haven't really processed it. I've been spending all my time at Scott and Kelly's house comforting Kelly and the children so that I haven't had time to really deal with this myself."

"How is Kelly dealing with it?" the doctor asks.

"She seems to be doing okay under the circumstances, I'd say."

"How about the children?"

"They're taking it hard, but I'm sure they'll be okay, too."

"James, you're probably aware of this, but there's a critical time following a major loss during which it's vital that parental figures be there for the children. You've become that parental figure whether you want that or not."

"I want to be that. I love those kids."

253

"I know, James, and this is a bonding time in the children's lives and this bonding window lasts, typically, for four to six months. You must make sure you're available to Kelly and the kids at every opportunity. It won't be easy."

"Easy is not something I'm used to."

I signal that it's okay to move on, so Dr. Janowitz turns to Cassandra; however, my concentration is elsewhere as my mind is focused on the Todds, so I sit there in a fog as Cassandra, Rick, Melissa, Leigh, and Jerry say what's on their minds.

"I just want to say," begins Leigh, "how proud I am of Jim for doing what he is doing for the Todds. He is ignoring his own pain and helping them. I find that very admirable. We should all have a friend so good."

"Nothing like this has ever happened to me. My grandparents died, but they were old. And I barely knew them. But a close friend, my first friend in Houston, this is new to me."

"If you need some moral support, James, you can always count on the group," Leigh says. "We are your friends too, after all. And me. You have been really kind to me. It has meant a lot."

Friday at work passes quickly as I have a lot of catching up to do. After work I pack my clothes and ride my bicycle over to Kelly's house to join her and the kids for dinner. Because it's late, Kelly and I decide that the drywall work will wait until Saturday morning. After dinner, as I clean up, Kelly checks her e-mail. We then sit and talk for a while before going to bed. The dog is nowhere to be seen. Gone. She has kenneled him for a week.

Saturday morning finds all of us awake early. After breakfast, as the children watch cartoons, I get started on the drywall taping, mudding, and sanding processes to prepare the attic for painting. In between checking her e-mails, Kelly is busy cleaning the house. She seems cheerful, which I guess is good, a sign either of some closure or denial.

Because I work straight through lunch, around 3:30 PM I decide to stop for the day. As I'm cleaning up outside, Kelly comes out to me and tells me her good news.

"Jim, I have something to tell you. You're the first one to know."

"I'm up for a little good news. Please tell me, what is it?"

"I'm engaged!" she gushes.

"Excuse me? Engaged in what?"

"Engaged to be married to my best friend. I don't know if you knew it or not, but Scott and I were having problems and had he not died, I would have sought a divorce."

"I didn't know anything about marital problems. Scott never said a thing."

"He didn't want anyone to know, I guess."

"So, you're actually engaged? To be married?"

"That's right," Kelly responds. "I can think of worse things than being married to my best friend."

"Your best friend. Who's the lucky guy?" I almost choke on the words.

"Corey Craig," Kelly answers gleefully, "my manager at work. You met him the night of the memorial."

Corey Fucking Craig, I say to myself in disbelief. Corey Fucking Creep. I remember him from the memorial service, slug-like, attaching himself to Kelly. Not an impressive physical specimen: about 5'7", brown balding head of hair, with a miserable mustache that looked like a bug died on his lip. Twenty years older than Kelly and looked every day of it. Loathsome in my view, but that's just me. She saw something in him. Oh, yeah, he's rich.

"Well tell me, how did all this happen?" I ask, trying not to be angry.

"We became friends when I started working for him. There was something there, Jim. I tried to fight it, but it just happened."

Through frequent e-mails and talks at work, their relationship grew over time to the point where Kelly was ready to leave Scott for Corey, and Corey was ready to leave his wife for Kelly. All those password-protected emails. No wonder she was always checking them.

"How long has Corey been married?"

"I think it's been eighteen years."

"Why would Corey want to leave an eighteen-year marriage?" I ask.

"He and his wife never had children, and he decided late in life that he wanted a family life. I'm offering him the ready-made family life he never had. And we're really compatible." Kelly answers.

I think to myself, how can she say that when I'm feeling the loss of my own future family?

"When did Corey propose?"

"He came by the house on Tuesday afternoon, the day before the memorial, and asked me to marry him. I couldn't think of any reason not to, so I accepted." Kelly says smiling.

Kelly explains that Corey then went home and announced to his wife that he wanted a divorce. Just like that. Wham bam, see you ma'am.

"He's moving into an apartment on this side of town next weekend," she adds gleefully. Glee is not an emotion appropriate to my mood. I begin to hate her just a little. It's like the star quarterback invited her to the Prom. You are a silly, unfeeling bitch, I think to myself.

"Congratulations," I say half-heartedly, my pain hidden by numbness. "I don't know quite what to say."

"Thanks!" Kelly responds smiling.

After she goes back inside the house, I finish cleaning the tools, then shower and change. While I am cleaning the taping knives, in a moment of self-destructive anger, I make a nice long cut in the palm of my right hand with the edge of the three-inch blade. It bleeds copiously, just as I knew it would. I watch my blood going down the drain diluted with water. I find the First Aid kit and wrap some gauze around the cut. The blood soaks through it quickly. Because I didn't eat lunch, Kelly plans to serve an early dinner; however, my bloody hand puts an end to that plan.

"Is there something wrong, Jim? Oh, my goodness what did you do to yourself?"

Yes, Kelly, I think to myself, something is very, very wrong. I feel like a fool.

"I cut myself cleaning my tools," I say. "I think I may need some stitches."

"Oh, James let me drive you to the emergency room. I'm sorry this happened."

Seven stitches and a tetanus shot later, when we get back from emergency care, I'm in no mood for food or conversation.

After they have their dinner, Kelly again checks her e-mail. Now her constant checking of e-mails makes sense. Connecting to Corey electronically. Rob, Amy, and I load the dishwasher.

When Kelly reappears, I say, "I need to go home and sleep in my own bed. This work today has really tired me out."

Kelly says nothing and nods her understanding. I give her a warm hug, then hug Rob and Amy and depart for the evening. On Sunday morning, I call Kelly and explain that I won't be coming over today due to not feeling well.

"I think I better keep this wound clean for a few days," I tell her.

Kelly says she understands. I spend the rest of the day Sunday in a severe depression, realizing that an important part of my life is over. There won't be any room for me — or Scott — in Kelly' new life.

On Monday morning, I call Leti and ask if Dr. Janowitz can see me on Tuesday after work, realizing that it's an off-week. Leti says she'll check with the doctor and call me back, which she does later that morning.

On Tuesday evening, Dr. Janowitz begins my therapy session by asking, "How are you doing this evening? What happened to your hand? You didn't hit someone I hope." He said that with a grin.

Without hesitation, I explode, "I cut it doing work at Scott's. I was upset about something that she told me. It's unbelievable, Dr. Janowitz, Kelly's engaged already! Scott was only dead six days before she accepted a marriage proposal from her boss at work! Jesus Christ, the body wasn't even cold! It was before the funeral. Can you imagine that!"

After providing more details, I explain how Kelly and Corey would e-mail messages to each other. They had this secret line of communication. Her password protected computer was safe from Scott's naïve eyes.

"She betrayed him. It's just that simple. Who knows what else she did?"

Dr. Janowitz remained silent. He wasn't taking notes; he just let me express my outrage.

"It wasn't normal e-mail!" I yell. "They would password protect a file that they passed to each other. Because only they knew the password, even if Scott did read Kelly's e-mails, he would never know about their secret file. He must have sensed something was going on. That fucking bitch!"

After talking for a while, I begin to calm down and look at the situation from a different angle.

"Scott died at work," I tell the doctor. "Yet Kelly didn't want to identify the body. Instead, she had one of Scott's co-workers do it. Why was that? I needed to see Scott for myself to see that he was really dead, and all this wasn't some sort of dream. The children didn't see the body. I didn't see the body. All that anyone saw of Scott was an urn picked out from a photograph. The cheapest urn she could find. How can we have closure with that?

"I should've known something was up by the way that Kelly cleaned out Scott's clothes. In just one day she completely rid herself of Scott and his memories. How can you write someone off just like that? How can you write off the father of your children that quickly? I am really searching for answers here, Dr. Janowitz."

I am searching for answers. "I just don't understand."

Dr. Janowitz spends the next twenty minutes helping me to process my feelings.

"I have something that might be of some solace, Jim. Will you allow me to share it with you? It's a brief verse from the Bible."

"Of course, knowing the Bible can be a source of faith, and I'm in short supply of that right now."

"It's from Philippians, an epistle to the citizens of Philippi from

Paul. Do you know it?"

"No, not really."

"Its message is to think about the things in your life, in your relationship with Scott, for example, that are meaningful to you. *Finally, brethren, whatever things are true, whatever things are noble, whatever things are just, whatever things are pure, whatever things are lovely, whatever things are of good report, if there is any virtue and if there is anything praiseworthy — meditate on these things.'*"

"I understand. I mean, I don't fully understand at all what happened, but it will help to remember the importance of Scott to me. There were many things praiseworthy about him, especially his ability to father Rob and Amy with love and devotion."

Near the end of our discussion, Dr. Janowitz again emphasizes the children, their vulnerability, and how long-lasting the death of their father will be to them.

"Even if it is very painful for you personally, you need to be there for Rob and Amy," he instructs. "Be there for the children."

Anger is always the easiest, the most available of emotions to me. It is the one I learned at my parents' knees, my mother's milk. It is the default emotion, even now, and it has become mine. Rage at the dying of the light, that's standard issue anger, I also rage at the birth of the light. Anger is the only emotion I trusted until Scott's death. A bubble exploded in his brain, and I am left to untangle what I feel. I am angry at him. I'm enraged at Kelly. That is a legitimate emotion that follows what I regard as her betrayal of Scott. Engaged within days of his death to some silly twit whom I despise without even knowing. And the betrayal of me. She has stolen my family from me, the bitch.

"What do you feel now, James, about Scott, I mean?" Dr. Janowitz asks.

"I feel abandoned."

"Anything else?"

"Irritated. Mad as hell at Kelly. Concern for Rob and Amy. I am outraged."

My situation, my dilemma, my illness has left me with little emotional affect. I feel the entanglement of confusion, accusations and deceit. I feel the burden of these things, and they weigh heavily on me.

"I feel something else, too. I've been trying to figure it out, and I think I have."

"What's that, James?"

"I am grieving. I feel sorrow," I answer.

"That's an appropriate feeling, James. You are grieving for your beloved friend."

I think I know in this moment that something has changed in me. This new thing — not violence, not furniture-throwing rage, not the bleakness of nighttime depression — but sorrow, was part of me, a piece of my healing truth.

From the place to which I had fallen, an abyss of my own creation, I began to rise, slowly, gradually, somehow lifted by the tragedy of Scott's death and the counterweight of my anguish.

THE FIRST DATE, THE FIRST DISGRACE

On the Wednesday, Thursday, and Friday following my emergency meeting with Dr. Janowitz, I remain in my office at work with my door closed as I try to process my feelings of loss: Scott, my "family," and Kelly's betrayal. Because my manager, Mike Brow, recognizes that this is a setback to previous behavior, on Friday morning he stops by my office.

"Is everything all right, Jim? How are things with Scott's family?"

"Not great."

I have a good relationship with Mike. There is a lot of pressure on him with the merger, but he has always looked out for me. On Thursday I had to warn him that I might be taking some additional vacation days or personal days to deal with Kelly and the kids. He behaved with marked concern and said that I should take off whatever time I needed.

I probably made a mistake when I told him the news about Kelly's sudden engagement. That would be office gossip for a long time.

"Kelly is engaged to her boss at work," I blurt out. "Apparently, they were having a sort of affair before Scott died. He was dead six days before they were engaged."

"Really? That's very strange. She didn't give the kids a chance to mourn for their dad. No respect for her husband. Terrible!"

"Do you think? I'm having some difficulty processing Scott's death and the whole situation with Kelly and how all of this will impact the children."

"How can I help, Jim?"

"I just need a little time to sort things out, Mike."

"I understand, Jim. If you want to talk to someone professionally, counseling is available via the Employee Assistance Program. I talked to them when my wife was so sick."

"Thanks, I think I just need to think and maybe cry a little, too."

Just before lunch, Kelly calls, "Jim, can you come over and spend the weekend? The kids really miss you."

"I guess I can," I answer. "What's going on?"

"I'd like you to watch Rob and Amy tonight so Corey and I can go out on a date to get to know each other better."

Even though it pains me, in the back of my mind I hear Dr. Janowitz's directions to be there for the children, I respond affirmatively.

"Yes, I can come by. I'll be a little late due to needing to work late on Friday, but I'll be there."

"Thanks," Kelly says. "I'll have dinner waiting for you."

"Thanks," I say softly as I hang up, the depression already setting in.

On my bicycle ride over to Kelly's house, I think about how the children will react to having a new dad, a total stranger to them, so soon after Scott's passing. Because the thought of Kelly spending "quality time" with Corey absolutely enrages me, I try my hardest to concentrate on the health and welfare of the children. It is very difficult for me to do.

Upon arriving at Kelly's house, I'm greeted in the usual fashion with warm hugs from Kelly, Rob, and Amy. I greet Corey with a nod rather than a firm handshake. I point to the bandage on my hand. The kids seem withdrawn and not sure what to make of "Uncle" Corey. They hold back emotionally and stand behind me almost as if they were hiding.

"Congratulations on your engagement. She's a great lady."

"Thanks," he says, the awkwardness of the situation apparent to all of us. I don't think the kids have any idea what an "engagement" is.

Because it's already approaching 8:00 PM, Kelly asks if I'd mind if they depart right away.

"No," I say. "Go have fun."

"There are warm-ups in the oven," Kelly tells me. "We should be back by midnight."

After a quick meal, I enter the living room and sit down on the couch with Rob and Amy, who are watching a television program on lions in Africa.

"Grrrrr!" I growl, startling them.

"Jimmy Snyder, don't do that!" Rob commands.

The three of us watch TV the rest of the evening until bedtime. They drape themselves over me, in need of physical contact and reassurance. I try to make things normal, just another night of TV with Jimmy Snyder. Unlike most nights, the kids push back a little on going to bed at their regular time this evening, so I tell them that they can stay up for a half-hour longer. Together we watch another TV show, this one on spiders in Africa. I then chase them upstairs to brush their teeth and go to bed.

At around midnight, Kelly and Corey return home. Kelly checks the kids as Corey and I make small talk. The two of them then say goodnight and Corey leaves.

"How was your evening?" I ask Kelly after she comes back inside the house.

"It was fabulous! It was really wonderful!" she exclaims.

"That's good," I say, somewhat limply.

"I'm going to ask you for another favor. Will you sit with the kids again tomorrow night?"

"Sure," I respond, feigning excitement. "They're no trouble. Plus, that'll give me more time to work in the attic."

Saturday finds me working the whole day in the attic, sanding and mudding the exposed tape. When I take a break, Kelly and I chat.

"It's funny, James, but the reason Corey proposed so soon after Scott died was because he was afraid you might have proposed."

"How would you feel about that?" I ask Kelly. I'm very interested in her answer.

"You're too much like Scott," Kelly tells me. "I need someone different. Besides, you're like a brother to me, Jim, and I can't see myself with my brother."

"Understand," I say, the only response I can muster.

On Saturday evening, Corey joins us for dinner, after which he and Kelly go out on another date. I make popcorn for the kids, who seem content to watch TV.

Kelly and Corey return around 10:30 PM and sit on the couch together as the three of us talk.

"Tonight, we went miniature golfing," Kelly tells me. "And I won!"

She giggles and prods Corey the way love birds do. I'm beginning to find them disgusting.

"She's pretty good," Corey responds smiling.

Looking at the two of them sitting there together turns my stomach, but I hide it well and pretend to be interested all the while we talk. Finally, at around 11:45 PM, Corey leaves.

After Corey leaves, Kelly says to me, "I'm going to have to do something about the dog. He's gotten really bad about shitting in the house. And I think Corey doesn't like him."

"You have to walk him more. He's an old dog, but he's not sick."

"I've been busy, and sometimes I forget. I love Casey but he's become a lot of trouble."

"Just don't do anything without talking to me about it. If necessary, I'll take him and figure out the logistics. I can always find a dog walker to take him out when I'm at work. He was Scott's and my dog, Kelly, we both raised him."

I hug Kelly goodnight and then hit the couch, my depression reaching its depth.

Early on Sunday morning, I'm awoken by Rob and Amy climbing on top of me.

"Jimmy Snyder, can we have some breakfast?" they ask in unison.

"Sure," I respond as I get up. "What would you like?"

"Can I have waffles?" Rob asks.

"Me, too!" Amy requests.

"Yes, you both may," I answer as I remove the frozen waffles from the freezer. In short order the toaster pops them out and the kids are fed. I then return to the couch until Kelly gets up.

Following Kelly's egg and pancake brunch, I decide to return home, my work at the Todds house finished for the weekend. I give warm hugs to Kelly, Rob, and Amy, and then ride home, defeated in love and maybe in life as well.

But God bless those sweet children.

TWO VERSIONS OF MY LIFE

At therapy on Tuesday evening, I talk with Dr. Janowitz about Kelly. I am very depressed about the course of events. I have lost Scott, and he has been replaced in Kelly's life and the kids' life with Corey, for whom I have formed a considerable enmity.

Dr. Janowitz encourages me not to abandon them; that despite my feelings of anger and frustration, this moment is critical for Rob and Amy.

I've become a little tired of that exhortation. I understand the theory of it, but the practice is painful, even humiliating. I'm thinking about something else, another of my failures.

After a moment of awkward silence, I continue. "Did I ever tell you about my pilot experience in the Air Force?"

"No," Dr. Janowitz answers. "I didn't think you were in the military."

"That's correct. I wasn't. However, I did try to join. As I was nearing graduation from Cleveland College, I approached a recruiter and told him that I wanted to fly F15's. Seeing that I wore glasses, the recruiter tried and tried and tried to convince me to go for a navigator position instead, for which the vision requirements were less strict. But I held my ground. I ended up receiving the pilot slot but failing the flight physical for a hearing loss. Go figure."

"How did you feel when you received the bad news?" Dr. Janowitz asks following my lead.

"Very disappointed," I answer. "But my point is I didn't give up. I didn't yield to the recruiter's pressure to go for a lesser position. Nor did I quit. I stuck with it for as far as it would go. And that's what I need to do here. As much as I want to walk away from that project and Kelly, I won't. I won't abandon those kids."

"Are you doing anything socially?" Dr. Janowitz asks changing the subject.

"Just going to work," I respond.

"I know you go to work, I mean, are you seeing anyone?"

"No, you know that," I answer sarcastically.

"The right relationship would be very good for you, Jim. With the right relationship, you could experience all the positives of being with someone you care about who cares about you. With the right relationship, we could probably lower the dosages of your medicines significantly."

"With the right relationship," I respond.

"Yes," the doctor continues, "With the right relationship."

"Exactly how do I meet this 'right relationship'?"

"Well, she's probably not going to come knocking on your door," Dr. Janowitz answers with a tinge of sarcasm. He is sometimes annoyed at me; we are sometimes, like tonight, annoyed at each other.

"What I'm saying, James, and I have said it before, you'll need to get out of your comfort zone and meet people. I think you should try internet dating. Many people are using it."

"I think there are mostly perverts on it."

"James, an amazing number of marriages start with internet dating. It's a way to meet people, particularly if you're a little isolated socially."

"I'll think about it."

"We'll talk more about it next time."

Changing the subject, he asks, "Are you exercising?"

"I'm still riding my bicycle after work. I've been riding my bike back and forth to the Todds house on weekends, and I try to get a longer ride in Sunday afternoon on my way home. I've been busy with the attic project. It's almost done, but with Corey in the picture, I'll probably be there less. I'll get a chance to ride more depending on what they do. I can't imagine Corey will want me around."

"Probably not. You would be a threat and a constant reminder of Scott."

"Anyway, I'm slowly getting into shape. I've lost about fifteen pounds, and people tell me I look ten years younger without the beard."

"I liked the beard, James. You looked very rabbinical."

I laugh at that. "I guess that's a compliment coming from you, Dr. Janowitz."

"Oh, it is. You looked fiercely intelligent and wise."

"I wish I were either of those things."

"Are you riding alone or with people?"

"I'm almost always alone."

"Would you be willing to ride with another person?"

Janowitz has a plan. I know him well enough by now to realize that he had found someone to ride with me. I was hoping it was Leigh.

"I'm open to that, I guess. Depends on the person."

"I have an idea. I have a new patient, very nice guy. He's a little older than you. He's from the Northeast, Boston or Vermont. He's in construction in some fashion. I think he's a construction manager on some big project over in River Oaks."

"Okay. So, what's your idea?"

"I bring him up because he is a bicyclist, and he is riding by himself as well. He doesn't feel comfortable riding by himself. He thinks it's dangerous, if he took a fall, for example. You know the hazards of bicycling as well as anyone."

"What's his name?"

"His name is Harry Boyarski. That's all I can tell you for the moment. But I think you two would get along, and you would have someone to ride with. A bike buddy, as it were. I took the liberty of mentioning the possibility to him. I hope you don't mind."

"I don't mind at all, but I suppose he is a world class rider. I ride for exercise. I'm not into competition."

"No, I think he does it for recreation, too. He's a weekend rider. He's here only temporarily for work, and I think he is a little lonely. Harry has given me permission to give his name and phone number to a bicyclist who might want to cycle with him. Maybe the two of you could work something out."

"I suppose I could call him."

"Why don't you give it a try? He's a very nice fellow."

"Nice fellow, huh? He's not gay, is he?"

"No. Not that that should matter, James."

"All right," I agree hesitantly. "I'll call this Harry the bicyclist fellow. I just hope he's not weird."

"He's not at all weird. He's a good guy. How are you doing on medicines?" The session is over when he asks that question.

"I'm okay."

"Thank you, Dr. Janowitz," I say as I'm on my way out.

"You will ride your bicycle this weekend, won't you?" the doctor shouts down the hallway after me.

"Yes, I will," I shout back. "Goodnight."

"Call Harry."

"I will."

Well, I think, driving home, Dr. Janowitz has become a

matchmaker. I guess it's all in a day's work. I don't like change; I've known that all my life. I am a man of extremely well-defined habits. In some ways, being able to cling to some sort of structure while enduring intense inner chaos is what preserves me. Fear is a big part of mental illness; fear of healing, fear of the consequences of healing. In my best, most lucid moments, I know I am fortunate to be healing. It doesn't have to be this way. I could have been on the evening news led into a police station in handcuffs. A dude whose homicidal ideations turned into really truly homicide. Still could do that, I guess. But driving home through the rainy Texas night — it never rains like this in Ohio — I feel my life is changing, slowly but profoundly. I wasn't afraid. Goodbye Kelly, hello Harry whatever the hell your name is.

HARRISON BOYARSKI, BICYCLIST

It was on that next Saturday morning, riding one of my favorite routes along I-10 that I decided that I would take Dr. Janowitz's suggestion and call Harry Boyarski. Normally, I would have been at Kelly's house (that's the way I've trained myself to think about it) but she and Corey were having a party for their co-workers. I was not invited to that BBQ. Kelly told me that she and Corey were going to Italy together in a few weeks.

"Jim, I know you're not happy about all this. But Corey is the next phase of my life."

"I know. But you don't love him, do you?"

"I don't know, yet. I didn't love Scott at the end, either. We had drifted apart."

"You had time to fix it."

"No, we didn't. Scott had almost no time left. We're going to go to Italy for ten days. The kids are going to stay with my mother."

"I could take care of them."

"No, Jim, they'll be better off with my mother. And one other thing, I'd like you to get the playroom done as soon as possible. Corey is willing to hire someone to finish the job if you can't handle it alone."

I am being squeezed out, that much is clear.

"No, there are only a few things left to do. I need to finish it myself. This was Scott's and my project, and I want it to end that way." I will not surrender that to anyone.

I am a solitary soul by inclination, for the most part happily solo, and have been all my life. My parents thought I was hiding something, but I wasn't. My instinct, the wary crouch of the prize fighter, is my emotional posture. Jab and move, jab and move. I wanted to stay vertical as long as I could. Lord knows, there might be one dread moment, in fact, when I will be flat-backed on the canvas, my mouth filled with blood, with the referee above me counting. But the man will never get to "ten." Here I am on my bicycle, struggling in the heat, sweating and not unhappy.

"Damn, Jim," I said surprisingly loudly to myself, "you have to get your sorry ass in shape."

I know this ride very well. It is an easy one, one of my Saturday morning rides. My Sunday rides are the more demanding ones, like Route 290. It is still very early in the morning, my favorite time to ride, especially in the Houston heat and humidity. I picked up the pace, knowing if I were going to have a riding partner, I needed to work on my wind and get the quads strengthened.

"Why not call this guy?" I say aloud. "If I don't like him, I don't have to ride with him."

I bent into the uphill ride, trying to get to the top of the hill without changing gears.

When I got home, even before I showered, I turned up the air conditioning and grabbed the phone. I dialed the number Dr. Janowitz had given me. The phone rang six or seven times, and I was waiting for the voice mail prompt, when someone picked up.

"This is Harry," Harry Boyarski said, a little breathlessly.

"Hi, Harry. My name is Jim Snyder. Dr. Janowitz gave me your number."

"Oh, yeah. Janowitz mentioned you."

"Is this a bad time?"

"It's fine. I'm a little out of breath because I just got back from the grocery store. I use the stairs rather than an elevator in the hope I can get some cardio work in on the cheap."

"So, Harry, tell me what you're looking for in a bike buddy."

It was my custom to always use Dr. Janowitz's title. I meant to be respectful to the man and his role in my life. Harry usually called him just Janowitz or old Janowitz. He meant no disrespect; that was just his style.

"So, Jim, I'm looking for a riding partner. I don't know Houston that well, and I don't know many good routes. I'm also a little skittish about riding by myself. Drivers are crazy in this town, man, worse than in Boston, and Boston is full of nasty drivers."

"I know what you mean. I've had a couple of close calls. What kind of rider are you? Do you want to race, I mean, to be in competition?"

"Too old, Jim. I'm just a spin-around-the-block, and a cold-beer-at-the-end-of-the- day, kind of guy."

"That's me, too. I work in an office all week, and I'm out of shape."

"I get that. I used to play tennis in college in Boston, but I hate to think what would happen if I picked up a racket now. Wouldn't be pretty."

"I'm going to be riding on the weekends, Harry. Probably Saturdays and most Sundays."

"Yeah, I'm running this construction job over in River Oaks. It's winding down, so the weekend is a good time for me."

"Okay, so how is next weekend? I'm finishing a little construction project myself, but it looks like I won't have access to the space for a few weeks."

"Oh, yeah, what are you doing?"

"My buddy Scott and I were renovating an attic space into a playroom for the kids. He was the real builder on the job, I was just a laborer, board holder. Unfortunately, he died suddenly a couple of weeks ago so I've been trying to finish it myself."

"Oh, man, I'm sorry to hear that. I've got some guys who might be willing to finish it if you need help."

"Nope. I'm going to do it myself. It's just a little taping and painting left. I think I have about three days' work at this point. So, for a couple of weeks my weekends are pretty much free. What's a good time for you?"

"I'll be honest, Jim, my schedule is a crazy one, and I never know when a plumber is going to fuck up something, so sometimes things get a little complicated. But, as of this moment, next weekend is wide open."

"Great. Do you want to say next Saturday then? Early, 7:00 AM or so?"

"That would work," Harry answers. "Hold on, Jim, while I look for something to write with."

I could hear a drawer opening and closing.

"Okay, Jim, give me your number so I can call you in case I need to work or something."

I gave him my work and home numbers. I wondered what the "or something" might be.

"I tell you what, Harry. Do you know where George Bush Park is?"

"No, but I can find it. I have a map around here somewhere. I'm sure one of the guys who works for me will know."

"Where do you live?"

"I live in Cinco Ranch."

"You're a ten-minute ride away. There is a gazebo in the center of the park. I'll meet you there."

"Great, Jim, I'll see you next Saturday."

After I hung up, I thought, he seemed okay, but you never know.

The next Saturday, I got to George Bush Park early. I'm usually always early, but I thought if I spotted him as he rode up and didn't like his looks I could make a getaway, unseen. I sat on the steps of the gazebo, wondering if this Boyarski person would really show up. I wondered what kind of bicycle he rode. Scott used to say that he could figure out a man's income by his watch and the kind of shoes he wore.

"Dead giveaways, Jimmy. Foolproof."

Bicyclists, particularly the dedicated enthusiasts, use the kind of bike you ride as an insight into your riding soul. Snobs, really, but I do have a fancy 12-speed Trek racing bike. It's probably more bike than I need, but at least I put up a good show.

I wonder what those bike snobs would have thought when they saw Harry Boyarski wobble into George Bush Park on an ancient Peugeot, well battered and hard ridden. The rider stopped at the entrance of the park and looked at the map, showing various features — gardens, playgrounds, and gazebo. He looked my way towards the gazebo, and I stood up and waved at him. He smiled and waved back and rode over to me.

"Jim, right?"

"Nice to meet you, Harry."

"Same with me. Man, that is a beautiful bike."

"I just got it last spring at an estate sale. It had been sitting in someone's attic for a couple of years."

"That's a Trek?"

"Yes. But I only paid seventy-five dollars for it. It needed a lot of work."

"That's a steal. You must have spent something to have it reconditioned if it was in bad shape."

"My friend Scott knew a bike mechanic who owed him a favor. Labor and parts to put it back into riding shape only cost me another two hundred bucks. I could never afford it if I had to pay full retail. This bike would be a couple grand new."

"It's a beauty. I hope you don't mind being with someone riding this piece of shit. I bought it very second hand from a carpenter. The carpenter was pretty much second hand, too."

"It's a ride. That's all that counts."

Harry's watch was an old Hamilton that he wore on a belt loop. And his shoes were muddy New Balances, with the right shoe frayed in the toe. I wondered what Scott would have made of that combination. Harry doesn't ooze prosperity, but then he isn't a Texan. Maybe wherever he is from oozes prosperity in a different way. Mostly, he seems like an old hippie, and maybe that is going to be okay.

"Let me sit down for a second here, Jim, to get my bearings."

"Sure. You feel okay?"

"I'm just a tiny bit out of shape. That's a nice outfit, by the way. I should get some riding shorts and a shirt. All I have is this helmet, also second hand, that came with the bike. At least it fits. By the way, saying I'm just a tiny bit out of shape is a wild understatement of my wretched physical condition."

He was wearing a pair of Navy blue sweatpants, and a faded red t-shirt that said, "Boston College." Probably not the right outfit for a long ride in the Texas heat, but okay for today, our test spin.

Boyarski has what I imagine to be the build of a tennis player. He is about six feet tall, thin, with dark hair, beginning to gray a little. I notice that he has large, beaten up hands. A worker's hands. He is handsome, I suppose, but I've never been a very good judge of that sort of thing. I notice his face and arms are very tan but his upper arms and chest below the neck are not. A farmer's tan.

"So how long have you been a patient of Janowitz, Jim?"

"I've been a patient of Dr. Janowitz for a long time. A long time. How about you?"

"A little less than a year. He's a good guy. Is it okay to talk about this?"

"Sure. Why not?"

"I don't know, a breach of confidentiality or something."

"Harry, you should know if we ride our bikes together it is very unlikely I'll talk to you about my therapeutic relationship with Dr. Janowitz."

"Okay, but I've never been in therapy before, so all this is new to me. Old Janowitz is a good guy, although I can't quite make him understand I'm not a Jew despite my name."

"Dr. Janowitz is a very special man. I think he saved my life."

"He's helped me dealing with some things. I guess we're both a little crazy, huh?"

"I was more than a little crazy, Harry."

"It happens. Stuff really happens. I was just kidding, by the way. I hope I didn't offend you."

"Not at all." Except I am offended, just a little.

I got up from the step and began to stretch.

"So, this is it? Time to ride?" Harry asks.

"Let's go."

"Lead the way, brother, but set a modest pace. I don't want to have a coronary on our first ride," Harry says.

I leave George Bush Park and turn onto Westheimer Parkway setting a relatively slow pace. I look back to see if Harry is behind me. He is but just. He is wobbling on his second-hand Peugeot, determined not to be left behind. So, it begins, these days of riding and talking and always with cold beer at the end. Many cold beers and much talk were to be our common destiny for the next few months. And beyond.

THE END OF SOMETHING

The next Friday afternoon, after work, I ride my Trek to the Todd's house. It is very hot and humid, Houston weather at the end of summer and a light rain is beginning. I don't like to ride in the rain but the forecast for the rest of the weekend is for good weather, so I put on my rain gear and hope I don't get too wet.

It's only been five weeks since Scott's death, and my world has changed dramatically. I feel like I'm walking around in someone else's nightmare. Instead of being at or near the center of the Todd family, Jimmy Snyder honorary uncle, I am an intruder into the evolving happy life of Kelly and Corey. I'm assuming they're fucking somewhere, but I don't know the details. Don't want to know them, frankly.

I put my bike in the garage and hang up my dripping rain gear. Kelly is in the kitchen when I enter the house.

"Hi, Jim. How was the ride?"

"Wet and slippery. I always feel really vulnerable on rainy days."

"It's supposed to clear up overnight. What are your plans for today?"

"As the Buddha said, Kelly, before Enlightenment I worked, after Enlightenment I worked. I guess I'm going to work. I have to finish a bit of mudding and sanding. Then I can prime and paint the ceilings and doors."

"What about the floors?"

"Scott was planning to sand and poly them himself. But that's way above my pay grade. I've checked into floor guys and made a list of three of them to bid on the job."

"How much will it cost?"

"I have no idea. A couple of thousand, I suppose for sanding the hardwood floors and three coats of poly?"

"Why three coats?"

"Little kids are hard on floors, I guess. I'm just passing along what Scott was planning to do."

"I think Corey mentioned something about paying for it. He wants to be a part of the project."

"That's his business. I don't give a shit what he pays for. This was, no, is Scott's and my job, and I'll always think of it that way."

"You miss Scott, don't you?"

"Of course. It's only been a few weeks."

"And you really don't like Corey."

"Kelly, I'm uncomfortable with this whole situation. I don't understand what you're doing with this guy."

"It just happened."

"I'm sorry but I don't buy that. You wanted it to happen and you made it happen. Men don't cheat on their wives and abandon an eighteen year marriage on a fucking whim, particularly when they are a twit like Corey."

"You think I seduced him?"

"It doesn't matter a rat's ass what I think. At this point you and Corey are like Bonnie and Clyde, a world historical couple and an embarrassment to me and a whole lot of other people. And, yes, I think you seduced him, although it didn't take much effort."

"You're being mean, now. I don't care about how anyone else thinks."

"Not even Rob and Amy? You don't care about what you're doing to them?"

"You're an asshole, Jim. And a crazy one at that. Did you forget to take your medication today?"

"I took plenty of medication. I'm fine."

"You're just jealous, Jim. You think I should have picked you."

"I'll be honest with you, Kelly. I think you should have but you didn't. Those kids love me and need me."

"I would have never picked you, ever. Not with your creepy paranoia and all that shit about Cindy and Janowitz and your really, really tiresome list of complaints and your whining. I know you're hurting, who the fuck isn't?"

"Don't start with this, Kelly. There's no coming back from where you're going."

"My husband just died, and I have to make some decisions. If you and Scott hadn't spent so much time getting your cocks rubbed on Friday nights, maybe he would have noticed that I had checked out emotionally."

"Kelly, don't do this. There are no second chances."

"Sure there are, Jim. 'No second chances' is just your little fucking insane fantasy, not mine. I have a second chance, and his name is Corey Craig. And it's definitely not Jimmy Snyder."

"By the way, where is Casey?"

"I couldn't deal with his shitting in the house anymore. Corey hated him so we put him down."

"You did what?"

"Corey took him to the vet, and had Casey euthanized. I couldn't watch it. I waited in the car."

"I told you not to do that. He was my dog as much as he was yours."

"Well, 'your' dog kept on shitting on my white carpets. Something had to be done."

"You know what Kelly, you are a fucking bitch."

We had come to the end of something in our friendship or whatever it was that existed between us. There were no second chances. Not for me.

"I'm just going to go back home."

"I think that's a very good idea. Corey is going to be here in a minute anyway."

When I get back to my apartment, I am in a deep depression. I sit in my wet rain gear, stunned and nearly hopeless. All the progress I feel I've made has vanished. I feel empty and very, very tired.

When the phone rings, I'm inclined to let the answering machine pick up, but I reach for the handset, thinking it might be important. It was Kelly.

"Jimmy," she says, "I'm so sorry for the things I said. I didn't really mean them. Can you forgive me?"

"Sure. We've both been under a lot of stress. There is nothing to forgive."

"I was really worried about you riding home in the rain. I almost got in the car to give you a ride."

"Why didn't you?"

"Corey wouldn't let me. We had a huge argument. If you don't mind, Jimmy, do you think you could stay away for a few days until things settle down?"

"I want to see the kids."

"I want you to see them, too. But just not right now."

"Okay. Not right now. Good night."

We had both said things that were hurtful, mostly because they were true. And, no, I am not going to forgive her. I am not the forgiving kind.

JAMES SNYDER, CHOCOLATIER

At group on Thursday evening, Dr. Janowitz begins by telling us that Leigh will not be in attendance because she is attending a conference in Austin.

"That's got to be fun, a bunch of mathematicians in a room together. Lots of wild algorithms in the state capital," Rick says.

"I'm sure it's a very distinguished group," Janowitz responds. "Apparently, Leigh is highly respected in her field."

"She is, Doctor, she's an expert or something about the Hodge Conjecture. Don't ask me about it. She tried to explain it to me, but I tuned out when she got to algebraic topology. It's all very, very abstract."

"I'm sure when Jim and Leigh go to Rolf's for a drink they don't just talk about mathematics. I bet they talk about us, too," Melissa says.

"She's way smarter than I am," I say, "and as a matter of fact we have talked about trigonometry. I have degrees in electrical engineering and aeronautical engineering, after all, Melissa. And we don't talk much about group. When we say anything it's mostly how wonderful you all are."

"Oh, Jim, you are not a very good liar. If we were wonderful, we wouldn't be here," Jerry says.

I just shrug. He is right, of course.

"That's impressive, Jim. And Dr. Janowitz promised me that there would be no mathematics in group. I was horrible at it. I guess we're lucky to have two brainiacs as groupmates," Rick says. "I'll bring my slide rule in next time."

"And I'll show you how to use it, Rick," I respond. "No charge."

"Okay," Dr. Janowitz says, "enough kidding around." He then

277

looks around the room and asks, "Who has some good news to share?"

When none of us volunteers, Dr. Janowitz turns to me saying, "Jim, why don't we start with you tonight, but before you talk about the chocolate project, I want to ask you how things are going with Kelly and the kids."

"She and shit for brains, I mean Corey, just got back from a trip to Italy. Ten days in Florence and the Tuscan foothills."

"Jim," says Dr. Janowitz, "let's just call him Corey."

"Okay. Anyway, this vacation was originally supposed to be an anniversary present to his wife, Trisha, the now-abandoned wife of eighteen years. The job that Scott and I started, the playroom job, is effectively finished but not quite. I don't think I'll be allowed to finish it. In fact, I don't think I'll be allowed back in the house. Corey doesn't like me around. He's living in an apartment close to Kelly, but he is going to move in with her any day now. Once they get married, which will be soon, I'll be invited to not be around. I'm being pushed to the sidelines. Even now, I rarely see the kids and it is very hurtful to me. I don't know what to do."

"It doesn't seem there is anything you can do. She has made some deeply stupid decisions," Melissa says.

"I don't think they're stupid at all," Jerry, the lawyer, says. "They are very calculated. Do you think Kelly loves Corey, Jim?"

"She said she didn't. Of course, she also said she didn't love Scott at the end."

"She's made a business decision. My question is, why isn't she marrying you?" Jerry asks. Not a fair question, I think. He is picking at a scab, my scab, unnecessarily.

I look up at Dr. Janowitz in embarrassment. I feel flushed and uneasy.

"She said I was too much like Scott."

Rick joins in, "Well, Jim, from what you told me about Scott, you're not at all like him. I get it you were good friends, but you seem very dissimilar. This is not a criticism of Scott, by the way. I know he was your dear friend."

Dr. Janowitz enters the discussion saying, "Kelly's choice is a complicated one, and as I see it had very little to do with James, I think. Everyone, Jim, Kelly and the kids, is trying to heal from the loss of someone they loved, Scott in this instance. I'm encouraging Jim, as should we all, to encourage Jim on his healing path. Kelly is finding her own path. Jim," Dr. Janowitz says looking at me, "you must do what you can to help Rob and Amy. They will be the ones most damaged in this process, if anyone is damaged. I know you'll do the right thing. Marriage with anyone right now would be problematic, especially with Kelly. Now, tell us about your chocolate empire in formation."

"I love those kids, Doctor. It's so damn sad."

"I know you love them, Jim. You'll do the right thing."

"Okay, chocolate," I begin again. "I have good news and bad news. I've spoken to you a little bit about my chocolate obsession. I think I've told you individually and as a group about the Easter eggs the ladies of my hometown church used to make for the holiday. Delicious and I wish I had one right now."

"I can't eat chocolate," Melissa says, "because of my diet. But they sound good."

"They are really good, Melissa, but they don't last long. They have to be refrigerated or eaten, otherwise they degrade very quickly. In short, they couldn't be a viable commercial project."

"Couldn't your Mom put them in a cooler and fly out here with them?" Jerry asks. "If we win the lottery we could buy an airplane ticket for her."

"She doesn't like to fly."

"Okay, Jim, we'll buy you a ticket, and you can pick them up."

"Rick" I ask, "can you arrange for us to win the lottery during Easter week?"

"Anything you want, Jim, for one of your Presbyterian Easter eggs."

"Anyway," I continue, "Dr. Janowitz has been encouraging me to think outside the box about my career. He knows I don't particularly like my job. Last week, when I was out riding my bicycle, I had a brainstorm. I couldn't wait to get home to try an experiment. I didn't have any peanut butter cups, so I ate a plain chocolate bar covered with peanut butter on both side of the chocolate. And I thought, wow is this good! I realized then that no candy company in the world puts chocolate inside the candy bar. It's always on the outside."

"Wouldn't it be gooey if it were on the inside?" Melissa asks.

"No, since the idea is the peanut butter would have the density of the chocolate."

"Can they do that?" Rick asks.

"I don't know yet. Let me just finish the concept part, Rick."

"My idea is to make a double decker or even a triple decker peanut butter cup. But I'm not going to limit myself to just peanut butter as the filling. There's peanut butter and jelly. Peanut butter and banana chips. Peanut butter with and caramel or peanuts or nougat. Or peanut butter and other type of fruit like cherries or raisins or apples."

"I like hazelnuts," Melissa says.

"Okay, hazelnuts," I reply. "The point is you're only limited by your imagination. All with chocolate as the dividing layer within the confection."

"Wow," says Jerry, "a chocolate visionary. That's a better mousetrap, Jim."

"I know, it seems obvious, you'd think someone would have done it by now."

"Maybe the chocolate makers have tried, and they can't get the formula right," Dr. Janowitz adds, a force for reason. Maybe I'm getting a little too amped up.

"That's possible, but have you ever noticed that major candy companies don't compete with one another? Only Hershey makes chocolate bars and peanut butter cups. Mars makes Snickers and M&Ms. Nestle makes Kit Kats to name a few."

"Stop," says Melissa. "I'm craving a Snickers bar right now."

"So, none of them compete with one another. By putting chocolate in the middle, it's possible to take them all on."

"Or they could buy you out for a billion dollars," Rick says.

"I don't want to get too deep into the details, but I've been doing a little research online and I think this idea is patentable. I know, one step forward, it seems, and one step back, or even a step and a half back. I've found the name of a food scientist by the name of Cyress in a place called Aimes College in Iowa. I called him last week and ran my idea past him. He likes the potential but was a little skeptical about finding a formula and a process that would work. I like him, but I'm a little distrustful. Trust has always been an issue with me. But things are breaking in my favor. So, my good news is that my researcher is willing to work with me to find out if this thing is feasible. I'm flying to Iowa in early October to meet him."

"Can you actually get a patent?" Rick interjects.

"Cyress thinks so, Rick," I respond.

"That is great news, Jim," Jerry says.

"Here, here!" Dr. Janowitz says loudly as the group responds.

"So, what's the bad news?" Melissa asks. She seems concerned for me.

"The bad news is that applying for the patents will cost every cent that I have, and even then, I won't be covering the worldwide market. I'm a little paranoid about spending more money, all my money."

"Jim, do you recall your diagnosis?" Dr. Janowitz asks.

"Yes," I answer quickly.

"Do you recall me telling you that you have a tendency toward paranoid thought processes?"

"Yes, but I'm not entirely sure what it means."

"Well, what that means is you tend to see things in their worst possible way. Instead of just being concerned, you go to the extreme and see this request in its worst possible light, as if Cyress is trying to steal your money and not move ahead to the next stage of the process. This could be life changing if it works out."

"But isn't paranoia helpful in business?"

"A little paranoia, perhaps," the doctor answers. "The key word being 'little.' In your case, Jim, you have a lot of paranoia to deal with."

"So, I shouldn't be concerned about the money?" I ask.

"Concerned, yes. Paranoid, no."

"Okay," I say. "I understand." I was basically terrified of losing my money in a crazy scheme.

"Jim, how much of the market will you be covering with your patents?" Jerry inquires.

"About two-thirds," I answer.

"And how big is the market in total?" Melissa asks.

"Today, about seventy-five billion US dollars."

"Wow!" Jerry concludes. "You could be an overnight multi-millionaire on royalties!"

"Let's hear it for Jim!" Dr. Janowitz proclaims as the group once again gets energized.

When all have calmed down, the doctor congratulates me and then talks about the hard work, dedication, and perseverance that I've put into this project. When he finishes, Leigh walks into the room, a little flushed from hurrying to make group.

"Leigh, I'm glad you could make it."

"Did I miss something important?"

"Jim was just explaining an idea he had about a chocolate bar."

"Oh, you mean, the peanut butter concoction. I think it's a great idea."

I look at Leigh, and she gives me one of her dazzling smiles.

"Jim, I guess you talk about trigonometry *and* chocolate with Leigh. How do I follow that?" Rick asks deadpan as he begins his turn to speak.

From Rick, we learn that the pain has started returning in his knee and lower back.

"Oh, that's not good. That's not a good sign at all!" Dr. Janowitz interrupts as he cautions Rick to be extra careful.

"I know, I know," Rick responds smiling. "I need to go back for more shots."

"You know," the doctor begins softly, "you can only go back for shots three times. After that, you'll have to live with the pain."

"Well, I'll try to be careful," Rick responds jovially, the seriousness of Dr. Janowitz's words lost on him.

"Tell us some good news tonight," Dr. Janowitz commands.

"We came close in the lottery. We matched three numbers and won a few dollars, and we were only one digit away on the other three numbers or we would've won the big one."

"Oh, damn, so close, that would have helped with my Cyress money," I say.

"How is your grandson, Rick?" Dr. Janowitz asks.

"He's doing well. I see him about once a week, usually on Saturdays."

"And your work?" the doctor continues.

"My relief work has slowed down a lot. I need to find something soon or we'll be standing in the soup line."

"Well, you seem very happy tonight, Rick," Dr. Janowitz says.

"Yes, I am happy," Rick responds. "I have my 'family.' You guys."

Dr. Janowitz turns to Jerry.

"Jerry," Dr. Janowitz queries, "How are you doing tonight?"

"Hi, everybody," Jerry says softly. "I'm not well."

"Tell us what's going on," the doctor encourages.

"I've been feeling down lately. I mean down. I don't want to do anything. I don't even want to get out of bed in the morning."

"Are you depressed?" Ricks asks sincerely.

"Yes, Rick," Jerry answers, "I believe I am depressed." No one does depression better than Jerry. When he begins to look down at the heels and a little scruffy, you know he's battling the Black Dog.

"What's going on in your life that has you down?" Dr. Janowitz asks.

"I don't know!" Jerry responds exasperatedly. "I look back over the last six or so months and there's nothing that I can point to that will explain why I'm depressed right now."

"Are you exercising?" the doctor asks.

"No, I don't have the motivation to exercise," Jerry answers.

"Are you still going to church?" Rick interjects. He is impatient with Jerry.

"What about Nita?" Rick asks before Jerry can answer. "Can't she get you motivated?"

"No, I sleep practically the whole weekend through. What's Nita got to do with it?"

"Jerry, it's pretty obvious you and Nita are an item."

"Rick," Nita says from the corner, "that's none of your business."

"I know, but what's the secret. I think we all know about it. Hey, let us be happy for you. What's the big deal?" Rick was enjoying this. But it is obvious there is something between them. Time to let the proverbial cat out of the proverbial bag.

"If it's obvious," Jerry says, "I think we can talk about it, Nita. We've been living together for a few weeks. We're talking about getting married."

"We're just thinking about it. Nothing definite," Nita adds hastily.

Dr. Janowitz says, "I didn't want to say anything until you were ready. Group, let's congratulate Jerry and Nita."

He started clapping and led us in applause. Leigh, I noticed, sat quietly with her hands in her lap. I joined in the applause. I'm not so sure about it.

"But, Jerry, we have to deal with your situation. When is your next individual session with me?" Dr. Janowitz asks.

"I don't have one scheduled."

"Please schedule one, the sooner the better," Dr. Janowitz advises. "I think we may need to make some adjustments."

"Okay," Jerry says, "I'll schedule an appointment for early next week."

"Melissa," Dr. Janowitz says as he turns to face her, "let's come to you next."

Melissa is also slightly depressed and upset that her weight loss has plateaued again, even though she continues to exercise regularly.

"Do you have any idea how frustrating it is to work your butt off in the gym every day of the week and not lose any weight?" she asks rhetorically as she looks up at the ceiling. "Let me tell you, it's really frustrating."

"It's not just exercise, Melissa," Leigh says. "You have to eat less."

"Easy for you to say, Leigh. What do you weigh, a hundred pounds?"

"I'm not being critical, Melissa, it's just a matter of the calories you take in versus the calories you burn."

"So, I eat some ice cream at the end of the day. Big deal. I'm not a mathematician. I don't want to count calories and divide by pi."

"Don't be angry, Melissa. And I'm not the one who is overweight. I'm just trying to be helpful."

"I know you are. Maybe some people are just meant to be overweight. Like me."

"What else is going on in your life?" Dr. Janowitz asks, refocusing the discussion.

"Ever since my relationship with Thomas ended," Melissa begins, "I've been concentrating on building my practice."

"Has it helped?" Rick asks.

"Yes, I'd say it's helped. But the strangest thing is, since I stopped caring if a man was pursuing me and began focusing solely on building my practice, I've had more offers for dates than I've ever had in my life!" Melissa says blushing.

"Why do you think that is?" the doctor asks.

"I honestly don't know," Melissa answers smiling. "But I like it and I hope it continues!"

Dr. Janowitz spends the final minutes of Melissa's turn talking with her about her budding love life.

"Okay, folks, I think that's good for tonight," says Dr. Janowitz. "We'll meet again in two weeks.

Before we leave the room, I notice that Melissa approaches Leigh. She whispers something in Leigh's ear, and they end the evening with a hug. Women. I don't get them.

IN WALKS HARRY BOYARSKI

Some nights in group are boring beyond belief. Sitting in the group room, in the places we habitually occupy, opening our sacks of sorrow and letting the anger and fear and anxiety out is mind numbing. Sitting in my chair, these tedious sessions are like waiting out a rain delay in a minor league baseball park in August: you want to get up and leave, but you never know, maybe in a few minutes the rain will stop, and the game will start. Tonight, it is still raining in Fall Creek, and the boys on the ball club are in the clubhouse, playing cards and eating baloney sandwiches.

From the group discussion, I learn that Nita and Jerry are planning to get married in late December and take their honeymoon in Hawaii over Christmas. They are both very excited about that, and we all wish them well.

Melissa announces, "I've lost another ten pounds. I have lost a total of thirty-five pounds. I'm still heavy, but I'm working on it."

With Dr. Janowitz leading the way, we all applaud her success. "You're doing wonderfully well, Melissa. You look great, and you seem to have so much more energy."

"I'm also trying to focus more on my orthopedic practice to try to develop it, but I'm having problems with employee turnover."

The grounds crew still hasn't budged; the tarp remains on the infield in rainy Fall Creek Park. Tonight, is excruciating. Leigh looks a little bored, too. She is unusually quiet tonight. I know that's she is being pursued by one of her colleagues. She's not ready for anything romantic, yet. I've learned quite a bit about her in our occasional drinks after group. She seems to trust me. I guess that's good. I know I have absolutely no chance with her. I appreciate her trust in me, and I find myself not talking about the past, not the tormented

James, but an emerging version of myself. I think I realize how damaged she is; how much she needs a person. I probably wouldn't have picked me for that. I know who I would have picked, but he's not here. Boyarski would have been ideal. Boyarski makes jokes in life, shy self-deprecating jokes. I like that about him. He is a mystery to me. He should be somewhere else other than Houston doing something other than building McMansions for Texas refinery vice presidents. Then it occurs to me: this Harry, my Harry, is the other Tran connection. Why didn't I think of that before?

Rick is his usual happy go lucky self and says that contract work is holding steady as the holidays approach. Rick is in his Rick uniform: well-pressed khakis and a polo shirt with the collar turned up like a refugee from a boy's prep school. He has not quite grown up. The class cut up, sometimes he doesn't know when to shut up. He's a great sitter by his swimming pool but with his fair skin, he is perpetually sunburned. I hope it's not high blood pressure.

"I plan to see my grandson over the holidays," he says. "And I hope to reunite with my daughter – my grandson's mother – at the same time."

He and his daughter haven't spoken for a long time, years. It is something that haunts him, this loss of contact.

During their time in group, Jerry proposed to Nita. They had been dating "secretly" for about six months. Not a well-kept secret, since it was obvious to everyone in the group something was stirring between them. I guess we all have our illusions, I have mine, God knows. Nita joyfully accepted and immediately began planning the wedding. Had Janowitz asked me, I would have said about them, "Wait. Hold on. I don't think this is a good idea."

He doesn't ask, and I am unwilling to volunteer that information. I know I'm not an expert in relationships, but it was obvious that they weren't suited to each other. Nita was continually disagreeing with Jerry in group. He held his tongue in response, but it was clear that he was uncomfortable. How different would it be around the breakfast table or the bedroom: Nita complaining about Jerry, and Jerry with a stricken smile on his face. He was a time bomb, and that's something I know a little bit about being.

Cassandra, who seems stressed, tells the group that it is not looking good for her son Henry's marriage. I notice that she has become a little careless in her appearance. Her hair is piled up on top of her head, with a few strands falling down across her forehead onto her face. I want to tell her to brush it out of her eyes but hold my tongue.

"Ted and I have very serious concerns for the mental health and well-being of Henry's two children due the psychotic behavior on the part of Henry's wife, Rose. She needs help."

The group is very supportive of Cassandra. We try, anyway.

"I think, Cassandra," Dr. Janowitz says, "that you and Ted should schedule an individual therapy session with me to talk about what is happening."

She wipes a tear from her eye and nods. She seems very fragile to me. I am trying to be empathetic, buy I find her weakness tiresome.

I was half expecting Harry to come tonight. Dr. Janowitz encouraged it, even though he would be joining a group already well established. I encouraged it, too, because it would be good to have a friendly, and new, face in these sessions. But he didn't seem interested.

Then there was a tentative rap on the conference room door, and Dr. Janowitz sprang up and opened it.

"Am I late?" A head pokes in beyond the door.

It is Harry Boyarski, a little disheveled looking. Of course, you're late, Harry, I think, you're always late.

"Harry, come in. You're only thirty minutes or so late. We still have plenty of time."

"Sorry," Harry says. "I had one of those meetings that wouldn't end."

The boys were leaving the clubhouse and beginning to warm up down the first base line. The rain delay was finally over. Play ball!

"Come in and welcome."

"Thanks."

"Group, we are going to have a new participant. I know this is a little unusual, but these are unusual circumstances. This is Harry Boyarski, and we've had individual sessions for a few months, and I thought a group experience would be helpful. So, Harry, why don't you introduce yourself."

"Good evening, I'm sorry I'm late. My name is Harry Boyarski, and as Doctor Janowitz said, I've been consulting with him for a few months. I'm from the Boston area, and I'm here in Houston on a short-term basis. I'm overseeing the construction of a house in River Oaks. It's been going on for a long time, far longer than I thought at the start of the job. It's a job that's making me a little crazy. Sorry," he says with a smile, "it's a job that's driving me to distraction."

The group, in unison, says, "Hello, Harry."

"Glad you're here, Harry," Rick says happily, "we need some fresh meat."

"I'm not sure how fresh I am, but I'm glad to be here. I've never been in one these sessions before, so I guess I'll just figure things out as we go along. Jimmy can help me. Hey Jim."

I wave at him.

"Oh yes," Dr. Janowitz says, "Harry and James are bicyclists. They are the demon bikers of South Texas. How many miles did you guys ride last weekend?"

"I'm not sure," I say, "what do you think, Harry?"

"Two hundred miles. Maybe more. That's what my calves are telling me, anyway."

"Well, Harry, I'm glad you're here," Dr. Janowitz says. "I daresay that we will all be glad you're here. What would you like to share with us tonight?"

"I'm not sure where to start. This is my first experience in the kind of situation."

"That's okay, Harry, we'll help you get used to the process," Rick says.

"Good. I should say first, that I was trained as an architect, but practiced for only a relatively short time. I don't think I was very good at it."

"Oh, that's just being modest, Harry," Dr. Janowitz says. "I've been in some of your houses north of Boston, and they are magnificent."

"I got lucky once or twice. What happened was I had some personal issues, and I decided to take a different path. I got into the construction management end of things. I'm pretty good at that. I have a buddy, a guy named Mike Monahan, with whom I went to school. He is an architect and a builder. He's the money guy. I'm in charge of the construction and he's in charge of everything else."

"How long have you been doing this, Harry?" Jerry asks.

"Ten years. That's a long time in architecture years. Too long. I'm under enormous pressure to complete jobs on time and within the budget. Better yet, to complete jobs early and under budget."

"How often does that happen?" Rick asks.

"Excellent question. Not often. Not often enough for Mickey Monahan. I started feeling very anxious, and I began to get what I now know are anxiety attacks. They started at night, but then they began to occur during the day as well. I was having a hard time functioning. I was really in a bad way, and that's why I'm seeing Dr. Janowitz. He encouraged me to join the group. He said you were a happy band of warriors for mental wellbeing."

"I'm taking Xanax for anxiety, Harry, and it's helped me. I'm Melissa, by the way."

"I'm taking that, too, but I don't like the side effects. I guess it helps. I seem to be feeling a little less panicked."

"It takes a few weeks for the medication to really work, Harry. We'll see where you're at in a few weeks. Thanks, Harry, and welcome," Dr. Janowitz says.

"I'm glad to be here at last," Harry adds.

"Before we come to the end of the evening, I have a small announcement to make," Dr. Janowitz says. "I will be traveling to Rome in March to visit the Pope."

We all look at him with surprise.

Because we know that Dr. Janowitz is Jewish, Rick kiddingly asks him if he is going there to convert the Pope to Judaism. The doctor laughs at this suggestion, but won't say any more about the purpose of his visit.

"It will be an honor to meet His Holiness. I'll tell you more about it when I get back."

We all organize our things and get up to leave. No one seems to be rushing out tonight. Harry looks at me and winks as if we were unindicted co-conspirators. It's good to have another friendly face in the group. I notice Harry nods at Leigh as she gets up to leave, and she waves at him going out the door. This is a little mystery I'm going to have to unravel.

Harry meets me at the door. "So, here I am, Jimmy."

"Here you are. I thought you were going to try to make it on time."

"I tried. Mrs. French needs to change her closets and I had to go over the change order with her husband. Can you believe it? She needs a separate closet for her shoes? She has four hundred pair. That's exactly three hundred ninety-seven more pairs than I have. Her husband was surprised by how much it was going to cost, but I don't care. I just want to get the hell out of there and go back to Boston."

"I'm glad you made it."

"Let's go get a drink. I could use a cold beer."

"We can go to Rolf's. It's just around the corner."

"I've heard about Rolf's. Cold beer and wiener schnitzel."

We walk to the restaurant in the humid Houston night. Harry opens the door for me, and I walk into the bar area. Leigh Hoffman is sitting at a table with a glass of what I know is Chardonnay in front of her. She sees us and smiles and waves, shyly, like a schoolgirl. She seems happy to see us. Harry has some explaining to do.

IT'S ALWAYS CHRISTMASTIME AT ROLF'S

"I guess we all know one another, thanks to Janowitz and Thomas Tran," Harry says with a goofy smirk after we sit at a table.

"I know you through Janowitz. I know you two know Janowitz through Tran, but how do you know each other and how do you know Tran?" I am puzzled and amused, sort of amused. Actually, I'm a little jealous.

"I met Harry in Tran's waiting room. We both had an appointment, and Thomas was held up in court, so we got to chatting and here we are. And so are you. It's kismet."

Harry looked around Rolf's. It was dark and a kind of a faux Bavarian beer hall with steins hanging from the ceilings and Christmas tree lights strung in the rafters and behind the bar. It was quiet. The waitress took our order and went away. She was not dressed like a Bavarian barmaid tonight. They save that for Octoberfest. It's hard to imagine how Rolf's survived in a place like Houston, maybe it had been around so long that it just entered the fabric of the city. That and the fact you could get a braised pig's knuckle any day of the week. If you were a pig's knuckle fancier, this is the place to be.

"It's loaded with gemutlichkeit, that's for sure. I like the Christmas tree lights."

"What's gemutlichkeit Harry?" Leigh asks.

"It's sort of friendliness, a sense of pleasure sharing something with friends. Like us, tonight."

The waitress bought Harry and me our beers.

"Would you mind telling me," he asks the waitress, "why do you keep the Christmas tree lights up?"

"There are three explanations that I heard: one, the old owner put them up a long time ago and didn't want to take them down because it was

290

too much work; two, he took them down one year and the regulars demanded that he put them back; and I've forgotten the third one. Anyway, they're up there and they're not coming down."

"You know," Leigh says, "I think it was the first one."

"It's festive," Harry responds. "Let's toast Rolf's where beer is in our glass and Christmas is always present in our hearts. Cheers. I mean, Prost!"

"And cheers to Thomas Tran," I say. "Prost! The one lawyer in Texas I can trust."

I tell them a bit about my legal struggles over the recent past. Harry has heard about it in the course of bike rides, and Leigh has heard about it in group. It seems like a long time ago. I didn't want to dwell in the past anymore. I don't want to dwell on Scott's death and Kelly's betrayal of Scott's memory. At least what I regard as betrayal. I tell them about meeting Vera Bowman in the bar of the Houstonian and the remarkable story she told Scott and me.

"I don't know if I believe her though," I say.

"I do," Leigh says. "Why she would she make something like that up?"

"The truth is a strange thing," Harry says. "It's not fastened to a granite cliff with chains. It is flexible and pliable, and I'm willing to bet most of what she told you is true. I've known Berliners and I'm sure as a young girl, she didn't understand how bad it was. Maybe the mother was actually raped; that wouldn't make her story less horrible. Maybe the mother killed many more Russians. The locals had a bounty on Russian deserters, I heard. And this wasn't catch and release. This was catch and kill. I think I believe it, too."

"Maybe we should talk about something else, guys. Something a little less sad."

We stare at each other for an awkward moment, and then Harry bursts out laughing.

"We need a tuba player in here. That would make me happy. Everyone loves a tuba player."

We ordered another drink. When the waitress returned to our table, she looked at us and said, "I discovered the third reason, why the lights were never taken down. When this place was first opened, there was a sign over the fireplace that said, 'It's always Christmastime at Rolf's.' That's what the cook told me, and he's been here since 1963." She seemed a little disappointed as she walked away.

"Well, boys, here's to Rolf's and the never-ending Yule," Leigh says, "and to finally getting the Tran Team together. We should have dinner here one night. I've never had a pig knuckle. It sounds disgusting but I'm sure it's delicious. What's tastier than pig fat?"

It is pleasant to be among friends. I am learning that time has very little importance. I have lost many things along my journey. Inevitably, I will grow old and weaken and fail. But here among these people, in the gemutlichkeit of a make-believe German restaurant, I feel a surprising awakening. Something occurs to me: I have a chance at being a happy man after all.

PLAYING BY THE NUMBERS

At group on Thursday, November 18, 2010, Dr. Janowitz selects me to go first. I boldly announce that I'm doing the internet dating thing. My group mates are very supportive. Nita even volunteers that she's been on IcingMeetsCake.com, a new dating site, and, while her results were mixed, she says that her overall experience was a positive one.

"This site is really designed for a younger crowd," Nita says. "And I think it might be a bit too young for me. But it's designed for foodies, and some of the members have a really amazing knowledge of the Houston food scene. There are some great places to eat these days. I went to a really cheap Vietnamese place last week with a guy who was a real loser. But the food was great, and he paid. It can be a lot of fun out there, Jim. Give it a chance."

I'm very encouraged by the support the group shows me.

"One of things you'll notice, Jim, is that the picture doesn't match the person," Nita adds.

From the group discussion, I learn that Nita and Jerry have scheduled their wedding date for Saturday, December 18th. They are very excited about getting married and it shows in their commentary. Rick is his usual happy, sappy self. He shares that his contract work has picked up and he is very excited by that.

"I'm seeing my grandson on a regular basis now, just as you predicted, Dr. Janowitz."

The group gives him a big round of applause.

Dr. Janowitz asks Cassandra how she is doing.

"My son's marital problems aren't improving, and I don't know what it will mean to me and Ted if Henry and his wife Rose divorce. I'm very concerned about the effects on my grandchildren by poor parenting by Henry's wife."

"You'll have to help them, Cassandra."

"I know, but so much is going on. My daughter Melanie is starting to have health problems and that is very concerning too, especially since Melanie and her husband live in California and are so far away. I don't know what to do. I need to be in California to help her, too."

"Schedule an extra session with me, Cassandra. We'll work on it," says Dr. Janowitz.

Melissa informs the group that she has lost another ten pounds and, while it's obvious to all of us that ten pounds is merely a drop in the bucket, we loudly applaud her for her efforts. She looks at Leigh, and Leigh gives her a big smile and an enthusiastic thumbs up. Women remain a mystery to me.

After group is over, I return home and get on my computer. I write to internet dating candidates one through five, hoping that at least one of them will write back. I then go to bed.

On Friday at work, I repeatedly check my personal e-mail account. At around 2:45 PM, I receive an e-mail from candidate number four, who says her real name is Jasmine. I immediately e-mail Jasmine back and, after several exchanges, she suggests that we meet for coffee on Saturday morning at the Starbucks on Westheimer Road. I readily agree.

That night I am so excited that I have great difficulty falling asleep. On Saturday morning I awake physically exhausted but mentally very alert. This will be my first real date in at least eight years. I am impressed with myself for doing this.

"Wow!" I say under my breath as I ponder how long it's been.

Not wanting to be late, I arrive at the designated Starbucks about fifteen minutes early. At a few minutes past nine, Jasmine arrives. She is every bit as attractive in person as she is in her profile, and I tell her that as I greet her with a handshake.

After we go get our coffees, we sit at a small table and talk. I learn that she is very active in a lot of social activities. She seems to have a pleasant personality; however, I sense that she is looking for a specific trait in her potential mate and I fear that I may not possess this attribute.

At the end of our conversation, I ask Jasmine, "May I call you?"

"Sure," she responds and writes her cell phone number on a napkin for me.

When I arrive home, I am flying high. I can't wait to call Jasmine to tell her how much I enjoyed meeting her; however, rather than calling at that instant, I decide to wait until the middle of the afternoon.

At a few minutes before three, I dial the phone. It rings six times and then rolls over to voice mail. I leave a message thanking Jasmine for meeting me in the morning and asking if she'd like to have dinner. Then I wait. And I wait. Dinner time passes and still the phone doesn't ring. I go to bed with the phone ringer on loud just in case she calls. But she doesn't.

On Monday mid-morning, I call Jasmine and leave a second voice mail message asking her to call me. Then I wait. And I wait. And I wait some more. I remain in my office near the telephone for practically the whole day, but she doesn't call. That evening I am very disappointed; however, trying to be the eternal optimist, I decide to call one last time.

In my third voice mail message, I again thank Jasmine for meeting me on Saturday, and I again ask that she call me back. This time when I hang up I realize that she's not going to call back. It dawns on me, at last, that she's not interested. With this realization comes an initial anger at being rejected and then a deep depression. Hello, old companion. Why give me her number if she did not want me to call? Women lie!

For the rest of the week and into the following week, the feeling of rejection hangs over me. I don't write to any other women. I don't even look at the website to see who's out there.

At my therapy session with Dr. Janowitz on Tuesday, November 30, I express great frustration with the whole internet dating scene.

"I think she was just leading me on. She wasn't interested in me at all."

Dr. Janowitz says, "James, this type of rejection is very common in internet dating. Every great salesman knows that when you're just starting out you must go through no, no, no, no, no, and so forth, until you get your first yes. With internet dating, you're selling yourself. You're marketing yourself. And you're bound to be rejected along the way. So, when that happens, the best thing you can do is pause, reflect, and then quickly move on to the next one. Internet dating is purely a numbers game."

"It's like the lottery," I respond dejectedly.

"Not exactly, but you need not be discouraged with one date that didn't turn out the way you wanted it to."

"That makes sense. I can deal with 'no' if there will eventually be a 'yes.'"

"There will be. Patience and persistence are the keys, James."

Armed with this encouragement, I go home and begin searching again.

WEDDING BELLS ANXIETY

December 2010 finds me focused on securing internet dates. To my astonishment, I have several first dates! For some reason, the second dates don't come. I find the process of internet dating intimidating, but for the moment at least, and with Dr. Janowitz's encouragement, I'm willing to stay with it. I'm astonished by the number of women on the market I find attractive. Eventually, Dr. Janowitz assures me, I'll make a genuine connection. For now, I don't share my failures with the group. I wonder why I can't.

In late December, I attend Nita and Jerry's wedding. Because they are different religions — Nita is Greek Orthodox, and Jerry is Episcopalian — they get married by the Justice of the Peace in downtown Houston. In addition to the bride and groom's families, all my groupmates are there except Leigh, as are Dr. Janowitz and his wife, Elaine. The ceremony is very nicely orchestrated. When it is over, we congratulate the new husband and wife and then retire to an old-fashioned Italian restaurant — Villa Mosconi — for the reception, a checkered tablecloths and spaghetti-and-meatballs kind of place.

At the reception, I notice that Jerry's family sits around one table, Nita's family sits around a second table, and the group members sit around a third table, with not a lot of interaction going on among tables. Because Jerry's family is smaller than Nita's, Dr. Janowitz and Elaine sit at his table. The bridal party sits at the head table. No one seems particularly happy.

In between courses, Melissa asks me how my internet dating is going.

"Have you been finding any nice girls, Jim?" she asks.

"Thus far, I've had four dates." I answer. "The first one was with a former Catholic nun who became disenfranchised with the Church, left it, and mothered a child out of wedlock, the father, an ex-priest who decided he was gay, then walked out on mommy and baby."

"You're kidding! Things are not so good in the Church. Glad I left the faith," Melissa says.

"I'm totally serious."

"What about your second date?"

"Date number two was with a woman who I call the female football player."

"Football player? Why is that?"

"Well, the photo on her profile is her from the neck up and she's very attractive. However, from the neck down she was built like a linebacker! Literally! On top of that, she wore these four-inch heels that made her walk funny. It was awkward."

"It seems like you're being a little tough on her, James," Ted says.

"Maybe. She was nice enough, I guess. She probably said something awful about me to her friends as well."

"Where did you go on your date?" Melissa asks. She was very curious.

"We met at a Chinese restaurant near where I work. Fortunately for me, none of my co-workers were there or I never would have lived it down. They can be real assholes."

"Tell us about date number three," Rick demands, leaning forward.

"My third date was with a woman whose photos must have been old because in her profile she said she was 'athletic and toned,' but when I met her, she was anything but."

"Was she heavy?" Cassandra asks.

"To put it mildly!"

"Hey, buddy," Melissa says, "don't forget I'm a plus-sized girl myself."

"She was really overweight, Melissa. Much heavier than you. Didn't mean to upset anybody."

"She had a pretty face, I bet," Melissa continues. "Men always say that about overweight women. And you boys probably have tiny penises. I'd love to hear the girls say something like: Mr. Needle Dick the Bug Fucker, that was my last date. A little underdeveloped down under."

"Okay, Melissa, let it go," Rick says. "Let him finish."

"What did you do?" Ted asks, joining the conversation.

"We met at a downtown Starbucks and while I really wanted to bail, I decided to stick it out as a character building exercise for myself."

"You're more of a gentleman that I would have been," Rick says.

"Needle Dick Rick," Melissa says.

"Okay, Melissa, I get it. What happened?"

"I drank my coffee very quickly."

"What about your fourth date?" Melissa asks.

"I call date number four the forty-year-old virgin."

"Why is that?" Melissa asks.

"Because she was very upfront in telling me that she was a virgin and would remain a virgin until she got married. She was also a Korean and was a bit strange."

"Strange in what way?" Ted asks.

"In the way Koreans are strange. I used to work for Koreans. Very serious. Very intense. She had been a sniper in the Korean army, and she looked it. She had a very focused expression, like I was in her crosshairs."

"I guess so," Ted comments. "You've had quite a time. You might want to try a different site."

"What do you make of all this, Harry? Your buddy is a real heartbreaker," Rick says, too loudly.

He was sitting at the end of the table, nursing a glass of wine.

"It's tough out there," Harry says. "I'm sure Jim did just fine."

"Did you ever do any internet dating?" Rick asks, pushing a bit.

And from some odd place, somewhere distant and very lonely, Harry looked up at Rick's beaming round face and said, "No."

"Where's Leigh tonight?"

"I don't know," Harry answers, "maybe she had a date."

"Aren't you two dating? I think you make a nice couple." Rick is pushing his luck with Harry.

"No," he answers quietly. By which he meant, I think, shut the fuck up.

After an awkwardly long pause, Melissa asks, "Are you going to continue internet dating, Jim?"

"I'm not sure," I answer in a resigned voice. "I think I've had enough. I want to talk to Dr. Janowitz before I completely stop, but I don't think internet dating is for me."

After the dessert is served, Nita, Jerry, and the Janowitz's join us at the group table for some photographs and a toast or two to the bride and groom. We talk for about twenty minutes and then decide to call it a night. Dr. Janowitz seems very happy about the wedding. His wife, Elaine, talks to Nita and Jerry about honeymoon plans. Nita and Jerry beam when they talk to the Janowitzes, happy to have them here as if it validated their love. They seem very happy, and despite my reservations, I truly wish them the best. I have no confidence it will work, but I am a hereditary doom and gloom guy.

"Your ceremony and reception were first class," Rick says to the newlyweds as we collect our coats.

"Here, here!" Ted and I add in unison.

I give Nita a big congratulatory hug and shake Jerry's hand. I have my doubts, but I would never say anything to anyone in the group, even to Harry. Harry and I leave the restaurant together and walk to our cars.

"Where is Leigh?" I ask Harry as we approach our cars.

"She's in Chicago."

"May I ask what she's doing there?"

"Cleaning up an old mess, I think. If you want the details, you're going to have to ask her about them yourself. I've been sworn to secrecy."

Harry is in a sour mood. We are both lost in our own thoughts and don't bother to say goodnight.

WOMEN ON WHEELS, OR
WHERE IN THE HELL IS HARRY?

On Saturday morning, I wake up around 5:45 AM and get dressed for cycling. However, rather than riding immediately, I remember my pledge to Dr. Janowitz, so instead sit down at my computer and surf the internet until 8:30 AM, at which time I get on my bicycle and head out. The sun is shining much brighter than the 6:15 AM start time I'm accustomed to, so I begin to sweat immediately.

After about twenty minutes of hard riding, I turn down a one-way street in a nearby residential neighborhood and come upon a group of four female riders who are moving slightly slower than I am.

"Good morning," I say as I catch up to them.

"Morning," they say in return.

"How long have you been out this morning?" one of the women asks as she notices my sweat-stained shirt.

"Only about twenty minutes," I answer. "I'm trying to get back into shape after a long layoff."

"So are we, out of shape, I mean," the second woman comments.

"Do you want to ride with us?" the third woman asks.

"How far are you going?" I did not recognize the opportunity.

"We just started," the second woman answers. "And we'll probably ride for another hour, probably about fifteen miles."

"Sure," I answer, finally getting it. "I'll ride with you, but only for as long as I can hold up."

"Deal!" the fourth woman says.

As we ride along, I introduce myself and learn that the women's names are Marcie, Jeanette, Bernadette, and Allison. During the ride we exchange pleasantries and I discover that all four women work for

Bank of America in different branches.

"We're part of the bank's cycling club," Jeanette tells me.

"Are you part of a riding club?" Marcie asks.

"No, I often ride alone due to the odd hours that I cycle."

"Oh, that's too bad," Allison quips. "You should consider joining a club."

"I definitely will," I answer sincerely. At least I think I was sincere.

"Sometimes I ride with a friend," I say, "but he had to work today."

During the ride, Jeanette, Allison, and Marcie talk almost non-stop about anything and everything, and I contribute to the conversation when I can. However, I notice that Bernadette remains rather quiet. Only as we near the end of the ride do I learn that Bernadette is the only single woman in the group.

"Ah," I say under my breath. "That explains it."

"Will you four be riding next Saturday?" I ask as we return to their starting point.

"Yes, but we'll be taking a different, longer route," Marcie answers.

"Would you like to join us?" Jeanette invites.

"Yes, I'd love to!" I answer emphatically and then exclaim, "y'all are a lot of fun!"

After we agree on a meeting spot, I turn to the women and say, "It was really nice meeting y'all," just like a real Texan.

"It was also nice meeting you, Jim," Allison says for the group. "We'll see you next Saturday."

"Thanks!"

Harry should have been here. He called me in the morning to tell me that he had to go to work. A broken pipe or window. He was always putting out brush fires on this project, and I could tell it was wearing him down. He was usually upbeat and easygoing, but in the last week or so he seemed withdrawn. I guess he was worried about the job, getting it done. I know he was anxious to get out of Texas. I'm not sure how well he would have liked the group, though. He would have been polite, but distant. As far as I could tell, he wasn't dating. Maybe he had a girlfriend in Boston. The only women we ever talked about were my internet dates. He said very little about them except to encourage me, like Dr. Janowitz, to be patient.

"Jimmy, you should realize that they're probably as nervous and confused as you are."

"Impossible."

"No, it's possible. You'll see."

301

Still, the bike ladies would have liked him and maybe liked me a little more, too, especially Bernadette, who was the youngest of the group and the cutest, too. Next week, he will meet them, I thought. And the ladies could see the two of us together, the mad bikers of South Texas!

HARRY HAS A SISTER

Over the next six days, I look forward to the weekend with increasing anticipation as I again want to ride with the four women.

On Saturday morning, I awake to the sound of thunder. When I peer out my bedroom window, I see nothing but raindrops everywhere.

"Shit!" I utter to myself. "No riding today."

Disappointed, I hope that the weather will cooperate next weekend.

Exactly one week later, I depart my house at 8:30 AM and follow the same route that I followed before. This time I'm riding with Harry Boyarski, but this time, however, there are no women to be found. Thinking that they may have left already on the same route as two weeks ago, I speed up to see if I can catch up to them.

"What are you doing, Jim?"

"I'm trying to find my bike ladies."

"Okay. Lead the way."

They are not there. Upon returning to their starting point, I think that maybe I left earlier than they did, so I pretend that my tires need air and linger in the area.

"Are we going to sit here all morning, Jimmy? They don't seem to be around."

"I'm thinking maybe they started late."

"Or early. Or they stayed in bed with their husbands."

"Yeah, I guess. Just a few more minutes."

The women do not appear, and I'm frustrated and disappointed.

"Maybe we'll see them next Saturday. I did promise Dr. Janowitz three weekends, after all," I say to Harry who is mounting his bike, "but if they don't show next weekend, that'll be it."

"I didn't promise old Janowitz anything. You can try to find them yourself next weekend. My last wild goose has long since been chased."

"One more weekend."

"Nope."

"We can take a quick look, and then go for a long ride if they're not here."

"Here's what I don't understand. Three of the four are married women. That usually — but God knows not always — means they are unavailable. And the fourth one, what's her name again?"

"Bernadette."

"Bernadette. Perfect. A nice little Catholic girl, I bet. Bless us and save us, Monsignor Snyder."

"I'm trying to be social. They are fun to ride with."

I can sense Harry's exasperation, but, as usual, his good humor revives.

"Okay, Jim, one more weekend and one last, and I mean last, wild goose."

"I have a feeling they'll show up."

"Of course, you do, because you're a freaking optimist."

"And what are you?"

"A pessimist, recovering. And I probably drink too much. That's what Lily says anyway. She insists I'm an alcoholic."

"Is that true?"

"I don't know, Jim. Maybe once, not anymore. I like a cold beer now and then."

I think I may have overstepped a boundary, so I don't say anything.

"So, let's ride, Harry. It's getting hot."

On a water break, we stretch out in the shade of an ancient oak.

"By the way, who is Lily? Your girlfriend in Boston?"

"Girlfriend, that's funny. I never told you about Lily? She's my little sister," Harry says, balancing the water bottle on his stomach. "Jimmy, if you want to be social, I should introduce you to her. She is very good at social. She's something special."

"I didn't know you had a sister."

"Well, now you do."

"What's she like?"

"She's like Lily. One of a kind. Sui generis."

"Lily's a nice name."

"She's a nice girl. Woman, I mean. But she's my baby sister, so I can still call her a girl."

"Is she married?"

"Divorced, but I don't think she is seriously looking. So, don't get any romantic ideas, buddy."

"Maybe I can meet her when we go to Boston?"

"Sure. Eventually."

"Does she live in Boston?"

"No, she lives in the old wreck of the family house on Cape Cod, on Buzzard's Bay to be precise. Very old money part of the Cape. The house is falling apart around her."

It was very hot, and it felt good to be in the cool of the shade. I was getting sleepy.

"What does she do?"

"It's sort of complicated. She does a lot of things. Mostly, I guess, she's a painter."

"You mean like an artist, of fine art?"

"Exactly. She paints, or used to paint anyway, dog portraits. That's a hell of a way to make money, isn't it? She's very successful among dog owners with more dollars than sense. She used to specialize in Labradors."

"That's amazing."

"It doesn't stop there. She's a day trader on various bourses around the world. She takes her doggie portrait money and buys stocks and bonds. She is brilliant and ruthless, my little sister. She hedges. She's long and she's short in the market. But she never capitulates, God bless her mercenary heart. Never, ever capitulates. She's made a fortune. I hope to God she managed to hang on to it."

"Why wouldn't she?"

"Men. She has execrable taste in them. Downhill skiers, hand models, every kind of boarding-school, trust-fund twit imaginable. She's taken a lot of losers out for a test drive."

"She probably wouldn't like me."

"She swears eighteen years with a shrink has given some insight into her choices. She's looking for a sober, kind fellow of Jesuitical temperament. Has to like dogs."

"I'm not sure what a Jesuitical temperament is Harry."

"A guy with a Jesuitical temperament, as an example, would spend three weekends on a bicycle chasing after a girl named Bernadette. That's a Jesuitical temperament, Monsignor Snyder, and you have one."

He smiled his goofy, lopsided smile.

"You'll meet her soon enough. Come on, let's finish the ride."

And we did. I followed Harry. He never did buy any real cycling shirts or shorts, but he had become a much stronger rider, even on his old bike. I watched his back bobbing in front of me, picking up the pace. I'm not sure what exactly is a Jesuitical temperament — I've never met a Jesuit — but I'm glad I have one. Monsignor Snyder, indeed.

THE INTERIM DIAGNOSIS

To get to where I am today was not the easiest thing to do. It was my intention, my anger-fueled need, to get completely into and out of my personal purgatory. That's why I bought the guns. I wanted to place the muzzle of my 9mm at the back of her lovely blond head and pull the trigger. I wanted to kill people: Cindy, for example, and then kill myself. Those thoughts frighten me now. I know I am in a lifeboat. I was helped into it by Dr. Janowitz. But it's all fragile, unsteady, capsizeable. At my individual therapy session on June 7, 2011, Dr. Janowitz presents his interim diagnosis. The doctor begins by telling me that my depression and paranoia are under control thanks to the medicines. Dr. Janowitz says he is pleased that I am beginning to self-monitor which allows for better communication, both of which are signs that I am taking control of my healing.

"Your behavior, James," he says, "is predictive of good results. It suggests an excellent recovery."

"Recovery? I don't think I'm recovered."

"Well, you have increased coping skills, increased stress tolerance, less anxiety, and less self-sequestration, I mean, less self-isolation. You have grown professionally in the workplace, don't you think?"

"I guess so. I hope so."

"And you no longer have the homicidal-like rage and the suicidal ideation of that first day we met. Do you remember that?"

"I do. I was full on crazy. It seems like a different life."

"Well, it is. You're transforming yourself from a wholly rage-driven and deeply damaged person to…We'll see what you transform to, James. But slowly, slowly. I have been at this a long time and it seems to me your prognosis for a full recovery is excellent based upon your very positive response to the treatment plan to date."

"If things are going so well — and I think they are — why am I still in therapy? I know I am 'better' than I was with Cindy. In those days, because of the improper counseling and the unavailability of the proper medication, I was forced to cope in a different way. I feel like I went into a cloud floating above myself, looking down at my life from some distant point. I became unreal to myself. I felt I couldn't maintain personal boundaries, especially with Cindy."

"And that, James, intensified your paranoia, anxiety, irrational thought, and psychosis, along with intense thoughts of suicide and homicide."

"And that's how I ended up here. Luckily."

"And that's how you ended up here."

"Do you think I was really capable of murder and suicide?"

"Most certainly. Yours was a deeply disturbed mind."

"Is still?"

"James, you are today, a much healthier human being emotionally. You are not fully healed; you will always need to be on your medication, for example. But there are improvements, of course, real ones, even major ones," Dr. Janowitz explains, "and there is a lot of work left to do. The areas we still need to work on are socialization, social functioning, and coping with the psychosocial stressors that cause you acute and chronic distress. In addition, we need to work on relationship development, and dating relationships."

"I understand, I guess. I think what I'll do next is…."

I pause for a moment to try to collect my thoughts. I don't know what to say next.

But Janowitz was never at a loss for words. He fills in the blanks. "Good, James, we have to think about moving forward. We should set goals to work toward."

"What kind of goals?" I ask earnestly.

"I think one of your goals should be to date more and have a relationship with an emotionally and physically available woman."

"That sounds good to me. No more strippers and ice queens," I say emphatically.

"You want to experience entrepreneurial success, to use your creativity. You want to pursue interests that are not tied to your nine to five job, isn't that correct?"

"Yes, very much."

"Let's think about that. You're inventive and extremely hard working. Maybe it's time to try your wings in another endeavor, like the chocolate project. You seem excited about that."

"I've got some ideas, too. The pressure is to do something other than draw a paycheck is building. The problem with the chocolate project is that I really don't have the capital to see it through."

"Excellent, James. Money is always going to be an issue, but in a city as rich as Houston, you can always raise capital if the idea looks like it can be successful. And a third goal would be to make more friends and become more involved in non-work-related activities, like community service, church. An excursion with a bike riding club, maybe riding with a group in Spain or France?"

"You know, Dr. Janowitz, Harry and I have been riding together. I have not had a close friend since Scott died. I mean, Harry and I are not close friends but we talk a lot. I talk a lot, that is, and he listens. Sometimes, he seems a little distant to me. I feel like I don't want to disappoint him. Plus, I don't want to get too close to someone now. I don't want to go lose someone like I lost Scott."

"James, Harry is a good man. He's been through some difficulties. I encourage you in this friendship, by the way. He is flawed and a little fragile, too, but he's a good guy. I can tell you that he really enjoys your rides together."

"He wants me to go East with him this fall. He says he's sick of Texas heat and roads. He wants to take a long trip in Vermont and Maine. And I think he has a house on Cape Cod. Some sort of fabulous old ruin."

"I think that would be great for both of you."

"I think I can get a couple weeks off in the fall. Need to burn some of that vacation time or I'll lose it."

"One other thing I should tell you, James. Harry is leaving the group. His job was a temporary one. As you know, he was the construction manager on one of those McMansions we see popping up like mushrooms after a rainstorm. It's almost completed. He's going back to Boston, I think."

I feel a twinge of anxiety. I feel deflated. Whom was I going to ride with now?

"He's going to talk about it at the next group, James. I think he will miss us. He did well in our sessions."

"I'll miss him," I say. "I will miss him very much."

"But you have your excellent bike-riding adventure to look forward to. Up and down those hills in New England. Flat tires, farm dogs chasing you, pickup trucks trying to run you off the road and cold beer at the end of the day! It will be wonderful."

"And then let's work on a real relationship," Dr. Janowitz continues. "You'll need a very special woman in your life. But we'll talk more about that next time. Your homework from today is to continue researching online dating. Will you do that for next time?"

"I'll try, but I'm not very good at it."

"You just have to be good at it once if it's the right woman."

As he always does near the end of my therapy sessions, Dr. Janowitz asks if I need any medicines. After I tell him that I'm okay until next time, we proceed to the reception area where I pay him his fee in cash, then I walk back out into my life.

THE WOUND THAT NEVER HEALS

As a gift for Dr. Janowitz, I've had a photograph framed for him for his office. I took it on one of my trips home to Ohio to visit my parents. I was out for a drive and went past an old farm that had fallen into ruin. I remembered this farm when I was kid, the Bukoskis had it then, and it was very prosperous. Mr. Bukoski, I think his name was Peter, had a big family, and one of his daughters was in my class in elementary school. Her name was Vicky, and she was the smartest girl in the class. I think she became a surgeon. Peter Bukoski was a recent Polish immigrant. Vicky, I remember, was very proud of him. He had been a cavalry officer in World War 2. That seems extraordinary to me, the Polish cavalry! In fact, she said, he had been in one of the last cavalry charges in history, men and horses against tanks: hopeless, heedless and insanely brave. That turned out not to be true, I discovered later, a myth repeated so often it became accepted as fact. The truth of it is that Peter Bukoski was a Polish cavalryman and fought with great distinction in the Battle of Krojanty. I learned that from his obituary. But he didn't charge tanks. He died very suddenly and very painfully of lung cancer. Apparently, he had been a heavy smoker all his life. Many of his old comrades, the ones who made it to the west, came to his funeral. Someplace in a box of clippings, I have a photograph of the funeral, hard and sad men gathered around an open grave.

I told Dr. Janowitz this story.

"After Peter died, the Bukoskis moved to Chicago, and they sold the land to a developer. The farm house and the barn and outbuildings fell into disrepair and then ruin. I took some photographs before they disappeared completely."

The one I gave him was of the barn, the building that had withstood the elements the best.

"This is wonderful, Jim. You've got a great eye."

311

"It's just a snapshot, but it means something to me. Vicky Bukoski and I always ended up in the back of the room."

"Where is she now, do you think?"

"I don't know, but I'm sure she's done well. She was a brilliant little girl."

"Thank you for this, Jim. Would you mind if I put it in the group therapy room? I'm sure everyone will be very pleased and impressed."

"You can put it wherever you want. I guess I am pleased with it."

"How are you doing today?"

He's asked me this question hundreds of times. In the past, I've been ready to express what I was feeling, which was often bitter, bitter anger and deep confusion. The drugs have helped, I realize. My moments of true and intense psychosis are rare these days, and these conversations over the years have given me some awareness of my behavioral issues.

"I'm actually okay, I think."

"Good. Anything you want to talk about?"

"Time."

"Okay. Let's talk about time."

"I am still terribly angry at Cindy and Joe Monteblanc. When I think about Damian, I find myself in a cold fury."

"But you don't want to kill them."

"No, not really. I mean, yes, I would like to kill them. But, no, I won't. That part is over."

"So, what about time?"

"How long does it take for me to say I'm cured of mental illness?"

"That's easy, Jim, you'll never be able to say that. Never."

"They stole my life from me. They stole my chance to be something other than a paper-pushing jerk off. I could have been in the CIA."

"This is true."

"I will never forgive them."

"Their trespasses," Dr. Janowitz says, "but I think you should."

"No."

"They have all gone on with their lives, Jim. You should try to do the same."

"Jim, you might think about it this way. However much you'd like to believe it, I don't think Monteblanc and Cindy were evil people. I don't think they meant to do you any harm."

"I don't accept that. I will never accept that."

"James, what you think you experienced in what you call 'The Incident' is what historians call 'The Unforgiving Moment,' that is when the thing one does or the events that occur cannot be corrected. I don't think it's true in this case."

"I don't want to listen to this."

"Hear me out, James. If you take a longer view and not the one with your face pressed up against the windshield, the incident is an embarrassing moment in what is in effect a clinic to train students in the processes of therapy. Some of these students are okay; some are great and some are flat out unsuited for the task. Cindy fell into the last category. But she was a graduate student trying to get a degree in a field for which she was utterly unsuited. Monteblanc is a bit of a charlatan, I agree, but in your interactions with him he could be seen as an overworked administrator trying to make due in a public institution that didn't provide the proper funding. Incompetent, overworked but not demons."

"They are poisoners. They destroyed LT."

"Very well, James, but please give some consideration to what I said. I wouldn't want you to go any further down the rabbit hole of anger and alienation that you already have gone. Those days are over, and you should be very proud of yourself for how far you have come."

"I will not surrender my anger. I will not forgive them. Just thinking of them even now, makes me furious."

I feel myself leaning forward in my chair, my hands balled into fists of rage.

"I will not fucking forget or forgive them," I say, as I slam my fists on the chair arms. "They wanted to destroy me."

Janowitz talks about building a new life, something about my new job and a career. Something about meeting the right woman. I can't listen. All I can hear is blood rushing from my brain, and all I can feel is my heart beating in my chest. Death is my only friend. I have been poisoned by demons and will always be poisoned. This has been my destiny all along.

"Aren't you looking forward to going on your bike adventure with Harry?"

Janowitz is fighting one of those skirmishes he fights every day, virtually every hour of every day. He is fighting to get me back into the moment. He is pulling me forward out of my despair and anger.

"And you're going to meet Harry's sister. What's her name?"

Harry has a sister. I know that. What is her name? Lily.

"Her name is Lily."

"That's a nice old-fashioned name."

"It is a nice name. I'm looking forward to the whole trip. It will be one of my last chances to ride with Harry."

"Oh, I'm sure you'll be spending time on Cape Cod and Maine or wherever Harry ends up. You've established a nice friendship."

"But not like Scott. I'll never have another friend like Scott."

"Perhaps not."

"And I'll never have another family like the Todds. That fucking bitch Kelly made sure that was destroyed for me."

313

"Yes, it would have been good for the kids to have you around as a loving presence in their lives. Have you heard from any of them, by the way?"

"Not a word. Not a goddamn word."

"That's too bad. Maybe we should talk more about it in group."

"Okay."

"How do you think group is going for you?"

"I'm adapting. I still feel awkward some times, but it seems to be working."

"I've told you this before, and I know you don't believe me. But that group was hand-picked for you. I worked very hard trying to get the right people together for you. It is like the endgame in a chess match."

"I don't know. That story seems like an urban myth about the group: a tale told so often it begins to have the aura of truth."

"It's true. Someday I'll convince you of that. Now, how are you doing with your medications?"

The session is ending.

"I'm doing fine. I'm good for a while."

Driving home, I have time to think about the last few years, the cycle of anger and depression. It's better, I think. I am less in the grasp of my mental illness. I know the medication, despite some side effects, has made a huge difference. I don't want to live a miserable existence. I have had some disappointments, I know, and many sad moments. And some of those disappointments, I realize, will last as long as life.

UNRAVELING

When things begin to unravel, in my experience, the unraveling starts slowly and then, without intervention, it speeds up to a blur. For example, when I was a kid and a young man, I'm sure the symptoms of my problem, my mental illness, were in place, nascent, waiting for some event or person to start the unraveling. Cindy and the incident, it seems, were what triggered my falling into paranoia and depression. But if it hadn't been Cindy, it would have been someone or something else. I was a piece of unexploded ordinance buried deep in a fallow field, waiting for the farmer's plow. Things fall apart, even in the group.

From Rick, we learn that his luck in the lottery has changed for the worse.

"I just can't seem to hit it anymore," Rick laments.

"Well, you can't win every time," Jerry says, attempting to console Rick.

That's what we do in group, offer consolation and advice.

"Yes, but my luck has never been this bad," Rick counters.

"Perhaps luck is like a circadian rhythm," Dr. Janowitz says. "It comes, and it goes."

"I guess that's possible," Rick says after a momentary pause. "But I'd like the group to make a little money. We could all go out for dinner or something."

"Tell us, what else is going on in your life to upset your natural rhythms," directs Dr. Janowitz.

"My knees have been causing me problems, my back hurts, I can't seem to get the amount of relief work I used to get, and I need new glasses."

"Well, that's enough to upset any natural system! What are you

315

going to do about these issues?"

"I'm going to go on a diet and lose weight and I'm going to get my vision checked," Rick answers.

"You should see an orthopedist about your knees, Rick. It might be something that if you catch right now won't bother you later," Melissa says.

"Very good, Melissa," Dr. Janowitz says. "Those are the right things to do."

"We can compare diets, Rick."

"Thanks, Melissa. I know how hard you're working at it."

From Cassandra, we learn that the grandchildren have bonded with her and Ted.

"We're so thankful!" Cassandra says. "The children are such a joy now. I mean, compared to before, they've really come around. Thank you, Dr. Janowitz."

"It's just as we predicted," the doctor responds. "Children have an amazing resilience. Tell us, what else is going on in your life?"

"I'm concerned about Ted. He seems to be withdrawing. I mean, he's spending most of his time day trading on the internet again. We don't go anywhere. We don't have friends over. We can't leave the house because he can't leave the computer. It's just really bothering me!"

"Oh, that's not good," Dr. Janowitz says. "When is your next individual session with me?"

"I don't have one scheduled," Cassandra responds.

"Tomorrow, please call my secretary and schedule one for you and Ted. Okay?"

"I'll do that."

Jerry and Nita's marriage, on shaky grounds from the start, has ended. Nita is not here tonight, which I take to be ominous. I like them both, but from the night of the wedding, I felt something was wrong. They forced their relationship, and the unraveling began early on in their marriage, and the unraveling went quickly.

From Jerry, we learn that his reconciliation with Nita did not work out and their divorce is turning ugly.

"I found out yesterday that over the Memorial Day holiday, when I thought we were reconciling, Nita installed spy software on my laptop and captured all of my passwords. She told me she used those passwords to copy my hard drive."

"That's horrible, Jerry. That's not fair," Rick says.

"I know, and if that weren't enough," Jerry continues, the anger rising in his voice, "before she moved out again, she took all of the money out of our checking account, leaving me no money to pay the bills that are coming due."

"Wow!" I say, "what got into Nita?"

"I wish I knew," Jerry answers. "All I want is a fair and equitable split. But she's not her usual self. Or maybe this is her usual self, but I just didn't see it."

"I don't think anyone saw it, Jerry. I will just say she is having a hard time," Dr. Janowitz adds.

"Are you going to keep the house?" Rick asks.

"I'm not sure. The mortgage is a lot for one person," Jerry responds.

"Do you have a lawyer?" I ask.

"Yes, Dr. Janowitz referred me to a good attorney. He's expensive, but I'll probably need him."

"If it's Thomas Tran," Harry says, "you won't find a better or more honest one."

"So, I take it Nita is not coming to group anymore?" Ricks asks.

"That appears to be the case," Jerry answers in a resigned voice.

"She said she'll join Dr. Janowitz's Monday night group instead."

Before turning to Melissa, Dr. Janowitz confirms that Nita has permanently left our group.

From Melissa, we learn that her ankle sprain has finally completely healed, and she has started exercising again.

"It's unbelievably debilitating to not be able to walk normally or exercise for almost four months," Melissa says as she alternates looks between Dr. Janowitz and the ceiling. "I couldn't believe how helpless I felt. And the thing is, I didn't realize how helpless I was at the time. It's only now that I'm healed and back into my old routine that I can look back and see the negative impacts the injury had on me."

"Are you still depressed?" Rick asks.

"You know," Melissa answers, "I think I'm over my depression. I think a lot of why I felt down was because of my injury. And now that I'm healed, I'm much more positive again."

"How are you doing in the men category?" Rick asks next.

"Rick," Leigh says, "she's not going to a meat market."

"I'm sorry Leigh and Melissa, but that's the way I am. I am a no bullshit guy."

"I think I'm okay. I met a nice fellow," Melissa answers as she starts to blush.

"Who's the lucky guy?" Jerry asks slyly.

"That's my secret," Melissa counters with a blush.

"Ah ha, so there is a man in your life," Rick says.

"Maybe I can talk about him next time," Melissa responds.

"Let them mind their own business, Melissa," Leigh says. "Talk about him only if you want to."

"They don't mean any harm. Really, it's okay," says Melissa.

"That's excellent, Melissa, I think you're doing really well," says Dr. Janowitz.

When it's my turn to speak, I share my frustration at the lack of progress made by my researcher. I've been trying to create a new enterprise, Lone Star Sweets and Treats, making my reversed peanut butter chocolate confection.

"The problem is that it is hard stabilizing the chocolate for the longer shelf life of a commercial product, and the process has been slow and expensive. Every time we get close to a solution, it ends in a failure. I'm not sure about this Cyress, dude. His credentials are okay, but he spends a lot of time in Iran."

"I encouraged this entrepreneurial venture," Dr. Janowitz says, "thinking it would help James' personal development. Plus, selfishly, I like chocolate."

He pushes his chair forward, so his chair is close to mine, "I forgot to mention that, Jim."

"I like it too, Doctor, that's not a problem." He is an amusing guy when he chooses to be.

"You're spending an awful lot of money on this guy," Jerry says. "Are you sure he's worth it?"

"No, I'm not sure. But I am certain that if I don't pursue this opportunity, I will regret it for sure."

"So, you're going to spend more money on this guy?" Rick queries.

"Yes, I think I am. I know all about sunk costs, but I believe that we've made too much progress to not continue further."

"How long will you pursue this?" Jerry inquires.

"Until we either have something patentable or I run out of money," I answer.

"Jim," says Rick, "we can plow our lottery profits into your chocolate scheme. I don't think anyone would object."

"That's quite a commitment," Melissa says. "You have so much to deal with, Jim. Do you think you can pull this off?"

"Yes, it is quite a commitment," I respond, "especially considering that I could have paid off my house with this money or taken some really nice vacations. This is maybe one of those middle of the night ideas I should have left in the middle of the night."

"Hey, Jim, you know that stuff WD 40?" Harry asks.

"Of course. I use it all the time."

"Well, it's called WD 40 because the WDs 1 through 39 were failures. And don't get me started about the filaments for light bulbs."

"I take your point, Harry."

"What else is going on in your life?" Dr. Janowitz asks.

"I'm afraid there's not much else going on," I respond. "I go to work. I come home. I work on my project. I ride my bike. And then I go to bed and do it all over again the next day."

"You need to get a life," Melissa says.

"No kidding. I do need to get a life. And I will. I promise."

"Harry?"

"I have some news. The never-ending job has ended. Mrs. French has all the gold-plated bidets and Brazilian marble countertops she can afford. Or at least Mr. French can afford. I'm going back to Boston soon. I got a nice big bonus. Can we have some cheers, please?"

The group laughed and cheered and clapped for Harry's success.

"And I'm willing to commit a substantial part of my bonus to Lone Star Sweets and Treats should a capital infusion be required. And I don't like peanut butter. In fact, I hate it."

"Thanks, Harry, I'll keep that in mind," I say.

"I'm going back to Boston, to Maine actually, to Bar Harbor where the rich people summer. You know you're with rich people when they use the word summer as a verb. In fact, sadly, this might be my last session with you. I'll be in Houston for a few more weeks packing up, and then I'll be back and forth to Maine getting that job organized. I appreciate what happened in this room. It's been a mystery to me this process, and the process is not complete, but I'm going in the right direction. I'm not very good at saying goodbye. I'll think about you all."

Even Janowitz seemed moved, and he is usually a reserved character. He has seen emotion pour out for months, and he usually rides it out like a champagne bottle bobbing in the salty sea.

"That's great, Harry. And you have another project you're going to in Maine?"

"I do. Another seaside attraction."

"Well, good luck."

"Leigh, you seem to be last again."

"I think I'm going to take a pass tonight and suggest we all go down to Rolf's and sample the …..What was that word you used about Rolf's Harry?"

"Gemutlichkeit. Happiness."

"Sample Rolf's gemutlichkeit, thank you, and wish our friend Harry bon voyage, bonne chance, and fare thee well."

"In that case, since we seem to be in a celebratory mood, I can tell you at last what happened with our delegation's meeting with His

Holiness Pope Benedict the Sixteenth. We are a group of Jews from all over the world dedicated to the preservation of the memory of the Holocaust. The Catholic Church, as you might know, has an uneasy time dealing with this subject. But Benedict is a man who knows history well. He is a philosopher and profoundly erudite. In coordination with the curators of the Vatican Museum, he accepted our gift of a painting by a holocaust survivor, the Israeli artist Ze'ev Neumann, a Hungarian Jew most of whose family were murdered by the Nazis. It is called 'The Word and the Words.' It is a large painting based on the Hebrew alphabet. His Holiness spoke very movingly, with Ze'ev at his side, about the necessity of remembering what happened to our people and others. The necessity of memory, he said, has never been as important as it is in this moment. It was one of the most remarkable days of my life."

Rick says, "Let's have a hand for the pope and the doc," and we clapped wildly for a moment. I'm not sure that was entirely appropriate, but we all left, deeply moved. Not just another night in group.

We spend a long time in Rolf's, and other than Harry and Leigh, I am the last to leave. They were talking about Chicago as I walked out the door.

REDEMPTION

"What, do you have a date at last, Harry? You've finally found that rich widow?"

He laughed.

We were going for a long Saturday ride. We've developed a pattern on bike ride Saturdays. Harry would put his bike in the back seat of his car, cram it in with the front wheel off, and drive to my apartment complex. This morning he had on an expensive suit, bespoke quality. His blue dress shirt had part of the tail untucked and he was tieless.

"What in the world are you wearing? And why are you wearing it?"

"Come on, Jimmy, can't a guy wear something other than blue jeans and a T-shirt? This is an old one, the last one, from my architect days. I had a lot of them. All fancy bespoke suits made in London. I used my father's tailor, that old crook. The tailor, that is, not my father, who had his own problems. I mean, my old man was a crook, too, in his own way. He developed commercial real estate, but somehow never got indicted for anything. I don't even want to tell you what this damn thing cost. My old firm paid for it, talking about crooks."

"All right. Why do you have it on now? You won't be happy riding a bike with a three-thousand-dollar suit on. Did you have a date last night?"

"Not really. A business meeting sort of. She's a widow, but she's only a little bit rich. That's a little bit Texas rich, of course. No gold-plated toilet seats or anything. Just some good old oil money."

"Good luck with that."

"James, I haven't had real a date since the second Reagan

Administration. I'll need more than luck. She's like the Prom Queen who wouldn't give me the time of day. After the appetizer she went to the ladies' room and grabbed a cab and went home. I didn't think it was going to end well, and it didn't."

"Is there really a rich widow?"

"No, not really. I mean, there are many rich widows, but none for me. Actually, I had a farewell dinner with my clients. You know, all hat and plenty of cows kind of clients. I gave them my final invoice last night."

"Were they surprised?"

"No, since I've sort of set them up for it, reminding them, because of their obsessive attention to detail, significant money was being spent. I mean, I didn't bring in Italian tilers to finish the pool house all the way from freaking Tuscany for nothing. So, it's beaucoup bucks. They can afford it. We had a farewell dinner at the Oilman's Club or whatever they call the fancy overpriced place the very wealthy eat in Houston. Big chunks of beef and French Champagne. It was fine. You want a crazily over-the-top job, you have to pay for it, right? I brought Leigh Hoffman as my guest. That might have been a mistake."

He took a deep breath and rubbed his hands together. Harry Boyarski was a handsome fellow, deeply tanned, with a head of thick black hair. He was fit, like an aging professional athlete who has taken good care of himself. He was the saddest-seeming man I have ever known. Women liked him; I had seen them reacting to him in bars and among other bicyclists. To their interest in him he was oblivious. He was not shy or confused among them, as I often was, just elsewhere. He was not seducible. I thought for a time, having seen this, he might have been gay. And I jokingly asked him, awkwardly, if that's why he was so uninterested.

"Leigh?" I am a little jealous. "You know, Rick thought there was a little spark there. Of course, at first, he thought you were gay."

"Hell, no, Jimmy. I like women fine. I had a lovely wife. I'm just not in the market right now. No point to it."

"What about Leigh?"

"She is a knockout! She looked stunning. The loveliest woman in the room."

"You spent the night together."

"Sort of. I had too much to drink. I don't handle Champagne well. I'd had a long day, and I got very drunk. Not embarrassing myself drunk in the restaurant, but hand around the shoulder and puke in the gutter on the way to the car drunk.

"Anyway, she brought me home, and let me sleep on her couch.

She was up early with coffee. I've never enjoyed a cup more by the way. We talked. I told her I was going back to Boston, and she seemed sorry about that. I'm sorry, too, that I won't get to know her better."

Something had happened, like a surge of current through a wire. Harry, who didn't speak much but always spoke well and interestingly, had something of consequence to say.

"Goddamn it, I'm an idiot," he says.

"But it's time go back to Boston," he continues. "I was a construction manager on this super fancy job for almost eighteen months. I've already been here six months longer than I anticipated, and the job, thank God, is finally, finally almost finished. Just a punch list that someone else can complete. I like my clients. They are demanding, but they are not unfair. And I have another job waiting for me in Maine, a big fancy house on the coast. So, I should go back to Boston. I have to make a living, unfortunately.

"Jimmy, when I came here a year and a half ago, I was in a bad way. Things had built up, the pressure of the job, which was enormous, and my own difficult history, had put me in a confusing place. I have always been a solitary sort of fellow. I'm like my mother that way, who was very private, very closed off emotionally. But I knew I had reached a breaking point, and that's when I found Dr. Janowitz and, eventually, ended up with you in the group.

"So, what was your problem, if I might ask?"

"The problem? You know I've talked in group about my job, and my family — difficult, odd, conflicted souls were my mother and father. I loved them, don't get me wrong, but I never felt especially safe with them. I know that's an awful thing to say, but that's the way I felt. Before my sister, Lily, was born, I always felt that I was an unwelcome guest in their house. I don't think they meant it. They were madly, wildly in love, but not, regrettably, with me. Things got a little better after Lily was around, since she is such a sweet and kind soul. It's funny, but from the time she was a tiny girl, she looked after me. Took care of her big brother. Somehow, by the grace God has given her, she intuited my pain.

"But that's not what drove me to the edge."

Harry looked at me. I smiled, but he was stone faced. He was far away.

"I was married once, a long time ago, by that I mean ten years ago, I guess that's a long time. My wife died of stomach cancer, a slow, horribly painful death. I met people on the cancer ward, which is a dreadful place, a literally dreadful place, who would say that they wished they could take the place of their cancer-ridden loved one.

Mom or dad or, in my case, wife. I never, ever entertained that delusion. I never want to suffer that sort of pain. I am heartsick, even now, when I think of it. At the end, the morphine could not touch it.

"We lived in Newburyport, just north of Boston. My wife was an administrator in a local college, a dean of something or other. She was always getting promotions because she was so competent and highly regarded. People loved her. I loved her. Her name was Emily. She was a dark-haired beauty. Even when she was dying she was beautiful. Like a luminous face in a Renaissance painting. I was part of a big architectural firm in Boston, all very waspy and proper. I was the house Jew, frankly. I let them think I was a Jew, anyway. My father was a Russian Jew, but my mother was Irish, and I was raised a Catholic. I think I still am a Catholic in many ways. I had gone to some of the right schools, and I knew a lot of people. It was all very tight-assed and proper, but I did well. By all accounts, we were happy: an attractive young couple, with a big old Queen Anne style Victorian in which to live, lovingly restored by me, a summer house in Maine, a place in Vermont where we skied. People envied us, I guess.

"One problem is that Emily chose not to have any children. She had a miserable childhood. Her mother, Phyllis, was a terror, a raging alcoholic and a kleptomaniac. She had plenty of money. She was a New England Brahmin. She liked to shoplift. And when she got drunk, she really liked to shoplift. She treated Emily like the hired girl. Emily was placed in the position of essentially raising her two younger brothers, totally worthless creatures in the end, but she protected them as best she could. When she went away to college, she studied in Scotland for some reason, although putting an ocean between her and her mother was as good a reason as any. She never looked back. She was an extraordinarily tough woman, my wife.

"So, she didn't want kids. She said she had already raised one family and didn't want to raise another."

Harry looked quickly at his watch, "We should get on the road soon."

"We've got plenty of time, Harry."

"I had an affair. I know people who have affairs always say this: it just happened. For a long time, I used to say that to myself, but, of course, it's one of the many lies you tell yourself and others when you are in the middle of it. We worked together. She was my assistant for a while. Her name was Jackie. Divorced with two kids. She was not a nice person. I lived with a nice person, so I found Jackie's anger, her general disagreeability, attractive. I was an idiot. She was a little chubby and blond and not particularly bright. What in the hell was I thinking? That's what my sister said when I told her. She and Emily were very close, and for a long time Lily would not speak to me, so furious was she with me. This went for two years, slightly more, I guess, and I finally did break it off. And then my wife got sick.

"From the start, it was hopeless. Stomach cancer is very hard to diagnose early. The symptoms that present can lead you down the wrong diagnostic rabbit hole. The correct diagnosis was a death sentence. There was no real treatment; none that she wanted to endure, anyway. The most optimistic assessment was that without treatment she had six weeks to live. It turned out she had four.

"The afternoon we heard the news, as I was driving back to Newburyport, from Mass General, she said to me, 'Do you want to tell me about it?'

"Of course, I knew what she was getting at, but I let the string play out. 'About what, Honey?'"

"'Harry, you know what I'm talking about, your little fling, your affair, what the fuck do you think I'm talking about?'

'I'm sorry. I love you. It didn't mean anything.'

'Christ, what does that mean?'

'It means, I love you. It just was one of those things that happened. It's over now.'

'Not for me, Harry. It is truly over for me, that's what we just heard, but what you did will never be over. Not until I die, which is soon. Then you can go back to her.'

'Don't say that.'

'Harry, I am going to goddamn die, which is so unfair. I loved you and you betrayed me with that fat, miserable creature. For Christ's sake, Harry, couldn't you at least have found a pretty one?'

'I'm sorry. It was a terrible mistake.'

'I'm sorry, too. You are a miserable son of a bitch.'"

"We finished the drive in silence. What was there to say? I was everything she said I was. I was a miserable son of a bitch."

"Things just went downhill. She got very, very sick. We brought in a nurse, but very quickly we realized she couldn't be cared for at home any longer. There was nothing to do but wait for her to die. I sat by her bed the last week. The last few days she was as sedated as heavily as she could be. Occasionally, the pain brought her back, momentarily.

"Two days before she died, she had a brief lucid moment. I was sitting in a chair by the bed, doing what I thought was right. I didn't want her to die alone. No one should die alone. She looked up at me, how beautiful she was."

"'Harry,' she said, 'you should go home now.'

'No. I'm going to stay with you.'

'Promise me one thing, that you'll take care of yourself. Promise me.'

'I promise.'

'No, really, promise me.'

'I will. I'll take care of myself.'

'Harry, I'm not going to forgive you. I'm sorry, I can't. I love you, though, I do love you.'

'I love you, Emily. I'm so sorry. I love you.'"

"And those were the last words we ever spoke to one another. And I am not forgiven, it seems, and will carry that memory to my grave.

"After she died, I got rid of the places in Maine and Vermont, quit my job, and rented the house in Newburyport to local couple. I have my lawyer looking after the place. I guess the renters are still there. I know I'll never live there are again. I traveled to Europe, revisiting all the places Emily and I had been as a young couple: Paris, Florence, Barcelona. Lots of places. Emily loved Florence. It is a wonderful city. That was what turned out to be my last stop before I came home. The last night I was there, I went out to dinner with some people I had met on the train from Milan. They were Scots, and I told them about how happy Emily had been in Edinburgh. It was a happy night, and we all got a little drunk. I was maybe the drunkest, but it was the first time I had enjoyed myself for a long time. The first time I had laughed in months.

"I was staying in this ancient house in Florence. Eight hundred years old, I think, full of ghosts and mice. I tried to sleep but I couldn't. I got up and sat at the rickety desk in the room. There was a bottle of Calvados that I had brought from Paris in my luggage. I dug it out and poured myself a drink. I was feeling the lightest, least burdened, I had in a long time. There were the remains of a sandwich I had for lunch, wrapped in some paper. And there was a rustling in the paper. A bold Florentine mouse, and they are bold, was helping himself to the remains of my meal. 'Eat away, wee mouse,' I said to him. He stuck his head from beneath the paper, and gave me a gaze that was fearless and, I thought, not unfriendly. That is the pathetic fallacy, I guess. Stranger that I was, a lost and lonely one at that, looked upon kindly by one of the least of God's creatures.

"It was in that early hour before dawn, that hour is called the hour of the wolf, by the way, in a miraculous city, that it came upon me that I would find neither solace nor forgiveness. The wrongs that I had done, the mistakes I made, could never be undone or unmade. And that if I could not find forgiveness, I could at least try to redeem myself somehow. Must do that. I'm trying to rediscover the things in myself that are redeemable.

"It is a beginning. My sister, my beautiful sister, said to me that I could redeem myself in acts of kindness and courage. It is easy for her, easier anyway, because she is both kind and courageous. I am not. Redemption."

"Have you found it? Redemption?"

"Of course not. But I'm trying. Damn it's going to be hot today."

"Okay, so put on your biking clothes and we'll start."

We rode a long way in the Texas heat.

JAMES SNYDER'S INFERNO:
A LETTER TO THE FUTURE

In one of my sessions with Dr. Janowitz, he suggested that it might be interesting in this moment in our relationship, now multiple years into therapy, that I stop for a moment and take a step back and think about my life and healing.

"It's a kind of mindfulness that I would encourage, James," he says. "Why don't you write a letter to James of the future?"

"What's the point of that?"

"I don't know. Does everything need to have a point?"

"For me, pretty much, yes."

"I don't think that's the case at all."

Dr. Janowitz was energetic tonight as he often is when he thinks he has a good idea that might lead to a breakthrough. With psychiatrists, I've learned, "breaking through" is a very big deal. He was tilted far back in his chair, alarmingly so.

"No, I think this is a very good idea," Dr. Janowitz continues. "What harm will it do? It might even be fun."

I've learned over time that when Dr. Janowitz has decided that something in my course of treatment would be useful, it usually is.

"All right," I say, "I'll give it a try."

So, this is my letter to James Snyder of the future. It is not about my expectations of the future but about my past, although I prefer to live in the present. That is the tense of preference for Michael Kruger, Vera Bowman and me.

Dear James,
Tonight, I'm thinking about journeys. I'm flying to Boston tomorrow and

eventually I'll end up in Vermont and Maine. I've never been to either place. I'm going to meet my friend from therapy and bike riding, Harry Boyarski, there and we are driving to Cape Cod and then to Vermont. We'll be riding our bikes in Vermont and Maine. We will be riding about two weeks, so I hope the weather is good. At least it won't be as hot as Texas. Harry tells me it will be all very hilly, leafy, and green. I'm also going to meet his sister, and I have a few anxieties about that.

Many years ago, thinking about journeys and anxieties, when I was in college as an undergraduate I studied engineering. It was a haze of calculations and theories and numbers. But as an underclassman, I also had to deal with the other part of the curriculum, the humanities. I was not very good at them, maybe because I wasn't really very human. I needed to take a literature course in my sophomore year.

There was a girl I was interested in, Marcia Meyers, a big red-headed woman. She played field hockey as I recall, and she was always sporting some sort of bandage around her wrist or knee. She was a girl you'd call handsome rather than pretty. She's a lawyer now in Columbus, Ohio. She used to send me Christmas cards. I never sent her any, so she stopped hers to me. I actually was a shit for a long time.

She was taking a class in medieval literature, and since I was interested in her and the thought of sitting next to her sweaty, sturdy body was quite a pleasant one, I enrolled in it, too. I think a lot of undergraduate boys enroll in courses to be next to an undergraduate girl. She stayed in the course - I'm sure she got an A - but I dropped out after two weeks.

I remember the professor's first lecture very well. I have always had a very good memory or did until I was put on all kinds of medication for my various emotional issues. He talked about, among other writers, Dante and The Divine Comedy, but especially the first volume of The Comedy, The Inferno. He called Dante's poem, "a deep and savage journey." That's what I've been on. In fact, ironically, I still have a copy of The Inferno in my apartment. It's one of the only books I still possess that for whatever reason hasn't been thrown out or ripped to shreds in one of my rages. I suppose I held out the hope I would read it, and Marcia Meyers would fall in love with me. Unlikely on both counts after all these years. I look at the opening lines occasionally, lines I take great comfort in, "Midway on the journey of our life, I woke to find myself in a dark wood, the right road lost." Boy, did Dante get it right.

I've been thinking about what I've gone through over the last many years, my evolution, the process of healing. As I think about it, I feel the old fear stirring, that my destiny is a terrible and lonely death. But the terror is beginning to ease. I've found my own Virgil to guide me through the Nine Circles of Hell, the unlikeliest of Virgils, a brilliant Jewish psychiatrist by the name of Solomon Janowitz. It's an interesting life, James, if you can stay on your feet.

I realize that shortly after my friend, and for a long time he was my only friend, Scott died and Kelly remarried, other problems started to swarm around me that I urgently had to deal with. My company was merging with another company. Identities were being changed at the highest levels of the system. They were re-organizing where I was. My job was in danger. My new immediate supervisor seemed to have had it in for me. He began to pick on me incessantly and actively worked to get me terminated. He threatened that he was going to do that and insisted that it was inexorable and that I couldn't stop it. I tried to transfer out. I tried other ways to escape. I didn't want to leave that job. This was something that was thrust upon me. The economy was tightening up. There was every danger with somebody out to get me who had more authority that I could be terminated. And I had to deal with the terminator.

Even today, dealing with the terminator causes so much anguish that I cannot help but think back to where I was following Kelly's marriage.

I remember the awful days when I was obsessed, and that understates my feeling, with Cindy and my anger toward her. Where is my life going? I'm going to lose my identity. My illness will progress, and nobody will be able to stop it. I won't know who I am. And if my illness progresses any further, I will lose all sense of bearing and ordinates.

But there have been so many discontinuities. I had a relationship with a woman who went to somebody else, who absolutely discarded me and ignored my feelings, and crushed me. But I survived. Then there was Scott's tragic death and my attempts at new relationships. In addition to the unrealized potential with Kelly, there were Laura, one of my suppliers, who was engaged but had fantasies about me; and Diana, a separated waitress in a bar from whom I contracted the clap, sorry to be so direct about that, but that's what happened; and Stephanie, a married woman who wanted to be "friends and lovers"; and Bianca, another married woman with whom I really wanted to have an affair, but Dr. Janowitz wisely talked me out of. The mystery of women is an ongoing one.

How will I meet new people? Will I be able to meet new people? Those were my concerns and to some extent still are. It's certainly going to be a continuing theme in my future. Other people seem to be having relationships, and I don't. Other people are dating. Other people are falling in love. I'm being tortured. I'm being excluded. I'm being the odd man out. And meanwhile there's music. There's music in the air. There's music on the radio. There's music in the neighborhood. They're writing songs of love, but not for me.

Will this dating of unavailable women become a theme for my years ahead? Will I ever meet a woman who is truly available for me? Will she have children? Will she want to have children with me? What if I don't want to have children? Will she still want to be with me?

Will I ever heal from this monster called mental illness? Will I be labeled "mentally ill" for the rest of my life? How will my "history of mental illness" be used against me?

Who will accept me if they knew the truth? Who would even like me if they knew the truth? I'll always be alone. I'll never have a girlfriend or a wife. No one will miss me when I'm gone.

Why did this have to happen to me? Why couldn't the Director have done his job and properly diagnosed me and then properly supervised my therapy sessions with Cindy? Why are Cindy and the Director allowed to continue pursuing their dreams of working in psychology, but I am denied a fair chance at pursuing my dream of working for the CIA? Why did the State of Texas protect Cindy and the Director when it was undeniably clear that they both had falsified medical records? Why is victimizing the victim a legally allowed defense? Why did Damian lie to me? Why wouldn't Damian prosecute Cindy?

What about my family? If I had acted out against Cindy and the others, my parents would literally have had to bury me. Do I really want that? Do I really want to put my parents and my brother and sister through that? How will society view them if the crazy man attacks his former therapists? Would that be fair to my family?

Will I ever heal? Will I ever be considered "normal"? Will I ever live a "normal" life? Is that even possible for me? There's so much pain. I'm so conflicted. Can Dr. Janowitz really help me? Or is he just stringing me along until he's ready to retire? What does my future hold?

On September 11th two jets just flew into the World Trade Center. The world experienced 9/11. But I already had my 9/11. I had my 9/11 early. Now the world is feeling what I've felt - the loss, the trauma, the violation, the anger, the betrayal of trust. The world is changing. We'll never be the same.

Why do I have trouble accepting and respecting people in positions of authority? Why do I automatically challenge titles? Is it a character flaw within my personality? Or is it learned behavior that can be changed?

These were my thoughts. I was deeply wounded and very ill. I still am. I thank God that I crossed paths with Thomas Tran who would lead me to Dr. Janowitz. I am not an ordinary person, whatever that means. I will never lead an ordinary life. I will need help all my life. I will need to take medication all my life. But at least I feel I am not alone. The terrible depth of depression is lifting. The default mode of murderous self-destructive anger has passed. I know that I am—was—capable of terrible things in that state of mind. But the darkness into which I had fallen, the darkness which I embraced, the hopelessness which was my life has dissipated. I'm still in the shadows, I guess, a bit anyway. I will always be there. I don't know, for example, if I'll ever find someone to love, a wife. And that makes me sad, but not psychotically angry. And it occurs to me that this is what healing feels like. I'm healing. That is a profound thing to say. It is a mystery and a gift from God.

Anyway, these are my thoughts on a rainy evening in Houston, Texas. That's what I feel about my life up to the moment. I've been trying to save as much money as I can, so you'll not be poor as an older man. I'm assuming you'll still be single. But I'm trying to make a lot more money, crazy money, and I haven't given up trying to find the right woman. And I've taken good care of my teeth. You can thank me for that when you go to the dentist.

Your friend,
James Snyder

IT HAPPENED ON BUZZARD'S' BAY

I cannot be certain of this, of course, but I believe I know what I will remember at the end of my life: the lovely October afternoon I met Lily Boyarski.

Harry Boyarski and I went up to the family house on Cape Cod. It stood overlooking Buzzard's Bay at the south end of the island. It was an old stone house with a slate roof. It was an imposing old wreck. My father, Harry said, bought this house for my mother.

"It's meant to be a summer house," Harry said. "The people who built it — Boston people — called it a cottage."

"It looks like it could use some work."

"Some! It should be bulldozed and returned to nature. The kitchen is the original to 1912. We put a modern stove and refrigerator in it, but the old stuff is still there. It's a museum."

A few slates had fallen to the terrace. Their shards had not been removed. The awning was in tatters.

"Why do you keep it?"

"My sister. She works here in the summer. Her husband, the unfortunate Ricky Louis Nanne, rhymes with Fanny, was going to fix it up. He was an architect. To my everlasting regret, I introduced them. He turned out to be a complete fraud and a world-class asshole. He worked with me. He was very handsome. They were a beautiful couple. My sister is a beautiful woman, James. You'll see. She'll knock your eyes out."

"What happened to Ricky Louis Nanne, rhymes with fanny?"

"He was swept away by the tide. Or Lily showed him the door. The latter."

"She kicked him out?"

"Out the door, down the street, and back to Turin."

333

"May I ask why?"

"Knowing my sister, it could have been for a number of reasons. She's a tough one. He cheated on her with a Harvard professor. Lady professor. And that was it."

"Should I be afraid of your sister?"

"I am," he says with a laugh, "she scares the shit out of me."

I laughed as he went to get us some beers.

Harry and I had promised ourselves, through the hot Texas summer, riding hundreds of miles along steaming highways, that we would ride together in New England. Now, in the bright autumn light of October, we were on our way to Vermont to ride in a cool place, in the hills and among the trees. We stopped here on Cape Cod. Harry wanted me to meet his sister, his younger sister.

Harry came back with the beers, frosty from the refrigerator. We sat down on some rickety patio chairs on the flagstone terrace overlooking Buzzard's Bay, which was gray and foam flecked.

"What did your father do, Harry?"

"Well, my great grandfather was a shoemaker. My grandfather owned shoes stores in the suburbs north of Boston. And my father was in real estate. This is the arc of Jews from Russia, it seems."

"Your family did well?"

"Oh, yeah. The truth is my grandfather was a bookie. That was the source, the fountainhead, of the Boyarski fortune."

"So why is the house in such bad shape?"

"The old man lost it all. Strip malls in New Jersey that went belly up. The only thing he didn't sell was this place, which is now an old ruin. Testimony to a great love affair."

"Your mother?"

"When she died the old man just gave up. My mother wasn't a Jew, did I ever tell you that?"

"I'm not sure."

"She was an Irish Catholic. She had some French blood because she had black hair and blue eyes. She was extraordinary."

"What was her name?"

"Her name was Ann. Ann Fitzgerald Boyarski. Annie, my old man called her. Jesus, he loved her."

He drank his beer and looked at the sea. He seemed lost for a moment.

"That's why we hang onto this old wreck. My sister keeps it up. But she won't change a thing. Sometimes I wonder if she changes the sheets."

"How does she do it?"

"She's so goddamn smart, it gives me a pain in my heart. She's taken what was left of the old man's money and restored it. She built it back up."

"How?"

"I'm not sure. She's had good advice. Money men give her advice because they are astonished by her beauty."

He yawned and stretched out his arm and rolled his neck as if it relaxed his back and shoulders.

"Am I going to meet her?"

"Sure, she's upstairs in her studio."

"That's right. She's a painter."

"She's the lioness of the third floor. That's where the staff used to live when there was staff. She's opened it up. It's quite nice."

He reached out slapped me on the knee.

"James, I have to run over to Provincetown."

"Why?"

"Because a mutual friend is having dinner with us tonight."

"Who is it?"

"A secret."

"Jesus Christ, you're going to pick up Leigh Hoffman."

"Possibly."

"You dog. You never told me a thing."

"There was nothing to tell. Still isn't anything to tell. Look, I'm running late. Go see Lily."

"Maybe I'll take a nap."

"No, my friend, you must pay a visit to our hostess on the third floor."

"Would I be intruding? I don't want to bother her."

"She'll let you know, my friend, ambiguity is not in my sister's nature."

"I want to do the right thing."

"Don't we all. Just go on up and ask her what she wants for dinner. I'll cook for us. No, she'll say chicken. Tell her I'm cooking chicken for dinner. Don't mention Leigh, however. I want it to be a surprise."

Over the months I had been friendly with Harry, I had spoken to Lily a few times. I told her something about my life, my struggles. She seemed interested in what I had to say, interested in the therapy I was undertaking. I had no illusions about her. She was my friend's sister, and I feared that when she met me she would be disappointed.

She had laughed when I told her how Harry had described her.

"James, I'm not like that. That's just Harry wanting me to be more like my mother. My mother was quite pretty, no doubt, and I look a little like her. Just a little."

The good thing was she knew I had been crazy, dangerously so, and was not frightened by that. I liked to talk to her, and now all I had to do was walk up two flights of stairs to say hello. Their old house was in bad shape, the plaster walls were cracked and bulging from a leak in the roof. Slate roofs are impossible to maintain, that I knew. The handrails and spindles were solid oak, but the varnish was darkened almost to black. The wainscoting was still in place from the second floor to the third. The wainscoting detail traditionally separated the real house from the servant's quarters. The master from the servant; the rich from the poor.

Lily had knocked down walls between the tiny bedrooms on the third floor, the maid's quarters, to make her studio. The windows in her studio faced west looking over Buzzard's Bay.

"Hello," I said, feeling foolish.

"Wait," a voice said, "don't come in yet."

"Why?"

"I'm not sure. Just wait, okay?"

"Lily?"

"Yes?"

"Is there a bathroom up here?"

"James, are you trying to tell me at the moment we first meet, you have to pee?"

"Yeah, and rather badly."

"Well come in. I was just cleaning up. But you'll just have to deal with the mess."

I walked into her studio through some draperies. There was no door.

Lily stepped forward and extended her hand.

"The toilet," she said, "is through that door."

She indicated a door behind her, painted a brilliant red. It looked a lacquered Chinese crimson.

"And after you've finished," she said, "would you like some wine? I'm done working for the day."

"Sure."

"James, have you ever met an artist that painted dogs?"

"I don't think so."

"Well, sir, now you have."

"Horses?"

"I've ridden them."

"Oh yes, you are a Texan. No, I mean, have you ever met someone who painted horses?"

"I'm guessing you're she, correct?"

"Absolutely, correct."

When I came out of the bathroom, Lily was sitting in an old armchair, which, like all the other furniture in the house was badly worn. She had an old crate in front of her, and on the crate were two glasses of wine.

"James, you are a fine-looking fellow, you know. You are too hard on yourself. And your ears, well, they are just ears."

"You're very pretty."

"Bullshit."

"No, really, I think you are."

"Bullshit. I used to be sort of pretty, but now I'm a paint-stained wretch. Look at me? Would you want to be seen with a woman with paint in her hair and on her glasses? Look at my hands. They are the hands of charwoman. I'm not sure what a charwoman is, but I'm sure they have red hands with banged up nails."

I walked to the window and looked over Buzzard's Bay. A cold front was moving in from the west and there was a chop on the water. The beach had little sand, grey rocks and beer cans. Lily walked up to me with the wine glasses.

"Here," she said, handing me the glass, "drink up. That wine cost me $9.99. I saved the good stuff for you."

"Thanks."

"And, yes," I said.

"Yes, to what?"

"Yes, you are the kind of woman I would like to be seen with."

She smiled and blushed a little. Her cheeks were a bright pink. She sat down on a couch in front of the window.

"Sit with me for a while, and then I have to take a shower."

"You have a wonderful place here. I don't know much about artists. Do you make any money doing this?"

"I'll give you some free advice, James. Never ask an artist if she makes any money being an artist. Never. Almost always the answer is no, and that pretty much ends the conversation."

"Sorry."

"It doesn't bother me. The answer for me is yes. But most serious artists don't think of me as an artist. They think of me as a decorator. I mean, I paint pictures of poodles. Although there is a very long and honored tradition of dog portraits."

"I just meant to say, I like this room. When we spoke on the phone, I tried to picture you in your studio."

"And?"

"Nothing this nice, I mean, interesting. Seems a little dark in here, though."

As the storm moved in the room was dark. There was only a desk lamp on a work table and a standing lamp that was not turned on.

"I only paint in sunlight. I can't really see to paint in artificial light."

"That makes sense."

"Do you know the story about Goya's candle hat?"

"No."

"Well Goya, the greatest of painters, loved to paint. He was obsessed with it. He didn't want to stop when it got dark. He was also very clever. Do you know what he did?"

"He wore a candle hat?"

"Exactly. He made himself a hat with candles. It was like a sombrero with candles around the brim. That's how he painted at night, with his candle hat. I can imagine his hair was full of candle wax. His eyebrows were flecked with it."

"Amazing."

"Oh, yes, James. It is amazing and crazy. But if you look at one of his paintings, you realize how he transformed a little pigment on a linen canvas — nothing really — into something beyond extraordinary. No one should be able to do it, but he did. A handful of artists, really, can do it."

Lily moved across the room and turned on the floor lamp, light filled the room.

"It makes me very happy to think of Goya in his candle hat. I'm good at what I do, this silly business of painting pooches. But I'm also a good painter. A serious painter, too."

"I'd like to see your serious work," I said.

"Maybe some time. I have to figure you out first."

"Whether or not I'm crazy?"

"No, something else. It's about trust."

She was wearing a man's Oxford cloth shirt, the shirt she painted in, and she took it off. She had a lovely, lithe body, small breasts. She pulled the kerchief that tied her hair back. Her hair was auburn and hung just down her back.

"What are you looking at, my friend? You can't be staring at my boobs because, as my former husband used to say, I don't have any."

"Sorry. I do think you're pretty."

"Used to be. Worn out, cast aside divorcee."

It seemed to me then that this was a place I wished to be. Not a home, exactly, but a refuge. And this quiet woman — as difficult as I am sure she was — was someone I could love. I could not say that, of course, I was still too tangled with my old life to say it.

"Say, James, how is the chocolate business? Are you very, very rich yet?"

"No. The chocolate business didn't work out."

"I didn't mean to tease you about your ears, by the way," she said. "They are really okay as ears. I'd paint your ears if you make your fortune."

We stood outside the circle of light, alone, separate.

In my own bleak madness, in my God-insulting rages, I had never imagined a moment like this. All I had wanted from the world was some sign, some indication I might be happy. Once I had wanted to die, but I didn't, and now I was here in this old house with this pretty woman. Rain rattled against the windows.

"Oh shit, I should go get cleaned up," she said.

"I'll go find Harry. I think he's going to make chicken or something."

"Chicken again. If Harry ever stopped eating chicken, chickens would make him King of All Poultry."

"He says the same thing about you, by the way. I'll see what the Chicken King is up to. I'm not sure if he's back yet though."

"Back yet? Where did he go?"

"Provincetown, I think."

"Why?"

"I can't tell you. I'm sworn to secrecy."

"What is this, an all boy's club, no girls allowed?"

"He's picking up a friend of ours from Houston. That's all I can tell you."

"Okay. You and your buddy Harry can keep your secret. But James, I'm glad you came here. I'm glad to finally meet you."

"Yeah, me too."

"And when you boys get back from your bicycling adventure, I want you to come back. I'll show you my paintings. You guys are assholes, by the way. Don't you know that the only people left in Vermont are transplanted New Yorkers? No laconic Rockwell models left up there if that's what you're looking for. There are cows, though, lots and lots of cows."

We laughed a moment. What a long way I have come. We could hear the wind and the surf outside, furious now. The storm had moved in across Buzzard's Bay.

The End

EPILOGUE

Out of legal necessity, this manuscript was a work of fiction; however, my life is very real. This was my story. I lived it in parts.

Twelve years ago when I first began drafting what would become this story, I did so as a therapeutic exercise to help me grasp the negativity and darkness that had befallen me as a result of my first therapeutic experience. Over time, my psychiatrist, through his unwavering commitment and steadfast approach, slowly and carefully calmed my intense rage. He showed me by his example that I too could one day re-enter the light and have a meaningful life.

The life lessons I learned through this therapeutic journey are to always believe in myself; to never give up; to value another opinion; to value another perspective from a related discipline, e.g., psychiatry versus psychology; to get the right diagnosis and the right treatment; that love is a curative driving force; and that the therapeutic alliance is sustaining even where there appears little else. I was a lost case, but not anymore! Today I'm a reconstituted soul; reconstituted with love and compassion and community.

For you who find yourselves in darkness, I encourage you to seek the most competent help available. Ask questions. Seek referrals. If you're not getting the answers you need, move on and try another therapist. But above all, have faith that you too can return to the light.

Experientially, I have discovered the truth in the words of Bishop Fulton J. Sheen, "Life is worth living!"